In
Sheikh

Their desire and passion knows no bounds…

In the Sheikh's Bed

THE SHEIKH'S CHOSEN WIFE

by
Michelle Reid

SURRENDER TO THE SHEIKH

by
Sharon Kendrick

DESERT AFFAIR

by
Kate Walker

MILLS & BOON®

MILLS & BOON and MILLS & BOON with the Rose Device
are registered trademarks of the publisher.
Harlequin Mills & Boon Limited,
Eton House, 18-24 Paradise Road, Richmond, Surrey, TW9 1SR

IN THE SHEIKH'S BED
© by Harlequin Enterprises II B.V., 2005

The Sheikh's Chosen Wife, Surrender to the Sheikh and
Desert Affair were first published in Great Britain by
Harlequin Mills & Boon Limited in separate, single volumes.

The Sheikh's Chosen Wife © Michelle Reid 2002
Surrender to the Sheikh © Sharon Kendrick 2001
Desert Affair © Kate Walker 2001

ISBN 0 263 84477 3

05-0705

Printed and bound in Spain
by Litografía Rosés S.A., Barcelona

Michelle Reid grew up on the southern edges of Manchester, the youngest in a family of five lively children. But now she lives in the beautiful county of Cheshire with her busy executive husband and two grown-up daughters. She loves reading, the ballet, and playing tennis when she gets the chance. She hates cooking, cleaning, and despises ironing! Sleep she can do without and produces some of her best written work during the early hours of the morning.

THE SHEIKH'S
CHOSEN WIFE

by

Michelle Reid

CHAPTER ONE

DRESSED to go riding, in knee-length black leather boots, buff pants, a white shirt and a white *gutrah* held to his dark head by a plain black *agal*, Sheikh Hassan ben Khalifa Al-Qadim stepped into his private office and closed the door behind him. In his hand he held a newly delivered letter from England. On his desk lay three more. Walking across the room, he tossed the new letter onto the top of the other three then went to stand by the grilled window, fixing his eyes on a spot beyond the Al-Qadim Oasis, where reclaimed dry scrubland had been turned into miles of lush green fig groves.

Beyond the figs rose the sand-dunes. Majestic and proud, they claimed the horizon with a warning statement. Come any closer with your irrigation and expect retaliation, they said. One serious sandstorm, and years of hard labour could be turned back into arid wasteland.

A sigh eased itself from his body. Hassan knew all about the laws of the desert. He respected its power and its driving passion, its right to be master of its own destiny. And what he would really have liked to do at this very moment was to saddle up his horse, Zandor, then take off for those sand-dunes and allow them to dictate his future for him.

But he knew the idea was pure fantasy. For behind him lay four letters, all of which demanded he make those decisions for himself. And beyond the relative sanctuary of the four walls surrounding him lay a palace in waiting; his father, his half-brother, plus a thousand and one other people, all of whom believed they owned a piece of his so-called destiny.

So Zandor would have to stay in his stable. His beloved sand-dunes would have to wait a while to swallow him up. Making a half-turn, he stared grimly at the letters. Only one

5

had been opened: the first one, which he had tossed aside with the contempt it had deserved. Since then he had left the others sealed on his desk and had tried very hard to ignore them.

But the time for burying his head in the sand was over.

A knock on the door diverted his attention. It would be his most trusted aide, Faysal. Hassan recognised the lightness of the knock. Sure enough the door opened and a short, fine-boned man wearing the traditional white and pale blue robes of their Arabian birthright appeared in its arched aperture, where he paused and bowed his head, waiting to be invited in or told to go.

'Come in, Faysal,' Hassan instructed a trifle impatiently. Sometimes Faysal's rigid adherence to so-called protocol set his teeth on edge.

With another deferential bow, Faysal moved to his master's bidding. Stepping into the room, he closed the door behind him then used some rarely utilised initiative by walking across the room to come to a halt several feet from the desk on the priceless carpet that covered, in part, the expanse of polished blue marble between the desk and the door.

Hassan found himself staring at the carpet. His wife had ordered it to be placed there, claiming the room's spartan appearance invited no one to cross its austere threshold. The fact that this was supposed to be the whole point had made absolutely no difference to Leona. She had simply carried on regardless, bringing many items into the room besides the carpet. Such as the pictures now adorning the walls and the beautiful ceramics and sculptures scattered around, all of which had been produced by gifted artists native to the small Gulf state of Rahman. Hassan had soon found he could no longer lift his eyes without having them settle on an example of local enterprise.

Yet it was towards the only western pieces Leona had brought into the room that his eyes now drifted. The low table and two overstuffed easy chairs had been placed by the other window, where she would insist on making him sit with her several times a day to enjoy the view while they drank tea and talked and touched occasionally as lovers do…

Dragging the *gutrah* from his head with almost angry fingers, Hassan tossed it aside then went to sit down in the chair behind his desk. 'Okay,' he said. 'What have you to tell me?'

'It is not good news, sir.' Faysal began with a warning. 'Sheikh Abdul is entertaining certain…factions at his summer palace. Our man on the inside confirms that the tone of their conversation warrants your most urgent attention.'

Hassan made no comment, but his expression hardened fractionally. 'And my wife?' he asked next.

'The Sheikha still resides in Spain, sir,' Faysal informed him, 'working with her father at the new resort of San Estéban, overseeing the furnishing of several villas about to be released for sale.'

Doing what she did best, Hassan thought grimly—and did not need to glance back at the two stuffed chairs to conjure up a vision of long silken hair the colour of a desert sunset, framing a porcelain smooth face with laughing green eyes and a smile that dared him to complain about her invasion of his private space. 'Trust me,' he could hear her say. 'It is my job to give great empty spaces a little soul and their own heartbeat.'

Well, the heartbeat had gone out of this room when she'd left it, and as for the soul…

Another sigh escaped him. 'How long do you think we have before they make their move?'

The slight tensing in Faysal's stance warned Hassan that he was not going to like what was coming. 'If you will forgive me for saying so, sir,' his aide apologised, 'with Mr Ethan Hayes also residing at her father's property, I would say that the matter has become most seriously urgent indeed.'

Since this was complete news to Hassan it took a moment for the full impact of this information to really sink in. Then he was suddenly on his feet and was swinging tensely away to glare at the sand-dunes again. Was she mad? he was thinking angrily. Did she have a death wish? Was she so indifferent to his feelings that she could behave like this?

Ethan Hayes. His teeth gritted together as an old familiar jealousy began mixing with his anger to form a much more volatile substance. He swung back to face Faysal. 'How long has Mr Hayes been in residence in San Estéban?'

Faysal made a nervous clearing of his throat. 'These seven days past,' he replied.

'And who else knows about this…? Sheikh Abdul?'

'It was discussed,' Faysal confirmed.

With a tight shifting of his long lean body, Hassan returned to his seat. 'Cancel all my appointments for the rest of the month,' he instructed, drawing his appointments diary towards him to begin scoring hard lines through the same busy pages. 'My yacht is berthed at Cadiz. Have it moved to San Estéban. Check that my plane is ready for an immediate take-off and ask Rafiq to come to me.'

The cold quality of the commands did nothing to dilute their grim purpose. 'If asked,' Faysal prompted, 'what reason do I give for your sudden decision to cancel your appointments?'

'I am about to indulge in a much needed holiday cruising the Mediterranean with my nice new toy,' Sheikh Hassan replied, and the bite in his tone made a complete mockery of the words spoken, for they both knew that the next few weeks promised to be no holiday. 'And Faysal…' Hassan stalled his aide as he was about to take his leave '…if anyone so much as whispers the word adultery in the same breath as my wife's name, they will not breathe again—you understand me?'

The other man went perfectly still, recognising the responsibility that was being laid squarely upon him. 'Yes, sir.' He bowed.

Hassan's grim nod was a dismissal. Left alone again, he leaned back in his chair and began frowning while he tried to decide how best to tackle this. His gaze fell on the small stack of letters. Reaching out with long fingers, he drew them towards him, picked out the only envelope with a broken seal and removed the single sheet of paper from inside. The content of the letter he ignored with the same dismissive contempt he had always applied to it. His interest lay only in the telephone number printed beneath the business logo. With an expression that said he resented having his hand forced like this, he took a brief glance at his watch, then was lifting up the telephone, fairly sure that his wife's lawyer would be in his London office at this time of the day.

The ensuing conversation was not a pleasant one, and the following conversation with his father-in-law even less so. He had just replaced the receiver and was frowning darkly over what Victor Frayne had said to him, when another knock sounded at the door. Hard eyes lanced towards it as the door swung open and Rafiq stepped into the room.

Though he was dressed in much the same clothes as Faysal was wearing, there the similarity between the two men ended. For where Faysal was short and thin and annoyingly effacing, Rafiq was a giant of a man who rarely kowtowed to anyone. Hassan warranted only a polite nod of the head, yet he knew Rafiq would willingly die for him if he was called upon to do so.

'Come in, shut the door, then tell me how you would feel about committing a minor piece of treason?' Hassan smoothly intoned.

Below the white *gutrah* a pair of dark eyes glinted. 'Sheikh Abdul?' Rafiq questioned hopefully.

'Unfortunately, no.' Hassan gave a half smile. 'I was in fact referring to my lovely wife, Leona…'

Dressed for the evening in a beaded slip-dress made of gold silk chiffon, Leona stepped into a pair of matching beaded mules then turned to look at herself in the mirror.

Her smooth russet hair had been caught up in a twist, and diamonds sparkled at her ears and throat. Overall, she supposed she looked okay, she decided, giving the thin straps at her shoulders a gentle tug so the dress settled comfortably over her slender frame. But the weight she had lost during the last year was most definitely showing, and she could have chosen a better colour to offset the unnatural paleness of her skin.

Too late to change, though, she thought with a dismissive shrug as she turned away from her reflection. Ethan was already waiting for her outside on the terrace. And, anyway, she wasn't out to impress anyone. She was merely playing stand-in for her father who had been delayed in London due to some urgent business with the family lawyer, which had left her and her father's business partner, Ethan, the only ones here to represent Hayes-Frayne at tonight's promotional dinner.

She grimaced as she caught up a matching black silk shawl and made for her bedroom door. In truth, she would rather not be going out at all tonight having only arrived back from San Estéban an hour ago. It had been a long day, and she had spent most of it melting in a Spanish heatwave because the air-conditioning system had not been working in the villa she had been attempting to make ready for viewing. So a long soak in a warm bath and an early night would have been her idea of heaven tonight, she thought wryly, as she went down the stairs to join Ethan.

He was half sitting on the terrace rail with a glass in his hand, watching the sun go down, but his head turned at her first step, and his mouth broke into an appreciative smile.

'Ravishing,' he murmured, sliding his lean frame upright.

'Thank you,' she replied. 'You don't look so bad yourself.'

His wry nod accepted the compliment and his grey eyes sparkled with lazy humour. Dressed in a black dinner suit and bow tie, he was a tall, dark, very attractive man with an easy smile and a famous eye for the ladies. Women adored him and he adored them but, thankfully, that mutual adoration had never raised its ugly head between the two of them.

Leona liked Ethan. She felt comfortable being with him. He was the Hayes in Hayes-Frayne, architects. Give

Ethan a blank piece of paper and he would create a fifty-storey skyscraper or a whole resort complete with sports clubs, shopping malls and, of course, holiday villas to die for, as with this new resort in San Estéban.

'Drink?' he suggested, already stepping towards the well stocked drinks trolley.

But Leona gave a shake of her head. 'Better not, if you want me to stay awake beyond ten o'clock,' she refused.

'That late? Next you'll be begging me to take you on to an all-night disco after the party.' He was mocking the fact that she was usually safely tucked up in bed by nine o'clock.

'Do you disco?' she asked him curiously.

'Not if I can help it,' he replied, discarding his own glass to come and take the shawl from her hand so he could drape it across her shoulders. 'The best I can offer in the name of dance is a soft shoe shuffle to something very slow, preferably in a darkened room, so that I don't damage my ego by revealing just how bad a shuffler I am.'

'You're such a liar.' Leona smiled. 'I've seen you dance a mean jive, once or twice.'

Ethan pulled a face at the reminder. 'Now you've really made me feel my age,' he complained. 'Next you'll be asking me what it was like to rock in the sixties.'

'You're not that old.' She was still smiling.

'Born in the mid-sixties,' he announced. 'To a free-loving mother who bopped with the best of them.'

'That makes you about the same age as Hass…'

And that was the point where everything died: the light banter, the laughter, the tail end of Hassan's name. Silence fell. Ethan's teasing grey eyes turned very sombre. He knew, of course, how painful this last year had been for her. No one mentioned Hassan's name in her presence, so to hear herself almost say it out loud caused tension to erupt between the both of them.

'It isn't too late to stop this craziness, you know,' Ethan murmured gently.

Her response was to drag in a deep breath and step right away from him. 'I don't want to stop it,' she quietly replied.

'Your heart does.'

'My heart is not making the decisions here.'

'Maybe you should let it.'

'Maybe you should mind your own business!'

Spinning on her slender heels Leona walked away from him to go and stand at the terrace rail, leaving Ethan behind wearing a rueful expression at the severity with which she had just slapped him down.

Out there at sea, the dying sun was throwing up slender fingers of fire into a spectacular vermilion sky. Down the hill below the villa, San Estéban was beginning to twinkle as it came into its own at the exit of the sun. And in between the town and the sun the ocean spread like satin with its brand-new purpose-built harbour already packed with smart sailing crafts of all shapes and sizes.

Up here on the hillside everything was so quiet and still even the cicadas had stopped calling. Leona wished that she could have some of that stillness, put her trembling emotions back where they belonged, under wraps, out of reach from pain and heartache.

Would these vulnerable feelings ever be that far out of reach? she then asked herself, and wasn't surprised to have a heavy sigh whisper from her. The beaded chiffon shawl slipped from her shoulders, prompting Ethan to come and gently lift it back in place again.

'Sorry,' he murmured. 'It wasn't my intention to upset you.'

I do it to myself, Leona thought bleakly. 'I just can't bear to talk about it,' she replied in what was a very rare glimpse at how badly she was hurting.

'Maybe you need to talk,' Ethan suggested.

But she just shook her head, as she consistently had done since she had arrived at her father's London house a year ago, looking emotionally shattered and announcing that her five-year marriage to Sheikh Hassan ben Khalifa Al-Qadim was over. Victor Frayne had tried every which way he could think of to find out what had happened. He'd even travelled out to Rahman to demand answers from Hassan, only to meet the same solid wall of silence he'd come up against with his daughter. The one thing Victor could say with any certainty was that Hassan was faring no better than Leona, though his dauntingly aloof son-in-law was more adept at hiding his emotions than Leona was. 'She sits here in London, he sits in Rahman. They don't talk to each other, never mind to anyone else! Yet you can feel the vibrations bouncing from one to the other across the thousands of miles separating them as if they are communicating by some unique telepathy that runs on pure pain! It's dreadful,' Victor had confided to Ethan. 'Something has to give some time.'

Eventually, it had done. Two months ago Leona had walked unannounced into the office of her family lawyer and had instructed him to begin divorce proceedings, on the grounds of irreconcilable differences. What had prompted her to pick that particular day in that particular month of a very long year no one understood, and Leona herself wasn't prepared to enlighten anyone. But there wasn't a person who knew her who didn't believe it was an action that had caused a trigger reaction, when a week later she had fallen foul of a virulent flu bug that had kept her housebound and bedridden for weeks afterwards.

But when she had recovered, at least she'd come back ready to face the world again. She had agreed to come here to San Estéban, for instance, and utilise her design skills on the completed villas.

She looked better for it too. Still too pale, maybe, but overall she'd begun to live a more normal day to day existence.

Ethan had no wish to send her back into hiding now she had come out of it, so he turned her to face him and pressed a light kiss to her brow. 'Come on,' he said briskly. 'Let's go and party!'

Finding her smile again, Leona nodded her agreement and

tried to appear as though she was looking forward to the evening. As they began to walk back across the terrace she felt a fine tingling at the back of her neck which instinctively warned her that someone was observing them.

The suspicion made her pause and turn to cast a frowning glance over their surroundings. She could see nothing untoward, but wasn't surprised by that. During the years she had lived in an Arab sheikhdom, married to a powerful and very wealthy man, she had grown used to being kept under constant, if very discreet, surveillance.

But that surveillance had been put in place for her own protection. This felt different—sinister. She even shivered.

'Something wrong?' Ethan questioned.

Leona shook her head and began walking again, but her frown stayed in place, because it wasn't the first time she'd experienced the sensation today. The same thing had happened as she'd left the resort site this afternoon, only she'd dismissed it then as her just being silly. She had always suspected that Hassan still kept an eye on her from a distance.

A car and driver had been hired for the evening, and both were waiting in the courtyard for them as they left the house. Having made sure she was comfortably settled, Ethan closed the side door and strode around the car to climb in beside her. As a man she had known for most of her adult life, Ethan was like a very fond cousin whose lean dark sophistication and reputed rakish life made her smile, rather than her heart flutter as other women would do in his company.

He'd never married. 'Never wanted to,' he'd told her once. 'Marriage diverts your energy away from your ambition, and I haven't met the woman for whom I'm prepared to let that happen.'

When she'd told Hassan what Ethan had said, she'd expected him to say something teasing like, May Allah help him when he does, for I know the feeling! But instead he'd looked quite sombre and had said nothing at all. At the time, she'd thought he'd been like that because he'd still been harbouring jealous suspicions about Ethan's feelings for her.

It had been a long time before she'd come to understand that the look had had nothing at all to do with Ethan.

'The Petronades yacht looks pretty impressive.' Ethan's smooth deep voice broke into her thoughts. 'I watched it sail into the harbour tonight while I was waiting for you on the terrace.'

Leandros Petronades was the main investor in San Estéban. He was hosting the party tonight for very exclusive guests whom he had seduced into taking a tour of the new resort, with an invitation to arrive in style on his yacht and enjoy its many luxurious facilities.

'At a guess, I would say it has to be the biggest in the harbour, considering its capacity to sleep so many people,' Leona smiled.

'Actually no, it wasn't,' Ethan replied with a frown. 'There's another yacht tied up that has to be twice the size.'

'The commercial kind?' Leona suggested, aware that the resort was fast becoming the fashionable place to visit.

'Not big enough.' Ethan shook his head. 'It's more likely to belong to one of Petronades' rich cronies. Another heavy investor in the resort, maybe.'

There were enough of them, Leona acknowledged. From being a sleepy little fishing port a few years ago, with the help of some really heavyweight investors San Estéban had grown into a large, custom-built holiday resort, which now sprawled in low-rise, Moorish elegance over the hills surrounding the bay.

So why Hassan's name slid back into her head Leona had no idea. Because Hassan didn't even own a yacht, nor had he ever invested in any of her father's projects, as far as she knew.

Irritated with herself, she turned her attention to what was happening outside the car. On the beach waterfront people strolled, enjoying the light breeze coming off the water.

It was a long time since she could remember strolling anywhere herself with such freedom. Marrying an Arab had brought with it certain restrictions on her freedom, which

were not all due to the necessity of conforming to expectations regarding women. Hassan occupied the august position
of being the eldest son and heir to the small but oil-rich Gulf
state of Rahman. As his wife, Leona had become a member
of Rahman's exclusive hierarchy, which in turn made everything she said or did someone else's property. So she'd
learned very quickly to temper her words, to think twice
before she went anywhere, especially alone. Strolling just for
the sake of just doing it would have been picked upon and
dissected for no other reason than interest's sake, so she had
learned not to do it.

This last year she hadn't gone out much because to be
seen out had drawn too much speculation as to why she was
in London and alone. In Rahman she was known as Sheikh
Hassan's pretty English Sheikha. In London she was known
as the woman who gave up every freedom to marry her
Arabian prince.

A curiosity in other words. Curiosities were blatantly
stared at, and she didn't want to offend Arab sensibilities by
having her failed marriage speculated upon in the British
press, so she'd lived a quiet life.

It was a thought that made Leona smile now, because her
life in Rahman had been far less quiet than it had become
once she'd returned to London.

The car had almost reached the end of the street where the
new harbour was situated. There were several large yachts
moored up—and Leandros Petronades' elegant white-hulled
boat was easy to recognise because it was lit up like a show-
boat for the party. Yet it was the yacht moored next to it that
caught her attention. It was huge, as Ethan had said—twice
the length and twice the height of its neighbour. It was also
shrouded in complete darkness. With its dark-painted hull, it
looked as if it was crouching there like a large sleek cat,
waiting to leap on its next victim.

The car turned and began driving along the top of the
harbour wall taking them towards a pair of wrought iron

gates, which cordoned off the area where the two yachts were tied.

Climbing out of the car, Leona stood looking round while she waited for Ethan to join her. It was even darker here than she had expected it to be, and she felt a distinct chill shiver down her spine when she realised they were going to have to pass the unlit boat to reach the other.

Ethan's hand found her arm. As they walked towards the gates, their car was already turning round to go back the way it had come. The guard manning the gates merely nodded his dark head and let them by without a murmur, then disappeared into the shadows.

'Conscientious chap,' Ethan said dryly.

Leona didn't answer. She was too busy having to fight a sudden attack of nerves that set butterflies fluttering inside her stomach. Okay, she tried to reason, so she hadn't put herself in the social arena much recently, therefore it was natural that she should suffer an attack of nerves tonight.

Yet some other part of her brain was trying to insist that her attack of nerves had nothing to do with the party. It was so dark and so quiet here that even their footsteps seemed to echo with a sinister ring.

Sinister? Picking up on the word, she questioned it impatiently. What was the matter with her? Why was everything sinister all of a sudden? It was a hot night—a beautiful night—she was twenty-nine years old, and about to do what most twenty-nine-year-olds did: party when they got the chance!

'Quite something, hmm?' Ethan remarked as they walked into the shadow of the larger yacht.

But Leona didn't want to look. Despite the tough talking-to she had just given herself, the yacht bothered her. The whole situation was beginning to worry her. She could feel her heart pumping unevenly against her breast, and just about every nerve-end she possessed was suddenly on full alert for no other reason than—

It was then that she heard it—nothing more than a whispering sound in the shadows, but it was enough to make her go perfectly still. So did Ethan. Almost at the same moment the darkness itself seemed to take on a life of its own by shifting and swaying before her eyes.

The tingling sensation on the back of her neck returned with a vengeance. 'Ethan,' she said jerkily. 'I don't think I like this.'

'No,' he answered tersely. 'Neither do I.'

That was the moment when they saw them, first one dark shape, then another, and another, emerging from the shadows until they turned themselves into Arabs wearing dark robes, with darkly sober expressions.

'Oh, dear God,' she breathed. 'What's happening?'

But she already knew the answer. It was a fear she'd had to live with from the day she'd married Hassan. She was British. She had married an Arab who was a very powerful man. The dual publicity her disappearance could generate was in itself worth its weight in gold to political fanatics wanting to make a point.

Something she should have remembered earlier, then the word 'sinister' would have made a lot more sense, she realised, as Ethan's arm pressed her hard up against him.

Further down the harbour wall the lights from the Petronades boat were swinging gently. Here, beneath the shadow of the other, the ring of men was steadily closing in. Her heart began to pound like a hammer drill. Ethan couldn't hold her any closer if he tried, and she could almost taste his tension. He, too, knew exactly what was going to happen.

'Keep calm,' he gritted down at her. 'When I give the word, lose your shoes and run.'

He was going to make a lunge for them and try to break the ring so she could have a small chance to escape. 'No,' she protested, and clutched tightly at his jacket sleeve. 'Don't do it. They might hurt you if you do!'

'Just go, Leona!' he ground back at her, then, with no more warning than that, he was pulling away, and almost in the same movement he threw himself at the two men closest to him.

It was then that all hell broke loose. While Leona stood there frozen in horror watching all three men topple to the ground in a huddle, the rest of the ring leapt into action. Fear for her life sent a surge of adrenaline rushing through her blood. Dry-mouthed, stark-eyed, she was just about to do as Ethan had told her and run, when she heard a hard voice rasp out a command in Arabic. In a state of raw panic she swung round in its direction, expecting someone to be almost upon her, only to find to her confusion that the ring of men had completely bypassed her, leaving her standing here alone with only one other man.

It was at that point that she truly stopped functioning— heart, lungs, her ability to hear what was happening to Ethan—all connections to her brain simply closed down to leave only her eyes in full, wretched focus.

Tall and dark, whip-cord lean, he possessed an aura about him that warned of great physical power lurking beneath the dark robes he was wearing. His skin was the colour of sun-ripened olives, his eyes as black as a midnight sky, and his mouth she saw was thin, straight and utterly unsmiling.

'Hassan.' She breathed his name into the darkness.

The curt bow he offered her came directly from an excess of noble arrogance built into his ancient genes. 'As you see,' Sheikh Hassan smoothly confirmed.

CHAPTER TWO

A BUBBLE of hysteria ballooned in her throat. 'But—why?' she choked in strangled confusion.

Hassan was not given the opportunity to answer before another fracas broke out somewhere behind her. Ethan ground her name out. It was followed by some thuds and scuffles. As she turned on a protesting gasp to go to him, someone else spoke with a grating urgency and Hassan caught her wrist, long brown fingers closing round fleshless skin and bone, to hold her firmly in place.

'Call them off!' she cried out shrilly.

'Be silent,' he returned in a voice like ice.

It shocked her, really shocked her, because never in their years together had he ever used that tone on her. Turning her head, she stared at him in pained astonishment, but Hassan wasn't even looking at her. His attention was fixed on a spot near the gates. With a snap of his fingers his men began scattering like bats on the wing, taking a frighteningly silent Ethan with them.

'Where are they going with him?' Leona demanded anxiously.

Hassan didn't answer. Another man came to stand directly behind her and, glancing up, she found herself gazing into yet another familiar face.

'Rafiq,' she murmured, but that was all she managed to say before Hassan was reclaiming her attention by snaking an arm around her waist and pulling her towards him. Her breasts made contact with solid muscle; her thighs suddenly burned like fire as they felt the unyielding power in his. Her eyes leapt up to clash with his eyes. It was like tumbling into oblivion. He looked so very angry, yet so very—

'Shh,' he cautioned. 'It is absolutely imperative that you do exactly as I say. For there is a car coming down the causeway and we cannot afford to have any witnesses.'

'Witnesses to what?' she asked in bewilderment.

There was a pause, a smile that was not quite a smile because it was too cold, too calculating, too—

'Your abduction,' he smoothly informed her.

Standing there in his arms, feeling trapped by a word that sounded totally alien falling from those lips she'd thought she knew so well, Leona released a constricted gasp then was totally silenced.

Car headlights suddenly swung in their direction. Rafiq moved and the next thing that she knew a shroud of black muslin was being thrown over her head. For a split second she couldn't believe what was actually happening! Then Hassan released his grasp so the muslin could unfurl right down to her ankles: she was being shrouded in an *abaya*.

Never had she *ever* been forced to wear such a garment! 'Oh, how could you?' she wrenched out, already trying to drag the *abaya* off again.

Strong arms firmly subdued her efforts. 'Now, you have two choices here, my darling.' Hassan's grim voice sounded close to her ear. 'You can either come quietly, of your own volition, or Rafiq and I will ensure that you do so—understand?'

Understand? Oh, yes, Leona thought painfully, she understood fully that she was being recovered like a lost piece of property! 'I'll never forgive you for this,' she breathed thickly.

His response was to wedge her between himself and Rafiq and then begin hustling her quickly forward. Feeling hot, trapped and blinded by the *abaya*, she had no idea where they were taking her.

Her frightened gasp brought Hassan's hand to cup her elbow. 'Be calm,' he said quietly. 'I am here.'

His reassurance was no assurance to Leona as he began urging her to walk ahead of him. The ground beneath her

feet gave way to something much less substantial. Through
the thin soles of her shoes she could feel a ridged metal
surface, and received a cold sense of some dark space yawning beneath it.

'What is this?' she questioned shakily.

'The gangway to my yacht,' Hassan replied.

His yacht, she repeated, and thought of the huge dark vessel squatting in the darkness. 'New toy, Hassan?' she hit out
deridingly.

'I knew you would be enchanted,' he returned. 'Watch
your step!' he cautioned sharply when the open toe of her
flimsy shoe caught on one of the metal ridges.

But she couldn't watch her step because the wretched
abaya was in the way! So she tripped, tried to right herself,
felt the slender heel of her shoe twist out from beneath her.
Instinct made her put out a hand in a bid to save herself. But
once again the *abaya* was in the way and, as she tried to
grapple with it, the long loose veil of muslin tangled around
her ankles and she lurched drunkenly forward. The sheer
impetus of the lurch lost Hassan his guiding grip on her arm.
As the sound of her own stifled cry mingled with the rough-
ness of his, Leona knew she hadn't a hope of saving herself.
In the few split seconds it all took to happen, she had a
horrible vision of deep dark water between the boat and the
harbour wall waiting to suck her down, with the wretched
abaya acting as her burial shroud.

Then hard hands were gripping her waist and roughly
righting her; next she was being scooped up and crushed hard
against a familiar chest. She curled into that chest like a
vulnerable child and began shaking all over while she listened to Hassan cursing and swearing beneath his breath as
he carried her, and Rafiq answering with soothing tones from
somewhere ahead.

Onto the yacht, across the deck, Leona could hear doors
being flung wide as they approached. By the time Hassan
decided that it was safe to set her down on her own feet
again, reaction was beginning to set in.

Shock and fright changed to a blistering fury the moment her feet hit the floor. Breaking free, she spun away from him, then began dragging the *abaya* off over her head with angry, shaking fingers. Light replaced darkness, sweet cool air replaced suffocating heat. Tossing the garment to the floor, she swung round to face her two abductors with her green eyes flashing and the rest of her shimmering with an incandescent rage.

Both Hassan and Rafiq stood framed by a glossy wood doorway, studying her with differing expressions. Both wore long black tunics beneath dark blue cloaks cinched in at the waist with wide black sashes. Dark blue *gutrahs* framed their lean dark faces. One neatly bearded, the other clean-shaven and sleek. Both held themselves with an indolent arrogance that was a challenge as they waited to receive her first furious volley.

Her heart flipped over and tumbled to her stomach, her feeling of an impossible-to-fight admiration for these two people, only helping to infuriate her all the more. For who were they—*what* were they—that they believed they had the right to treat her like this?

She began to walk towards them. Her hair had escaped from its twist and was now tumbling like fire over her shoulders, and somewhere along the way she had lost her shawl and shoes. Without the help of her shoes, the two men towered over her, indomitable and proud, dark brown eyes offering no hint of apology.

Her gaze fixed itself somewhere between them, her hands closed into two tightly clenched fists at her side. The air actually stung with an electric charge of anticipation. 'I demand to see Ethan,' she stated very coldly.

It was clearly the last thing either was expecting her to say. Rafiq stiffened infinitesimally, Hassan looked as if she could not have insulted him more if she'd tried.

His eyes narrowed, his mouth grew thin, his handsome sleek features hardened into polished rock. Beneath the dark robes, Leona saw his wide chest expand and remain that way as, with a sharp flick of a hand, he sent Rafiq sweeping out of the room.

As the door closed them in, the sudden silence stifled almost as much as the *abaya* had done. Neither moved, neither spoke for the space of thirty long heart-throbbing seconds, while Hassan stared coldly down at her and she stared at some obscure point near his right shoulder.

Years of loving this one man, she was thinking painfully. Five years of living the dream in a marriage she had believed was so solid that nothing could ever tear it apart. Now she couldn't even bring herself to focus on his face properly in case the feelings she now kept deeply suppressed inside her came surging to the surface and spilled out on a wave of broken-hearted misery. For their marriage was over. They both knew it was over. He should not have done this to her. It hurt so badly that he could treat her this way that she didn't think she was ever going to forgive him for it.

Hassan broke the silence by releasing the breath he had been holding onto. 'In the interests of harmony, I suggest you restrain from mentioning Ethan Hayes in my presence,' he advised, then simply stepped right past her to walk across the room to a polished wood counter which ran the full length of one wall.

As she followed the long, lean, subtle movement of his body through desperately loving eyes, fresh fury leapt up to save her again. 'But who else would I ask about when I've just watched your men beat him up and drag him away?' she threw after him.

'They did not beat him up.' Flicking open a cupboard door, he revealed a fridge stocked with every conceivable form of liquid refreshment.

'They fell on him like a flock of hooligans!'

'They subdued his enthusiasm for a fight.'

'He was defending me!'

'That is my prerogative.'

Her choked laugh at that announcement dropped scorn all

over it. 'Sometimes your arrogance stuns even me!' she informed him scathingly.

The fridge door shut with a thud. 'And your foolish refusal to accept wise advice when it is offered to you stuns me!'

Twisting round, Hassan was suddenly revealing an anger that easily matched her own. His eyes were black, his expression harsh, his mouth snapped into a grim line. In his hand he held a bottle of mineral water which he slammed down on the cabinet top, then he began striding towards her, big and hard and threatening.

'I don't know what's the matter with you,' she burst out bewilderedly. 'Why am I under attack when I haven't done anything?'

'You dare to ask that, when this is the first time we have looked upon each other in a year—yet all you can think about is Ethan Hayes?'

'Ethan isn't your enemy,' she persisted stubbornly.

'No.' Thinly said. Then something happened within his eyes that set her heart shuddering. He came to a stop a bare foot away from her. 'But he is most definitely yours,' he said.

She didn't want him this close and took a step back. 'I don't know what you mean,' she denied.

He closed the gap again. 'A married woman openly living with a man who is not her husband carries a heavy penalty in Rahman.'

'Are you daring to suggest that Ethan and I *sleep* together?' Her eyes went wide with utter affront.

'Do you?'

The question was like a slap to the face. 'No we do not!'

'Prove it,' he challenged.

Surprise had her falling back another step. 'But you know Ethan and I don't have that kind of relationship,' she insisted.

'And, I repeat,' he said, 'prove it.'

Nerve-ends began to fray when she realised he was being serious. 'I can't,' she admitted, then went quite pale when she felt forced to add, 'But you know I wouldn't sleep with him, Hassan. You *know* it,' she emphasised with a painfully thickening tone which placed a different kind of darkness in his eyes.

It came from understanding and pity. And she hated him for that also! Hated and loved and hurt with a power that was worse than any other torture he could inflict.

'Then explain to me, please,' he persisted nonetheless, 'when you openly live beneath the same roof as he does, how I convince my people of this certainty you believe I have in your fidelity?'

'But Ethan and I haven't spent one night alone together in the villa,' she protested. 'My father has always been there with us until he was delayed in London today!'

'Quite.' Hassan nodded. 'Now you understand why you have been snatched from the brink of committing the ultimate sin in the eyes of our people. There,' he said with a dismissive flick of the hand. 'I am your saviour, as is my prerogative.'

With that, and having neatly tied the whole thing off to his own satisfaction, he turned and walked away— Leaving Leona to flounder in his smooth, slick logic and with no ready argument to offer.

'I don't believe you are real sometimes,' she sent shakily after him. 'Did it never occur to you that I didn't want *snatching from the brink*?'

Sarcasm abounding, Hassan merely pulled the *gutrah* from his head and tossed it aside, then returned to the bottle of water. 'It was time,' he said, swinging the fridge door open again. 'You have had long enough to sulk.'

'I wasn't sulking!'

'Whatever,' he dismissed with a shrug, then chose a bottle of white wine and closed the door. 'It was time to bring the impasse to an end.'

Impasse, Leona repeated. He believed their failed marriage was merely stuck in an *impasse*. 'I'm not coming back to you,' she declared, then turned away to pretend to take an interest in her surroundings, knowing that his grim silence was denying her the right to choose.

They were enclosed in what she could only presume was a private stateroom furnished in subtle shades of cream faced with richly polished rosewood. It was all so beautifully designed that it was almost impossible to see the many doors built into the walls except for the wood-framed doors they had entered through. And it was the huge deep-sprung divan taking pride of place against a silk-lined wall, that told her exactly what the room's function was.

Although the bed was not what truly captured her attention, but the pair of big easy chairs standing in front of a low table by a set of closed cream velvet curtains. As her heart gave a painful twist in recognition, she sent a hand drifting up to her eyes. Oh, Hassan, she thought despairingly, don't do this to me...

She had seen the chairs, Hassan noted, studying the way she was standing there looking like an exquisitely fragile, perfectly tooled art-deco sculpture in her slender gown of gold. And he didn't know whether to tell her so or simply weep at how utterly bereft she looked.

In the end he chose a third option and took a rare sip at the white wine spritzer he had just prepared for her. The forbidden alcohol content in the drink might be diluted but he felt it hit his stomach and almost instantly enter his bloodstream with an injection of much appreciated fire.

'You've lost weight,' he announced, and watched her chin come up, watched her wonderful hair slide down her slender back and her hand drop slowly to her side while she took a steadying breath before she could bring herself to turn and face him.

'I've been ill—with the flu,' she answered flatly.

'That was weeks ago,' he dismissed, uncaring that he was revealing to her just how close an eye he had been keeping on her from a distance. The fact that she showed no surprise told him that she had guessed as much anyway. 'After a virus such as influenza the weight recovery is usually swift.'

'And you would know, of course,' she drawled, mocking the fact that he had not suffered a day's illness in his entire life.

'I know *you*,' he countered, 'and your propensity for slipping into a decline when you are unhappy…'

'I was *ill*, not unhappy.'

'You missed me. I missed you. Why try to deny it?'

'May I have one of those?' Indicating towards the drink he held in his hand was her way of telling him she was going to ignore those kind of comments.

'It is yours,' he explained, and offered the glass out to her.

She looked at the glass, long dusky lashes flickering over her beautiful green eyes when she realised he was going to make her come and get the drink. Would she do it? he wondered curiously. Would she allow herself to come this close, when they both knew she would much rather turn and run?

But his beautiful wife had never been a coward. No matter how she might be feeling inside, he had never known her to run from a challenge. Even when she had left him last year she had done so with courage, not cowardice. And she did not let him down now as her silk stockinged feet began to tread the cream carpet until she was in reach of the glass.

'Thank you.' The wine spritzer was taken from him and lifted to her mouth. She sipped without knowing she had been offered the glass so she would place her lips where his lips had been.

Her pale throat moved as she swallowed; her lips came away from the glass wearing a seductively alluring wine glossed bloom. He watched her smother a sigh, watched her look anywhere but directly at him, was aware that she had not looked him in the face since removing the *abaya*, just as she had stopped looking at him weeks before she left Rahman. And he had to suppress his own sigh as he felt muscles tighten all over his body in his desire to reach out, draw her close and make her look at him!

But this was not the time to play the demanding husband. She would reject him as she had rejected him many times a year ago. What hurt him the most about remembering those bleak interludes was not his own angry frustration but the grim knowledge that it had been herself she had been denying.

'Was the Petronades yacht party an elaborate set-up?' she asked suddenly.

A brief smile stretched his mouth, and it was a very self-mocking smile because he had truly believed she was as concentrated on his close physical presence as he was on hers. But, no. As always, Leona's mind worked in ways that continually managed to surprise him.

'The party was genuine.' He answered the question. 'Your father's sudden inability to get here in time to attend it was not.'

At least his honesty almost earned him a direct glance of frowning puzzlement before she managed to divert it to his right ear. 'But you've just finished telling me that I was snatched because my father was—'

'I know,' he cut in, not needing to hear her explain what he already knew—which was that this whole thing had been very carefully set up and co-ordinated with her father's assistance. 'There are many reasons why you are standing here with me right now, my darling,' he murmured gently. 'Most of which can wait for another time to go into.'

The *my darling* sent her back a defensive step. The realisation that her own father had plotted against her darkened her lovely eyes. 'Tell me now,' she insisted.

But Hassan just shook his head. 'Now is for me,' he informed her softly. 'Now is my moment to bask in the fact that you are back where you belong.'

It was really a bit of bad timing that her feet should use that particular moment to tread on the discarded *abaya*, he supposed, watching as she looked down, saw, then grew angry all over again.

'By abduction?' Her chin came up, contempt shimmering along her finely shaped bones. 'By plots and counter-plots and by removing a woman's right to decide for herself?'

He grimaced at her very accurate description. 'We are by
nature a romantic people,' he defended. 'We love drama and
poetry and tragic tales of star-crossed lovers who lose each
other and travel the caverns of hell in their quest to find their
way back together again.'

He saw the tears. He had said too much. Reaching out, he
caught the glass just before it slipped from her nerveless
fingers. 'Our marriage is a tragedy,' she told him thickly.

'No,' he denied, putting the hapless glass aside. 'You
merely insist on turning it into one.'

'Because I hate everything you stand for!'

'But you cannot make yourself hate the man,' he added,
undisturbed by her denunciation.

Leona began to back away because there was something
seriously threatening about the sudden glow she caught in
his eyes. 'I left you, remember?'

'Then sent me letters at regular intervals to make sure I
remembered you,' he drawled.

'Letters to tell you I want a divorce!' she cried.

'The content of the letters came second to their true purpose.' He smiled. 'One every two weeks over the last two
months. I found them most comforting.'

'Gosh, you are so conceited it's a wonder you didn't marry
yourself!'

'Such insults.' He sighed.

'Will you stop stalking me as if I am a hunted animal?'
she cried.

'Stop backing away like one.'

'I do not want to stay married to you.' She stated it
bluntly.

'And I am not prepared to let you go. There,' he said. 'We
have reached another impasse. Which one of us is going to
win the higher ground this time, do you think?'

Looking at him standing there, arrogant and proud yet so
much her kind of man that he made her legs go weak, Leona
knew exactly which one of them possessed the higher
ground. Which was also why she had to keep him at arm's

length at all costs. He could fell her in seconds, because he was right; she didn't hate him, she adored him. And that scared her so much that when his hand came up, long fingertips brushing gently across her trembling mouth, she almost fainted on the sensation that shot from her lips to toe tips.

She pulled right away. His eyebrow arched. It mocked and challenged as he responded by curling the hand around her nape.

'Stop it,' she said, and lifted up her hand to use it as a brace against his chest.

Beneath dark blue cotton she discovered a silk-smooth, hard-packed body pulsing with heat and an all-too-familiar masculine potency. Her mouth went dry; she tried to breathe and found that she couldn't. Helplessly she lifted her eyes up to meet with his.

'Seeing me now, hmm?' he softly taunted. 'Seeing this man with these eyes you like to drown in, and this nose you like to call dreadful but usually have trouble from stopping your fingers from stroking? And let us not forget this mouth you so like to feel crushed hotly against your own delightful mouth.'

'Don't you dare!' she protested, seeing what was coming and already beginning to shake all over at the terrifying prospect of him finding out what a weak-willed coward she was.

'Why not?' he countered, offering her one of his lazily sensual, knowing smiles that said he knew better than she did what she really wanted—and he began to lower his dark head.

'Tell me first.' Sheer desperation made her fly into impulsive speech. 'If I am here on this beautiful yacht that belongs to you—is there another yacht just like it out there somewhere where your second wife awaits her turn?'

In the sudden suffocating silence that fell between them Leona found herself holding her breath as she watched his face pale to a frightening stillness. For this was provocation of the worst kind to an Arab and her heart began pounding madly because she just didn't know how he was going to respond. Hassan possessed a shocking temper, though he had never unleashed it on her. But now, as she stood here with her fingers still pressed against his breastbone, she could feel the danger in him—could almost taste her own fear as she waited to see how he was going to respond.

What he did was to take a step back from her. Cold, aloof, he changed into the untouchable prince in the single blink of an ebony eyelash. 'Are you daring to imply that I could be guilty of treating my wives unequally?' he responded.

In the interim wave of silence that followed, Leona stared at him through eyes that had stopped seeing anything as his reply rocked the very axis she stood upon. She knew she had prompted it but she still had not expected it, and now she found she couldn't breathe, couldn't even move as fine cracks began to appear in her defences.

'You actually went and did it, and married again,' she whispered, then completely shattered. Emotionally, physically, she felt herself fragment into a thousand broken pieces beneath his stone-cold, cruel gaze.

Hassan didn't see it coming. He should have done, he knew that, but he had been too angry to see anything but his own affronted pride. So when she turned and ran he didn't expect it. By the time he had pulled his wits together enough to go after her Leona was already flying through the door on a flood of tears.

The tears blinded what was ahead of her, the *abaya* having prevented her from taking stock of her surroundings as they'd arrived. Hassan heard Rafiq call out a warning, reached the door as Leona's cry curdled the very air surrounding them and she began to fall.

What he had managed to prevent by the skin of his teeth only a half-hour before now replayed itself before his helpless eyes. Only it was not the dark waters of the Mediterranean she fell into but the sea of cream carpet that ran from room to room and down a wide flight of three shallow stairs that led down into the yacht's main foyer.

CHAPTER THREE

CURSING and swearing in seething silence, Hassan prowled three sides of the bed like a caged tiger while the yacht's Spanish medic checked her over.

'No bones broken, as far as I can tell,' the man said. 'No obvious blow to the head.'

'Then why is she unconscious?' he growled out furiously.

'Shock—winded,' the medic suggested, gently laying aside a frighteningly limp hand. 'It has only been a few minutes, sir.'

But a few minutes was a lifetime when you felt so guilty you wished it was yourself lying there, Hassan thought harshly.

'A cool compress would be a help—'

A cool compress. 'Rafiq.' The click of his fingers meant the job would be done.

The sharp sound made Leona flinch. On a single, lithe leap Hassan was suddenly stretched out across the bed and leaning over her. The medic drew back; Rafiq paused in his step.

'Open your eyes.' Hassan turned her face towards him with a decidedly unsteady hand.

Her eyes fluttered open to stare up at him blankly. 'What happened?' she mumbled.

'You fell down some stairs,' he gritted. 'Now tell me where you hurt.'

A frown began to pucker her smooth brow as she tried to remember.

'Concentrate,' he rasped, diverting her mind away from what had happened. 'Do you hurt anywhere?'

She closed her eyes again, and he watched her make a mental inventory of herself then give a small shake of her head. 'I think I'm okay.' She opened her eyes again, looked directly into his, saw his concern, his anguish, the burning fires of guilt—and then she remembered *why* she'd fallen.

Aching tears welled up again. From coldly plunging his imaginary knife into her breast, he now felt it enter his own. 'You really went and did it,' she whispered.

'No, I did not,' he denied. 'Get out,' he told their two witnesses.

The room emptied like water down a drain, leaving them alone again, confronting each other again. It was dangerous. He wanted to kiss her so badly he could hardly breathe. She was his. He was hers! They should not be in this warring situation!

'No—remain still!' he commanded when she attempted to move. 'Don't even breathe unless you have to do so! Why are females so *stupid*?' he bit out like a curse. 'You insult me with your suspicions. You goad me into a response, and when it is not the one you want to hear you slay me with your pain!'

'I didn't mean to fall down the stairs,' she pointed out.

'I wasn't talking about the fall!' he bit out, then glared down into her confused, hurt, vulnerable eyes for a split second longer. 'Oh, Allah give me strength,' he gritted, and gave in to himself and took her trembling mouth by storm.

If he had kissed her in any other way Leona would have fought him with her very last breath. But she liked the storm; she *needed* the storm so she could allow herself to be swept away. Plus he was trembling, and she liked that too. Liked to know that she still had the power to reduce the prince in him to this vulnerable mass of smashed emotion.

And she'd missed him. She'd missed feeling his length lying alongside her length, had missed the weight of his thighs pressing down on her own. She'd missed his kiss, hungry, urgent, insistent…wanting. Like a banquet after a year of long, hard fasting, she fed greedily on every deep, dark, sensual delight. Lips, teeth, tongue, taste. She reached for his chest, felt the strong beat of his heart as she glided her palms beneath the fabric of his top robe where only the thin cotton of his tunic came between them and tightly muscled, satin-smooth flesh. When she reached his shoulders her fingers curled themselves into tightly padded muscle then stayed there, inviting him to take what he liked.

He took her breasts, stroking and shaping before moving on to follow the slender curve of her body. Long fingers claimed her hips, then drew her against the force of his. Fire bloomed in her belly, for this was her man, the love of her life. She would never, ever, find herself another. What he touched belonged to him. What he desired he could have.

What he did was bring a cruelly abrupt end to it by rising in a single fluid movement to land on his feet beside the bed, leaving her to flounder on the hard rocks of rejection while he stood there with his back to her, fighting a savage battle with himself.

'Why?' she breathed in thick confusion.

'We are not animals,' he ground back. 'We have issues to deal with that must preclude the hungry coupling at which we already know we both excel.'

It served as a dash of water in her face; and he certainly possessed good aim, Leona noted as she came back to reality with a shivering gasp. 'What issues?' she challenged cynically. 'The issue of what we have left besides the excellent sex?'

He didn't answer. Instead he made one of her eyebrows arch as he snatched up her spritzer and grimly downed the lot. There was a man at war with himself as well as with her, Leona realised, knowing Hassan hardly ever touched alcohol, and only then when he was under real stress.

Sitting up, she was aware of a few aches and bruises as she gingerly slid her feet to the floor. 'I want to go home,' she announced.

'This is home,' he replied. 'For the next few weeks, anyway.'

Few weeks? Coming just as gingerly to her feet, Leona stared at his rigid back—which was just another sign that

Hassan was not functioning to his usual standards, because no Arab worthy of the race would deliberately set his back to anyone. It was an insult of the worst kind.

Though she had seen his back a lot during those few months before she'd eventually left him, Leona recalled with a familiar sinking feeling inside. Not because he had wished to insult her, she acknowledged, but because he had refused to face what they had both known was happening to their marriage. In the end, she had taken the initiative away from him.

'Where are my shoes?'

The surprisingly neutral question managed to bring him swinging round to glance at her feet. 'Rafiq has them.'

Dear Rafiq, Leona thought wryly, Hassan's ever-loyal partner in crime. Rafiq was an Al-Qadim. A man who had attended the same schools, the same universities, the same everything as Hassan had done. Equals in many ways, prince and lowly servant in others. It was a complicated relationship that wound around the status of birth and the ranks of power.

'Perhaps you would be kind enough to ask him to give them back to me.' Even she knew you didn't *command* Rafiq to do anything. He was a law unto himself—and Hassan. Rafiq was a maverick. A man of the desert, yet not born of the desert; fiercely proud, fiercely protective of his right to be master of his own decisions.

'For what purpose?'

Leona's chin came up, recognising the challenge in his tone. She offered him a cool, clear look. 'I am not staying here, Hassan,' she told him flatly. 'Even if I have to book into a hotel in San Estéban to protect your dignity, I am leaving this boat now, tonight.'

His expression grew curious, a slight smile touched his mouth. 'Strong swimmer, are you?' he questioned lazily.

It took a few moments for his taunt to truly sink in, then she was moving, darting across the room and winding her way between the two strategically placed chairs and the accompanying table to reach for the curtains. Beyond the glass, all she could see was inky darkness. Maybe she was on the seaward side of the boat, she told herself in an effort to calm the sudden sting of alarm that slid down her spine.

Hassan quickly disabused her of that frail hope. 'We left San Estéban minutes after we boarded.'

It was only then that she felt it: just the softest hint of a vibration beneath the soles of her feet that told of smooth and silently running engines. This truly was an abduction, she finally accepted, and turned slowly back round to face him.

'Why?' she breathed.

It was like a replay of what had already gone before, only this time it was serious—more serious than Leona had even begun to imagine. For she knew this man—knew he was not given to flights of impulse just for the hell of it. Everything he did had to have a reason, and was always preceded by meticulous planning which took time he would not waste, and effort he would not move unless he felt he absolutely had to do.

Hassan's small sigh conveyed that he too knew that this was where the prevarication ended. 'There are problems at home,' he informed her soberly. 'My father's health is failing.'

His father… Anger swiftly converted itself into anxious concern for her father-in-law. Sheikh Khalifa had been frail in health for as long as she had known him. Hassan doted on him and devoted most of his energy to relieving his father of the burdens of rule, making sure he had the best medical attention available and refusing to believe that one day his father would not be there. So, if Hassan was using words like 'failing', then the old man's health must indeed be grave.

'What happened?' She began to walk towards him. 'I thought the last treatment was—'

'Your interest is a little too late in coming,' Hassan cut in, and with a flick of a hand halted her steps. 'For I don't recall you showing any concern about what it would do to his health when you left a year ago.'

That wasn't fair, and Leona blinked as his words pricked a tender part of her. Sheikh Khalifa was a good man—a kind man. They had become strong, close friends while she had lived at the palace. 'He understood why I felt I needed to leave,' she responded painfully.

You think so? Hassan's cynical expression derided. 'Well, I did not,' he said out loud. 'But, since you decided it was the right thing for you to do, I now have a serious problem on my hands. For I am, in effect, deemed weak for allowing my wife to walk away from me, and my critics are making rumbling noises about the stability of the country if I do not display some leadership.'

'So you decided to show that leadership by abducting me, then dragging me back to Rahman?' Her thick laugh poured scorn over that suggestion, because they both knew taking her back home had to be the worst thing Hassan could possibly do to prove that particular point.

'You would prefer that I take this second wife who makes you flee in pain when the subject appears in front of you?'

'She is what you need, not me.' It almost choked her to say the words. But they were dealing with the truth here, painful though that truth may be. And the truth was that she was no longer the right wife for the heir to a sheikhdom.

'I have the wife I want,' he answered grimly.

'But not the wife you *need*, Hassan!' she countered wretchedly.

His eyes flicked up to clash with her eyes. 'Is that your way of telling me that you no longer love me?' he challenged.

Oh, dear God. Lifting a trembling hand up to cover her eyes, Leona gave a shake of her head in refusal to answer. Without warning Hassan was suddenly moving at speed down the length of the room.

'Answer me!' he insisted when he came to a stop in front of her.

Swallowing on a lump of tears, Leona turned her face away. 'Yes,' she whispered.

His sudden grip on her hand dragged it from her eyes. 'To my face,' he instructed, 'You will tell me this to my face!'

Her head whipped up, tear darkened eyes fixing painfully on burning black. 'Don't—' she pleaded.

But he was not going to give in. He was pale and he was hurt and he was furiously angry. 'I want to hear you state that you feel no love for me,' he persisted. 'I want you to tell that wicked lie to my face. And then I want to hear you beg forgiveness when I prove to you otherwise! Do you understand, Leona?'

'All right! So, I love you! Does that make it all okay?' she cried out. 'I love you but I will not stay married to you! I will *not* watch you ruin your life because of me!'

There—it was out. The bitter truth. On voicing it, she broke free and reeled away, hurting so much it was almost impossible to breathe. 'And your life?' he persisted relentlessly. 'What happens to it while you play the sacrificial lamb for mine?'

'I'll get by,' she said, trying to walk on legs that were shaking so badly she wasn't sure if she was going to fall down.

'You'll marry again?'

She shuddered and didn't reply.

'Take lovers in an attempt to supplant me?'

Harsh and cruel though he sounded, she could hear his anguish. 'I need no one,' she whispered.

'Then you mean to spend the rest of your life watching me produce progeny with this second wife I am to take?'

'Oh, dear heaven.' She swung around. 'What are you trying to do to me?' she choked out tormentedly.

'Make you see,' he gritted. 'Make you open your eyes and *see* what it is you are condemning us both to.'

'But I'm not condemning you to anything! I am giving you my blessing to do what you want with your life!'

If she'd offered to give him a whole harem he could not have been more infuriated. His face became a map of hard angles. 'Then I will take what I want!' It was a declaration of intent that propelled him across the space between them. Before Leona knew what was coming she was locked in his arms and being lifted until their eyes were level. Startled green irises locked with burning black passion. He gave her one small second to read their message before he was kissing her furiously. Shocked out of one kind of torment, she found herself flung into the middle of another—because once again she had no will to fight. She even released a protesting groan when her feet found solid ground again and he broke the urgent kiss.

Her lips felt hot, and pulsed with such a telling fullness that she had to lick them to try and cool them down. His breath left his body on a hiss that brought her eyes flickering dazedly up to his. Thick dark lashes rested over ebony eyes that were fixed on the moist pink tip of her tongue. A slither of excitement skittered right down the front of her. Her breasts grew tight, her abdomen warming at the prospect of what all of this meant.

Making love. Feeling him deep inside her. No excuses, no drawing back this time. She only had to look at Hassan to know this was it. He was about to stake his claim on what belonged to him.

'You will regret this later,' she warned unsteadily, because she knew how his passions and his conscience did not always walk in tandem—especially not where she was concerned.

'Are you denying me?' he threw back in a voice that said he was interested in the answer, but only out of curiosity.

Well, Leona asked herself, are you?

The answer was no, she was not denying him anything he wanted to take from her tonight. Tomorrow was another day, another war, another set of agonising conflicts. Reaching up, she touched a gentle finger to his mouth, drew its shape, softened the tension out of it, then sighed, went up on tiptoe and gently joined their mouths.

His hands found the slender frame of her hips and drew her against him; her hands lifted higher to link around his neck so her fingers could slide sensually into his silk dark hair. It was an embrace that sank them into a long deep loving. Her dress fell away, slithering down her body on a pleasurable whisper of silk against flesh. Beneath she wore a dark gold lace bra, matching high-leg briefs and lace-topped stockings. Hassan discovered all of this with the sensual stroke of long fingers. He knew each pleasure point, the quality of each little gasp she breathed into his mouth. When her bra fell away, she sighed and pressed herself against him; when his fingers slid beneath the briefs to cup her bottom she allowed him to ease her into closer contact. They knew each other, *loved* each other—cared so very deeply about each other. Fight they might do—often. They might have insurmountable problems. But nothing took away the love and caring. It was there, as much part of them as the life-giving oxygen they took into their lungs.

'You want me,' he declared.

'I've always wanted you,' she sadly replied.

'I am your other half.'

And I am your broken one, Leona thought, releasing an achingly melancholy sigh.

Maybe he knew what she was thinking, because his mouth took burning possession that gave no more room to think at all. It came as an unwelcome break when he lowered her down onto the bed then straightened, taking her briefs with him. Her love-flooded eyes watched his eyes roam over her. He was no longer being driven by his inner devils, she realised as she watched him removing his own clothing. Her compliance had neutralised the compelling need to stake his claim.

So she watched him follow her every movement as she made a sensual love-play out of removing her stockings from her long slender legs. His dark robe landed on the floor on top of her clothing; the tunic eventually went the same way. Beneath waited a desert-bronzed silk-smooth torso, with a muscled structure that set her green eyes glowing with pleasure and made her fingers itch to touch. Those muscles rippled and flexed as he reached down to grasp the only piece of clothing he had left to remove. The black shorts trailed away from a sexual force that set her feminine counterpart pulsing with anticipation.

He knew what was happening, smiled a half-smile, then came to lean over her, lowering his raven head to place a kiss there that was really a claim of ownership. She breathed out a shivering breath of pleasure and he was there to claim that also. Then she had all of him covering her. It was the sweetest feeling she had ever experienced. He was her Arabian lover. The man she had seen across a crowded room long years ago. And she had never seen another man clearly since.

He seduced her mouth, he seduced her body, he seduced her into seducing him. When it all became too much without deeper contact, he eased himself between her thighs and slowly joined them.

Her responsive groan made him pause. 'What?' he questioned anxiously.

'I've missed you so much.' She sighed the words out helplessly.

It was a catalyst that sent him toppling. He staked his claim on those few emotive words with every driving thrust. She died a little. It was strange how she did that, she found herself thinking as the pleasure began to run like liquid fire. They came as one, within the grip of hard, gasping shudders and afterwards lay still, locked together, as their bodies went through the pleasurable throes of settling back down again.

Then nothing moved, not their bodies nor even their quiet breathing. The silence came—pure, numbing, unbreakable silence.

Why?

Because it had all been so beautiful but also so very empty. And nothing was ever going to change that.

Hassan moved first, levering himself away to land on his feet by the bed. He didn't even spare her a glance as he walked away. Sensational naked, smooth and sleek, he touched a finger to the wall and a cleverly concealed door sprung open. As he stepped through it Leona caught a glimpse of white tiling and realised it was a bathroom. Then the door closed, shutting him in and her completely out.

Closing her eyes, she lifted an arm up to cover them, and pressed her lips together to stop them from trembling on the tears she was having to fight. For this was not a new situation she was dealing with here. It had happened before—often— and was just one of the many reasons why she had left him in the end. The pain had been too great to go on taking it time after time. His pain, her pain—she had never been able to distinguish where one ended and the other began. The only difference here tonight was that she'd somehow managed to let herself forget that, until this cold, solitary moment.

Hassan stood beneath the pulsing jet of the power shower and wanted to hit something so badly that he had to brace his hands against the tiles and lock every muscle to keep the murderous feeling in. His body was replete but his heart was grinding against his ribcage with a frustration that nothing could cure.

Silence. He hated that silence. He hated knowing he had nothing worth saying with which to fill it in. And he still had to go back in there and face it. Face the dragging sense of his own helplessness and—worse—he had to face hers.

His wife. His woman. The other half of him. Head lowered so the water sluiced onto his shoulders and down his back, he tried to predict what her next move was going to be, and came up with only one grim answer. She was not going to stay. He could bully her as much as he liked, but in the end she was still going to walk away from him unless he could come up with something important enough to make her stay.

Maybe he should have used more of his father's illness, he told himself. A man she loved, a man she'd used to spend hours of every day with, talking, playing board games or just quietly reading to him when he was too weak to enjoy anything else.

But his father had not been enough to make her want to

stay the last time. The old fool had given her his blessing, had missed her terribly, yet even on the day he'd gone to see him before he left the palace he had still maintained that Leona had had to do what she'd believed was right.

So who was in the wrong here? Him for wanting to spend his life with one particular woman, or Leona for wanting to do what was right?

He hated that phrase, *doing what was right.* It reeked of duty at the expense of everything: duty to his family, duty to his country, duty to produce the next Al-Qadim son and heir.

Well, I don't need a son. I don't need a second wife to produce one for me like some specially selected brood mare! I need a beautiful red-haired creature who makes my heart ache each time I look at her. I *don't* need to see that glazed look of emptiness she wears after we make love!

On a sigh he turned round, swapped braced hands for braced shoulders against the shower wall. The water hit his face and stopped him breathing. He didn't care if he never breathed again—until instinct took over from grim stubbornness and forced him to move again.

Coming out of the bathroom a few minutes later, he had to scan the room before he spotted her sitting curled up in one of the chairs. She had opened the curtains and was just sitting there staring out, with her wonderful hair gleaming hot against the pale damask upholstery. She had wrapped herself in a swathe of white and a glance at the tumbled bed told him she had dragged free the sheet of Egyptian cotton to wear.

His gaze dropped to the floor by the bed, where their clothes still lay in an intimate huddle that was a lot more honest than the two of them were with each other.

'Find out how Ethan is.'

The sound of her voice brought his attention back to her. She hadn't moved, had not turned to look at him, and the demand spoke volumes as to what was really being said. Barter and exchange. She had given him more of herself than she had intended to do; now she wanted something back by return.

Without a word he crossed to the internal telephone and found out what she wanted to know, ordered some food to be sent in to them, then strode across the room to sit down in the chair next to hers. 'He caught an accidental blow to the jaw which knocked him out for a minute or two, but he is fine now,' he assured her. 'And is dining with Rafiq as we speak.'

'So he wasn't part of this great plan of abduction you plotted with my father.' It wasn't a question, it was a sign of relief.

'I am devious and underhand on occasion but not quite that devious and underhand,' he countered dryly.

Her chin was resting on her bent knees, but she turned her head to look at him through dark, dark eyes. Her hair flowed across her white-swathed shoulders, and her soft mouth looked vulnerable enough to conquer in one smooth swoop. His body quickened, temptation clawing across flesh hidden beneath his short robe of sand-coloured silk.

'Convincing my own father to plot against me wasn't devious or underhand?' she questioned.

'He was relieved I was ready to break the deadlock,' he informed her. 'He wished me well, then offered me all the help he could give.'

Her lack of comment was one in itself. Her following sigh punctuated it. She was seeing betrayal from her own father, but it just was not true. 'You knew he worried about you,' he inserted huskily. 'Yet you didn't tell him why you left me, did you?'

The remark lost him contact with her eyes as she turned them frontward again, and the way she stared out into the inky blackness beyond the window closed up his throat, because he knew what she was really seeing as she looked out there.

'Coming to terms with being a failure is not something I wanted to share with anyone,' she murmured dully.

'You are not a failure,' he denied.

'I am infertile!' She flashed out the one word neither of them wanted to hear.

It launched Hassan to his feet on a surge of anger. 'You are not infertile!' he ground out harshly. 'That is not what the doctors said, and you know it is not!'

'Will you stop hiding from it?' she cried, scrambling to her feet to stand facing him, with her face as white as the sheet she clutched around her and her eyes as black as the darkness outside. 'I have one defunct ovary and the other one ovulates only when it feels like it!' She spelt it out for him.

'Which does not add up to infertility,' he countered forcefully.

'After all of these years of nothing, you can still bring yourself to say that?'

She was staring up at him as if he was deliberately trying to hurt her. And, because he had no answer to that final charge, he had to ask himself if that had been his subconscious intention. The last year had been hell to live through and the year preceding only marginally better. Married life had become a place in which they'd walked with the darkness of disappointment shadowing their past and future. In the end, Leona had not been able to take it any more so she'd left him. If she wanted to know what failure really felt like then she should have trodden in his shoes as he'd battled with his own failure to relieve this woman he loved of the heavy burden she was forced to carry.

'We will try other methods of conception,' he stated grimly.

If it was possible her face went even whiter. 'My eggs harvested like grains of wheat and your son conceived in a test tube? Your people would never forgive me for putting you through such an indignity, and those who keep the Al-Qadim family in power will view the whole process with deep suspicion.'

Her voice had begun to wobble. His own throat closed on

the need to swallow, because she was right, though he did not want her to be. For she was talking about the old ones, those tribal leaders of the desert who really maintained the balance of power in Rahman. They lived by the old ways and regarded anything remotely modern as necessary evil to be embraced only if all other sources had been exhausted. Hassan had taken a big risk when he'd married a western woman. The old ones had surprised him by deciding to see his decision to do so as a sign of strength. But that had been the only concession they had offered him with regard to his choice of wife. For why go to such extremes to father a son he could conceive as easily by taking a second wife?

Which was why this subject had always been so sensitive, and why Leona suddenly shook her head and said, 'Oh, why did you have to bring me back here?' Then she turned and walked quickly away from him, making unerringly for the bathroom he had so recently used for the same purpose—to be alone with her pain.

CHAPTER FOUR

Two hours, Leona noticed, as she removed her slender gold watch from her wrist with badly trembling fingers and laid it on the marble surface along with the diamonds from her ears and throat. Two hours together and already they were tearing each other to pieces.

On a sigh she swivelled round to sink down onto the toilet seat and stare dully at her surroundings. White. Everything was white. White-tiled walls and floor, white ceramics—even the sheet she had discarded lay in a soft white heap on the floor. The room needed a bit of colour to add some—

She stopped herself right there, closing her eyes on the knowledge that she had slipped into professional mode and knowing she had done it to escape from what she should really be thinking about.

This situation, this mad, foolish, heart-flaying situation, which was also so bitter-sweet and special. She didn't know whether to laugh at Hassan's outrageous method of bringing them together, or sob at the unnecessary agony he was causing the both of them.

In the end she did both, released a laugh that turned into a sob and buried the sound in her hands. Each look, each touch, was an act of love that bound them together. Each word, each thought, was an act of pain that tore them apart at the seams.

Then she remembered his face when he had made the ultimate sacrifice. Chin up, face carved, mouth so flat it was hardly a mouth any more. When the man had had to turn himself into a prince before he could utter the words, 'We will try other methods of conception,' she had known they had nothing left to fight for.

What was she supposed to have done? Made the reciprocal sacrifice to their love and offered to remain his first wife while he took a second? She just could not do it, could not live with the agony of knowing that when he wasn't in her bed he would be lying in another. The very idea was enough to set her insides curling up in pained dismay while her covered eyes caught nightmare visions of him trying to be fair, trying to pretend it wasn't really happening, that he wasn't over the moon when the new wife conceived his first child. How long after that before his love began to shift from her to this other woman with whom he could relax—enjoy her without feeling pain every time he looked at her?

'No,' she whispered. 'Stop it.' She began to shiver. It just wasn't even an option, so she must stop thinking about it! He knew that—he *knew it*! It was why he had taunted her with the suggestion earlier. He had been angry and had gone for the jugular and had enjoyed watching her die in front of him! It had always been like this: exploding flashes of anger and frustration, followed by wild leaps into sensual forgetfulness, followed by the low-of-low moments when neither could even look at the other because the empty truth was always still waiting there for them to re-emerge.

Empty.

On a groan she stood up, and groaned again as tiny muscles all over her body protested at being forced into movement. The fall, the lovemaking, or just the sheer stress of it all? she wondered, then wearily supposed it was a combination of all three.

So why do it? Why put them both back into a situation they had played so many times before it was wretched? Or was that it? she then thought on a sudden chill that shot down her backbone. Had he needed to play out the scene this one last time before he could finally accept that their marriage was over?

Sick. She felt sick. On trembling legs she headed quickly for the shower cubicle and switched the jet on so water sluiced over her body. Duty. It was all down to duty. His duty to produce an heir, her duty to let him. With any other man the love would be enough; those *other methods of conception* would be made bearable by the strength of that love. But she'd fallen in love with a prince not a man. And the prince had fallen in love with a barren woman.

Barren. How ugly that word was. How cold and bitter and horribly cheap. For there was nothing barren about the way she was feeling, nor did those feelings come cheap. They cost her a part of herself each time she experienced them. Like now, as they ate away at her insides until it was all she could do to slide down into a pathetic huddle in the corner of the shower cubicle and wait for it all to recede.

Where was she? What was she doing in there? She had been shut inside the bathroom for half an hour, and with a glance at his watch, Hassan continued to pace the floor on the vow that if she didn't come out in two minutes he was going in there after her.

None of this—*none* of it—was going the way he had planned it. How had he managed to trick himself into diluting just how deep their emotions ran, how painful the whole thing was going to be? He hit his brow with the palm of his hand, then uttered a few choice curses at his arrogant belief that all he'd needed to do was hook her up and haul her back in for the rest to fall into place around them.

All he'd wanted to do was make sure she was safe, back here where she belonged, no matter what the problems. So instead he'd scared the life out of her, almost lost her to the depths of the ocean, fought like the devil over issues that were so old they did not need raking over! He'd even lied to score points, had watched her run in a flood of tears, watched her fly through the air down a set of stairs he now wished had never been put there. Shocked, winded and dazed by the whole crazy situation, he had then committed his worst sin and had ravished her. Now she had locked herself away behind a bathroom door because she could not deal with him daring to make an offer they both knew was not, and never had been, a real option!

What was left? Did he unsheath his ceremonial scabbard and offer to finish them both off like two tragic lovers?

Oh, may Allah forgive him, he prayed as his blood ran cold and he leapt towards the bathroom door. She wouldn't. She was made of stronger stuff, he told himself as he lifted a clenched fist to bang on the door just as it came open.

She was wearing only a towel and her hair was wet, slicked to her beautiful head like a ruby satin veil. Momentarily shocked by the unexpected face-to-face confrontation, they both just stared at each other. Then he bit out, 'Are you all right?'

'Of course,' she replied. 'Why shouldn't I be?'

He had no answer to offer that did not sound insane, so he took another way out and reached for her, pulled her into his arms and kissed her—hard. By the time he let her up for air again she was breathless.

'Hassan—'

'No,' he interrupted. 'We have talked enough for one night.'

Turning away, he went over to the bed to retrieve the pearl-white silk robe he had laid out ready for her. During her absence the room had been returned to its natural neatness, at his instruction, and a table had been laid for dinner in the centre, with the food waiting for them on a heated trolley standing beside it.

He saw her eyes taking all of this in as he walked back to where she was standing. She also noticed that the lights had been turned down and candles had been lit on the table. She was no fool; she knew he had set the scene with a second seduction in mind and he didn't bother to deny it.

'Here,' he said, and opened the robe up between his hands, inviting her to slip into it.

There was a pause where she kept her eyes hidden beneath the sweep of her dusky lashes. She was trying to decide how to deal with this and he waited in silence, more than willing to let the decision be hers after having spent the previous few minutes listing every other wrong move he had made until now.

'Just for tonight,' she said, and lifted those lashes to show him the firmness of that decision. 'Tomorrow you take me back to San Estéban.'

His mouth flexed as the urge to say, Never, throbbed on the end of his tongue. 'Tomorrow we—talk about it,' he offered as his only compromise, though he knew it was no compromise at all and wondered if she knew it too.

He suspected she did, suspected she knew he had not gone to all of this trouble just to snatch a single night with her. But those wonderful lashes fluttered down again. Her soft mouth, still pulsing from his kiss, closed over words she decided not to say, and with only a nod of her head she lost the towel, stepped forward and turned to allow him to help feed her arms into the kimono-type sleeves of the robe.

It was a concession he knew he did not deserve. A concession he wanted to repay with a kiss of another kind, where bodies met and senses took over. Instead, he turned her to face him, smoothed his fingers down the robe's silken border from slender shoulders to narrow waist, then reached for the belt and tied it for her.

His gentle ministrations brought a reluctant smile to her lips. 'The calm before the storm,' she likened dryly.

'Better this than what I really want to do,' he very ruefully replied.

'You mean this?' she asked, and lifted her eyes to his to let him see what was running through her head, then reached up and kissed him, before drawing away again with a very mocking smile.

As she turned to walk towards the food trolley she managed to trail her fingers over that part of him that was already so hard it was almost an embarrassment. The little vixen. He released a soft laugh. She might appear subdued on the surface, but underneath she still possessed enough spirit to play the tease.

They ate poached salmon on a bed of spinach, and beef stroganoff laden with cream. Hassan kept her glass filled with the crisp dry white wine she liked, while he drank sparkling water. As the wine helped mellow her mood some more, Leona managed to completely convince herself that all she wanted was this one wonderful night and she was prepared to live on it for ever. By the time the meal was finished and he suggested a walk on the deck, she was happy to go with him.

Outside the air was warm and as silken as the darkness that surrounded them. Both in bare feet, dressed only in their robes, they strolled along the deck and could have been the only two people on board it was so quiet and deserted.

'Rafiq is entertaining Ethan—up there,' Hassan explained when she asked where everyone else was. Following his gaze, Leona could see lights were burning in the windows of the deck above.

'Should we be joining them?'

'I don't think they would appreciate the interruption,' he drawled. 'They have a poker game planned with several members of the crew, and our presence would dampen their—enthusiasm.'

Which was really him saying he didn't want to share her with anyone. 'You have an answer for everything, don't you?' she murmured.

'I try.' He smiled.

It was a slaying smile that sent the heat of anticipation burning between the cradle of her hip-bones, forcing her to look away so he wouldn't see just how susceptible she was even to his smile. Going to lean against the yacht's rail, she looked down to watch the white horses chase along the dark blue hull of the boat. They were moving at speed, slicing through the water on slick silent power that made her wonder how far they were away from San Estéban by now.

She didn't ask, though, because it was the kind of question that could start a war. 'This is one very impressive toy, even for an oil-rich sheikh,' she remarked.

'One hundred and ninety feet in length,' he announced, and came to lean beside her with his back against the rail. 'Twenty-nine feet across the beam.' His arm slid around her waist and twisted her to stand in front of him so she could follow his hand as he pointed. 'The top deck belongs mainly to the control room, where my very efficient captain keeps a smoothly running ship,' he said. 'The next down belongs to the sun deck and main reception salons designed to suitably luxurious standards for entertaining purposes. We stand upon what is known as the shade deck, it being cast mostly in the shade of the deck above,' he continued, so smoothly that she laughed because she knew he was really mocking the whole sumptuous thing. 'One half is reserved for our own personal use, with our private staterooms, my private offices etcetera,' he explained, 'while the other half is split equally between outer sun deck, outer shade deck, plus some less formal living space.'

'Gosh, you're so lucky to be this rich.' She sighed.

'And I haven't yet finished this glorious tour,' he replied. 'For below our feet lies the cabin deck, complete with six private suites easily fit for the occupation of kings. Then there is the engine room and crew's quarters below that. We can also offer a plunge pool, gymnasium and an assortment of nautical toys to make our weary lot a happier one.'

'Does it have a name, this sheikh's floating palace?' she enquired laughingly.

'Mmm. *Sexy Lady*,' he growled, and lowered his head so he could bury his teeth in the side of her neck where it met her shoulder.

'You're joking!' she accused, turning round in his arms to stare at him.

'Okay.' He shrugged. 'I am joking.'

'Then what is she called?' she demanded, as her heart skipped a beat then stopped altogether because he looked so wonderful standing here with his lean dark features relaxed and smiling naturally for the first time. She loved him quite desperately—how could she not? He was her—

The laughter suddenly died on her lips, his expression telling her something she didn't want to believe. 'No,' she breathed in denial. He couldn't have done—he *wouldn't*...

'Why not?' he challenged softly.

'Not in this case!' she snapped at him, not knowing quite what it was that was upsetting her. But upset she was; her eyes felt too hot, her chest too tight, and she had a horrible feeling she was about to weep all over his big hard beautiful chest!

'It is traditional to name a boat after your most cherished loved-one,' he pointed out. 'And why am I defending myself when I could not have paid you a better compliment than this?'

'Because...' she began shakily.

'You don't like it,' he finished for her.

'No!' she confirmed, then almost instantly changed her mind and said. 'Yes, I like it! But you shouldn't have! Y-you—'

His mouth crushed the rest of her protest into absolute oblivion, which was where it belonged anyway, because she didn't know what she was saying, only that a warm sweet wave of love was crashing over her and it was so dangerously seductive that—

She fell into it. She just let the wave close over her head and let him drown her in the heat of his passion, the power of his arms and the hunger of his kiss.

'Bed?' he suggested against her clinging mouth.

'Yes,' she agreed, then fed her fingers into his hair and her tongue between his ready lips. A groan broke low in his throat; it was husky and gorgeous; she tasted it greedily. A hand that knew her so very well curved over her thighs, slid up beneath her wrap, then cupped her bottom so he could bring her into closer contact with his desire. It was all very hot and very hungry. With a flick of a few scraps of silk they could be making love right here against the yacht's rail and in front of however many unseen eyes that happened to be glancing this way.

Hassan must have been thinking similarly because he suddenly put her from him. 'Bed,' he repeated, two dark streaks of colour accentuating his cheekbones and the fevered glitter in his eyes. 'Can you walk, or do I carry you?'

'I can run,' she informed him candidly, and grabbed hold of his hand, then turned to stride off on long slender legs with his husky laugh following as she pulled him behind her.

Back in their stateroom, now magically cleared of all evidence that they had eaten, they parted at the end of the bed, one stepping to one side of it, one to the other. Eyes locking in a needle-sharp, sensual love game, they disrobed together, climbed into the bed together and came together.

Hot, slow and deep, they made love into the night and didn't have to worry about empty spaces in between because one loving simply merged into another until—finally—they slept in each other's arms, legs entwined and faces so close on the pillows that the sleep was almost a long kiss in itself.

Leona came awake to find the place beside her in the bed empty and felt disappointment tug at her insides. For a while she just lay there, watching the sunlight seeping in through the window slowly creep towards her across the room, and tried not to let her mind open up to what it was bringing with it.

After a night built on fantasy had to come reality, not warm, like the sun, but cold, like the shadow she could already feel descending upon her even as she tried to hold it back for a little while longer.

A sound caught her attention. Moving her head just a little, she watched Hassan walk out of the bathroom wearing only a towel, his sun-brown skin fashioned to look almost like skillfully tanned leather. For such a dark man he was surprisingly free of body hair, which meant she could watch unhindered each beautifully toned muscle as he strode across to one of the concealed doors in the wall and sprung it open at a touch to reveal a wardrobe to provide for the man who had everything. A drawer was opened and he selected a pair of white cotton undershorts, dropped the towel to give her a glimpse of lean tight buttocks before he pulled the shorts on. A pair of stone-washed outer shorts followed. Zipped and buttoned, they rested low on a waist that did not know the meaning of spare flesh to spoil his sleek appearance. A casual shirt came next, made of such fine white Indian cotton she could still see the outline of his body through it.

'I can feel you watching me,' he remarked without turning.

'I like to look at you,' Leona replied. And she did; rightly or wrongly in their present situation, he was a man to watch whatever he was doing, even fastening buttons as he was doing now.

Shirt cuffs left open, he turned to walk towards the bed. The closer he came the faster her heart decided to beat. 'I like to look at you, too,' he murmured, bracing his hands on either side of head so he could lean down and kiss her.

He smelt clean and fresh and his face wore the smooth sheen of a wet razor shave. Her lips clung to his, because she was still pretending, and her arms reached up so she could clasp them round the back of his neck. 'Come back to bed with me,' she invited.

'So that you can ravish me? No way,' he refused. 'As the wise ones will tell you, my darling, too much of a good thing is bad for you.'

He kissed her again to soften the refusal, and his mouth was smiling as he straightened away, but as his hands reached up to gently remove her hands she saw the toughening happening behind his eyes. Hassan had already made contact with reality, she realised.

With that he turned away and strode back to the wall to spring open another set of doors which revealed clothes for the woman who wanted for nothing—except her man. And already she felt as if he had moved right out of her reach.

'Get up and get dressed,' he instructed as he walked towards the door. 'Breakfast will be served on the sun deck in fifteen minutes.'

As she watched him reach for the door handle the shadow

of reality sank that bit deeper into her skin. 'Nothing has changed, Hassan,' she told him quietly. 'When I leave this room I won't be coming back to it again.'

He paused, but he did not turn to glance back at her. 'Everything has changed,' he countered grimly. 'You are back where you belong. This room is only part of that.' Then he was gone, giving her no chance to argue.

Leona returned to watching the sun inch its way across the cream carpet for a while. Then, on a sigh, she slid out of the bed and went to get herself ready to face the next round of argument.

In another room not that far away Hassan was facing up to a different opponent. Ethan Hayes was standing there in the clothes he had arrived in minus the bow tie, and he was angry. In truth Hassan didn't blame him. He was wearing a bruise on his jaw that would appal Leona if she saw it, and he had a thick head through being encouraged to imbibe too much alcohol the night before.

'What made you pull such a crazy stunt?' he was demanding.

Since Hassan had been asking himself the same thing, he now found himself short of an adequate answer. 'I apologise for my men,' he said. 'Their…enthusiasm for the task got the better of them, I am afraid.'

'You can say that again.' Ethan touched his bruised jaw. 'I was out for the count for ten minutes! The next thing I know I am stuck on a yacht I don't want to be on, and Leona is nowhere to be seen!'

'She's worried about you, too, if that is any consolation.'

'No, it damn well isn't,' Ethan said toughly. 'What the hell was wrong with making contact by conventional methods? You scared the life out of her, not to mention the life out of me.'

'I know, and I apologise again.' Not being a man born to be conciliatory, being forced to be so now was beginning to grate, and his next cool remark reflected that. 'Let it be said that you will be generously compensated for the… disruption.'

Ethan Hayes stiffened in violent offence. 'I don't want compensation,' he snapped. 'I want to see for myself that Leona is okay!'

'Are you daring to imply that I could harm my wife?'

'I don't know, do I?' Ethan returned in a tone deliberately aimed to provoke. 'Overenthusiasm can be infectious.'

Neither man liked the other, though it was very rare that either came out from behind their polite masks to reveal it. But, as the sparks began to fly between the two of them, this meeting was at risk of being one of those times. Leona might prefer to believe that Ethan Hayes was not in love with her. But, as a man very intimate with the symptoms, Hassan knew otherwise. The passion with which he spoke her name, the burn that appeared in his eyes, and the inherent desire to protect her from harm all made Ethan Hayes' feelings plain. And, as far as Hassan was concerned, the handsome Englishman's only saving grace was the deep sense of honour that made him respect the wedding ring Leona wore.

But knowing this did not mean that Hassan could dismiss the other man's ability to turn her towards him if he really set his mind to it. He had the build and the looks to turn any woman's head.

Was he really afraid of that happening? he then asked himself, and was disturbed to realise that, yes, he was afraid. Always had been, always would be, he admitted, as he fought to maintain his polite mask because, at this juncture, he needed Ethan Hayes' cooperation if he was going to get him off this boat before Leona could reach him.

So, on a sigh which announced his withdrawal from the threatening confrontation, he said grimly, 'Time is of the essence,' and went on to explain to the other man just enough of the truth to grab his concern.

'A plot to get rid of her?' Ethan was shocked and Hassan could not blame him for being so.

'A plot to use her as a lever to make me concede to certain

issues they desire from me,' he amended. 'I am still holding onto the belief that they did not want to turn this into an international incident by harming her in any way.'

'Just snatching her could do it,' Ethan pointed out.

'Only if it became public property,' Hassan responded. 'They would be betting on Victor and myself holding our silence out of fear for Leona's safety.'

'Does she know?' Ethan asked.

'Not yet,' Hassan confessed. 'And not at all if I can possibly get away with it.'

'So why does she think she's here?'

'Why do you think?' Hassan countered, and gained some enjoyment out of watching Ethan stiffen as he absorbed the full masculine depth of his meaning. 'As long as she remains under my protection no one can touch her.'

Ethan's response took him by surprise because he dared to laugh. 'You've no chance, Hassan,' he waged. 'Leona will fight you to the edge and back before she will just sit down and do what you want her to do simply because you've decided that is how it must be.'

'Which is why I need your support in this,' Hassan replied. 'I need you to leave this boat before she can have an opportunity to use your departure as an excuse to jump ship with you.'

He got it. In the end, and after a bit more wrangling, he watched Ethan Hayes turn to the door on a reluctant agreement to go. And, oddly, Hassan admired him for trusting him enough to do this, bearing in mind the year that had gone before.

'Don't hurt her again.' Almost as if he could read his thoughts, Ethan issued that gruff warning right on cue.

'My wife's well-being is and always has been of paramount importance to me,' Hassan responded in a decidedly cooler tone.

Ethan turned, looked him directly in the eye, and for once the truth was placed in the open. 'You hurt her a year ago. A man gets only one chance at doing that.'

The kid gloves came off. Hassan's eyes began to glint. 'Take a small piece of advice,' he urged, 'and do not presume to understand a marital relationship until you have tried it for yourself.'

'I know a broken-hearted woman when I see one,' Ethan persisted.

'And has she been any less broken-hearted in the year we have been apart?'

Game, set and match, Hassan recognised, as the other man conceded that final point to him, and with just a nod of his head Ethan went out of the door and into the capable hands of the waiting Rafiq.

At about the same time that Rafiq was escorting Ethan to the waiting launch presently tied up against the side of the yacht, Leona was slipping her arms into the sleeves of a white linen jacket that matched the white linen trousers she had chosen to wear. Beneath the jacket she wore a pale green sun top, and she had contained her hair in a simple pony-tail tied up with a green silk scarf. As she turned towards the door she decided that if she managed to ignore the throbbing ache happening inside her then she was as ready as she ever could be for the battle she knew was to come with Hassan.

Stepping out of the stateroom, the first person she saw was a bearded man dressed in a long white tunic and the usual white *gutrah* on his head.

'Faysal!' Her surprise was clear, her smile warm. Faysal responded by pressing his palms together and dipping into the kind of low bow that irritated Hassan but didn't bother Leona at all simply because she ignored it. 'I didn't know you were here on the boat. Are you well?' she enquired as she walked towards him.

'I am very well, my lady,' he confirmed, but beneath the beard she had a suspicion he was blushing uncomfortably at the informal intimacy she was showing him.

'And your wife?' she asked gently.

'Oh, she is very well,' he confirmed with a distinct softening in his formal tone. 'The—er—problem she suffered has gone completely. We are most grateful to you for taking the trouble to ensure she was treated by the best people.'

'I didn't do anything but point her in the right direction, Faysal.' Leona smiled. 'I am only grateful that she felt she could confide in me.'

'You saved her life.'

'Many people saved her life.' Daring his affront, she crossed the invisible line Arab males drew between themselves and females and reached out to press her hands against the backs of his hands. 'But you and I were good conspirators, hmm, Faysal?'

'Indisputably, my lady.' His mouth almost cracked into a smile but he was too stressed at having her hands on his, and in the end she relented and moved away.

'If you would come this way…' he bowed '…I am to escort you to my lord Hassan.'

Ah, my lord Hassan, Leona thought, and felt her lighter mood drop again as Faysal indicated that she precede him down the steps she had taken a tumble on the night before. On the other side of the foyer was a staircase which Leona presumed led up to the deck above.

With Faysal tracking two steps behind her, she made her way up and into the sunlight flooding the upper deck, where she paused to take a look around. The sky was a pure, uninterrupted blue and the sea the colour of turquoise. The sun was already hot on her face and she had to shade her eyes against the way it was reflecting so brightly off the white paintwork of the boat.

'You managed to make Faysal blush, I see,' a deep voice drawled lazily.

Turning about, she found that Faysal had already melted away, as was his habit, and that Hassan was sitting at a table laid for breakfast beneath the shade of a huge white canvas awning, studying her through slightly mocking eyes. Her heart tried to leap in her breast but she refused to let it.

'There is a real human being hiding behind all of that strict protocol, if you would only look and see him.'

'The protocol is not my invention. It took generations of family tradition to make Faysal the man he is today.'

'He worships you like a god.'

'And you as his angel of mercy.'

'At least he felt I was approachable enough that he could bring his concerns to me.'

'After I had gently suggested it was what he should do.'

'Oh,' she said; she hadn't realised that.

'Come out of the sun before you burn.'

It was hot, and he was right, but Leona felt safer keeping her distance. She had things to say, and she began with the one subject guaranteed to alter his mellow mood into something else entirely. 'I was hoping that Ethan would be here with you,' she said. 'Since he isn't, I think I will go and look for him.'

Like a sign from Allah that today was not going to be a good day, at that moment the launch powered up and slipped its ties to the yacht.

Attention distracted, Leona glanced over the side, then went perfectly still.

Hassan knew what she was seeing even before he got up to go and join her. Sure enough, there was Ethan standing on the back of the launch. As the small boat began to pick up speed he glanced up, saw them and waved a farewell.

'Wave back, my darling,' he urged smoothly. 'The man will appreciate the assurance that all is well.'

'You rat,' she whispered.

'Of the desert,' he dryly replied, then compounded his sins by bringing an arm to rest across her stiff shoulders and lifting his other to wave.

Leona waved also, he admired her for that because it showed that, despite how angry she was feeling, she was—as always—keeping true to her unfailing loyalty to him.

In the eyes of other people, anyway. He extended that statement as the two of them stood watching Ethan and his passage away from them decrease in size, until the launch was nothing more than an occasional glint amongst many on the ocean. By then Leona was staring beyond the glint, checking the horizon for a glimpse of land that was not there. She was also gripping the rail in front of them with fingers like talons and wishing they were around his throat, he was sure.

'Try to think of it this way,' he suggested. 'I have saved us the trouble of yet another argument.'

CHAPTER FIVE

'WE HAVE to put into port some time,' Leona said coldly. She twisted out from beneath his resting arm then began walking stiffly towards the stairs, so very angry with him that she was quite prepared to lock herself in the stateroom until they did exactly that.

Behind the rigid set of her spine, she heard Hassan release a heavy sigh. 'Come back here,' he instructed. 'I was joking. I know we need to talk.'

But this was no joke, and they both knew it. He was just a ruthless, self-motivated monster, and as far as she was concerned, she had nothing left to— Her thoughts stopped dead. So did her feet when she found her way blocked by a giant of a man with a neat beard and the hawklike features of a desert warrior.

'Well, just look what we have here,' she drawled at this newly arrived target for her anger. 'If it isn't my lord sheikh's fellow conspirator in crime.'

Rafiq had opened his mouth to offer her a greeting, but her tone made him change his mind and instead he dipped into the kind of bow that would have even impressed Faysal, but only managed to sharpen Leona's tongue.

'Don't you dare efface yourself to me when we both know you don't respect me at all,' she sliced at him.

'You are mistaken,' he replied. 'I respect you most deeply.'

'Even while you throw an *abaya* over my head?'

'The *abaya* was an unfortunate necessity,' he explained, 'For you sparkled so brilliantly that you placed us in risk of discovery from the car headlights. Though please accept my apologies if my actions offended you.'

He thought he could mollify her with an apology? 'Do you know what you need, Rafiq Al-Qadim?' she responded. 'You need someone to find you a wife—a real harridan who will make your life such a misery that you won't have time to meddle in mine!'

'You are angry, and rightly so,' he conceded, but his eyes had begun to glint at the very idea of anyone meddling with his life. 'My remorse for the incident with the *abaya* is all yours. Please be assured that if you had toppled into the ocean I would have arrived there ahead of you.'

'But not before me, I think,' another voice intruded. It was very satisfying to hear the impatience in Hassan's tone. He was not a man who liked to be upstaged in any way, which was what Leona had allowed Rafiq to do. 'Leona, come out of the sun,' he instructed. 'Allowing yourself to burn because you are angry is the fool's choice.'

Leona didn't move but Rafiq did. In two strides he was standing right beside her and quite effectively blocking her off from the sun with his impressive shadow.

Which only helped to irritate Hassan all the more. 'Your reason for being up here had better be a good one, Rafiq,' he said grimly.

'Most assuredly,' the other man replied. 'Sheikh Abdul begs an urgent word with you.'

Hassan's smile was thin. 'Worried, is he?'

'Protecting his back,' Rafiq assessed.

'Sheikh Abdul can wait until I have eaten my breakfast.' Levering himself away from the yacht's rail, he walked back to the breakfast table. 'Leona, if you are not over here by the time Rafiq leaves you will not like the consequences.'

'Threats now?' she threw at him.

'Tell the sheikh I will speak to him later,' he said, ignoring her remark to speak to Rafiq.

Rafiq hesitated, stuck between two loyalties and clearly unsure which one to heed. He preferred to stay by Leona's side until she decided to leave the sun, but he also needed to deliver Hassan's message; so a silence dropped and tension rose. Hassan picked up the coffee pot and poured himself a cup while he waited. He was testing the faith of a man who had only ever given him his absolute loyalty, and that surprised and dismayed Leona because, tough and cold though she knew Hassan could be on occasion, she had never known him to challenge Rafiq in this way.

In the end she took the pressure off by stepping beneath the shade of the awning. Rafiq bowed and left. Hassan sent her a brief smile. 'Thank you,' he said.

'You didn't have to challenge him like that,' she admonished. 'It was an unfair use of your authority.'

'Perhaps,' he conceded. 'But it served its purpose.'

'The purpose of reminding him of his station in life?'

'No, the purpose of making you remember yours.' He threw her a hard glance. 'We both wield power in our way, Leona. You have just demonstrated your own by giving Rafiq the freedom to leave with his pride intact.'

He was right, though she didn't like being forced to realise it.

'You can be so cruel sometimes.' She released the words on a sigh. To her surprise Hassan countered it with a laugh.

'You call me cruel when you have just threatened him with a wife? He has a woman,' he confided, coming to stand right behind her. 'A black-haired, ruby-eyed, golden-skinned Spaniard.' Reaching round with his hands, he slipped free the single button holding her jacket shut, then began to remove the garment. 'She dances the flamenco and famously turns up men's temperature gauges with her delectably seductive style.' His lips brushed the slender curve of her newly exposed shoulder. 'But Rafiq assures me that nothing compares to what she unleashes when she dances only for him.'

'You've seen her dance?' Before she could stop herself, Leona had turned her head and given him just what he had been aiming for, she realised, too late to hide the jealous green glow in her eyes.

A sleek dark brow arched, dark eyes taunting her with his

answer. 'You like to believe you can set me free but you are really so possessive of me that I can feel the chains tightening, not slackening.'

'And you are so conceited.' She tried to draw back the green eyed monster.

'Because I like the chains?' he quizzed, and further disarmed her.

It wasn't fair, Leona decided; he could seduce her into a mess of confusion in seconds: Ethan, the launch, her sense of righteous indignation at the way she was being manipulated at just about every turn; she was in real danger of becoming lost in the power he had over her. She tried to break free from it. From *her* chains, she recognised.

'I prefer tea to coffee,' she murmured, aiming her concentration at the only neutral thing she could find, which was the table set for breakfast.

The warm sound of his laughter was in recognition of her diversion tactics. Then suddenly he wasn't laughing, he was releasing a gasp of horror. 'You are bruised!' he claimed, sending her gaze flittering to the slight discolouring to her right shoulder that she had noticed herself in the shower earlier.

'It's nothing.' She tried to dismiss it.

But Hassan was already turning her round and his black eyes were hard as they began flashing over every other exposed piece of flesh he could see. 'Me, or the fall?' he demanded harshly.

'The fall, of course.' She frowned, because she couldn't remember a single time in all the years they had been together that Hassan had ever marked her, either in passion or anger, yet he had gone so pale she might have accused him of beating her.

'Any more?' he asked tensely.

'Just my right hip, a little,' she said, holding her tongue about the sore spot at the side of her head, because she could see he wasn't up to dealing with that information. '—Hassan, will you stop it?' she said gasping when he dropped down in front of her and began to unfasten her white trousers. 'It isn't that bad!'

He wasn't listening. The trousers dropped, his fingers were already gently lifting the plain white cotton of her panty line out of the way so he could inspect for himself. 'I am at your feet,' he said in pained apology.

'I can see that,' she replied with a tremor in her voice that had more to do with shock than the humour she'd tried to inject into it. His response was so unnecessary and so very enthralling. 'Just get up now and let me dress,' she pleaded. 'Someone might come, for goodness' sake!'

'Not if they value their necks,' he replied, but at least he began to slide her trousers back over her slender hip-bones.

It had to be the worst bit of timing that Faysal should choose that moment to make one of his silent appearances. Leona was covered—just—but it did not take much imagination for her to know what Faysal must believe he was interrupting. The colour that flooded her cheeks must have aided that impression. Hassan went one further and rose up like a cobra.

'This intrusion had better be worth losing your head for!' he hissed.

For a few awful seconds Leona thought the poor man was going to prostrate himself in an agony of anguish. He made do with a bow to beat all bows. 'My sincerest apologies,' he begged. 'Your most honourable father, Sheikh Khalifa, desires immediate words with you, sir.'

Anyone else and Hassan would have carried out his threat, Leona was sure. Instead his mouth snapped shut, his hands took hold of her and dumped her rudely into a chair.

'Faysal, my wife requires tea.' He shot Leona's own diversion at the other man. Glad of the excuse to go, Faysal almost ran. To Leona he said, 'Eat,' but he wasn't making eye contact, and the two streaks of colour he was wearing on his cheekbones almost made her grin because it was so rare that anyone saw Sheikh Hassan Al-Qadim disconcerted.

'You dare,' he growled, swooping down and kissing her

twitching mouth, then he left quickly with the promise to return in moments.

But moments stretched into minutes. She ate one of the freshly baked rolls a white liveried steward had brought with a pot of tea, then drank the tea—and still Hassan did not return.

Eventually Rafiq appeared with another formal bow and Hassan's apologies. He was engaged in matters of state.

Matters of state she understood having lived before with Hassan disappearing for hours upon end to deal with them.

'Would you mind if I joined you?' Rafiq then requested.

'Orders of state?' she quizzed him dryly.

His half-smile gave her an answer. Her half-smile accompanied her indication to an empty chair. She watched him sit, watched him hunt around for something neutral to say that was not likely to cause another argument. There was no such thing, Leona knew that, so she decided to help him out.

'Tell me about your Spanish mistress,' she invited.

It was the perfect strike back for sins committed against her. Rafiq released a sigh and dragged the *gutrah* from his head, then tossed it aside. This was a familiar gesture for a man of the Al-Qadim household to use. It could convey many things: weariness, anger, contempt or, as in this case, a relayed throwing in of the towel. 'He lacks conscience,' he complained.

'Yet you continue to love him unreservedly, Rafiq, son of Khalifa Al-Qadim,' she quietly replied.

An eyebrow arched. Sometimes, in a certain light, he looked so like Hassan that they could have been twins. But they were not. 'Bastard son,' Rafiq corrected in that proud way of his. 'And you continue to love him yourself, so we had best not throw those particular stones,' he advised.

Rafiq had been born out of wedlock to Sheikh Khalifa's beautiful French mistress, who'd died giving birth to him. The fact that Hassan had only been six months old himself at the time of Rafiq's birth should have made the two half-brothers bitter enemies as they grew up together, one certain of his high place in life, the other just as certain of what would never be his. Yet in truth the two men could not have been closer if they'd shared the same mother. As grown men they had formed a united force behind which their ailing father rested secure in the knowledge that no one would challenge his power while his sons were there to stop them. When Leona came along, she too had been placed within this ring of protection.

Strange, she mused, how she had always been surrounded by strong men for most of her life: her father, Ethan, Rafiq and Hassan; even Sheikh Khalifa, ill though he now was, had always been one of her faithful champions.

'Convince him to let me go,' she requested quietly.

Ebony eyes darkened. 'He had missed you.'

So did green. 'Convince him,' she persisted.

'He was lonely without you.'

This time she had to swallow across the lump those words helped to form in her throat before she could say, 'Please.'

Rafiq leaned across the table, picked up one of her hands and gave it a squeeze. 'Subject over,' he announced very gently.

And it was. Leona could see that. It didn't so much hurt to be stonewalled like this but rather brought it more firmly home to her just how serious Hassan was.

Coming to his feet, Rafiq pulled her up with him. 'Where are we going?' she asked.

'For a tour of the boat in the hopes that the diversion will restrain your desire to weaken my defences.'

'Huh,' she said, for the day had not arrived when anyone could weaken Rafiq in any way involving his beloved brother. But she did not argue the point about needing a diversion.

He turned to collect his *gutrah*. The moment it went back on his head, the other Rafiq reappeared, the proud and remote man. 'If you would be so good as to precede me, my lady. We will collect a hat from your stateroom before we begin…'

Several hours later she was lying on one of the sun loungers on the shade deck, having given in to the heat and changed into a black and white patterned bikini teamed with a cool white muslin shirt. She had been shown almost every room the beautiful yacht possessed, and been formally introduced to Captain Tariq Al-Bahir, the only other Arab as far as she could tell in a twenty-strong crew of Spaniards. This had puzzled her enough to question it. But 'Expediency,' had been the only answer Rafiq would offer before it became another closed subject.

Since then she had eaten lunch with Rafiq and Faysal, and had been forced, because of Faysal's presence, to keep a lid on any other searching questions that might be burning in her head, which had been Rafiq's reason for including the other man, she was sure. And not once since he'd left her at the breakfast table had she laid eyes on Hassan—though she knew exactly where he was. Left alone to lie in the softer heat of the late afternoon, she was free to imagine him in what would be a custom built office, dealing with *matters of state*.

By phone, by fax, by internet—her mouth moved on a small smile. Hyped up, pumped up and doing what he loved to do most and in the interim forgetting the time and forgetting her! At other times she would have already been in there *reminding* him that there was a life other than *matters of state*. Closing her eyes, she could see his expression: the impatient glance at her interruption; the blank look that followed when she informed him of the time; the complaining sigh when she would insist on him stopping to share a cup of coffee or tea with her; and the way he would eventually surrender by reaching for her hand, then relaxing with a contented sigh…

In two stuffed chairs facing the window in his palace office—just like the two stuffed chairs strategically placed in the yacht's stateroom. Her heart gave a pinch; she tried to ignore what it was begging her to do.

*   *   *

Hassan was thinking along similar lines as he lay on the lounger next to hers. She was asleep. She didn't even know he was here. And not once in all the hours he had been locked away in his office had she come to interrupt.

Had he really expected her to? he asked himself. The answer that came back forced him to smother a hovering sigh because he didn't want to make a noise and waken her. They still had things to discuss, and the longer he put off the evil moment the better, as far as he was concerned, because he was going to get tough and she was not going to like it.

Another smothered sigh had him closing his eyes as he reflected back over the last few hours in which he had come as close as he had ever done to causing a split between the heads of the different families which together formed the Arabian state of Rahman.

Dynastic politics, he named it grimly. Al-Qadim and Al-Mukhtar against Al-Mahmud and Al-Yasin, with his right to decide for himself becoming lost in the tug of war. In the end he had been forced into a compromise that was no compromise at all—though he had since tried to turn it into one with the help of an old friend.

Leona released the sigh he had been struggling to suppress, and Hassan opened his eyes in time to see her yawn and stretch sinuously. Long and slender, sensationally curved yet exquisitely sleek. The colour of her hair, the smoothness of her lovely skin, the perfectly proportioned contours of her beautiful face. The eyes he could not see, the small straight nose that he could, the mouth he could feel against his mouth merely by looking at it. And—

Be done with it, he thought suddenly, and was on his feet and bending to scoop her into his arms.

She awoke with a start, saw it was him and sent him a sleepy frown. 'What are you doing?' she protested. 'I was comfortable there—'

'I know,' he replied. 'But I wish to be comfortable too, and I was not.'

He was already striding through the boat with a frown that

was far darker than hers. Across the foyer, up the three shallow steps. 'Open the door,' he commanded and was surprised when she reached down and did so without argument. He closed it with the help of a foot, saw her glance warily towards the bed. But it was to the two chairs that he took her, set her down in one of them, then lowered himself into the other with that sigh he had been holding back for so long.

'I suppose you have a good reason for moving me here,' she prompted after a moment.

'Yes,' he confirmed, and turned to look into those slumber darkened green eyes that tried so hard to hide her feelings from him but never ever quite managed to succeed. The wall of his chest contracted as he prepared himself for what he was about to say. 'You have been right all along.' He began with a confession. 'I am being pressured to take another wife…'

She should have expected it, Leona told herself as all hint of sleepy softness left her and her insides began to shake. She had always *known* it, so why was she feeling as if he had just reached out with a hand and strangled her heart? It was difficult to speak—almost impossible to speak—but she managed the burning question. 'Have you agreed?'

'No,' he firmly denied. 'Which is why you are here with me now—and more to the point, why you have to stay.'

Looking into his eyes, Leona could see that he was not looking forward to what he was going to say. She was right.

'A plot was conceived to have you abducted,' he told her huskily, 'the intention being to use your capture as a weapon with which to force my hand. When I discovered this I decided to foil their intentions by abducting you for myself.'

'Who?' she whispered, but had a horrible feeling she already knew the answer.

'Did the plotting? We are still trying to get that confirmed,' he said. 'But whoever it was they had their people watching your villa last night, waiting for Ethan and your father to leave for the party on the Petronades yacht. Once they had assured themselves that you were alone they meant to come in and take you.'

'Just like that,' she said shakily, and looked away from him as so many things began to fall into place. 'I felt their eyes on me,' she murmured. 'I knew they were there.'

'I suspected that you would do,' Hassan quietly commended. 'It is the kind of training we instilled into you that you never forget.'

'But this was different.' She got up, wrapped her arms around her body. 'I *knew* it felt different. I should have heeded that!'

'No—don't get upset.' Following suit, Hassan stood up and reached for her. She was as pale as a ghost and shaking like a leaf. 'My people were also there watching over you,' he assured. 'The car driver was my man, as was the man at the gate. I had people watching their people. There was not a single moment when you were not perfectly safe.'

'But to dislike me so much that they should *want* to take me!' Hurt beyond belief by that knowledge, Leona pushed him away, unwilling to accept his comfort. It had been hard enough to come to terms with it, when she'd believed he had snatched her back for his own purposes. But to discover now that he had done it because there was a plot against her was just too much to take. 'What is it with you people that you can't behave in a normal, rational manner?' she threw at him, eyes bright, hurt and accusing. 'You should have phoned *me* not my father!' she cried. 'You should have agreed to a divorce in the first place, then none of this would have happened at all!'

The *you people* sent Hassan's spine erect; the mention of divorce hardened his face. 'You are one of *my people*,' he reminded her curtly.

'No, I am not!' she denied with an angry shake of her head. 'I am just an ordinary person who had the misfortune to fall in love with the *extra*ordinary!'

'At least you are not going back to denying you love this

extraordinary person,' he noted arrogantly. 'And stop glaring at me like that!' he snapped. 'I am not your enemy!'

'Yes, you are!' Oh, why had she ever set eyes on this man? It would have been so much easier to have lived her life without ever having known him! 'So what happens now?' she demanded. 'Where do we go from here? Do I spend the rest of my days hiding from dark strangers just because you are too stubborn to let me go?'

'Of course not.' He was standing there frowning impatiently. 'Stop trying to build this into more than it actually is—'

More? 'Don't you think it is enough to know that I wasn't safe to be walking the streets in San Estéban? That my life and my basic human rights can be reduced to being worth nothing more than a mere pawn in some wretched person's power game?'

'I am sorry it has to come to this—'

Well, that just wasn't good enough! 'But you are no better yourself!' she threw at him angrily. 'Up to now you've used abduction, seduction and now you've moved onto intimidation to bring the wayward wife into line.' She listed. 'Should I be looking for the hidden cameras you are using so that you can show all of Rahman what a strong man you can be? Do I need to smile now?' she asked, watching his face grow darker with the sarcasm she tossed at him—and she just didn't care! 'Which way?' she goaded. 'Do I need to let Rafiq shroud me in an *abaya* again and even go as far as to abase myself at your exalted feet just to save your wretched face?'

'Say any more and you are likely to regret it,' he warned very grimly.

'I regret knowing you already!' Her eyes flashed, her body shook and her anger sparkled in the very air surrounding her. 'Next I suppose you will have me thrown into prison until I learn to behave myself!'

'This is it—' he responded, spreading his arms out wide in what was an outright provocation. 'Your prison. Now stop shouting at me like some undignified fishwife,' he snapped. 'We need to—'

'I want my life back without you in it!' Leona cut loudly across him.

What she got was the prince. The face, the eyes, his mood and his manner changed with the single blink of his long dark eyelashes. When his shoulders flexed it was like a dangerous animal slowly raising its hackles, and the fine hairs on her body suddenly became magnetised as she watched the metamorphosis take place. Her breathing snagged; her throat grew tight. He was standing perhaps three yards away from her but she could suddenly feel his presence as deeply as if he was a disturbing inch away.

'You want to live your life without me, then you may do so,' he announced. 'I will let you go, give you your divorce. There, it is done. *Inshallah.*' With a flick of the hand he strode across the room and calmly ordered tea!

It was retaliation at its most ruthless and it left her standing there utterly frozen with dismay. *Inshallah.* She couldn't even wince at what that single word represented. The will of Allah. Acceptance. A decision. The end. Hassan was agreeing to let her go and she could neither move nor breathe as the full power of that decree made its stunning impact.

She had not deserved that, Hassan was thinking impatiently as he stood glaring down at the telephone. She had been shocked, angry, hurt. Who would not be when they discovered that people they cared about, people they had tried to put before themselves, had been plotting to use them ruthlessly in a nasty game called politics? She had every right to vent her feelings—he had expected it! It was the reason why he had found them privacy before telling her the truth!

Or part of the truth, he then amended, all too grimly aware that there was yet more to come. But the rest was going to have to wait for a calmer time, for this moment might be silent but it certainly was not calm, because—

Damn it, despite the sensible lecture he was angry! There

was not another person on this planet who dared to speak to him as she had just done, and the hell if he was going to apologise for responding to that!

He flicked a glance at her. She hadn't moved. If she was even breathing he could see no evidence of it. Her hair was untidy. Long silken tendrils had escaped from the band she'd had it tied up in all day and were now caressing her nape, framing her stark white profile to add a vulnerability to her beauty that wrenched hard on his heart-strings. Her feet were bare, as were her slender arms and long slender legs. And she was emulating a statue again, only this time instead of art-deco she portrayed the discarded waif.

He liked the waif. His body quickened; another prohibited sigh tightened his chest. Curiosity replaced anger, though pride held his arrogant refusal to be the first one to retract his words firmly in place. She moved him like no other woman. She always had done. Angry or sad, hot with searing passion or frozen like ice as she was now.

Inshallah. It was Allah's will that he loved this woman above all others. Let her go? Not while he had enough breath in his body to fight to hold onto what was his! Though he wished he could see evidence that there was breath inside hers.

He picked up an ornament, measured the weight of the beautifully sculpted smooth sandstone camel then put it back down again to pick up another one of a falcon preparing to take off on the wing. And all the time the silence throbbed like a living pulse in the air all around them.

Say something—talk to me, he willed silently. Show me that my woman is still alive in there, he wanted to say. But that pride again was insisting he would not be the one to break the stunning deadlock they were now gripped in.

The light tap at the door meant the ordered tea he didn't even want had arrived. It was a relief to have something to do. She didn't move as he went to open the door, still hadn't moved when he closed it again on the steward he'd left firmly outside. Carrying the tray to the low table, he put it down, then turned to look at her. She still hadn't moved.

Inshallah, he thought again, and gave up the battle. Walking over to her, he placed a hand against her pale cheek, stroked his thumb along the length of her smooth throat then settled it beneath her chin so he could lift her face up that small inch it required to make her look at him.

Eyes of a lush dark vulnerable green gazed into sombre night-dark brown. Her soft mouth parted; at last she took a breath he could hear and see. 'Be careful what you wish for,' she whispered helplessly.

His legs went hollow. He understood. It was the way it had always been with them. 'If true love could be made to order, we would still be standing here,' he told her gravely.

At which point the ice melted, the gates opened and in a single painfully hopeless move she coiled her arms around his neck, buried her face into his chest and began to weep.

So what do you do with a woman who breaks her heart for you? You take her to bed. You wrap her in yourself. You make love to her until it is the only thing that matters any more. Afterwards, you face reality again. Afterwards you pick up from where you should never have let things go astray.

The tea stewed in the pot. Evening settled slowly over the room with a display of sunset colours that changed with each deepening stage of their sensual journey. Afterwards, he carried her into the shower and kept reality at bay by loving her there. Then they washed each other, dried each other, touched and kissed and spoke no words that could risk intrusion for as long as they possibly could.

It was Leona who eventually approached reality. 'What now?' she asked him.

'We sail the ocean on our self-made island, and keep the rest of the world out,' he answered huskily.

'For how long?'

'As long as we possibly can.' He didn't have the heart to

tell her he knew exactly how long. The rest would wait, he told himself.

It was a huge tactical error, though he did not know that yet. For he had not retracted what he had decreed in a moment of anger. And, although Leona might appear to have set the words aside, she had not forgotten them. Nor had she forgotten the reason she was here at all: there were people out there who wanted to harm her.

But for now they pretended that everything was wonderful. Like a second honeymoon in fact—if an unusual one with Rafiq and Faysal along for company. They laughed a lot and played like any other set of holidaymakers would. Matters of state took a back seat to other more pleasurable pursuits. They windsurfed off the Greek islands, snorkelled over shipwrecks, jet-skied in parts of the Mediterranean that were so empty of other human life that they could have had the sea to themselves.

One week slid stealthily into a second week Leona regained the weight she had lost during the empty months without Hassan, and her skin took on a healthy golden hue. When matters of state refused to be completely ignored, Rafiq was always on hand to help keep up the pretence that everything was suddenly and miraculously okay.

Then it came. One heat-misted afternoon when Hassan was locked away in his office, and Faysal, Leona and Rafiq were lazing on the shade deck sipping tall cool drinks and reading a book each. She happened to glance up and received the shock of her life when she saw that they were sailing so close to land it felt as if she could almost reach out and touch it.

'Oh, good grief,' Getting up she went to stand by the rail. 'Where are we, Rafiq?'

'At the end of our time here alone together,' a very different voice replied.

CHAPTER SIX

LEONA turned to find Hassan was standing not far away and Rafiq was in the process of rising to his feet. One man was looking at her; the other one was making sure that he didn't. Hassan's words shimmered in the air separating them and Rafiq's murmured, 'Excuse me, I will leave you to it,' was as revealing as the speed with which he left.

The silence that followed his departure pulsed with the flurried pace of her heartbeat while Leona waited for Hassan to clarify what he had just said.

He was still in the same casual shorts and shirt he had been wearing when she had last seen him, she noticed. But there, the similarity between this man and the man who had kissed the top of her head and strolled away to answer Faysal's call to work a short hour ago ended. For there was a tension about him that was almost palpable, and in his hand he held a gold fountain pen which offered up an image of him getting up from his desk to come back here at such speed that he hadn't even had time to drop the pen.

'We arrived here sooner than I had anticipated,' he said, confirming her last thought.

'It would be helpful for me to know where *here* is,' she replied in a voice laden with the weight of whatever it was that was about to come at her.

And come it did. 'Port Said,' he provided, saw her startled response of recognition and lowered his eyes on an acknowledging grimace that more or less said the rest.

Port Said lay at the mouth of the Suez Canal, which linked the Mediterranean with the Red Sea. If they were coming into the port, then there could only be one reason for it:

Hassan was ready to go home and their self-made, sea-borne paradise was about to disintegrate.

He had noticed the pen in his hand and went to drop it on the lounger next to the book she had left there. Then he walked over to the long white table at which they had eaten most of their evening meals over the last two weeks. Pulling out a chair, he sat down, released a sigh, then put up a hand to rub the back of his neck as if he was trying to iron out a crick.

When he removed it again he stretched the hand out towards her. 'Join me,' he invited.

Leona shook her head and instead found her arms crossing tightly beneath the thrust of her breasts. 'Tell me first,' she insisted.

'Don't be difficult,' he censured. 'I want you here, within touching distance when I explain.'

But she didn't want to be within touching distance when he said what she knew he had to say. 'You are about to go home, aren't you?'

'Yes,' he confirmed.

It was all right challenging someone to tell you the truth when you did not mind the answer, but when you did mind it— 'So this is it,' she stated, finding a short laugh from somewhere that was not really a laugh at all. 'Holiday over…'

Out there the sun glistened on the blue water, casting a shimmering haze over the nearing land. It was hot but she was cold. It was bright but she was standing in darkness. The end, she thought. The finish.

'So, how are you going to play it?' she asked him. 'Do you drop me off on the quay in the clothes I arrived in and wave a poignant farewell as you sail away. Or have I earned my passage back to San Estéban?'

'What are you talking about?' Hassan frowned. 'You are my wife, yet you speak about yourself as a mistress.'

Which was basically how she had been behaving over the

last two weeks, Leona admitted to herself. '*Inshallah*,' she murmured.

The small sarcasm brought him back to his feet. As he strode towards her she felt her body quicken, felt her breasts grow tight and despised herself for being so weak of the flesh that she could be aroused by a man who was about to carry out his promise to free her. But six feet two inches of pedigree male to her five feet seven was such a lot to ignore when she added physical power into the equation, then included mental power and sexual power. It really was no wonder she was such a weakling where he was concerned.

And it didn't stop there, because he came to brace his hands on the rail either side of her, then pushed his dark face close up to hers. Now she could feel the heat of him, feel his scented breath on her face. She even responded to the ever-present sexual glow in his eyes though it had no right to be there—in either of them.

'A mistress knows when to keep her beautiful mouth shut and just listen. A wife does her husband the honour of hearing him out before she makes wildly inaccurate claims,' he said.

'You've just told me that our time here is over,' she reminded him with a small tense shrug of one slender shoulder. 'What else is there left for you to say?'

'What I said,' he corrected, 'was that our time here *alone* was over.'

The difference made her frown. Hassan used the moment to shift his stance, grasp both of her hands and pry them away from the death grip they had on her arms. Her fingers left marks where they had been clinging. He frowned at the marks and sighed at her pathetically defiant face. Then, dropping one of her hands, he turned and pulled her over to the table, urged her down into the chair he had just vacated and, still without letting go of her other hand, pulled out a second chair upon which he sat down himself.

He drew the chair so close to her own that he had to spread his thighs wide enough to enclose hers. It was a very effective way to trap his audience, especially when he leaned forward and said, 'Now, listen, because this is important and I will not have you diverting me by tossing up insignificant comments.'

It was automatic that she should open her mouth to question that remark. It was predictable, she supposed, that Hassan should stop her by placing his free hand across her parted lips. 'Shh,' he commanded, 'for I refuse to be distracted yet again because the anguish shows in your eyes each time we reach this moment, and your words are only weapons you use to try and hide that from me.'

'Omniscient' was the word that came to mind to describe him, she thought, as her eyes told him she would be quiet. His hand slid away from her face, leaving its warm imprint on her skin. He smiled a brief smile at her acquiescence, then went so very serious that she found herself holding onto her breath.

'You know,' he began, 'that above all things my father has always been your strongest ally, and it is for him that I am about to speak…'

The moment he mentioned Sheikh Khalifa her expressive eyes clouded with concern.

'As his health fails, the more he worries about the future of Rahman,' he explained. 'He frets about everything. You, me, what I will do if the pressures currently being brought to bear upon me force me to make a decision which could change the rule of Rahman.'

'You mean you have actually considered giving up your right to succession?' Leona gasped out in surprise.

'It is an option,' he confessed. 'And one which became more appealing after I uncovered the plot involving you, which was aimed to make me do as other people wish,' he added cynically. 'But for my father's sake I assured him that I am not about to walk away from my duty. So he decided to fret about my happiness if I am forced to sacrifice you for the sake of harmony, which places me in a frustrating no-win situation where his peace of mind is concerned.'

'I'm sorry,' she murmured.

'I don't want your sympathy, I want your help,' he stated with a shortness that told her how much he disliked having to ask. 'He loves you, Leona, you know that. He has missed you badly since you left Rahman.'

'I didn't completely desert him, Hassan.' She felt pushed into defending herself. 'I've spoken to him every day via the internet.' Even here on the yacht she had been using Faysal's computer each morning to access her e-mail. 'I even read the same books he is reading so that we can discuss them together. I—'

'I know,' Hassan cut in with a wry smile. 'What you say to him he relays to me, so I am fully aware that I am a bully and a tyrant, a man without principle and most definitely my father's son.'

'I said those things to tease a laugh out of him,' she defended.

'I know this too,' he assured her. 'But he likes to make me smile with him.' Reaching up, he stroked a finger along the flush of discomfort that had mounted her cheeks. 'And let me face it,' he added, removing the finger, 'your communication with him was far sweeter than your communication with me.'

He was referring to the letters he'd received from her lawyer. 'It was over between us. You should have left it like that.'

'It is not over between us, and I *cannot* leave it like that.'

'Your father—'

'Needs you,' he grimly inserted. '*I* need you to help me ease his most pressing concerns. So I am asking you for a full and open reconciliation of our marriage—for my father's sake if not for yours and mine.'

Leona wasn't a fool. She knew what he was *not* saying here. 'For how long?'

He offered a shrug. 'How long is a piece of string?' he posed whimsically. Then, because he could see that the answer was not enough, he dropped the whimsy, sat right back in his seat and told her curtly, 'The doctors give him two months—three at most. In that period we have been warned to expect a rapid deterioration as the end draws near. So I ask you to do this one thing for him and help to make his passage out of this world a gentle one…'

Oh, dear heaven, she thought, putting a hand up to her eyes as the full weight of what he was asking settled over her. How could she refuse? She didn't even want to refuse. She loved that old man as much as she loved her own father. But there were other issues here which had not been aired yet, and it was those that kept her agreement locked inside.

'The other wife they want for you,' she prompted, 'am I to appear to accept her imminent arrival also?'

His expression darkened. 'Do me the honour of allowing me some sensitivity,' he came back. 'I have no wish to sacrifice your face for my own face. And I find it offensive that you could suspect that I would do.'

Which was very fine and noble of him but— 'She is still there, hovering in the shadows, Hassan,' Leona said heavily. She could even put a name to the woman, though he probably didn't know that she could. 'And taking me back to Rahman does not solve your problems with the other family leaders unless you take that other wife.'

'The old ones and I have come to an agreement,' he informed her. 'In respect for my father, they will let the matter ride while he is still alive.'

'Then what?'

'I will deal with them when I have to, but for the next few months anyway, my father's peace of mind must come first.'

And so, he was therefore saying, should it for her. 'Will you do this?'

The outright challenge. 'Did you really think that I would not?' She sighed, standing up and pushing her chair away so that she could step around him.

'You're angry.' His eyes narrowed on her sparkling eyes and set expression.

Anger didn't nearly cover what she was really feeling. 'In principle I agree to play the doting wife again,' she said. 'But in fact I am now going to go away and *sulk* as you like to call it. Because no matter how well you wrap it all up in words of concern, Hassan, you are as guilty for using me in much the same way my foiled abductors intended to use me, and that makes you no better than them, does it?'

With that she turned and walked away, and Hassan allowed her to, because he knew she was speaking the truth so had nothing he could offer in his own defence.

Within seconds Rafiq appeared with a question written into the hard lines of his face.

'Don't ask,' he advised heavily. 'And she does not even know the half of it yet.'

'Which half does she not know,' Rafiq asked anyway.

'What comes next,' Hassan replied, watching his half-brother's eyes slide over his left shoulder. He spun to see what he was looking at, then began cursing when he saw how close they were to reaching their reserved berth in Port Said. 'How long?' he demanded.

'You have approximately one hour before the first guests begin to arrive.'

A small hour to talk, to soothe, to plead yet again for more charity from a woman who had given enough as it was. 'You had better prepare yourself to take my place, Rafiq,' he gritted. 'Because, at this precise moment, I am seriously considering jumping ship with my wife and forgetting I possess a single drop of Al-Qadim blood.'

'Our father may not appreciate such a decision,' Rafiq commented dryly.

'That reminder,' Hassan turned to snap, 'was not necessary.'

'I was merely covering for myself,' his half brother defended. 'For I have no wish to walk in your shoes, my lord Sheikh.'

About to go after Leona, Hassan paused. 'What do you wish for?' he questioned curiously.

'Ah.' Rafiq sighed. 'At this precise moment I wish for midnight, when I should be with *my* woman in a hotel room in Port Said. For tonight she flies in to dance for visiting royalty by special request. But later she will dance only for me and I will worship at her feet. Then I will worship other parts of her until dawn, after which I will reluctantly return here, to your exalted service, my lord sheikh,' he concluded with a mocking bow.

Despite the weight of his mood, Hassan could not resist a smile. 'You should change your plans and bring her to dinner,' he suggested. 'The sheer sensation she would cause would be a diversion I would truly appreciate.'

'But would Leona?' Rafiq pondered.

Instantly all humour died from Hassan's face. 'Leona,' he predicted. 'is in no frame of mind to appreciate anything.'

And on that grim reminder, he went off to find *his* woman, while half wishing that he was the one treading in Rafiq's shoes.

He found her without difficulty, shut behind the bathroom door and hiding in the steam being produced by the shower. The fact that she had not bothered to lock the door spoke volumes as to her mood. Hassan could visualise the angry way she would have walked in here, throwing the door shut behind her then taking the rest of her anger out on the heap of clothes he could see tossed onto the floor.

So what did he do now? Go back to the bedroom and wait for her to reappear, or did he throw caution to the wind, strip off and just brave her fiery den?

It was not really a question since he was already taking off his clothes. For this was no time to be feeble. Leona had agreed *in principle*, so now she was about to learn the consequences of that. With a firming of his mouth he opened the shower-cubicle door, stepped inside and closed it again.

She was standing just out of reach of the shower jets with her head tipped back as she massaged shampoo into her hair. Streams of foaming bubbles were sliding over wet gold skin, collecting around the tips of her tilted breasts and snaking through the delightful valley in between to pool in the perfect oval of her navel, before spilling out to continue their way towards the chestnut cluster marking the apex with her slender thighs.

His body awoke; he allowed himself a rueful smile at how little it took to make him want this beautiful creature. Then she realised he was there and opened her eyes, risking soap burn so that she could kill him with a look.

'What do you want now?' she demanded.

Since the answer to that question was indubitably obvious, he didn't bother with a reply. Instead he reached for the container of foaming body soap, pumped a generous amount into the palm of his hand and began applying it to her skin. Her hands dropped from her hair and pressed hard against his chest in an effort to push him away.

'Thank you,' he said, and calmly pumped some soap onto his own chest as if it was a foregone conclusion that she would wash him. 'Sharing can turn the simplest of chores into the best of pleasures, do you not think?'

The green light in her eyes took on a distinctly threatening gleam. 'I think you're arrogant and hateful and I want you to get out of here,' she coldly informed him.

'Close your eyes,' he advised. 'The shampoo is about to reach them.'

Then, even as she lifted a hand to swipe the bubbles away, he reached up and directed the shower head at her so that the steamy spray hit her full in the face. While gasping at the shock, he made his next move, turned the spray away and replaced it with his mouth.

For a sweet, single moment he allowed himself to believe he'd made the easy conquest. It usually worked. On any other occasion it would have worked as a tasty starter to other ways of forgetfulness. But this time he received a sharp dig in the ribs for his optimism, and a set of teeth closed threateningly on his bottom lip until he eased the pressure and lifted his head. Her eyes spat fire and brimstone at him.

He arched an eyebrow and glided a defiant hand down to the silken warmth of her abdomen.

'You are treading on dangerous ground, Sheikh,' she warned him.

'I am?'

She ignored the message in his tone. 'I have nothing I want to say to you. So why don't you leave me alone?'

'But I was not offering to talk,' he explained, and boldly slid the hand lower.

'You are not doing *that* either!' Squirming away like a slippery snake, she ended up pressed against the corner of the cubicle, eyes like green lasers trying their best to obliterate him. One arm was covering her breasts, the other hand was protecting other parts. She looked like some sweet, cowering virgin, but he was not fooled by the vision. This beautiful wife of his possessed a temper that could erupt without warning. At the moment it was merely simmering.

'Okay.' With an ease that threw her into frowning confusion, he conceded the battle to her, pumped more soap onto his chest and began to wash while trying to ignore the obvious fact that a certain part of him was as hard as a rock and begging he do something about it. 'We did not really have time, anyway. Our guests arrive in less than an hour...'

'Guests?' she looked up sharply. 'What guests?'

'The guests we are about to transport to Rahman to attend the anniversary of my father's thirtieth year of rule, which will take place in ten days' time,' he replied while calmly sluicing the soap from his body as if he had not dropped yet another bomb at her feet. 'Here.' He frowned. 'Wash the shampoo from your hair before you really do hurt your eyes.' And he stepped back to allow her access to the spray.

Leona didn't move; she didn't even notice that he had. She was too busy suffering from one shock too many. 'How long have you known you were taking on guests?'

'A while.' Reaching up to unhook the shower head from the wall, he then pulled her towards him to began rinsing the shampoo from her hair for himself.

'But you didn't feel fit to tell me before now?'

'I did not feel fit to do anything but enjoy being with you.' Pushing up her chin, he sent the slick, clean pelt of her hair sliding down her spine with the help of the shower jet. 'Why?' He asked a question of his own. 'Would knowing have had any bearing on your decision to come back to Rahman with me?'

Would it? Leona asked herself, when really she did not need to, because she knew her answer would have been the same. He was rinsing the rest of her now and she just stood there and let him do it. Only a few minutes ago his smallest touch had infused her with that need to feel him deep inside her, now she could not remember what the need felt like. As she waited for him to finish administering to her wooden form, she noticed that his passion had died too.

'I suppose I had better know if there is anything else you haven't bothered to tell me,' she murmured eventually.

His pause before speaking could have been a hesitation over his answer, or it could have been a simple pause while he switched off the shower. 'Just the names of our guests,' he said. 'And that can wait until we have dealt with the more urgent task of drying ourselves and getting dressed.'

With that he opened the shower door and stepped out to collect a towel, which he folded around her before offering her another one for her hair. For himself he reached for a towelling bathrobe, pulled it on and headed for the door.

'Hassan...' she made him pause '...the rest of this trip and your father's celebration party—am I being put on public show for a specific purpose?'

'Some people need to be shown that I will not be coerced in any way,' he answered without turning. 'And my father wants you there. This will be his last anniversary. I will deny him nothing.'

At Hassan's request, she was wearing a calf-length white silk tunic studded with pearl-white sequins that shimmered when she moved. In accordance with Arabian tradition, the tunic had a high neckline, long sleeves and a pair of matching slender silk trousers that covered her legs. On her head she had draped a length of fine silk, and beneath it her hair had been carefully pleated into a glossy, smooth coronet. Her make-up was so understated you could barely tell it was there except for the flick of black mascara highlighting the length of her eyelashes and the hint of a gloss to her soft pink mouth.

Beside her stood the Prince. Dressed in a white silk tunic and gold silk top robe, on his head he wore a white *gutrah* ringed by three circles of gold. To her other side and one short pace behind stood Rafiq, dressed almost exactly the same as his brother only without the bands of gold. And as they waited in the boat's foyer, Leona was in no doubt that the way they were presented was aimed to make a specific statement.

Sheikh Hassan ben Khalifa Al-Qadim and his wife the Sheikha Leona Al-Qadim—bestowed upon her at her request, for the woman of Arabia traditionally kept their father's name—were ready to formally receive guests, whether those guests were friends or foes.

Rafiq was their guardian, their protector, their most respected brother and trusted friend. He possessed his own title, though he had never been known to use it. He possessed the right to wear the gold bands of high office, but no one had ever seen them circling his head. His power rode on the back of his indifference to anything that did not interest him. His threat lay in the famed knowledge that he would lay down his life for these two people standing in front of him, plus the father he loved without question.

His presence here, therefore, made its own loud statement; come in friendship and be at peace; come in conflict and beware.

Why? Because the first person to tread the gangway onto the yacht was Sheikh Abdul Al-Yasin and his wife, Zafina. Hassan and Rafiq knew that Sheikh Abdul was behind the plot to abduct Leona, but the sheikh did not know the brothers knew. Which was why he felt safe in taking the bait handed out for this trip—namely a meeting of the chiefs during a cruise on the Red Sea, in which his aim was to beat Hassan into submission about this second wife he was being so stubborn in refusing.

What none of them knew was that Leona suspected it was Sheikh Abdul who had planned her abduction. Because she knew about Nadira, his beautiful daughter, who had been held up to her many times as the one chosen to take that coveted place in Sheikh Hassan's life as his second wife.

'Ah—Hassan!' The two men greeted and shook hands pleasantly enough. 'You will be pleased to know that I left your father in better sorts than of late. I saw him this morning before I caught my flight to Cairo.'

'I must thank you for keeping him company while we have been away,' Hassan replied.

'No thanks—no thanks.' Sheikh Abdul refused them. 'It was my privilege—Leona…' He turned towards her next, though offered no physical contact as was the Arab way. He bowed instead. 'You have been away too long. It is good to see you here.'

'Thank you.' She found a smile, wished she dared search for the comfort of Hassan's hand, but such shows of weakness would be pounced upon and dissected when she was not there to hear it happen.

'Rafiq.' His nodded greeting was distinctly wary. 'You made a killing with your stock in Schuler-Kleef, I see.'

'My advice is usually sound, sir,' Rafiq replied respectfully. 'I take it you did not buy some for yourself?'

'I forgot.'

Through all of this, Sheikh Abdul's wife, Zafina, stood back in total silence, neither stepping forward to follow the line of introduction nor attempting to remind her husband of her presence. It was such a quiescent stance, one that Leona had grown used to from the women of Rahman when they were out in the company of their men.

But it was a quiescence that usually only lasted as long as it took them to be alone with the other women. Then the real personalities shot out to take you by surprise. Some were soft and kind, some cold and remote, some alive with fun. Zafina was a woman who knew how to wield her power from within the female ranks and had no hesitation in doing so if it furthered her own particular cause. It was due to her clever machinations that her son had married another sheikh's most favoured daughter.

She'd had Hassan marked for her daughter, Nadira, from the day the child had been born. Therefore, in her eyes, she had every reason to dislike Leona. And, tranquil though she might appear right now, Leona could feel resentment flowing towards her in waves.

'Zafina.' She stepped forward, deciding to take the polite stand. 'You are well, I trust? Thank you for taking time out of your busy life to join us here.'

'The pleasure is all mine, Sheikha,' the older woman replied. But then her husband was listening and so was the coveted Sheikh Hassan. 'You have lost weight, I think. But Sheikh Khalifa tells me you have been sick?'

Someone had told her at any rate, but Leona suspected it was not Hassan's father. Thankfully other guests began to arrive. Sheikh Jibril Al-Mahmud and his timid wife, Medina, who looked to her husband before she dared so much as breathe.

Sheikh Imran Al-Mukhtar and his youngest son, Samir, arrived next. Like a light at the end of a tunnel, Samir put the first genuine smile on everyone's face because he broke right through every stiff convention being performed in the yacht's foyer, and headed directly for Leona. 'My princess!' he greeted, picked her up in his arms then swung her around.

'Put her down,' his father censured. 'Rafiq has that glint in his eye.'

'Not Hassan?' Samir questioned quizzically.

'Hassan knows what belongs to him, Rafiq is merely overprotective. And everyone else simply disapproves of your loose ways.'

And there it was, tied up in one neat comment, Hassan

noted as he watched Leona laugh down into Samir's handsome young face. Al-Qadim and Al-Mukhtar set apart from Al-Mahmud and Al-Yasin. It promised to be an interesting trip. For the first time in two weeks they used the formal dining room on the deck above. White-liveried stewards served them through many courses, and the conversation around the table was pleasant and light, mainly due to Samir, who refused to allow the other men to sink into serious discussion, and even the other women unbent beneath his boyish charm.

But Leona was quiet. From his end of the table Hassan watched her speak when spoken to, smiling in all the right places. He watched her play the perfect hostess in that easy, unassuming way he remembered well, where everyone's needs were predicted and met before they knew they were missing something. But occasionally, when she thought no one was attending her, he watched the corners of her mouth droop with short releases of the tension she was experiencing.

Sad. Her eyes were sad. He had hurt her with his dripping-tap method of feeding information to her. Now here she sat, having to pretend everything was perfect between them, when really she wanted to kill him for waiting until the last minute to spring all of this.

His heart clenched when he caught sight of her impulsive grin as she teasingly cuffed Samir for saying something outrageous. She had not laughed with him like that since the first night they'd been together again. No matter how much she had smiled, played, teased—loved him—during the last two weeks, he had been aware of an inner reserve that told him he no longer had all of her. Her spirit was missing, he named it grimly. It had been locked away out of his reach.

I love you, he wanted to tell her. But loving did not mean much to a woman who felt that she was trapped between a rock and a hard place.

A silence suddenly reigned. It woke him up from his own thoughts to notice that Leona was staring down at the plate in front of her and Samir had frozen in dismay. What had he missed? What had been said? Muscles began tightening all over him. Rafiq was looking at him for guidance. His skin began to crawl with the horrible knowledge that he had just missed something supremely important, and he could not think of a single thing to say!

His half-brother took the initiative by coming to his feet. 'Leona, you will understand if I beg to leave you now,' he petitioned as smooth as silk, while Hassan, who knew him better than anyone, could see him almost pulsing with rage.

Leona's head came up as, with a flickering blink of her lashes, she made the mammoth effort to pull herself together. 'Oh, yes, of course, Rafiq,' she replied, having absolutely no idea, Hassan was sure, why Rafiq was excusing himself half-way through dinner, and at this precise moment she didn't care. It was a diversion. She needed the diversion. It should have been himself who provided it.

'I need a word before you leave,' he said to Rafiq, and got to his feet. 'Samir, do the honours and replenish my wife's glass with wine.'

The poor young man almost leapt at the wine bottle, relieved to have something to do. As Rafiq walked past Hassan, with a face like fury, Hassan saw Leona reach out and gently touch Samir's hand, as if to assure him that everything was all right.

'What did I miss in there?' he rapped out at Rafiq as soon as they were out of earshot.

'If I did not like Samir I would strangle him,' Rafiq responded harshly. 'Leona asked him how his mother was. He went into a long and humorous story about her sitting in wait for his sister to give birth. Leona dealt with that. She even laughed in all the right places. But then the fool had to suggest it was time that she produced your son and heir.'

'He cannot have known what he was saying,' Hassan said angrily.

'It was not the question which threw Leona, it was the resounding silence that followed it and the bleak expression

upon your face! Where were you, man?' Rafiq wanted to
know. It was so rare that he used that tone with Hassan, that
the censure in it carried twice the weight.

'My mind had drifted for a few seconds,' he answered
tensely.

'And the expression?'

'Part of the drift,' he admitted heavily.

'You were supposed to be on the alert at all times for
attacks of this kind.' Rafiq was not impressed. 'It was risk
enough to bring onto this boat the man who wishes her ill,
without you allowing your mind to drift.'

'Stop spitting words at my neck and go to your dancer,'
Hassan snapped back impatiently. 'You know as well as I
do that neither Abdul or Jibril would dare to try anything
when they are here for the specific purpose of talking me
round!'

It's okay, Leona was telling herself. I can deal with it. I've
always known that deep inside he cared more than he ever
let me see. So, he had been caught by surprise and showed
the truth to everyone. *I* was caught by surprise and showed
it myself.

'Samir,' she murmured gently. 'If you pour me any more
wine I will be sozzled and fall over when I have to stand
up.'

'Hassan wants your glass kept full.' He grimly kept on
pouring.

'Hassan was attempting to fill an empty gap in the conversation, not put me under the table,' she dryly pointed out.

Samir sat back with a sigh. 'I want to die a thousands
deaths,' he heavily confessed.

Hassan arrived back at the table. Leona felt his glance sear
a pointed message at her down the table's length. She refused
to catch his eye, and smiled and smiled until her jaw ached.

After that, the rest of the dinner passed off without further
incident. But by the time the ladies left the men alone and
removed to the adjoining salon Leona was in no mood for a

knife-stabbing session. So she was actually relieved that Medina and Zafina chose to stab at her indirectly by discussing Zafina's daughter, Nadira, whose beauty, it seemed, had multiplied during the last year. And as for her grace and quiet gentle ways—she was going to make some lucky man the perfect wife one day.

At least they didn't prose on about how wonderful she was with children, Leona thought dryly, as the conversation was halted when Hassan brought the men through within minutes of the ladies leaving them.

The evening dragged on. She thought about the other days and nights still to come and wondered if she was going to get through them all in one piece. Eventually the other two women decided they were ready to retire. A maid was called and within minutes of them leaving Leona was happy to follow suit. As she stepped outside, Hassan joined her. It was the first time he had managed to get her alone since the incident at the dinner table.

'I am at your feet,' he murmured contritely. 'I was miles away and had no idea what had taken place until Rafiq explained it to me.'

She didn't believe him, but it was nice of him to try the cover-up, she supposed. 'Samir wins hands down on apologies,' she came back. 'He wants to die a thousands deaths.'

With that she walked away, shaking inside and not really sure why she was. She got ready for bed and crawled between the cool cotton sheets, sighed, punched the pillow, then attempted to fall asleep. She must have managed it, because the next thing she knew a warm body was curling itself in behind her.

'I don't recall our new deal involving having to share a bed,' she said coldly.

'I don't recall offering to sleep elsewhere,' Hassan coolly returned. 'So go back to sleep.' The arm he folded around her aimed to trap. 'And, since I am as exhausted as you are, you did not need the silk pyjamas to keep my lecherous desires at bay…'

'I really hate you sometimes.' She wanted the last word.

'Whereas I will love you with my dying breath. And when they lay us in our final resting place in our crypt of gold it will be like this, with the scent of your beautiful hair against my face and my hand covering your lying little heart. There,' he concluded, 'is that flowery enough to beat Samir's one thousand deaths?'

Despite not wanting to, she giggled. It was her biggest mistake. The exhausted man became an invigorated man. His lecherous desires took precedence.

Did she try to stop him? No, she did not. Did she even want to? No, again. Did he know all of that before he started removing the pyjamas?' Of course he did. And there was something needle-piercingly poignant in this man losing touch with everything but this kind of loving as he came inside her, cupped her face with his hands and held her gaze with his own, as he drove them towards that other resting place.

CHAPTER SEVEN

MORNING came too soon, to Leona's regret. Although here, shut inside this room and wrapped in the relative sanctuary of Hassan's arms, she could let herself pretend for a little while longer that everything was perfect.

He was perfect, she observed tenderly as she studied the lean smooth lines of his dark golden face. He slept quietly—he always had done—lips parted slightly, black lashes lying still against the silken line of his cheekbones. Her heart began to squeeze and her stomach muscles joined in. This deep-rooted attraction he had always inspired in her had never diminished no matter what else had come in between.

She released a sigh that feathered his face and made his nose twitch. And it was such a nose, she thought with a smile, irresistibly reaching up to run a fingertip down its long silken length.

'Life can have its perfect moments,' a sleepy voice drawled.

Since she had been thinking much the same herself, Leona moved that bit closer so she could brush a kiss on his mouth.

Eyelashes drifted upward, revealing ebony irises packed with love. 'Does the kiss mean you have forgiven me for dropping all of this on you?'

'Shh,' she whispered, 'or you will spoil it.'

'Kiss me again, then,' he insisted. So she did. Why not? she asked herself. This was her man. Rightly or wrongly he was most definitely hers here and now.

It was a shame the ring of the telephone beside the bed had to intrude, or one thing would have led to another before they should have needed to face reality again. As it was, Hassan released a sigh and reached out to hook up the receiver. A few seconds later he was replacing it again and reaching out to touch her kiss-warmed mouth with a look of regret.

'Duty calls,' he murmured.

Ah, duty, Leona thought, and flopped heavily onto her back. Perfect moment over, pretence all gone. Stripped clean to his smooth dark golden skin, it was the prince who rose up from the bed and without saying another word disappeared into the bathroom.

He came out again ten minutes later, wrapped in fluffy white cotton and looking as handsome as sin. Wishing his pull wasn't as strong on her senses, she got up with a definite reluctance to face the day mirrored on her face, pulled on her wrap and went to take her turn in the bathroom.

But Hassan stopped her as she walked past him, his hand gently cupping her chin. He smelt of soap and minted toothpaste as he bent to kiss her cheek. 'Fifteen minutes, on the sun deck,' he instructed as he straightened again. 'For breakfast with an added surprise.'

The 'added surprise' made Leona frown. 'You promised me you had no more surprises waiting to jump out at me,' she protested.

'But this one does not count,' he said with a distinctly worrying gleam in his eye. 'So hurry up, wear something deliciously stylish that will wow everyone, and prepare yourself to fall on my neck.'

'Fall on his neck,' Leona muttered to herself as she showered. She had developed a distinct aversion to surprises since arriving on this wretched boat so she was more likely to strangle him.

In a pale blue sundress made of a cool cotton, and with her red hair floating loose about her shoulders—because she felt like wearing it as a banner, which made a statement about…something, though she wasn't absolutely sure what—Leona walked out onto the sun deck to find Rafiq there but no Hassan.

He looked up, smiled, then stood to pull out a chair for

her. He was back in what she called his off-duty clothes, loose-fitting black chinos and a white V-neck tee shirt that did things to his muscled shape no one saw when he was covered in Arab robes.

'Was your mother an Amazon, by any chance?' she enquired caustically, because his father was a fine boned little man and Rafiq had to have got his size from someone.

The waspishness in her tone earned her a sharp glance. 'Did you climb out of bed on the wrong side, by any chance?' he threw back.

'I *hate* surprises,' she announced as she sat down.

'Ah,' Rafiq murmured. 'So you have decided to take it out on me because I am unlikely to retaliate.'

He was right, and she knew it, which didn't help this terrible, restless tension she was suffering from. 'Where is Hassan?' She strove for a nicer tone and managed to half succeed. 'He said he would be here.'

'The pilot who will guide us through the Suez Canal has arrived,' Rafiq explained. 'It is an expected courtesy for Hassan to greet him personally.'

Glancing outwards, Leona saw Port Said sprawling out in front of them like a vast industrial estate. It was not the prettiest of views to have with your breakfast, even though they seemed to have got the best of the berths, moored way off to one side in a separate harbour that looked as if it was reserved for the luxury private crafts.

'And the rest of our guests?' she enquired next, aware that she probably should have asked about them first.

'Either still asleep or breakfasting in their suites.'

Mentioning sleep had a knock-on effect on him, and in the next moment Rafiq was stifling a yawn. It was only then that Leona recalled his slick retreat from the fray the evening before.

'Up all night?' The spike was back in her voice.

He didn't reply, but the rueful way his mouth tilted suddenly made her think of Spanish dancers. 'I hope she was good.' She took a tart stab in the dark.

'Delightful.' He smiled. It was yet another blow to her fragile ego that her one solid ally had deserted her last night for another woman. 'Here,' he said gently, and began to pour her out a cup of tea. 'Maybe this will help soothe your acid little tongue.'

Something needed to, Leona silently admitted as she picked up the cup. She had never felt so uptight and anxious, and it all was down to Hassan and surprises she did not want and people she did not want to be with and a marriage she did not—

The slightly sweet scent of Earl Grey suddenly turned her stomach. She must have gone pale because Rafiq began frowning. 'What is the matter?' he demanded.

'I think the milk must be off,' she explained, hastily putting the cup back on its saucer then pushing it away.

The sickly sensation left her almost as suddenly as it had hit. Problem solved in her mind, she wasn't convinced when Rafiq picked up the jug to sniff at the milk and announced, 'It seems fine to me.'

But he rose anyway and went to replace the milk with fresh from the cartons kept in the refrigerator situated just inside the salon. Then Hassan appeared and the incident was forgotten because, after dropping a kiss on her forehead, he went to pull out the chair next to Rafiq, who was just returning to the table with the fresh jug of milk. For a moment Leona was held captivated by how much alike the two men were. Even their clothes were similar, only Hassan wore beige chinos and a black tee shirt.

Men of beauty no matter what clothes they were wore, she mused a trifle breathlessly, knowing that she would be hard put to it to find two more perfect specimens. So why do I love them both so differently? she asked herself as she watched them sit down. Life would certainly have been a whole lot simpler if she'd fallen in love with Rafiq instead of Hassan. No strict calls to duty, no sheikhdom to rule, no onus to produce the next son and heir to his vast power and untold fortune.

But she loved Rafiq as a brother, not as a lover—just as he loved her as a sister. Plus, he had his mysterious dancer, she added wryly, as she poured herself another cup of tea in a clean cup, then reached for a slice of toast.

'You look pale. What's wrong?' Glancing up, she found Hassan's eyes were narrowed on her profile.

'She hates surprises.' Rafiq offered a reply.

'Ah. So I am out of favour,' Hassan drawled. 'Like the milk and the butter…' he added with the sharp eyes that should have been gold, like a falcon's, not a bottomless black that made her feel as if she could sink right into them and never have to come back out again.

'The milk was off, it turned my stomach, so I decided not to risk it or the butter,' she said, explaining the reason why she was sipping clear tea and nibbling on a piece of dry toast.

Keeping dairy produce fresh was an occupational hazard in hot climates, so Hassan didn't bother to question her answer—though Leona did a moment later when a pot of fresh coffee arrived for Hassan and the aroma sent her stomach dipping all over again.

Hassan saw the way she pushed her plate away and sat back in the chair with the paleness more pronounced, and had to ask himself if her pallor was more to do with anxiety than a problem with the milk. Maybe he should not be teasing her like this. Maybe no surprise, no matter how pleasant was going to merit putting her through yet more stress. He glanced at his watch. Ten more minutes. Was it worth him hanging on that long?

'You look stunning,' he murmured.

She turned her head, her wonderful hair floating out around her sun-kissed shoulders and the perfect heart-shape of her face. Her eyes were like emeralds, to match the one she wore on her finger, glowing with a passion she could never quite subdue no matter how low she was feeling. Kiss me, her small, soft, slightly sulky mouth seemed to say.

'I am *de trop*.' Rafiq broke through the moment and rose

to his feet. 'I will go and awaken Samir and drag him to the gym for an hour before I allow him breakfast.'

Neither bothered to answer even if they heard him, which Rafiq seriously doubted as he went to leave. Then a sound beyond the canvas awning caught his attention, diverting him towards the rail. A car was coming down the concrete quay towards them, its long black sleekly expensive lines giving him a good idea as to who was inside it.

This time he made sure he commanded attention by lightly touching Hassan's shoulder. 'Your surprise is arriving,' he told him, then left as Hassan stirred himself and Leona blinked herself back from wherever she had gone to.

Getting up, Hassan went to capture one of her hands and urged her out of her chair. 'Come,' he said, and keeping hold of her hand walked them down the stairs, across the foyer, out onto the shade deck and to the rail beside the gangway, just in time to watch a beautiful creature with pale blonde hair step out of the car and onto the quayside.

Beside him he felt Leona's breath catch on a gasp, felt the pulse in her wrist begin to race. 'Evie,' she whispered. 'And Raschid,' she added as Sheikh Raschid Al-Kadah uncoiled his long lean body out of the car.

'They're sailing with us?' Now her eyes were shining with true pleasure, Hassan noted with deep satisfaction. Now she was looking at him as if he was the most wonderful guy in the world, instead of the most painful to be around.

'Will their presence make your miserable lot easier to bear?'

Her reply was swift and uninhibited. She fell upon him with a kiss he would have given half of his wealth for. Though it did not need wealth, only the appearance of her closest friend and conspirator against these—arrogant Arabian men, as she and Evie liked to call Raschid and himself.

'After six years, I would have expected the unrestrained passion to have cooled a little,' a deep smooth, virtually accent-free voice mocked lazily.

'Says the man with his son clutched in one arm and his daughter cradled in the other,' mocked a lighter, drier voice.

Son and daughter. Hassan stiffened in shock, for he had not expected the Al-Kadahs to bring along their children on this cruise. Leona, on the other hand, was pulling away from him, turning away from him—hiding away from him? Had his pleasant surprise turned into yet another disaster? He turned to see what she was seeing and felt his chest tighten so fiercely it felt as if it was snapping in two. For there stood Raschid, as proud as any man could be, with his small son balanced on his arm while the beautiful Evie was in the process of gently relieving him of his small pink three-month-old daughter.

They began walking up the gangway towards them, and it was his worst nightmare unfolding before his very eyes, because there were tears in Leona's as she went to meet them. Real tears—bright tears when she looked down at the baby then up at Evangeline Al-Kadah before, with aching description, she simply took the other woman in her arms and held her.

Raschid was watching them, smiling, relaxed while he waited a few steps down the gangway for them to give him room to board the boat. He saw nothing painful in Leona's greeting, nor the way she broke away to gently touch a finger to the baby girl's petal soft cheek.

'I didn't know,' she was saying softly to Evie. 'Last time I saw you, you weren't even pregnant!'

'A lot can happen in a year,' Raschid put in dryly, bringing Leona's attention his way.

The tableau shifted. Evie moved to one side to allow her husband to step onto the deck so he could put his son to the ground, leaving his arms free to greet Leona properly. 'And aren't you just as proud as a peacock?' She laughed, defying the Arab male-female don't-touch convention by going straight into Raschid's arms.

What was wrong with Hassan? Leona wondered, realising that he hadn't moved a single muscle to come and greet their

latest guests. She caught his eye over one of Raschid's broad
shoulders, sent him a frowning look that told him to pull
himself together. By the time he was greeting Evie Leona
was squatting down to say hello to the little boy who now
clutched his mother's skirt for safety. Dark like his father;
golden-eyed like his father. The fates had been kind to these
two people by allowing them to produce a son in Raschid's
image and a daughter who already looked as if she was going
to be a mirror of her mother.

'Hello, Hashim.' She smiled gently. They had met before
but she was sure the small boy would not remember. 'Does
that thumb taste very nice?'

He nodded gravely and stuck the thumb just that quarter
inch further between sweetly pouting lips.

'My name is Leona,' she told him. 'Do you think we can
be friends?'

'Red,' he said around the thumb, looking at her hair. 'Sun-
shine.'

'Thank you.' She laughed. 'I see you are going to be a
dreadful flirt, like your papa.'

Mentioning his papa sent the toddler over to Raschid,
where he begged to be picked up again. Raschid swung him
up without pausing in his conversation with Hassan, as if it
was the most natural thing in the world for him to have his
son on his arm.

Tears hit again. Leona blinked them away. Hassan gave a
tense shift of one shoulder and in the next moment his arm
was resting across her shoulders. He was smiling at Evie, at
her baby, at Raschid. But when Leona noticed that he was
not allowing himself to so much as glance at Raschid's son
it finally hit her what was the matter with him. Hassan could
not bear to look at what Raschid had, that which he most
coveted.

Her heart dropped to her stomach to make her feel sick
again. The two men had been good friends since— -for ever.
Their countries lay side by side. And they shared so many
similarities in their lives that Leona would have wagered ev-

erything that nothing could drive a wedge between their friendship.

But a desire for what one had that the other did not, in the shape of a boy-child, could do it, she realised, and had to move away from Hassan because she just couldn't bear to be near him and feel that need pulsing in him.

'May I?' she requested of Evie, holding out her arms for the baby.

Evie didn't hesitate in handing the baby over. Soft and light and so very fragile. It was like cradling an angel. 'How old is she?' she asked.

'Three months,' Evie supplied. 'As quiet as a mouse, as sweet as honey—and called Yamila Lucinda after her two grandmothers, but we call her Lucy because it's cute.'

At the sound of her mother's voice, Lucy opened her eyes to reveal two perfect amethysts the same as Evie's, and Leona found herself swallowing tears again.

You're so lucky, she wanted to say, but remarks like that were a potential minefield for someone in her situation. So she contented herself with lifting the baby up so she could feel her soft cheek against her own and hoped that no one noticed the small prick of tears she had to blink away.

A minute later and other guests began appearing on the shade deck to find out who else had joined them. Sheikh Raschid earned himself looks of wary surprise from some. From all he was awarded the respect accorded to a man who held absolute rule in his own Gulf state of Behran. His children brought down other barriers; the fact that Evie had achieved what Leona had not, in the shape of her small son, earned her warm smiles instead of stiffly polite ones that conveyed disapproval. Still, most of the tension from the evening before melted away in the face of the newcomers, and Leona was deeply grateful to them for succeeding in neutralising the situation.

When it was decided that they would move up to the sun deck, with its adjoining salon, to take refreshment and talk in comfort, Leona quickly shifted herself into hostess mode and led the way upstairs with her small bundle in her arms and her husband walking at her shoulder.

He didn't speak, and she could sense the same mood about him he had donned when he'd come face to face with Raschid and his son. It hurt. Though she strove not to show it. But his manner made such a mockery out of everything else he had said and done.

They arrived on the upper deck as the yacht slipped smoothly from its moorings and began making its way towards the mouth of the Suez Canal. Medina Al-Mahmud suddenly appeared in front of Leona and politely begged to hold the baby. She was a small, slight woman with nervous eyes and a defensive manner, but as Leona placed the little girl in her arms Medina sent her a sympathetic look which almost broke her composure in two.

She did not want people's pity. Oh, how she had come to hate it during her last year in Rahman when the rumours about her had begun flying. With a desperate need of something else to do other than stand here feeling utterly useless, she walked into the salon to pick up the internal phone and order refreshments.

It was really very bad timing for Hassan to follow her. 'I must offer you my deepest apologies,' he announced so stiffly it was almost an insult. 'When I arranged this surprise for you I did not expect the Al-Kadahs to bring their children with them.'

She was appalled to realise that even Hassan believed her an object of such pity. 'Oh, stop being so ultra-sensitive,' she snapped. 'Do you really believe that I could resent them their beautiful children because I cannot have them for myself?'

'Don't say that!' he snapped back. 'It is not true, though you drive me insane by insisting it is so!'

'And you stop burying your head in the sand, Hassan,' she returned. 'Because we both know that you know it is you who lies to yourself!'

With that she stalked off, leaving him to simmer in his

own frustration while she went to check that the accommodation could stretch to two more guests than they had expected. Faysal already had the matter in hand, she discovered, finding several people hurriedly making ready a pair of adjoining suites, while others unpacked enough equipment, brought by the Al-Kadahs, to keep an army of young children content.

On her way back upstairs she met Rafiq and Samir. Rafiq studied her narrowly, his shrewd gaze not missing the continuing paleness in her face. He was probably questioning whether one sniff at suspect milk could upset her stomach for so long when in actual fact it had never been the milk, she had come to realise, but sheer anxiety and stress.

Samir, on the other hand, noticed nothing but a target for his wit. By the time the three of them had joined the others, Samir had her laughing over a heavily embroidered description of himself being put through the agonies of hell in the gym by a man so fit it was a sin.

After that she played the circulating hostess to the hilt and even endured a whole ten minutes sitting with Zafina listening to her extol the virtues of her daughter, Nadira. Then Evie rescued her by quietly asking if she would show her to their room, because the baby needed changing.

With Hashim deciding to come with them, they went down to the now beautifully prepared twin cabins and a dark-eyed little nurse Evie had brought with them appeared, to take the children into the other room. The moment the two women were alone Evie swung round on Leona and said, 'Right, let's hear it. Why did Hassan virtually beg and bribe us to come along on this trip?'

At which point; Leona simply broke down and wept out the whole sorry story. By the time she had hiccuped to a finish they were curled up on the bed and Evie was gently stroking her hair.

'I think you are here to make me feel better.' She finally answered Evie's original question. 'Because anyone with eyes can see that the Al-Mahmuds and the Al-Yasins wish me on another planet entirely. Hassan doesn't know that I've always known that Nadira Al-Yasin is the people's preferred wife for him.'

'I've been there. I know the feeling,' Evie murmured understandingly. 'I suppose she's beautiful, biddable and loves children.'

Leona nodded on a muffled sob. 'I've met her once or twice. She's quite sweet,' she reluctantly confessed.

'Just right for Hassan, I suppose.'

'Yes,'

'And, of course, you are not.'

Leona shook her head.

'So why are you here, then?' Evie challenged.

'You tell me,' she suggested, finding strength in anger and pulling herself into a sitting position on the bed. 'Because I don't know! Hassan says I am here for this reason, then he changes it to another. He is stubborn and devious and an absolute expert at plucking at my heart strings! His father is ill and I adore that old man so he uses him to keep me dancing to his secret tune!'

'Raschid's father died in his arms while I held Raschid in my arms,' Evie told her sadly. 'Wretched though it was, I would not have been anywhere else. He needed me. Hassan needs you too.'

'Oh, don't defend him,' Leona protested, 'It makes me feel mean, yet I know I would have gone to his father like a shot with just that request. I didn't need all of this other stuff to make me do it.'

'But maybe Hassan needed this other stuff to let him make you do it.'

'I'm going to sit you at the dinner table between Mrs Yasin and Mrs Mahmud tonight if you don't stop trying to be reasonable,' Leona said warningly.

'Okay, you've made your point,' Evie conceded. 'You need a loyal champion, not a wise one.' Then, with a complete change of manner, 'So get yourself into the bathroom and tidy yourself up before we go and fight the old dragons together.'

Leona began to smile. 'Now you're talking,' she enthused, and, stretching out a long leg, she rose from the bed a different person than the one who'd slumped down on it minutes ago. 'I'm glad you're here, Evie,' she murmured huskily.

It was a remark she could have repeated a hundred times over during the following days when everyone did try to appear content to simply enjoy the cruise with no underlying disputes to spoil it.

But in truth many undercurrents were at work. In the complicated way of Arab politics, there was no natural right to succession in Rahman. First among equals was the Arab way of describing a collective of tribe leaders amongst which one is considered the most authoritative. The next leader did not necessarily have to be the son of the one preceding him, but choice became an open issue on which all heads of the family must agree.

In truth everyone knew that Hassan was the only sensible man for the job simply because he had been handling the modern thrusts of power so successfully for the last five years as his father's health had begun to fail. No one wanted to tip the balance. As it stood, the other families had lived well and prospered under Al-Qadim rule. Rahman was a respected country in Arabia. Landlocked though it was, the oil beneath its desert was rich and in plenty, and within its borders were some of the most important oases that other, more favourably placed countries, did not enjoy.

But just as the sands shifted, so did opinions. Al-Mahmud and Al-Yasin might have lived well and prospered under thirty years of Al-Qadim rule, but they had disapproved of Hassan's choice of wife from the beginning. Though they could not fault the dedication Hassan's wife had applied to her role, nor ignore the respect she had earned from the Rahman people, she was frail of body. She had produced no sons in five years of marriage, and then had made Hassan appear weak to his peers when she'd walked away from him of her own volition. Divorce should have followed swiftly. Hassan had refused to discuss it as an option. Therefore, a second wife should have been chosen. Hassan's refusal to pander to what he called the ways of the old guard had incensed many. Not least Sheikh Abdul Al-Yasin who had not stopped smarting from the insult he'd received when Hassan had not chosen his daughter, Nadira, who had been primed from birth to take the role.

With Hassan's father's health failing fast, Sheikh Abdul had seen an opportunity to redress this insult. All it required was for Hassan to agree to take on a second wife in order to maintain the delicate balance between families. It was that simple. Everyone except Hassan agreed that his marriage to Nadira Al-Yasin would form an alliance that would solve everyone's problems. Hassan could keep his first wife. No one was asking him to discard this beautiful but barren woman. But his first son would come from the womb of Nadira Al-Yasin, which was all that really mattered.

The alternatives? Sheikh Jibril Al-Mahmud had a son who could be considered worthy of taking up the mantle Hassan's father would leave vacant. And no one could afford to ignore Sheikh Imran Al-Mukhtar and his son, Samir. Samir might be too young to take on the mantle of power but his father was not.

This, however only dealt with the male perspective. As the sheikhs fought their war with words on each other during long discussions, ensconced in one of the staterooms, the women were waging a similar war for their own reasons. Zafina Al-Yasin wanted Leona out and her daughter, Nadira, in. Since Hassan was not allowing this, then she would settle for her daughter taking second place. For the power lay in the sons born in a marriage, not the wives. So critical remarks were dropped at every opportunity to whittle away at Leona's composure and a self-esteem that was already fragile due to her inability to give Hassan what he needed most in this world.

In the middle of it all stood Sheikh Raschid and his wife, Evie offering positive proof that west could successfully join with east. For Behran had gone from strength to strength since their marriage and was fast becoming one of the most influential States in Arabia. But they had a son. It was the cog on which everything else rotated.

It took two days to navigate the Suez Canal, and would take another five to cross the Red Sea to the city of Jeddah on the coast of Saudi Arabia. By the time they had reached the end of the Canal, battle lines had been clearly marked for those times when the war of words would rage or a truce would be called. Mornings were truce times, when everyone more or less did their own thing and the company could even be called pleasant.

In the afternoons most people took a siesta, unless Samir grew restless and chivvied the others towards more enjoyable pursuits.

'Just look at them,' Evie murmured indulgently one afternoon as they stood watching Samir, Rafiq, Raschid and Hassan jet-skiing the ocean like reckless idiots, criss-crossing each other's wash with a daring that sometimes caught the breath. 'They're like little boys with exciting new toys.'

They came back to the boat, refreshed, relaxed—and ready to begin the first wave of strikes when the men gathered to drink coffee in one of the staterooms while the women occupied another.

Dinner called a second truce. After dinner, when another split of the sexes occurred, hostilities would resume until someone decided to call it a day and went to bed.

Bed was a place you could neither describe as a place of war nor truce. It gave you a sanctuary in which you had the chance to vent all of the things you had spent the day suppressing. But when the person in the bed with you saw you as much the enemy as every one else did, then you were in deep trouble. As Hassan acknowledged every time he slid into bed beside Leona and received the cold shoulder if he so much as attempted to touch her or speak.

She was angry with him for many reasons, but angriest most for some obscure point he had not managed to expose. He was aware that this situation was difficult, that she would rather be anywhere else other than trapped on this yacht right now. He knew she was unhappy, that she was only just managing to hide that from everyone else. That she was eating little and looking contradictorily pale when in truth her skin was taking on a deeper golden hue with every passing day. He knew that Zafina and Medina used any opportunity presented to them to compare her situation unfavourably with Evie's. And he wished Raschid had shown some sensitivity to that prospect when he'd made the decision to bring his children along!

The children were a point of conflict he could not seem to deal with. This evening, for instance, when Raschid had brought his son into the salon to say goodnight to everyone, Hashim had run the length of the room with his arms open wide in demand for a hug from Leona. She had lifted him up in her arms and received all of his warm kisses to her face with smiles of pleasure while inside, Hassan knew, the ache of empty wishes must be torture for her.

When she hurt, he hurt. When he had no remedy to ease that pain, he had to turn away from its source or risk revealing to her the emptiness of helplessness he suffered whenever he saw her hugging a son that was not their own.

But in trying to protect Leona from himself he had forgotten the other pairs of eyes watching him. The Al-Mahmuds and the Al-Yasins had seen, read and drawn their own conclusions.

'A sad sight, is it not?' Abdul had dared to say.

Leona had heard him, had known what he'd been referring to, and had been shunning Hassan ever since.

'Talk to me, for Allah's sake.' He sighed into the darkness.

'Find another bed to sleep in.'

Well, they were words, he supposed, then sighed again, took the bull by the horns and pushed himself up to lean over her, then tugged her round to face him. 'What is it that you want from me?' he demanded. 'I am trying my best to make this work for us!'

Her eyes flicked open; it was like gazing into pools of broken ice. 'Why go to all this trouble when I am still going to leave you flat the first moment I know I can do it without hurting your father?'

'Why?' he challenged.

'We've already been through the *whys* a hundred times! They haven't changed just because you have decided to play the warlord and win the battle against your rotten underlings without giving an inch to anyone!'

'Warlord?' His brow arched. 'How very pagan.' He made sure she knew he liked the sound of that title in a very physical way.

'Oh, get off me,' she snapped, gave a push and rolled free of him, coming to her feet by the bed. Her hair floated everywhere, and the cream silk pyjamas shimmied over her slender figure as she walked down the room and dumped herself into one of the chairs, then dared to curl up in it as if he would allow her to sleep there!

'Come back here, Leona,' he commanded wearily.

'I regret ever agreeing to be here,' she answered huskily.

Husky meant tears. Tears made him want to curse for making a joke of what they had been talking about when any fool would have known it was no time for jokes! On yet another sigh he got out of the bed, then trod in her footsteps and went to squat down in front of her.

'I'm sorry,' he said, 'that this situation is so difficult for you. But my father insisted that the family heads must talk to each other. I have no will to refuse him because in truth his reasons are wise. You know I have no automatic right to succession. I must win the support of the other family leaders.'

'Stop being so stubborn and just let me go and you would not have to win over anyone,' she pointed out.

'You know...' he grimaced '...I think you are wrong

there. I think that underneath all the posturing they want me to fight this battle and win, to prove the strength of my resolve.'

She brushed a tear off her cheek. Hassan had wanted to do it for her, but instinct was warning him not to. 'Tonight Zafina asked me outright if I had any idea of the life I was condemning you to if I held onto a marriage destined to have no children.'

His eyes flashed with raw anger, his lips pressing together on an urge to spit out words that would make neither of them feel any better. But he made a mental note that from tomorrow Leona went nowhere without himself or Rafiq within hearing.

'And I saw your face, Hassan,' she went on unsteadily. 'I heard what Abdul said to you and I know why he said it. So why are you being so stubborn about something we both know is—'

He shut her up in the most effective way he knew. Mouth to mouth, tongue to tongue, words lost in the heat of a much more productive form of communication. She fought him for a few brief seconds, then lost the battle when her flailing fingers made contact with his naked flesh.

He had no clothes on, she had too many, but flesh-warmed silk against naked skin achieved a sensual quality he found very pleasurable as he lifted her up and settled her legs around his hips.

'You are such an ostrich,' she threw into his face as he carried her back to bed. 'How long do you think you can go on ignoring what—!'

He used the same method to shut her up again. By then he was standing by the bed with her fingernails digging into his shoulders, her hair surrounding him and her long legs clinging to his waist with no indication that they were going to let go. If he tried for a horizontal position he would risk hurting her while she held him like this.

So—who needed a bed? he thought with a shrug as his fingers found the elastic waistband to her pyjama bottoms and pushed the silk far enough down her thighs to gain him access to what he wanted the most. She groaned as he eased himself into her, and the kiss deepened into something else.

Fevered was what it was. Fevered and hot and a challenge to how long he could maintain his balance as he stood there with his hands spanning her slender buttocks, squeezing to increase the frictional pleasure, and no way—no way— would he have believed three nights without doing this could leave him so hungry. Twelve months without doing this had not affected him as badly.

'You're shaking.'

She'd noticed. He wasn't surprised. He wasn't just shaking, he was out of control, and he could no longer maintain this position without losing his dignity as well as his mind. So he lowered her to the bed with as much care as he could muster, pushed her hair from her face and stared blackly into her eyes.

'You tell me how I deny myself this above all things?' he demanded. 'You, only you, can do this to me. It is only you I want to do it with.'

The words were spoken between fierce kisses, between possessive thrusts from his hips. Leona touched his face, touched his mouth, touched his eyes with her eyes. 'I'm so very sorry,' she whispered tragically.

It was enough to drive an already driven man insane. He withdrew, got up, swung away and strode into the bathroom, slammed shut the door then turned to slam the flat of his palm against the nearest wall. Empty silences after the loving he had learned to deal with, but tragic apologies in the middle were one large step too far!

Why had she said it? She hadn't meant to say it! It was just one of those painful little things that had slipped out because she had seen he was hurting, and the look had reminded her of the look he had tried to hide from her when she had been cuddling Hashim.

Oh, what were they doing to each other? Leona asked

herself wretchedly. And scrambled to her feet as the sickness she had been struggling with for days now came back with a vengeance, leaving her with no choice but to make a run for the bathroom with the hope that he hadn't locked the door.

With one hand over her mouth and the other trying to recover her slipping pyjama bottoms, she reached the door just as it flew open to reveal a completely different Hassan than the one who had stormed in there only seconds ago.

'You may have your wish,' he informed her coldly. 'As soon as it is safe for me to do so, I will arrange a divorce. Now I want nothing more to do with you.'

With that he walked away, having no idea that her only response was to finish what she had been intending to do and make it to the toilet bowl before she was sick.

CHAPTER EIGHT

LEONA was asleep when Hassan let himself back into the room the next morning. She was still asleep when, showered and dressed, he left the room again half an hour later, and in a way he was glad.

He had spent the night stretched out on a lounger on the shade deck, alternating between feeling angry enough to stand by every word he had spoken and wanting to go back and retract what he had left hanging in the air.

And even now, hours later, he was not ready to choose which way he was going to go. He'd had enough of people tugging on his heartstrings; he'd had enough of playing these stupid power games.

He met Rafiq on his way up to the sun deck. 'Set up a meeting,' he said. 'Ten o'clock in my private office. We are going for broke.'

Rafiq sent him one of his steady looks, went to say something, changed his mind, and merely nodded his head.

Samir was already at the breakfast table, packing food away at a pace that made Hassan feel slightly sick—a combination of no sleep and one too many arguments, he told himself grimly.

Leona still hadn't put in an appearance by the time everyone else had joined them and finished their breakfast. Motioning the steward over, he instructed him to ring the suite.

'I'll go,' Evie offered, and got up, leaving her children to Raschid's capable care.

And he was capable. In fact it irritated Hassan how capable his friend was at taking care of his two children. How did he run a Gulf state the size of Behran and find time to learn how to deal with babies?

The sun was hot, the sky was blue and here he was, he acknowledged, sitting here feeling like a grey day in London.

'Hassan…'

'Hmm?' Glancing up, he realised that Sheikh Imran had been talking to him and he hadn't heard a single word that he had said.

'Rafiq tells us you have called a meeting for ten o'clock'

'Yes.' He glanced at his watch, frowned and stood up. 'If you will excuse me, this is the time I call my father.'

To reach his office required him to pass by his suite door. It was closed. He hesitated, wondering whether or not to go in and at least try to make his peace. But Evie was in there, he remembered, and walked on, grimly glad of the excuse not to have to face that particular problem just now. For he had bigger fish to fry this morning.

Faysal was already in the office. 'Get my father on the phone for me, Faysal,' he instructed. 'Then set the other room up ready for a meeting.'

'It is to be today, sir?' Faysal questioned in surprise.

'Yes, today. In half an hour. My father, Faysal,' he prompted before the other man could say any more. He glanced at his watch again as Faysal picked up the telephone. Had Leona stayed in their suite because she didn't want to come face to face with him?

But Leona had not stayed in their suite because she was sulking, as Hassan so liked to call it. She was ill, and didn't want anyone to know.

'Don't you dare tell anyone,' she warned Evie. 'I'll be all right in a bit. It just keeps happening, and then it goes away again.'

'How long?' Evie looked worried.

'A few days.' Leona shrugged. 'I don't think I've got any-thing your children might catch, Evie,' she then anxiously assured her. 'I'm just—stressed out, that's all.'

'Stressed out.' Evie was looking at her oddly.

'It's playing havoc with my stomach.' Leona nodded and took another sip of the bottled water Evie had opened for her. 'Who would not be feeling sick if they were stuck on this boat with a load of people they liked as little as those people liked them? You and your family excluded, of course,' she then added belatedly.

'Oh, of course.' Evie nodded and sat down on the edge of the bed, a bed with one half that had not been slept in. Hassan had not come back last night, and Leona was glad that he hadn't.

'I hate men,' she announced huskily.

'You mean you hate one man in particular.'

'I'll be glad when this is over and he just lets me go.'

'Do you really think that is likely?' Evie mocked. 'Hassan is an Arab and they give up on nothing. Arrogant, possessive, stubborn, selfish and sweet,' she listed ruefully. 'It is the moments of sweetness that are their saving grace, I find.'

'You're lucky, you've got a nice one.'

'He wasn't nice at all on the day I sent him packing,' Evie recalled. 'In fact it was the worst moment of my life when he turned to leave with absolutely no protest. I knew it was the end. I'd seen it carved into his face like words set in stone...'

'I know,' Leona whispered miserably. 'I've seen the look myself...'

Evie had seen the same look on Hassan's face at the breakfast table. 'Oh, Leona.' She sighed. 'The two of you have got to stop beating each other up like this. You love each other. Can't that be enough?'

Raschid was not in agreement with Hassan's timing. 'Think about this,' he urged. 'We have too much time before we reach dry land. Time for them to fester on their disappointment.'

'I need this settled,' Hassan grimly insisted. 'Leona is a mess. The longer I let the situation ride the more hesitant I appear. Both Abdul and Zafina Al-Yasin are becoming so over-confident that they think they may say what they please. My father agrees. It shall be done with today. *Inshallah*,' he concluded.

'*Inshallah*, indeed,' Raschid murmured ruefully, and went away to prepare what he had been brought here specifically to say.

An hour later Evie was with her children, Medina and Zafina were seated quietly in one of the salons sipping coffee while they awaited the outcome of the meeting taking place on the deck below, and Leona and Samir were kitting up to go jet-skiing when Sheikh Raschid Al-Kadah decided it was time for him to speak.

'I have listened to your arguments with great interest and some growing concern,' he smoothly began. 'Some of you seem to be suggesting that Hassan should make a choice between his country and his western wife. I find this a most disturbing concept—not only because I have a western wife myself, but because forward-thinking Arabs might be setting such outmoded boundaries upon their leaders for the sake of what?'

'The blood line,' Abdul said instantly.

Some of the others shifted uncomfortably. Raschid looked into the face of each and every one of them and challenged them to agree with Sheikh Abdul. It would be an insult to himself, his wife and children if they did so. None did.

'The blood line was at risk six years ago, Abdul.' He smoothly directed his answer at the man who had dared to offer such a dangerous reason. 'When Hassan married, his wife was accepted by you all. What has changed?'

'You misunderstand, Raschid,' Jibril Al-Mahmud quickly inserted, eager to soothe the ruffled feathers of the other man. 'My apologies, Hassan, for feeling pressed to say this.' He bowed. 'But it is well known throughout Rahman that your most respected wife cannot bear a child.'

'This is untrue, but please continue with your hypothesis,' Hassan invited calmly.

Flustered, Jibril looked back at Raschid. 'Even in your

country a man is allowed, if not expected, to take a second wife if the first is—struggling to give him sons,' he pointed out. 'We beg Hassan only take a second wife to secure the *family* line.' Wisely, he omitted the word 'blood'.

'Hassan?' Raschid looked to him for an answer.

Hassan shook his head. 'I have the only wife I need,' he declared.

'And if Allah decides to deny you sons, what then?'

'Then control passes on to my successor. I do not see the problem.'

'The problem is that your stance makes a mockery of everything we stand for as Arabs,' Abdul said impatiently. 'You have a duty to secure the continuance of the Al-Qadim name. Your father agrees. The old ones agree. I find it insupportable that you continue to insist on giving back nothing for the honour of being your father's son!'

'I give back my right to succession,' Hassan countered. 'I am prepared to step down and let one or other of you here take my place. There,' he concluded with a flick of the hand, 'it is done. You may now move on to discuss my father's successor without me...'

'One moment, Hassan...' It was Raschid who stopped him from rising. Worked in and timed to reach this point in proceedings, he said, 'I have some objections to put forward against your decision.'

Hassan returned to his seat. Raschid nodded his gratitude for this, then addressed the table as a whole. 'Rahman's land borders my land. Your oil pipeline runs beneath Behran soil and mixes with my oil in our co-owned holding tanks when it reaches the Gulf. And the old ones criss-cross our borders from oasis to oasis with a freedom laid down in a treaty drawn up and signed by Al-Kadah and Al-Qadim thirty years ago. So tell me,' he begged, 'with whom am I expected to renegotiate this treaty when an Al-Qadim is no longer in a position to honour his side of our bargain?'

It was an attack on all fronts. For Rahman was landlocked. It needed Behran to get its oil to the tankers that moored up at its vast terminals. The treaty was old and the tariffs laid down in it had not been changed in those thirty years Raschid had mentioned. Borders were mere lines on maps the old ones were free to ignore as they roamed the desert with their camel trains.

'There is no question of altering the balance of power here in Rahman,' It was Sheikh Jibril Al-Mahmud who declaimed the suggestion. He looked worried. Crown Prince Raschid Al-Kadah was not known as a bluffing man. 'Hassan has our complete loyalty, respect and support.'

'Ah,' Raschid said. 'Then I am mistaken in what I have been hearing here. My apologies.' He bowed. 'I believed I was hearing Hassan about to step down as his father's natural successor.'

'Indeed no such thing ever crossed our minds.' You could almost see Sheikh Jibril shifting his position into the other camp as he spoke. 'We are merely concerned about future successors and question whether it is not time for Hassan to consider taking steps to—'

'As the old ones would say,' Raschid smoothly cut in, 'time is but a grain of sand that shifts in accordance with the wind and the will of Allah.'

'*Inshallah*,' Sheikh Jibril agreed, bringing Sheikh Abdul's house of cards tumbling down.

'Thank you,' Hassan murmured to Raschid a few minutes later, when the others had left them. 'I am in your debt.'

'There is no debt,' Raschid denied. 'I have no wish to see the spawn of Sheikh Abdul Al-Yasin develop in to the man who will then deal with my son. But, as a matter of interest only, who is your successor?'

'Rafiq,' Hassan replied.

'But he does not want the job.'

'He will nonetheless acquire it,' Hassan said grimly.

'Does he know?'

'Yes. We have already discussed it.'

Raschid nodded thoughtfully, then offered a grim smile.

'Now all you have to do, my friend, is try to appear happy that you have achieved your goal.'

It was Hassan's cue to begin smiling, but instead he released a heavy sigh and went to stand by the window. Outside, skimming across the glass-smooth water, he could see two jet-skis teasing each other. Leona's hair streamed out behind her like a glorious banner as she stood, half bent at the knees, turning the machine into a neat one-hundred-and-eighty-degree-spin in an effort to chase after the reckless Samir.

'The victory could be an empty one in the end,' he murmured eventually. 'For I do not think she will stay.'

Raschid's silence brought Hassan's head round. What he saw etched into the other man's face said it all for him. 'You don't think she will, either, do you?' he stated huskily.

'Evie and I discussed this,' Raschid confessed. 'We swapped places with you and Leona, if you like. And quite honestly, Hassan, her answer made my blood run cold.'

Hassan was not surprised by that. East meets west, he mused as he turned back to the window. Pride against pride. The love of a good, courageous woman against the—

'In the name of Allah,' he suddenly rasped out as he watched Leona's jet-ski stop so suddenly that she was thrown right over the front of it.

'What?' Raschid got to his feet.

'She hit something,' he bit out, remaining still for a moment, waiting for her to come up. It didn't happen. His heart began to pound, ringing loudly in his ears as he turned and began to run. With Raschid close on his heels he took the stairs two at a time, then flung himself down the next set heading for the rear of the boat where the back let down to form a platform into the water. Rafiq was already there, urgently lowering another jet ski into the water. His taut face said it all; Leona still had not reappeared. Samir had not even noticed; he was too busy making a wide, arching turn way out.

Without hesitation he wrenched the jet-ski from Rafiq and

was speeding off towards his wife before his brother had realised what he had done. Teeth set, eyes sharp, he made an arrow-straight track towards her deadly still jet-ski as behind him the yacht began sounding its horn in a warning call to Samir. The sound brought everyone to the boatside, to see what was going on.

By the time Hassan came up on Leona's jet-ski, Rafiq was racing after him on another one and Samir was heading towards them at speed. No one else moved or spoke or even breathed as they watched Hassan take a leaping dive off his moving machine and disappear into the deep blue water. Three minutes had past, maybe four, and Hassan could not understand why her buoyancy aid had not brought her to the surface.

He found out why the moment he broke his dive down and twisted full circle in the water. A huge piece of wood, like the beam from an old fishing boat, floated just below the surface—tangled with fishing net. It was the net she was caught in, a slender ankle, a slender wrist, and she was frantically trying to free herself.

As he swam towards her, he saw the panic in her eyes, the belief that she was going to die. With his own lungs already wanting to burst, he reached down to free her foot first, then began hauling her towards the surface even as he wrenched free her wrist.

White, he was white with panic, overwhelmed by shock and gasping greedily for breath. She burst out crying, coughing, spluttering, trying desperately to fill her lungs through racking sobs that tore him to bits. Neither had even noticed the two other jet-skis warily circling them or that Raschid and a crewman were heading towards them in the yacht's emergency inflatable.

'Why is it you have to *do* this to me?' he shouted at her furiously.

'Hassan,' someone said gruffly. He looked up, saw his brother's face, saw Samir looking like a ghost, saw the inflatable almost upon them, then saw—really saw—the woman he held crushed in his arms. After that the world took on a blur as Rafiq and Samir joined them in the water and helped to lift Leona into the boat. Hassan followed, then asked Raschid and the crewman to bring in the other two men on the jet-skis. As soon as the jet-skis left the inflatable, he turned it round and, instead of making for the yacht, he headed out in the Red Sea.

Leona didn't notice, she was lying in a huddle still sobbing her heart out on top of a mound of towels someone had had the foresight to toss into the boat, and he was shaking from teeth to fingertips. His mind was shot, his eyes blinded by an emotion he had never experienced before in his life.

When he eventually stopped the boat in the middle of no-where, he just sat there and tried hard to calm whatever it was that was raging inside of him while Leona tried to calm her frightened tears.

'You know,' he muttered after a while, 'for the first time since I was a boy, I think I am going to weep. You have no idea what you do to me, no idea at all. Sometimes I wonder if you even care.'

'It was an accident,' she whispered hoarsely

'So was the trip on the gangway! So was the headlong fall down the stairs! What difference does it make if it was an accident? You still have no idea what you do to me!'

Sitting up, she plucked up one the towels and wrapped it around her shivering frame.

'Are you listening to me?' he grated.

'No,' she replied. 'Where are we?'

'In the middle of nowhere where I can shout if I want to, cry if I want to, and tell the rest of the world to get out of my life!' he raged. 'I am sick of other people meddling in it. I am sick of playing stupid, political games. And I am sick and tired of watching you do stupid madcap things just because you are angry with me!'

'Hassan—'

'What?' he lashed back furiously, black eyes burning,

body so taut it looked ready to snap in two. He was soaking wet and he was trembling—not shivering like herself.

'I'm all right,' she told him gently.

He fell on her like a ravaging wolf, setting the tiny boat rocking and not seeming to care if they both ended up in the water again. 'Four minutes you were under the water—I timed it!' he bit out between tense kisses.

'I'm accident prone; you know I am,' she reminded him. 'The first time we met I tripped over someone's foot and landed on your lap.'

'No.' He denied it. 'I helped you there with a guiding hand.'

She frowned. He grimaced. He had never admitted that before. 'I had been watching you all evening, wondering how I could get to meet you without making myself appear over-eager. So it was an opportunity sent from Allah when you tripped just in front of me.'

Leona let loose a small, tear-choked chuckle. 'I tripped in front of you on purpose,' she confessed. 'Someone said you were an Arabian sheikh, rich as sin, so I thought to myself. That will do for me!'

'Liar,' he murmured.

'Maybe.' She smiled.

Then the teasing vanished from both of them. Eyes darkened, drew closer, then dived into each other's to dip into a place so very special it actually hurt to make contact with so much feeling at once.

'Don't leave me—ever.' He begged her promise.

Leona sighed as she ran her fingers through his wet hair. Her throat felt tight and her heart felt heavy. 'I'm frightened that one day you will change your mind about me and want more from your life. Then what will I be left with?'

'Ethan Hayes is in love with you,' he said.

'What has that got to do with this?' She frowned. 'And, no, he is not.'

'You are frightened I will leave you. Well, I am frightened

that you will one day see a normal man like Ethan and decide
he has more to offer you than I ever can.'

'You are joking,' she drawled.

'No, I am not.' He sat up, long fingers reaching out to
pluck absently at the ropework around the sides of the boat.
'What do I offer you beside a lot of personal restrictions,
political games that can get nasty enough to put your well-
being at risk, and a social circle of friends you would not
pass the day with if you did not feel obliged to do so for my
sake.'

'I liked most of our friends in Rahman,' she protested,
sitting up to drape one of the towels around her head because
the sun was too hot. 'Those I didn't like, you don't particularly like, and we only used to see them at formal func-
tions.'

'Or when we became stuck on a boat with them with no
means of escape.'

'Why are we having this conversation in this small boat
in the middle of the Red Sea?' she questioned wearily.

'Where else?' He shrugged. 'In our stateroom where there
is a convenient bed to divert us away from what needs to be
said?'

'It's another abduction,' she murmured ruefully.

'You belong to me. A man cannot abduct what is already
his.'

'And you're arrogant.' She sighed.

'Loving you is arrogant of me?' he challenged.

Leona just shook her head and used the corner of the towel
to dry her wet face. Her fingers were trembling, and she was
still having a struggle to calm her breathing. 'Last night you
promised me a divorce.'

'Today I am taking that promise back.'

'Here…' she held her arm out towards him. '…can you
do something about this?'

Part of the netting she had been tangled in was still clinging to her wrist. The delicate skin beneath it was red and
chafed. 'I'm sorry I said what I did last night,' he murmured.

'I'm sorry I said what I did,' Leona returned. 'I didn't even mean it the way it came out. It's just that sometimes you look so very...'

'Children are a precious gift from Allah,' Hassan interrupted, dark head sombrely bent over his task. 'But so is love. Very few people are fortunate enough to have both, and most only get the children. If I had to choose then I would choose, to have love.'

'But you are an Arabian sheikh with a duty to produce the next successor to follow on from you, and the choice no longer belongs to you.'

'If we find we want children then we will get some,' he said complacently, lifting up her wrist to break the stubborn cord with the sharp snap of his teeth. 'IVF, adoption... But only if *we* want them.' He made that fine but important point. 'Otherwise let Rafiq do his bit for his country,' he concluded with an indifferent shrug.

'He would give you one of his stares if he heard you saying that.' Leona smiled.

'He is an Al-Qadim, though he chooses to believe he is not.'

'He's half-French.'

'I am one quarter Spanish, and one quarter Al-Kadah,' he informed her. 'You, I believe, are one half rampaging Celt. I do not see us ringing bells about it.'

'All right, I will stay,' she murmured.

Dark eyes shrouded by a troubled frown lifted to look at her. 'You mean stay as in for ever, no more argument?' He demanded clarification.

Reaching up, she stroked her fingers through his hair again. 'As in you've got me for good, my lord Sheikh,' she said soberly. 'Just make sure you don't make me regret it.'

'Huh.' The short laugh was full of bewildered incredulity. 'What suddenly brought on this change of heart?'

'The heart has always wanted to stay, it was the mind that was causing me problems. But...look at us, Hassan.' She sighed 'sitting out in the middle of the sea in a stupid little boat beneath the heat of a noon-day sun because we would rather be here, together like this, than anywhere else.' She gave him her eyes again, and what always happened to them happened when he looked deep inside. 'If you believe love can sustain us through whatever is waiting for us back there, then I am going to let myself believe it too.'

'Courage,' he murmured, reaching out to gently cup her cheek. 'I never doubted your courage.'

'No,' she protested when he went to kiss her. 'Not here, when I can feel about twenty pairs of eyes trained on us from the yacht.'

'Let them watch,' he decreed, and kissed her anyway. 'Now I want the privacy of our stateroom, with its very large bed,' he said as he drew away again.

'Then, let's go and find it.'

They were halfway back to the yacht before she remembered Samir telling her about the planned meeting. 'What happened?' she asked anxiously.

Hassan smiled a brief, not particularly pleased smile. 'I won the support I was looking for. The fight is over. Now we can begin to relax a little.'

As a statement of triumph, it didn't have much satisfaction running through it. Leona wanted to question him about it, but they were nearing the yacht, so she decided to wait until later because she could now clearly see the sea of faces watching their approach—some anxious, some curious, some wearing expressions that set her shivering all over again. Not everyone was relieved that Hassan had plucked her out of the ocean, she realised ruefully.

Rafiq and a crewman were waiting on the platform to help them back on board the yacht. 'I'll walk,' she insisted when Hassan went to lift her into his arms. 'I think I have looked foolish enough for one day.'

So they walked side by side through the boat, wrapped in towels over their wet clothing. Neither spoke, neither touched, and no one accosted them on their journey to their stateroom. The door shut them in. Hassan broke away from her side and strode into the bathroom. Leona followed, found the jets in the shower already running. She dropped the towels, Hassan silently helped her out of the buoyancy aid that had not been buoyant enough and tossed it in disgust to the tiled floor. Next came her tee shirt, her shorts, the blue one-piece swimsuit she was wearing beneath.

It was another of those calms before the storm, Leona recognised as she watched him drag his shirt off over his head and step out of the rest of his clothes. His face was composed, his manner almost aloof, and there wasn't a single cell in her body that wasn't charged, ready to accept what had to come.

Tall and dark, lean and sleek. 'In,' he commanded, holding open the shower-cubicle door so that she could step inside. He followed, closed the door. And as the white-tiled space engulfed them in steam he was reaching for her and engulfing her in another way.

Think of asking questions about how much he had conceded to win his support from the other sheikhs? Why think about anything when this was warm and soft and slow and so intense that the yacht could sink and they would not have noticed. This was love, a renewal of love; touching, tasting, living, breathing, feeling love. From the shower they took it with them to the bed, from there they took it with them into a slumber which filtered the rest of the day away.

Questions? Who needed questions when they had this depth of communication? No more empty silences between the loving. No more fights with each other or with themselves about the wiseness of being together like this. When she received him inside her she did so with her eyes wide open and brimming with love and his name sounding softly on her lips.

Beyond the room, in another part of the yacht, Raschid looked at Rafiq. 'Do you think he has realised yet that today's victory has only put Leona at greater risk from her enemies?' he questioned.

'Sheikh Abdul would be a fool to show his hand now, when he must know that Hassan has chosen to pretend he had no concept of his plot to take her.'

'I was not thinking of Abdul, but his ambitious wife,' Raschid murmured grimly. 'The woman wants to see her daughter in Leona's place. One only had to glimpse her expression when Hassan brought them back to the yacht to know that she has not yet had the sense to give up the fight…'

CHAPTER NINE

LEONA was thinking much the same thing when she found herself faced by Zafina later that evening.

Before the confrontation the evening had been surprisingly pleasant. Leona made light of her spill into the sea, and the others made light of the meeting that had taken place as if the battle, now decided, had given everyone the excuse to relax their guard.

It was only when the women left the men at the table after dinner that things took a nasty turn for the worse. Evie had gone to check on her children and Leona used the moment to pop back to the stateroom to freshen up. The last person she expected to see as she stepped out of the bathroom was Zafina Al-Yasin, standing there waiting for her.

Dressed in a traditional jewel-blue *dara'a* and matching *thobe* heavily embroidered with silver studs, Zafina was here to cause trouble. It did not take more than a glance into her black opal eyes to see that.

'You surprise me with your jollity this evening.' The older woman began her attack. 'On a day when your husband won all and you lost everything I believed you stood so proudly for, I would have expected to find you more subdued. It was only as I watched you laugh with our men that it occurred to me that maybe, with your unfortunate accident and Sheikh Hassan's natural concern for you, he has not made you fully aware of what it was he has agreed to today?'

Not at all sure where she was going to be led with this, Leona demanded cautiously, 'Are you implying that my husband has lied to me?'

'I would not presume to suggest such a thing,' Zafina denied with a slight bow of respect meant in honour of Hassan, not Leona herself. 'But he may have been a little...economical with some of the details in an effort to save you from further distress.'

'Something you are not prepared to be,' Leona assumed.

'I believe in telling the truth, no matter the pain it may course.'

Ah, Leona thought, the truth. Now there was an interesting concept.

'In the interest of fair play, I do feel that you should be fully informed so that you may make your judgements on your future with the full facts at hand.'

'Why don't you just get to the point of this conversation, Zafina?' Leona said impatiently.

'The point is…this…' Zafina replied, producing from inside the sleeve of her *dara'a* a piece of paper, which she then spread out on the bed.

Leona did not want to, but she made herself walk towards it, made herself look down. The paper bore the Al-Qadim seal of office. It bore the name of Sheikh Khalifa.

'What is it?' she asked, oddly unwilling to read the closely lined and detailed Arabian script that came beneath.

'A contract drawn up by Sheikh Khalifa himself, giving his blessing to the marriage between his son Sheikh Hassan and my daughter Nadira. This is my husband's copy. Sheikh Khalifa and Sheikh Hassan have copies of their own.'

'It isn't signed,' Leona pointed out.

'It will be,' Zafina stated certainly, 'as was agreed this morning at the meeting of the family heads. Sheikh Khalifa is dying. His loving son will deny him nothing. When we reach Rahman the signing will take place and the announcement will be made at Sheikh Khalifa's celebration banquet.'

He will deny him nothing… Of everything Zafina had said, those words were the only ones that held the poison. Still, Leona strove to reject them.

'You lie,' she said. 'No matter what this piece of paper says, and no matter what you imply. I know Hassan. I know my father-in-law, Sheikh Khalifa. Neither would even think of deceiving me this way.'

'You think not?' She sounded so sure, so confident. 'In the eyes of his country, Sheikh Hassan must prove his loyalty to them is stronger than his desire to pander to your western principles.'

More certain on having said it, Leona turned ice-cold eyes on the other woman. 'I will tell Hassan about this conversation. You do realise that?' she warned.

Zafina bowed her head in calm acquiescence. 'Face him,' she invited. 'Tell him what you know. He may continue to keep the truth from you for his father's sake. He may decide to confess all then fall on your mercy, hoping that you will still go to Rahman as his loyal first wife to help save his face. But mark my words, Sheikha,' she warned, 'my daughter will be Sheikh Hassan's wife before this month is out, and she will bear him the son that will make his life complete.'

Stepping forward, she retrieved her precious contract. 'I have no wish to see you humiliated,' she concluded as she turned towards the door. 'Indeed I give you this chance to save your face. Return to England. Divorce Hassan,' she advised. 'For, whether you do or not, he will marry my daughter, at which point I think we both know that your usefulness will be at an end.'

Leona let her go without giving her the satisfaction of a response, but as the door closed behind Zafina she began to shake. No, she told herself sternly, you will not let that woman's poison eat away at you. She's lying. Hassan would not be so deceitful or so manipulative. He loves you, for goodness' sake! Haven't you both just spent a whole afternoon re-avowing that love?

I will deny him nothing... Hassan's own words, exactly as spoken only days ago. Her stomach turned, sending her reeling for the bathroom. Yet she stopped herself, took a couple of deep controlling breaths and forced herself to think, to trust in her own instincts, to believe in Hassan!

He would not do it. Hands clenched into tense fists at her

sides, she repeated that. *He would not do it!* The woman is evil. She is ambitious. She cannot accept failure.

She used your own inadequacies against you. How dare you so much as consider anything she said as worthy of all of this anguish?

You promised to believe in him. How dare you let that promise falter because some awful woman wants you out of his life and her daughter in it?

A contract. What was the contract but a piece of paper with words written upon it? Anyone could draw up a contract; it was getting those involved to sign it that was the real test!

She would tell Hassan, let him deny it once and for all, then she could put all of this behind her and—

No she wouldn't. She changed her mind. She would not give that woman the satisfaction of causing more trouble between the families, which was what was sure to happen if Hassan did find out what Zafina had said.

Trust was the word. Trust she *would* give to him.

The door opened. She spun around to find Hassan standing there. Tall and dark, smooth and sleek, and so heart-achingly, heart-breakingly, precious to her.

'What is wrong?' He frowned. 'You look as pale as the carpet.'

'N-nothing,' she said. Then, because it was such an obvious lie, she admitted, 'H-headache, upset stomach…' Two tight fists unclenched, one hand going to cover her stomach the other her clammy forehead. 'Too much food tonight. T-too much water from my dip in the sea, maybe. I…'

He was striding towards her. Her man. Her beautiful, grim-faced man. He touched her cheek. 'You feel like ice.' He picked up her chafed wrist between gentle finger and thumb. 'Your pulse is racing like mad! You need the medic.' He spun towards the telephone. 'Get undressed. You are going to bed…'

'Oh…no, Hassan!' she cried out in protest. 'I will be okay in a couple of minutes! Please…' she pleaded as he picked up the telephone. 'Look!' she declared, as he glared at her from beneath frowning black brows. 'I'm feeling better already. I—took something a few minutes ago.' With a mammoth gathering together of self-control, she even managed to walk over to him without stumbling and took the receiver from his hand.

'No,' she repeated. 'I will not spoil everyone's enjoyment tonight. I've caused enough fuss today as it is.' And she would not give Zafina a moment's smug satisfaction. 'Walk me back along the deck.' Firmly she took his hand. 'All I need is some fresh air.'

He wasn't sure. But Leona ignored his expression and pulled him towards the door. Actually the walk did her more good than she had expected it to do. Just being with him, feeling his presence, was enough to help reaffirm her belief that he would never, ever, do anything so cruel as to lie about a second wife.

He's done it before, a small voice inside her head reminded her.

Oh, shut up! she told it. I don't want to listen. And she pasted a bright smile on her face, ready to show it to their waiting guests—and Zafina Al-Yasin—as she and Hassan stepped back into the salon.

Zafina wasn't there, which in a way was a relief and in another was a disappointment, because she so wanted to outface the evil witch. She had to make do with shining like a brilliant star for those left to witness it, and she wondered once or twice if she was going to burn out. And she was never more relieved when it became time to retire without causing suspicion that this was all just a dreadful front.

Raschid and Imran had collared Hassan. So she was free to droop the moment she hit the bedroom. Within ten minutes she was curled up in bed. Within another ten she was up again and giving in to what had been threatening to happen since Zafina's visit. Fortunately Hassan was not there to witness it. By the time he came to bed she had found escape in sleep at last, and he made no move to waken her, so morning arrived all too soon, and with it returned the nauseous sensation.

She got through the day by the skin of her teeth, and was pleasant to Zafina, who was not sure how to take that. She spent most of her morning with Evie and her children, taking comfort from the sheer normality of their simple needs and amusements. It was while she was playing with Hashim that the little boy inadvertently brushed against her breasts and she winced at their unexpectedly painful response.

Evie noticed the wince. 'You okay?' she enquired.

Her shrug was rueful. 'Actually, I feel a bit grotty,' she confessed. 'I ache in strange places after my fight with the fishing net yesterday, and I think the water I swallowed had bugs.'

'The same bugs that got you the day before that?' Evie quizzed.

'Okay,' she conceded. 'So I'm still stressed out.'

'Or something,' Evie murmured.

Leona's chin came up, 'What's that supposed to mean?' she demanded.

It was Evie's turn to offer a rueful shrug, then Raschid walked into the room and the conversation had to be shelved when he reminded them that lunch was being served.

After lunch came siesta time. Or, for those like Hassan and Raschid, time to hit the phones and deal with matters of state. Leona had never been so glad of the excuse to shut herself away in her room because she was really beginning to feel ill by then. Her head ached, her bones ached, her stomach was objecting to the small amount of food she had eaten for lunch.

Maybe it was a bug, she mused frowningly as she drew the curtains across the windows in an effort to diffuse the light that was hurting her eyes. Stripping off her top clothes, she then crawled into the bed.

Maybe she should have steered well clear of Evie's children just in case she had picked up something catching, she then added, and made herself a promise to mention it to Evie later just before she slipped into a heavy sleep.

She came awake only as a scarlet sunset seeped into the room. The last sunset before they reached Jeddah, she recalled with relief. And found the reminder gave her a fresh burst of energy that she took with her into the bathroom where she indulged in a long leisurely shower then took her time getting ready for dinner. She chose to wear a calf-length tunic made of spearmint-blue silk with a matching pair of slender-cut trousers.

Hassan arrived in the room with a frown and his mind clearly preoccupied.

'Hello stranger,' she said.

He smiled. It was an amazing smile, full of warmth, full of love—full of lazy suggestions as he began to run his eyes over her in that dark possessive way that said, Mine, most definitely mine. It was the Arab-male way. What the man did not bother to say with words he could make up for with expressive glances.

'No,' Leona said to this particular look. 'I am all dressed up and ready to play hostess, so keep your lecherous hands to yourself.'

'Of course, you do know that I could easily change your mind?' he posed confidently.

Jokes. Light jokes. Warm smiles and tender communication. Would this man she knew and loved so well look at her like this yet still hold such terrible secrets from her?

No, of course he would not, so stop thinking about it! 'Save it until later,' she advised, making a play of sliding the silk scarf over her hair.

His eyes darkened measurably. It was strange how she only now noticed how much he liked seeing her dressed Arabian style. Was it in his blood that he liked to see his woman modestly covered? Was it more than that? Did he actually prefer—?

No. She stopped herself again. Stop allowing that woman's poison to get to you.

'Wait for me,' he requested when she took a step towards the door. 'I need only five minutes to change, for I showered ten minutes ago, after allowing that over-energetic Samir talk me into a game of softball on the sun deck.'

'Who won?' she asked, changing direction to go and sit on the arm of one of the chairs to wait as requested.

'I did—by cheating,' he confessed.

'Did he know you cheated?'

'Of course,' Hassan replied. 'But he believes he is in my debt so he allowed me to get away with it.'

'You mean you played on his guilty conscience over my accident,' she accused.

He turned another slashing grin on her. It had the same force as an electric charge aimed directly at her chest. Heat flashed across her flesh in a blanket wave of sensual static. Followed by another wave of the same as she watched him strip off western shirt and shorts to reveal sleek brown flesh just made for fingers to stroke. By the time he had replaced the clothes with a white tunic he had earned himself a similar possessive glance to the one he had given her.

See, she told herself, you can't resist him in Arab dress. It has nothing to do with what runs in the blood. She even decided to tease him about it. 'If there is one thing I have learned to understand since knowing you, it is why men prefer women in dresses.'

'This is not a dress,' he objected.

Getting up, she went to stand in front of him and placed her palms flat against the wall of his chest to feel warm skin, tight and smooth, and irresistible to seeking hands that wanted to stroke a sensual pathway over muscled contours to his lean waist.

'I know what it is, my darling,' she murmured seductively. 'It is a sinful temptation, and therefore no wonder that you don't encourage physical contact between the sexes.'

His answering laugh was low and deep, very much the sound of a man who was aware of his own power to attract. 'Remind Samir of that, if you will,' he countered dryly. 'He is very lucky I have not beaten him to a pulp by now for the liberties he takes with my wife.'

But Samir, Leona discovered as soon as they entered the main salon, was more interested in extolling the liberties Hassan had taken with him. 'He cheats. He has no honour. He went to Eton, for goodness' sake, where they turn desert savages into gentlemen!'

'Oh…' Leona lifted her head to mock her husband. 'So that's what it is I love most about you.'

'The gentleman?'

'The savage,' she softly corrected.

He replied with a gentle cuff to her chin. Everyone laughed. Everyone was happy. Zafina tried very hard to hide her malicious glare.

They ate dinner beneath the stars that night. Leona was surprised to see a bed of ice holding several bottles of champagne waiting on a side table. Some of her guests drank alcohol; some of them did not. Wine was the favoured choice for those who did imbibe. But even when there had been cause to celebrate yesterday evening champagne had not been served.

'What's going on?' she asked Hassan as he saw her seated.

'Wait and see,' he replied frustratingly, and walked away to take his own seat at the other end of the table.

Ah, the last supper, she thought then, with a pinch of acid wit. And, believing she had her answer, she turned her attention to her meal, while Rafiq continued his opinions of men in high positions who could lower themselves to cheat.

The first spoonful of what was actually a delicious Arabian soup set Leona's stomach objecting. 'Never mind,' she said to soothe Samir's dramatically ruffled feathers as she quietly laid aside her spoon. 'Tomorrow you and I will race on the jet-skis and I promise that I, as an English gentlewoman, will not cheat.'

'Not on this trip, I am afraid,' Hassan himself inserted smoothly. 'All water sports are now stopped until we can replace the buoyancy aids with something more effective.'

Leona stared down the table at him. 'Just like that?' she protested. 'I have an unfortunate and one-in-a-million-chance accident and you put a stop on everyone else's fun?'

'You almost drowned. The life jacket did not do what it is designed to do. A million-to-one chance of it happening again makes the odds too great.'

'That is the voice of the master,' Samir noted.

'You heard it too, hmm?' Leona replied.

'Most indubitably,' Hassan agreed.

After that the conversation moved on to other things. Soup dishes were removed and replaced with a fish dish she didn't even attempt to taste. A richly sauced Arab dish followed, with a side bowl each of soft and fluffy steamed white rice.

The rice she thought she could just about manage to eat, Leona decided, listening intently to the story Imran Al-Mukhtar was telling her as she transferred a couple of spoonfuls of rice onto her plate then added a spoonful of sauce just for show.

One spoonful of soup, two forkfuls of rice. No fish. No attempt to even accept a sample of the thick honey pudding to conclude. Hassan watched it all, took grim note, glanced to one side to catch Evie's eye. She sent him a look that said that she had noticed too.

'The Sheikha Leona seems a little…pale,' Zafina Al-Yasin, sitting to one side of him, quietly put in. 'Is she not feeling quite herself?'

'You think so?' he returned with mild surprise. 'I think she looks exquisite. But then, I am smitten,' he allowed. 'It makes a difference as to how you perceive someone, don't you think?'

A steward came to stand at his side then, thankfully relieving him from continuing such a discussion.

With a nod of understanding he sent the steward hurrying over to the side table where he and his assistants began deftly uncorking the bottles of champagne. Picking up a spoon, he gave a couple of taps against a wine glass to capture everyone's attention.

'My apologies for interrupting your dinner,' he said, 'but in a few minutes our captain will sound the yacht's siren. As you can see, the stewards are in the process of setting a glass of champagne before each of you. It is not compulsory that you actually drink it,' he assured with a grin for those who never imbibed no matter what the occasion, 'but as a courtesy, in the time-honoured tradition of any sailing vessel. I would be most honoured if you would stand and join me by raising your glass in a toast. For we are about to cross the Tropic of Cancer...'

With the perfect timing of a man who was adept at such things, the siren gave three short sharp hoots at the same moment that Hassan rose to his feet. On a ripple of surprise everyone rose up also. Some drank, some didn't, but all raised their glasses. Then there was a mass exodus to the yacht's rail, where everyone stood gazing out into the inky dark Red Sea as if they expected to see some physical phenomenon like a thick painted line to mark this special place.

Of course there was none. It did not seem to matter. Moving to place his hands on the rail either side of his wife, Hassan bent to place his lips to her petal-smooth cheek.

'See anything?' he questioned teasingly.

'Oh, yes,' she replied. 'A signpost sticking out of the water. Did you miss it?'

His soft laugh was deep and soft and seductive. As she tilted back to look at him the back of her head met with his shoulder. She was smiling with her eyes. He wanted to drown in them. Kiss me, they were saying. An Arab did not kiss in front of guests, so a raised eyebrow ruefully refused the invitation. It was the witch in her that punished him for that refusal when one of her hands slid backwards and made a sensual sweep of one of his thighs.

Sensation spat hot pricks of awareness like needles deep into his flesh. She was right about the *dishdasha*, he conceded, it had to be one of the ancient reasons why his culture frowned upon close physical contact with the opposite sex whilst in the company of others.

'I will pay you back for that later,' he warned darkly.

'I am most seriously worried, my lord Sheikh,' she replied provokingly.

Then, in the way these things shifted, the private moment was broken when someone spoke to him. He straightened to answer Jibril Al-Mahmud who, since the meeting had spent every minute he could possibly snatch trying to squeeze himself back into Hassan's good graces. Leona took a sip at her champagne. That dreadful intruder, Samir, claimed the rest of her attention. He was, Hassan recognised, just a little infatuated with Leona, which offered another good reason why he would be happy when their cruise ended tomorrow.

Jibril's timid little wife came to join them. She smiled nervously at him and, because he felt rather sorry for her, Hassan sent her a pleasant smile back, then politely asked about her family. Raschid joined in. Evie and Imran went to join Leona and Samir. Abdul and Zafina were the last to join his own group but at least they did it, he acknowledged.

Tonight there was no splitting of the sexes. No lingering at the table for the men. They simply mingled, talked and lingered together. And, had it not been for one small but important detail, Hassan would have declared the evening—if not the whole cruise—a more than satisfactory success.

That small but important detail was Leona. Relaxed though she might appear, content though she might appear, he could see that the strain of the whole ordeal in general had begun to paint soft bruises around her eyes. He didn't like to see them there, did not like to notice that every so often the palm of her hand would go to rest against the flat of her stomach, as if to soothe away an inner distress.

Nor had he forgotten that she had barely eaten a morsel of food all day. He frowned down at his champagne glass, still brimming with its contents. Tomorrow they reached Jeddah. Tomorrow he would take her to visit a doctor, he decided grimly. If there was one rule you were taught never to ignore when you lived in a hot country, it was the rule about heeding any signs of illness. Maybe it was nothing.

Maybe it was all just down to stress. But maybe she had picked up something in the water when she fell in. Whatever—tomorrow he would make sure that they found out for definite.

It was a decision he found himself firmly repeating when they eventually retired to their stateroom and the first thing that Leona did was wilt.

'You are ill,' he said grimly.

'Just tired,' she insisted.

'Don't take me for a fool, Leona,' he ground back. 'You do not eat. You are clearly in some sort of discomfort. And you *look* ill.'

'All right.' She caved in. 'So I think I have developed a stomach bug. If we have time when we reach Jeddah tomorrow I will get something for it.'

'We will make time.'

'Fine.' She sighed.

He sighed. 'Here, let me help you…' She even looked too weary to undress herself.

So he did it for her—silently, soberly, a concentrated frown darkening his face. She smiled and kissed him. It really was too irresistible to hold the gesture in check. 'Don't turn into a minx just because I am indulging you,' he scolded, and parted the tunic, then let it slide to her feet.

'But I like it when you indulge me,' she told him, her eyes lowered to watch him reach for the front clasp holding the two smooth satin cups of her cream bra together. As the back of his knuckles brushed against the tips of her breasts she drew back with a sharp gasp.

'What?' he demanded.

'Sensitive.' She frowned. He frowned. They both glanced down to see the tight distension of her nipples standing pink and proud and wilfully erect. A small smug smile twitched at the corner of his mouth. Leona actually blushed.

'I'll finish the rest for myself,' she decided dryly.

'I think that would be wise,' Hassan grinned, and pulled

the *dishdasha* off over his head to show her why he had said that.

'I don't know.' She was almost embarrassed by how fiercely one responded to the closeness of the other. 'I'm supposed to be ill and tired and in need of much pampering.'

A set of warm brown fingers gently stroked the flush blooming in her cheek. 'I know of many ways to pamper,' he murmured sensually. 'Slow and gentle. Soft and sweet…'

His eyes glowed darkly with all of those promises; hers grew darker on the willingness to accept. The gap between them closed, warm flesh touched warm flesh, mouths came together on a kiss. Then he showed her. Deep into the night he showed her a hundred ways to pamper a woman until she eventually fell asleep in his arms and remained there until morning came to wake them up.

At breakfast she actually ate a half-slice of toast with marmalade and drank a full cup of very weak tea—hopefully without giving away the fact that it was a struggle not to give it all back up.

Little Hashim came to beg to be allowed to sit on her lap. Leona placed him there and together they enjoyed sharing the other half of her slice of toast, while Hassan looked on with a glaze across his eyes and Evie posed a sombre question at her husband, Raschid, with expressive eyes.

He got up and stepped around the table to lay a hand on Hassan's shoulder. The muscles beneath it were fraught with tension. 'I need a private word with you, Hassan,' he requested. 'If you have finished here?'

The same muscle flexed as Hassan pulled his mind back from where it had gone off to. 'Of course,' he said, and stood up. A moment later both men were walking away from the breakfast table towards the stairs which would take them down to the deck below and Hassan's private suite of offices.

Most watched them go. Many wondered why Sheikh Raschid felt it necessary to take Sheikh Hassan to one side. But none, friend nor foe—except for Evie, who kept her attention firmly fixed on the small baby girl in her arms—came even close to guessing what was about to be discussed.

By the time Raschid came to search his wife out she was back in their suite. She glanced anxiously up at him. Raschid lifted a rueful shoulder, 'Well, it is done,' he said. Though neither of them looked as if the statement pleased them in any way.

Well, it is done. That more or less said it. *Well it is done,* now held Hassan locked in a severe state of shock. He couldn't believe it. He wanted to believe it, but did not dare let himself because it changed everything: the view of his life; the view of his marriage.

He had to sit down. The edge of his desk was conveniently placed to receive his weight, and his eyes received the cover of a trembling hand. Beyond the closed door to his office his guests and the tail end of the cruise carried on regardless, but here in this room everything he knew and felt had come to a complete standstill.

He couldn't move. Now his legs had been relieved of his weight, they had lost the ability to take it back again. Inside he was shaking. Inside he did not know what to feel or what to think. For he had been here in this same situation before— many times—and had learned through experience that it was a place best avoided at all costs.

Hope—then dashed hopes. Pleasure—then pain. But this was different. This had been forced upon him by a source he had good reason to trust and not to doubt.

Doubt. Dear heaven, he was very intimate with the word doubt. Now, as he removed the hand from his eyes and stared out at the glistening waters he could see through the window, he found doubt being replaced by the kind of dancing visions he had never—ever—allowed himself to see before.

A knock sounded at the door, then it opened before he had a chance to hide his expression. Rafiq walked in, took one look at him and went rock solid still.

'What is it?' he demanded. 'Father?'

Hassan quickly shook his head. 'Come in and close the door,' he urged, then made an effort to pull himself together—just in case someone else decided to take him by surprise.

Leona.

Something inside him was suddenly threatening to explode. He didn't know what, but it scared the hell out of him. He wished Raschid had said nothing. He wished he could go back and replay the last half hour again, change it, lose it—

'Hassan…?' Rafiq prompted an explanation as to why he was witnessing his brother quietly falling apart.

He looked up, found himself staring into mirrors of his own dark eyes, and decided to test the ground—test those eyes to find out what Leona would see in his eyes if she walked in here right now.

'Evie—Raschid,' he forced out across a sand-dry throat. 'They think Leona might be pregnant. Evie recognises the signs…'

CHAPTER TEN

SILENCE fell. It was, Hassan recognised, a very deathly silence, for Rafiq was already showing a scepticism he dared not voice.

Understanding the feeling, Hassan released a hard sigh, then grimly pulled himself together. 'Get hold of our father,' he instructed. 'I need absolute assurance from him that I will not be bringing Leona back to a palace rife with rumour attached to her return.' From being hollowed by shock he was now as tight as a bowstring. 'If he has any doubts about this, I will place her in Raschid's safekeeping, for she must be protected at all cost from any more anguish or stress.'

'I don't think Leona will—'

'It is not and never has been anyone else's place to *think* anything about my wife!' The mere fact that he was lashing out at Rafiq showed how badly he was taking this. 'Other people's thinking has made our life miserable enough! Which is why I want you to speak to our father and not me,' he explained. 'I will have this conversation with no one else. Leona must be protected from ever hearing from anyone else that I am so much as suspecting this. If I am wrong then only I will grieve over what never was. If I am correct, then she has the right to learn of her condition for herself. I will not take this away from her!'

'So I am not even to tell our father,' Rafiq assumed from all of that.

'He and Leona communicate daily by e-mail,' Hasssan explained. 'The old man may be too puffed up with excitement to hold back from saying something to her.'

'In the state you are in, all of this planning may well be a waste of time,' Rafiq remarked with a pointed glance at his watch. 'In one hour we arrive in Jeddah. If you do not pull yourself together Leona will need only to look at your face to know that something catastrophic has taken place.'

Hassan knew it. Without warning he sank his face into his hands. 'This is crazy,' he muttered thickly.

'It is certainly most unexpected,' his brother agreed. 'And a little too soon for anyone, including the Al-Kadahs, to be making such confident judgements?' he posed cautiously.

Behind his hands Hassan's brain went still. Behind the hands it suddenly rushed ahead again, filling him with the kind of thoughts that made his blood run cold. For Rafiq was right: three weeks was not long enough—not to achieve what he was suggesting. As any man knew, it took only a moment to conceive a child. But which man—whose child?

On several hard curses he dragged his hand down. On several more he climbed to his feet then strode across the room to pull open the door that connected him with his aide.

'Faysal!' The man almost jumped out of his skin. 'Track down my father-in-law, wherever he is. I need to speak with him urgently.'

Slam. The door shut again. 'May Allah save me from the evil minds of others,' he grated.

'I do not follow you.' Rafiq frowned.

'Three weeks!' Hassan muttered. 'Three weeks ago Leona was sleeping in the same house as Ethan Hayes! It was one of the problems which forced me into bringing her to this yacht, if you recall...'

Leona didn't see Hassan until a few minutes before they were due to arrive in Jeddah. By then most of their guests were assembled on the shade deck taking refreshment while watching the yacht make the delicate manoeuvres required to bring such a large vessel safely into its reserved berth in the harbour.

In respect of Saudi Arabian custom everyone was wearing traditional Arab daywear, including little Hashim, who looked rather cute in his tiny white tunic and *gutrah*.

Hassan arrived dressed the same way; Rafiq was less than a step behind him. 'Hello, strangers.' Leona smiled at both of them. 'Where have you two been hiding yourselves all morning?'

'Working.' Rafiq smiled, but Hassan didn't even seem to hear her, and his gaze barely glanced across her face before he was turning to speak to Samir's father, Imran.

She frowned. He looked different—not pale, exactly, but under some kind of grim restraint. Then little Hashim demanded, 'Come and see,' and her attention was diverted. After that she had no time to think of anything but the formalities involved in bidding farewell to everyone.

A fleet of limousines stood in line along the concrete jetty waiting to speed everyone off to their various destinations. Accepting thanks and saying goodbye took over an hour. One by one the cars pulled up and took people away in a steady rota. Sheikh Abdul and Zafina first—relieved, Leona suspected, to be getting away from a trip that had not been a pleasant one for them, though their farewells were polite enough.

Sheikh Imran and Samir were the next to leave. Then she turned to smile at Sheikh Jibril and his wife, Medina, who made very anxious weight of their farewell, reminding Hassan several times that he had complete loyalty. In Jibril's case money talked much louder than power. He had no desire to scrape his deep pockets to pay Sheikh Raschid for the privilege of sending his oil across his land.

Raschid and his family were the last ones to leave. As with everyone else it would be a brief parting, because they would come together again next week, when they attended Sheikh Kalifa's anniversary celebration. Only this time the children would be staying at home with their nurse. So Leona's goodbyes to them were tinged with a genuine regret, especially for Hashim, who had become her little friend during their cruise. So, while she was promising to come and visit with him soon, she missed the rather sober exchanges between the others.

Eventually they left. Their car sped away. Rafiq excused himself to go and seek out Faysal, and Hassan said he had yet to thank his captain and walked away leaving her standing there, alone by the rail, feeling just a little bit rejected by the brevity with which he had treated her.

Something was wrong, she was sure, though she had no idea exactly what it could be. And, knowing him as well as she did, she didn't expect to find out until he felt ready to tell her. So with a shrug and a sigh she went off to follow Hassan's lead and thank the rest of the staff for taking care of everyone so well. By the time they came together again there was only time left to make the dash to the airport if they wanted to reach Rahman before nightfall.

Rafiq and Faysal travelled with them, which gave Hassan the excuse—and Leona was sure it *was* an excuse—to keep conversation light and neutral. A Lear jet bearing the gold Al-Qadim insignia waited on the runway to fly them over Saudi Arabia and into Rahman. The Al-Qadim oasis had its own private runway. A four-wheel drive waited to transport them to the palace whose ancient sandstone walls burned red against a dying sun.

Home, Leona thought, and felt a lump form in her throat because this was home to her. London…England—both had stopped being that a long time ago.

They swept through the gates and up to the front entrance. Hassan helped her to alight. As she walked inside she found herself flanked by two proud males again and wanted to lift her head and say something teasing about *abayas*, but the mood didn't allow for it somehow.

'My father wishes to see us straight away.' Hassan unwittingly explained the sombre mood. 'Please try not to show your shock at how much he has deteriorated since you were last here.'

'Of course,' she replied, oddly hurt that he felt he needed to say that. Then she took the hurt back when she saw the old sheikh reclining against a mound of pillows on his favourite divan.

His sons strode forward; she held back a little to allow them the space to greet him as they always did, with the old sheikh holding out both hands and both hands being taken, one by each son. In all the years she had known Sheikh Kalifa she had never seen him treat his two sons less than equal. They greeted each other; they talked in low-toned Arabic. They touched, they loved. It was an honour and a privilege to be allowed to witness it. When the old sheikh decided to acknowledge her presence he did so with a spice that told her that the old spirit was still very much alive inside his wasted frame.

'So, what do you think of my two warriors, huh?' he asked. 'They snatch you back with style and panache. A worthy woman cannot but be impressed.'

'Impressed by their arrogance, their cheek, and their disregard for my safety,' Leona responded, coming forward now that he had in effect given her permission to do so. 'I almost drowned—twice—and was tossed down a set of stairs. And you dare to be proud of them.'

No one bothered to accuse her of gross exaggeration, because he laughed, loving it, wishing he could have been there to join in. Reclaiming his hands, he waved his sons away and offered those long bony fingers to Leona.

'Come and greet me properly,' he commanded her. 'And you two can leave us. My daughter-in-law and I have things to discuss.'

There was a pause, a distinct hesitation in which Hassan looked ready to argue the point. The old man looked up at him and his son looked down; a battle of the eyes commenced that made Leona frown as a strange kind of tension began to sizzle in the air. Then Hassan conceded by offering a brief, grim nod and left, with Rafiq making the situation feel even stranger when, as he left with him, he placed a hand on Hassan's shoulder as if to reassure him that it would be okay.

'What was all that about?' she enquired as she reached down to brush a kiss on her father-in-law's hollowed cheek.

'He worries about you,' the old sheikh answered.

'Or he worries about you,' she returned.

He knew what she was referring to and flicked it away with a sigh and a wave of a hand. 'I am dying,' he stated bluntly. 'Hassan knows this—they both do. Neither likes knowing they can do nothing to stop it from happening.'

'But you are resigned?' Leona said gently.

'Yes. Come—sit down here, in your chair.' Discussion over, he indicated the low cushion-stuffed chair she had pulled up beside his divan years ago; it had remained there ever since. 'Now, tell me,' he said as soon as she was settled, 'have you come back here because Hassan bullied you into doing so, or because you still love him?'

'Can it be both?' she quizzed him.

'He needs you.'

'Rahman doesn't.'

'Ah,' he scathed, 'that stupid man, Abdul, thought he could force our hand and soon learned that he could not.'

'So it was Sheikh Abdul who plotted to take me,' Leona murmured ruefully.

Eyes that were once a rich dark brown but were now only pale shadows sharpened. 'He did not tell you,' he surmised on an impatient sigh. 'I am a fool for thinking he would.'

'Maybe that is why he didn't want to leave me alone with you,' Leona smilingly replied. 'Actually, I had already guessed it,' she then admitted, adding quietly, 'I know all about Nadira, you see.'

The name had a disturbing effect on Sheikh Khalifa: he shifted uncomfortably, pulled himself up and reached out to touch her cheek. 'Rahman needs my son and my son needs you. Whatever has to happen in the future I need to know that you will always be here supporting him when I can no longer do so.'

Strange words, fierce, dark, compelling words that sealed her inside a coating of ice. What was he saying? What did he mean? Was he telling her that Nadira was still Hassan's only real option if he wanted to continue in his father's foot-steps?

But before she could ask him to elaborate, as after most brief bursts of energy, Sheikh Khalifa suddenly lay back exhausted against the cushions and, without really thinking about it, Leona slipped back into her old routine. She picked up the book lying face down on the table beside him and began reading out loud to him.

But her mind was elsewhere. Her mind was filling up with contracts and Hassan's method of feeding her information on a need-to-know only basis. She saw him as he had been that same morning, relaxed, at peace with both her and himself. Then Raschid had begged a private word. When he'd eventually reappeared later it had been as if he had changed into a different man—a tense, preoccupied and distant man.

A man who avoided eye contact, as if he had something to hide...

The old sheikh was asleep. Leona put down the book.

Doubts; she hated to feel the doubts return. It was no use, she told herself, she was going to have to tackle Hassan about what Zafina had said to her. Once he had denied everything she could put the whole stupid thing away, never to be dredged up again.

And if he didn't deny it? she asked herself as she left the old sheikh's room to go in search of the younger one. The coating of ice turned itself into a heavy cloak that weighed down her footsteps as she walked in between pale blue walls on a cool, polished sandstone flooring.

She didn't want to do this, she accepted as she trod the wide winding staircase onto the landing where pale blue walls changed to pale beige and the floor became a pale blue marble.

She didn't want to reveal that she could doubt his word, she thought dully as she passed between doors made of thick cedar fitted tightly into wide Arabian archways, the very last one of which led through to Hassan's private suite of offices.

Her head began to ache; her throat suddenly felt strange:

hot and tight. She was about five yards away when the door suddenly opened and Hassan himself stepped out. Slender white tunic, flowing blue *thobe*, no covering on his raven-dark head. He saw her and stopped, almost instantly his expression altered from the frowningly preoccupied to… nothing.

It was like having a door slammed in her face. Her doubts surged upwards along with her blood pressure; she could feel her pulse throbbing in her ears. A prickly kind of heat engulfed her whole body—and the next thing that she knew, she was lying on the pale blue marble floor and Hassan was kneeling beside her.

'What happened?' he rasped as her eyes fluttered open.

She couldn't answer, didn't want to answer. She closed her eyes again. His curse wafted across her cheeks. One of his hands came to cover her clammy forehead, the other took a light grasp of her wrist then he was grimly sliding his arms beneath her shoulders and knees and coming to his feet.

'Ouch,' she said as her breasts brushed his breastbone.

Hassan froze. She didn't notice because from absolutely nowhere she burst into tears! What was the matter with her? she wondered wretchedly. She felt sick, she felt dizzy, she hurt in places she had never hurt before! From another place she had never known existed inside her, one of her clenched fists aimed an accusing blow at his shoulder.

Expecting him to demand what he had done to deserve it, she was thrown into further confusion when all he did was release a strained groan from deep in his throat, then began striding back the way from which she had come. A door opened and closed behind them. Lifting her head from his shoulder, she recognised their old suite of rooms.

Laying her on the bed, he came to lean over her. 'What did my father say to you?' he demanded. 'I knew I should not have left you both alone! Did he say you should not have come back, is that it?'

Her eyes flew open, tear-drenched and sparkling. 'Is that what he thinks?'

'Yes—no!' His sigh was driven by demons. But what demons—? The demons of lies? 'In case you did not notice,
he does not think so clearly any more,' he said tightly.

'Sheikh Abdul was behind the plot to abduct me; there is
nothing unclear about that, as far as I can see.'

'I knew it was a mistake.' Hassan sighed, and sat down
beside her.

He looked tired and fed up and she wanted to hit him
again. 'You lied to me again,' she accused him.

'By omission,' he agreed. 'And Abdul's involvement
cannot be proved,' he added. 'Only by hearsay which is not
enough to risk a war between families.'

'And you've always got the ready-typed contract involving
Nadira if things really do get out of hand…'

This time she saw the freeze overtake him. This time she
got the answer she had been desperately trying to avoid.
Sitting up, Leona ignored the way her head spun dizzily.
Drawing up her knees, she reached down to ease the straps
of her sandals off the backs of her heels, then tossed them
to the floor.

'He told you about that also?' Hassan asked hoarsely.

She shook her head. 'Zafina did.'

'When?'

'Does it really matter when?' she derided. 'It exists. I saw
it. You felt fit not to warn me about it. What do you think
that tells me about what is really going on around here?'

'It means nothing,' he claimed. 'It is just a meaningless
piece of paper containing words with no power unless several
people place their signatures against it.'

'But you have a copy.'

He didn't answer.

'You had it in your possession even before you came to
Spain to get me,' she stated, because she knew it was the
truth even though no one had actually told her so. 'What was
it—firm back-up in case Raschid failed to bail you out of
trouble? Or does it still carry a lot of weight around with it?'

'You could try trusting me,' he answered.

'And you, my lord sheikh, should have tried trusting me, then maybe it would not be the big problem it is.' With that, she climbed off the bed and began walking away.

'Where are you going?' He sighed out heavily. 'Come back here. We need to—'

The cold way she turned to look at him stopped the words; the way she had one hand held to her forehead and the other to her stomach paled his face. 'I am going to the bathroom to be sick,' she informed him. 'Then I am going to crawl into that bed and go to sleep. I would appreciate it if you were not still here when I get to do that.'

And that, Hassan supposed, had told him. He watched the bathroom door close behind her retreating figure.

He got up and strode over to the window beyond which an ink dark evening obliterated everything beyond the subtle lighting of the palace walls.

So where do we go from here? he asked himself. When Zafina Al-Yasin had picked her weapon, she'd picked it well. For Hassan could think of nothing more likely to shatter Leona's belief in his sincerity than a document already drawn up and ready to be brought into use should it become necessary. She would not now believe that he had agreed to the drawing up of such a document merely to buy him time. Why should she when he had refrained from telling her so openly and honestly before she'd found out by other means?

Sighing, he turned to leave the room. It was simpler to leave her alone for now. He could say nothing that was going to change anything, because he had another problem looming, he realised, One bigger and more potentially damaging than all that had tried to damage his marriage before.

He had a contract bearing his agreement to take a second wife. He had a wife whom he suspected might be carrying his first child. Leona was never going to believe that the former was not an insurance policy to protect him against the failure of the latter.

'Faysal,' he said as he stepped into his aide's office, which guarded the entrance to his own, 'get Rafiq for me, if you please…'

'You look pale like a ghost,' the old sheikh remarked.

'I'm fine,' Leona assured him.

'They tell me you fainted the other day.'

'I still had my sea legs on,' Leona explained. 'And how did you find out about it?' she challenged, because as far as she knew no one but herself and Hassan had been there at the time!

'My palace walls are equipped with a thousand eyes.' He smiled. 'So I also know that when he is not with me my son walks around wearing the face of a man whose father is already dead.'

'He is a busy man doing busy, important things,' Leona said with a bite that really should have been resisted.

'He also has a wife who sleeps in one place while he sleeps in another.'

Getting in practice, Leona thought nastily. 'Do you want to finish this chapter or not?' she asked.

'I would prefer you to confide in me,' the old sheikh murmured gently. 'You used to do so all the time, before I became too sick to be of any use to anyone…'

A blatant plucking of her heartstrings though it was, Leona could see the concern in his eyes. On a sigh, she laid the book aside, got up to go and sit down beside him and picked up one of his cool, dry, skeletal hands to press a gentle kiss to it.

'Don't fret so, old man,' she pleaded gently. 'You know I will look after your two sons for you. I have promised, haven't I?'

'But you are unhappy. Do you think this does not fret me?'

'I—struggle with the reasons why I am here,' she explained, because she wasn't going to lie. It wasn't fair to lie to him. 'You know the problems. They are not going to go away just because Hassan wants them to.'

'My son wants you above all things, daughter of Victor Frayne,' he said, using the Arab way of referring to her, because by their laws a woman kept her father's name after marriage. 'Don't make him choose to prove this to you…'

CHAPTER ELEVEN

DON'T make him choose... The next day, those words played inside Leona's head like a mantra, because she had just begun to realise that Hassan might not be forced to choose anything.

Sickness in the morning, sickness in the evening, a certain tenderness in her breasts and other changes in her body that she could no longer ignore were trying to tell her something she was not sure she wanted to know.

Pregnant. She could be pregnant. She *might* be pregnant. She absolutely refused to say that she was *most definitely* pregnant. How could she be sure, when her periods had never been anything but sporadic at best? Plus it had to be too soon to tell. It had to be. She was just wishing on rainbows—wasn't she?

A month. She had been back in Hassan's life for a tiny month—and not even a full month! Women just didn't know that quickly if they had conceived, did they? She didn't know. At this precise moment she didn't know anything. Her brain was blank, her emotions shot and she was fighting an ever-growing battle with excitement that was threatening to turn her into a puff of smoke!

It was this morning that had really set her suspicions soaring, when she'd climbed out of bed feeling sick and dizzy before her feet had managed to touch the floor. Then, in the shower, she'd seen the changes in her breasts, a new fullness, darkening circles forming round their tips. She'd *felt* different too—inside, where it was impossible to say how she felt different, only that she did.

Instinct. What did she know about the female instinct in such situations?

Doubt. She had to doubt her own conclusions because the specialists had given her so little hope of it ever happening for them.

But even her skin felt different, her hair, the strange, secret glint she kept on catching in her own eyes whenever she looked in a mirror. She'd stopped looking in the mirror. It was easier not to look than look and then see, then dare— *dare* to hope.

I want Hassan, she thought on a sudden rocketing rise of anxiety.

I don't want Hassan! she then changed her mind. Because if he saw her like this he would know something really drastic was worrying her and she couldn't tell him—didn't dare tell him, raise his hopes, until she was absolutely sure for herself.

She needed one of those testing kits, she realised. But, if such a thing was obtainable, where could she get one from without alerting half of Rahman? There was not a chemist's in the country she could walk into and buy such an obvious thing without setting the jungle drums banging from oasis to oasis and back again.

But I need one. I *need* one! she thought agitatedly.

Ring Hassan, that tiny voice inside her head persisted. Tell him your suspicions, get him to bring a pregnancy testing kit home with him.

Oh, yes, she mocked that idea. I can just see Sheikh Hassan Al-Qadim walking into a chemist's and buying one of those!

Rafiq, then. No, *not* Rafiq! she all but shouted at herself. Oh, why could there not be some more women in this wretched house of Al-Qadim? Why do I have to be surrounded by men?

Maids. There were dozens of maids she could call upon— all of whom would be just as proficient at belting out the message across the whole state.

As if she'd conjured her up a knock sounded on the door and one of the maids walked into the room. She was carrying a dress that Leona had ordered to be delivered from one of her favourite couturier's in the city.

'It is very beautiful, my lady,' the maid said shyly.

And very red, Leona thought frowningly. What in heaven's name had made her choose to buy red? Made by a local designer to a traditional Arabian design, the dress was silk, had matching trousers and *thobe*, and shimmered with beautifully embroidered golden threads. And she never, ever wore red!

'The sheikha will shine above all things tomorrow night,' the maid approved.

Tomorrow night, Leona repeated with a sinking heart as the maid carried the dress into her dressing room. For tomorrow night was *the* night of Sheikh Kalifa's anniversary celebration, which meant she had a hundred guests to play hostess to when really all she wanted to do was—

Oh, she thought suddenly, where is my head? And she turned to walk quickly across the room towards the telephone which sat beside the bed.

Pregnant.

Her feet pulled to a stop. Her stomach twisted itself into a knot then sprang free again, catching at her breath. It was a desperate sensation. Desperate with hope and with fear and a thousand other things that—

The maid appeared again, looked at her oddly because she was standing here in the middle of the room, emulating a statue. 'Thank you, Leila,' she managed to say.

As soon as the door closed behind the maid she finished her journey to the telephone, picked up her address book, flicked through its pages with trembling fingers, then stabbed in a set of numbers that would connect her with Evie Al-Kadah in Behran.

Hassan was fed up. He was five hours away from home, on his way back from Sheikh Abdul's summer palace, having just enjoyed a very uncomfortable meeting in which a few home truths had been aired. He should be feeling happy, for the meeting had gone very much his way, and in his possession he now had the sheikh's copy of one ill-judged contract and the satisfaction of knowing the man and his wife now understood the error of their ways.

But it had required a five-hour drive out to mountains of Rahman to win this sense of grim satisfaction, which meant they now had to make the same journey back again. And Rafiq might feel *he* needed the physical exercise of negotiating the tough and challenging terrain but, quite frankly, so did he. He felt tense and restless, impatient to get back to Leona now that he could face her with an easy conscience.

So the flat tire they suffered a few minutes later was most unwelcome. By the time they had battled in soft sand on a rocky incline to jack the car up and secure it so they could change the wheel time was getting on, and the sun was beginning to set. Then, only a half-mile further into their journey, they became stuck in deep soft sand. And he couldn't even blame Rafiq for this second inconvenience because he had taken over the driving for himself. Proficient though they were at getting themselves out of such difficulties, time was lost, then more time when they were hit by a sandstorm that forced them to stop and wait until it had blown past.

Consequently, it was very late when they drove through the gates of the palace. By the time he had washed the sand from his body before letting himself quietly into the bedroom he found Leona fast asleep.

Did he wake her or did he go away? he pondered as he stood looking down on her, lying there on her side, with her glorious hair spilling out behind her and a hand resting on the pillow where his head should be.

She murmured something, maybe because she sensed he was there, and the temptation to just throw caution to the wind, slide into the bed and awaken her so he could confide his suspicions then discover whether she felt he was making any sense almost got the better of him.

Then reality returned, for this was not the time for such an emotive discussion. It could backfire on him and deeply hurt her. And tomorrow was a day packed with strife enough for both of them, without him adding to it with what could be merely a foolish dream.

Anyway, he had some damage limitation to perform, preferably before this new development came into the open—just in case.

So, instead of waking her, he turned away, unaware that behind him her eyes had opened to watch him leave. The urge to call him back tugged at her vocal cords. The need to scramble out of the bed and go after him to confide her suspicions stretched nerve ends in every muscle she possessed.

But, no, it would not be fair to offer him hope where there might be none. Better to wait one more day until she knew for sure one way or another, she convinced herself.

So the door between their two rooms closed him away from her—just as it had closed him away before, when he had decided it was better to sleep elsewhere than risk another argument with her.

Maybe he was right. Maybe the common sense thing to do was stay out of each other's way, because they certainly didn't function well together unless they were in bed!

They had a battleground, not a marriage, she decided, and on that profound thought she turned her back on that wretched closed door and refused to look back at it.

The next day continued in much the same fashion. He avoided her. She avoided him. They circulated the palace in opposing directions like a pair of satellites designed never to cross paths. By six o'clock Leona was in her room preparing for the evening ahead. By seven she was as ready as she supposed she ever would be, having changed her mind about what to wear a hundred times before finally deciding to wear the red outfit.

When Hassan stepped into the room a few minutes later he took her breath away. Tall, lean and not yet having covered his silky dark hair, he was wearing a midnight blue long tunic with a standing collar braided in gold. At his waist a wide sash of gold silk gave his body shape and stature, and the jewel encrusted shaft belonging to the ceremonial scabbard he had tucked into his waistband said it all.

Arrogance personified. A prince among men. First among equals did not come into it for her because for her he was it—the one—her only one. As if to confirm that thought her belly gave a skittering flutter as if to say, And me, don't forget me.

Too soon for that, too silly to think it, she scolded herself as she watched him pause to look at her. As always those dark eyes made their possessive pass over her. As always they liked what they saw.

'Beautiful,' he murmured.

Tell me about it, she wanted to say, but she couldn't, didn't dare say anything in case the wrong thing popped anxiously out.

So the twist his mouth gave said he had misread her silence. 'Forgiveness, my darling, is merely one sweet smile away,' he drawled as he walked towards her.

'But you have nothing to forgive me for!' she protested, glad now to use her voice.

'Throwing me out of your bed does not require forgiveness?' An eyebrow arched, the outfit, the coming occasion, turning the human being into a pretentious monster that made her toes curl inside her strappy gold shoes. With life, that was what they curled with. Life.

I love this man to absolute pieces. 'You left voluntarily,' she told him. 'In what I think you would describe as a sulk.'

'Men do not sulk.'

But you are not just any man, she wanted to say, but the comment would puff up his ego, so she settled for, 'What do they do, then?'

'Withdraw from a fight they have no hope of winning.' He smiled. Then on a complete change of subject, he said, 'Here, a peace offering.' And he held out a flat package wrapped in black silk and tied up with narrow red ribbon.

Expecting the peace offering to be jewellery, the moment

she took possession of the package she knew it was too light. So…what? she asked herself, then felt her heart suddenly drop to her slender ankles as a terrible suspicion slid snake-like into her head.

No, she denied it. Evie just would not break such a precious confidence. 'What is it?' she asked warily.

'Open it and see.'

Trembling fingers did as he bade her, fumbling with the ribbon and then with the square of black silk. Inside it was a flat gold box, the kind that could be bought at any gift shop, nothing at all like she had let herself wonder, and nothing particularly threatening about it, but still she felt her breath snag in her chest as she lifted the lid and looked inside.

After that came the frown while she tried to work out why Hassan was giving her a box full of torn scraps of white paper. Then she turned the top one over, recognised the insignia embossed upon it and finally realised what it was.

'You know what they are?' he asked her quietly.

'Yes.' She swallowed.

'All three copies of the contract are now in your possession,' he went on to explain anyway. 'All evidence that they were ever composed wiped clean from Faysal's computer hard disk. There, it is done. Now we can be friends again.' Without giving her a chance to think he took the gift and its packaging back from her and tossed it onto the bed.

'But it doesn't wipe clean the fact that it was written in the first place,' she pointed out. 'And nor does it mean it can't be typed up again in five short minutes if it was required to be done.'

'You have said it for yourself,' Hassan answered. 'I must require it. I do not require it. I give you these copies for ceremonial purposes, only to *show* you that I do not require it. Subject over, Leona,' he grimly concluded, 'for I will waste no more of my time on something that had only ever been meant as a diversion tactic to buy me time while I decided what to do about Sheikh Abdul and his ambitious plans.'

'You expect me to believe all of that, don't you?'

'Yes.' It was a coldly unequivocal yes.

She lifted her chin. For the first time in days they actually made eye contact. And it was only as it happened that she finally began to realise after all of these years *why* they avoided doing it when there was dissension between them. Eye contact wiped out everything but the truth. The *love* truth. The *need* truth. The absolute and utter *total* truth. I love him; he loves me. Who or what else could ever really come between that?

'I think I'm pregnant,' she whispered.

It almost dropped him like a piece of crumbling stone at her feet. She saw the shock; she saw the following pallor. She watched his eyes close and feared for a moment that *he* was actually going to faint.

For days he had been waiting for this moment, Hassan was thinking. He had yearned for it, had begged and had prayed for it. Yet, when it came, not only had he not been ready, the frightened little remark had virtually knocked him off his feet!

'I could kill you for this,' he ground out hoarsely. 'Why here? Why now, when in ten short minutes we are expected downstairs to greet a hundred guests?'

His response was clearly not the one she had been expecting. Her eyes began to glaze, her mouth to tremble. 'You don't like it,' she quavered.

'Give me strength.' He groaned. 'You stupid, unpredictable, aggravating female. Of course I like it! But look at me! I am now a white-faced trembling mess!'

'You just gave me something I really needed. I wanted to give you something back that you needed,' she explained.

'Ten minutes before I face the upper echelons of Arabian society?'

'Well, thanks for being concerned about how I am feeling!' she flashed back at him.

She was right. 'You've just knocked me for six,' he breathed unsteadily.

'And I might be wrong, so don't start going off the deep end about it!' she snapped, and went to turn away.

Oh, Allah, help him, what was he doing here? With shaking hands he took hold of her by her silk-swathed shoulders and pulled her against him. She was trembling too. And she *felt* different, slender and frail and oh, so precious.

He kissed her— What else did a man do when he was so blown away by everything about her?

'I should not have dropped it on you like this,' she murmured repentantly a few seconds later.

'Yes, you should,' he argued. 'How else?'

'It might come to nothing.' Anxiety was playing havoc with her beautiful eyes.

'We will deal with the something or the nothing together.'

'I am afraid of the nothing,' she confessed to him. 'I am afraid I might never get the chance to feel like this again.'

'I love you,' he said huskily. 'Can that not be enough?'

'For you?' She threw the question back at him, clinging to his eyes like a vulnerable child.

'We know how I feel, Leona,' he said ruefully. 'In fact, the whole of Rahman knows how I feel about you. But we hardly ever discuss how you feel about the situation I place you in here.'

'I just don't want you to have to keep defending my place in your life,' she told him. 'I hate it.'

Hassan thought about the damage-control exercise he had already set into motion, and wished he knew how to answer that. 'I like defending you.' His words seemed to say it all for him.

'You won't tell anyone tonight, will you?' she flashed up at him suddenly. 'You will keep this our secret until we know for sure.'

'Do you really think I am that manipulative?' He was shocked, then uncomfortable, because he realised that she knew him better than he knew himself. 'Tomorrow we will bring in a doctor,' he decided, looking for an escape from his own manipulative thoughts.

But Leona shook her head. 'It would be all over Rahman in five minutes if we did that. Look what happened when I went to see him to find out why I couldn't conceive?'

'But we have to know—'

'Evie is bringing me a pregnancy testing kit with her,' she told him, too busy trying to smooth some semblance of calmness into herself to notice how still he had gone. 'I rang her and explained. At least I can trust her not to say anything to anyone.'

'What did she say?' Hassan enquired carefully.

'She said I should make sure I tell you. Which I've done.' She turned a wry smile on him. 'Now I wish that I hadn't because, looking at you, I have a horrible feeling you are going to give the game away the moment anyone looks at you.'

Confess all, he told himself. Tell her before the Al-Kadahs tell her that you already suspected all of this, days ago. A knock at the door was a thankful diversion. Going to open it, he found Rafiq standing there dressed very much like himself—only he was wearing his *gutrah*.

'Our guests are arriving,' he informed him. 'You and Leona should be downstairs.'

Guests. Dear heaven. His life was in crisis and he must go downstairs and be polite to people. 'We will be five minutes only.'

'You are all right?' Rafiq frowned at him.

No, I am slowly sinking beneath my own plots and counter-plots. 'Five minutes,' he repeated, and closed the door again.

Leona was standing by a mirror, about to fix her lipstick with a set of very unsteady fingers. The urge to go over there and stop her so that he could kiss her almost got the better of him. But one kiss would most definitely lead to another and another. In fact he wanted to be very primitive and drag her off by her beautiful hair to his lair and smother her in kisses. So instead he stepped back into the other room and came back a moment later wearing white silk on his head, held by triple gold thongs, to find that Leona had also covered her hair with a gold-spangled scarf of red silk.

The red should have clashed with her hair but it didn't. It merely toned with the sensual colour on her lips. She lifted her eyes to look at him. He looked back at her. A different man, a different woman. It was amazing what a piece of silk laid to the head could do for both of them, because neither was now showing signs of what was really going on inside them.

His smile, therefore, was rueful. 'Showtime,' he said.

And showtime it was. As on the yacht, but on a grander scale, they welcomed heads of state from all over Arabia, diplomats from further afield. Some brought their wives, sons and even their daughters, and some came alone. Some women were veiled; all were dressed in the exotic jewelled colours favoured by Arabian women.

Everyone was polite, gracious, and concerned about Sheikh Khalifa's well-being. He had not yet put in an appearance, though he had every intention of doing so eventually. This was his night. He had in fact planned it as much as he could from his sick bed. Today his doctor had insisted he be sedated for most of the day to conserve his energy. But he had looked bright-eyed and excited when Leona had popped in to see him just before she had gone to get ready.

'Rafiq should be doing this with us,' Leona said to Hassan when she realised that his brother was nowhere to be seen.

'He has other duties,' he replied, then turned his attention to the next person to arrive at the doors to the great hall. A great hall that was slowly filling with people.

Sheikh Abdul arrived without his wife, Zafina, which seemed a significant omission to Leona. He was subdued but polite to her, which was all she could really expect from him, she supposed. They greeted Sheikh Jibril and his wife, Medina, Sheikh Imran, and of course Samir.

When Sheikh Raschid Al-Kadah and his wife, Evie, arrived, there were some knowing glances exchanged that made Leona want to blush. But the real blushing happened every time Hassan glanced at her and his eyes held the burning darkness of their secret.

'Don't,' she whispered, looking quickly away from him.

'I cannot help it,' he replied.

'Well, try.' A sudden disturbance by the door gave her someone new to divert her attention, only to have her heart stop in complete surprise.

Two men dressed in black western dinner suits, white shirts and bow ties. She flicked her eyes from one smiling male face to the other, then on a small shriek of delight launched herself into the arms of her father.

Tall, lean and in very good shape for his fifty-five years, Victor Frayne caught his daughter to him and accepted her ecstatic kisses to his face. 'What are you doing here? Why didn't you tell me? Ethan—' One of her hands reached out to catch one of his. 'I can't believe this! I only spoke to you this morning. I thought you were in San Estéban!'

'No, the Marriott, here.' Her father grinned at her. 'Thank your husband for the surprise.'

Hassan. She turned, a hand each clinging to her two surprises. 'I love you,' she said impulsively.

'She desires to make me blush,' Hassan remarked, and stepped forward, took his wife by her waist, then offered his hand to his father-in-law and to Ethan Hayes. 'Glad you could make it,' he said.

'Happy to be here,' Ethan replied with only a touch of dryness to his tone to imply that there was more to this invitation than met the eye.

Leona was just too excited to notice. Too wrapped up in her surprise to notice the ripple of awareness that went through those people who had dared to believe rumours about her relationship with her father's business partner. Then, with the attention to fine detail which was Hassan's forte, another diversion suddenly appeared.

People stopped talking, silence reigned as Rafiq arrived,

pushing a wheelchair bearing Sheikh Khalifa ben Jusef Al-Qadim.

He looked thin and frail against the height and breadth of his youngest son. A wasted shadow of his former self. But his eyes were bright, his mouth smiling, and in the frozen stasis that followed his arrival, brought on by everyone's shock at how ill he actually looked, he was prepared and responded. 'Welcome…welcome everyone,' he greeted. 'Please, do not continue to look as if you are attending my funeral, for I assure you I am here to enjoy myself.'

After that everyone made themselves relax again. Some who knew him well even grinned. As Rafiq wheeled him towards the other end of the room the old sheikh missed no one in reach of his acknowledgement. Not even Leona's father, whom he had only met once or twice. 'Victor,' he greeted him. 'I have stolen your daughter. She is now my most precious daughter. I apologise to you, but I am not sorry, you understand?'

'I think we can share her,' Victor Frayne allowed graciously.

'And…ah…' he turned his attention to Ethan '…Mr Hayes, it is my great pleasure to meet Leona's very good friend.' He had the floor, as it should be. So no one could miss the messages being broadcast here. Even Leona began to notice that something was going on beneath the surface here. 'Victor…Mr Hayes…come and see me tomorrow. I have a project I believe will be of great interest to you… Ah, Rafiq, take me forward, for I can see Sheikh Raschid…'

He progressed down the hall like that. As Leona watched, she gently slipped her arm around Hassan's waist. She could feel the emotion pulsing inside him. For this was probably going to be the old Sheikhs final formal duty.

But nothing, nothing prepared her for the power of feeling that swept over everyone as Rafiq and his father reached the other end of the hall where Sheikh Khalifa's favourite divan had been placed upon a raised dais, ready for him to enjoy the party in reasonable comfort.

Rafiq bent and lifted his father into his arms and carried the frail old man up the steps then gently lowered his father down again. As he went to straighten, the sheikh lifted a pale bony hand to his youngest son's face and murmured something to him which sent Rafiq to his knees beside the divan and sent his covered head down.

The strong and the weak. It was a painful image that held everyone in its thrall because in those few seconds it was impossible to tell which man held the strength and which one was weaker.

'Hassan, go to him,' Leona said huskily. 'Rafiq needs you.'

But Hassan shook his head. 'He will not thank me,' he replied. And he was right; Leona knew that.

Instead Hassan turned his attention to causing yet another diversion by snapping his fingers to pull a small army of servants into use.

They came bearing trays of delicately made sweets and Arabian coffee and *bukhoor* burners, which filled the air with the smell of incense. The mood shifted, took on the characteristics of a traditional *majlis*, and the next time Leona looked the dais was surrounded by the old sheikhs from the desert tribes sitting around on the provided cushions while Sheikh Khalifa reclined on his divan enjoying their company.

Hassan took her father and Ethan with him and circulated the room, introducing them to their fellow guests. The timid Medina Al-Mahmud attached herself to Leona's side like a rather wary limpet and, taking pity on her, Leona found herself taking the older woman with her as they moved from group to group.

It was a success. The evening was really looking as if it was going to be a real success. And then from somewhere behind her she heard Sheikh Abdul say, 'A clever ploy. I am impressed by his strategy. For how many men here would now suspect Mr Hayes as his lovely wife's lover?'

She pretended not to hear, smiled her bright smile and just kept on talking. But the damage was done. The evening was ruined for her. For it had not once occurred to her that her father and Ethan were here for any other purpose than because Hassan wanted to please her.

Evie appeared at her side to save her life. 'Show me where I can freshen up,' she requested.

As Leona excused herself from those she was standing with, a hand suddenly gripped her sleeve. 'You heard; I saw your face. But you must not listen,' Medina advised earnestly. 'For he has the bad mouth and his wife is in purdah after Sheikh Hassan's visit yesterday.'

Sheikh Hassan's visit? Curiouser and curiouser, Leona thought grimly as she took a moment to reassure Medina before moving away with Evie Al-Kadah.

'What was that all about?' Evie quizzed.

'Nothing.' Leona dismissed the little incident.

But from across the room Hassan saw the green glint hit her eyes and wondered what had caused it. Had Evie let the proverbial cat out of the bag, or was it the timid Medina who had dared to stick in the knife?

He supposed he would soon find out, he mused heavily, and redirected his attention to whoever it was speaking to him, hoping he had not missed anything important.

The evening moved on; the old sheikh grew tired. His two sons appeared by the side of his divan. He did not demur when Hassan gently suggested he bid goodnight to everyone. Once again Rafiq lifted him into his wheelchair with the same gentleness that would be offered a fragile child. His departure was achieved quietly through a side door, as the old Sheikh himself had arranged.

Leona was standing with her father and Ethan as this quiet departure took place. 'How long?' Victor asked her gravely.

'Not very long,' she answered, then chided herself because Sheikh Khalifa wished his thirtieth celebration to be an occasion remembered for its hospitality, not as his obituary.

It was very late by the time people began leaving. Even later before Leona felt she could dare to allow herself a sigh of relief at how relatively pain-free the whole evening had turned out to be.

Which suddenly reminded her of something she still had to do that might not be as pain free. Her heart began thudding as Hassan came to take her hand and walk her towards the stairs. She could feel his tension, knew that his mind had switched onto the same wavelength as her own. Hand in hand they trod the wide staircase to the floor above. The door to the private apartments closed behind them.

'Did Evie bring—'

'Yes,' she interrupted, and moved right away from him. Now the moment of truth had arrived Leona found she was absolutely terrified. 'I don't want to know,' she admitted.

'Then leave it for now,' Hassan answered simply.

She turned to look anxiously at him. 'But that's just being silly.'

'Yes,' he agreed. 'But tomorrow the answer will still be the same, and the next day and the next.'

Maybe it was a good thing that the telephone began to ring. Hassan moved away from her to go and answer it. Thirty seconds later he was sending her a rueful smile. 'My father is restless,' he explained. 'Over-excited and in need of talk. Will you mind if I go to him, or shall I get Rafiq to—?'

'No,' she said quickly. 'You go.' She really was a pathetic coward.

'You won't…do anything without me with you?' he murmured huskily.

She shook her head. 'Tomorrow,' she promised. 'W-when I am feeling less tired and able to cope with…' *The wrong answer*, were the words she couldn't say.

Coming back to her, Hassan gave her a kiss of understanding. 'Go to bed,' he advised, 'Try to sleep. I will come back just as soon as I can.'

He was striding towards the door when she remembered. 'Hassan… My father and Ethan were invited here for a specific purpose, weren't they?'

He paused at the door, sighed and turned to look at her. 'Damage limitation,' he confirmed. 'We may not like it. We may object to finding such a demeaning act necessary. But the problem was there, and had to be addressed. *Inshallah*.' He shrugged, turned and left.

CHAPTER TWELVE

INSHALLAH—as Allah wills. It was, she thought, the perfect throwaway answer to an uncomfortable subject. On a dissatisfied sigh she moved across the room to begin to prepare for bed.

Already tucked out of sight in the drawer of her bedside cabinet lay the offerings Evie had brought with her from Behran. Just glancing at the drawer was enough to make her shudder a little, because the pregnancy testing kit had too much power for her comfort. So she turned away to pull on her pyjamas, slid into bed and switched off the light without glancing at the cabinet again. Sleep came surprisingly quickly, but then it had been a long day.

When she woke up, perhaps an hour later, she thought for a few moments that Hassan must have come back and disturbed her when he'd got into the bed. But there was no warm body lying beside her. No sign of life in evidence through the half-open bathroom door.

Then she knew. She didn't know how she knew, but suddenly she was up and pulling on a robe, frantically trying the belt as she hurried for the door. It was as if every light in the palace was burning. Her heart dropped to her stomach as she began racing down the stairs.

It was the sheikh. Instinct, premonition, call it what you wanted; she just knew there was something badly wrong.

On bare feet she ran down the corridor and arrived at his door to find it open. She stepped inside, saw nothing untoward except that neither the sheikh nor Hassan was there. Then she heard a noise coming from the room beyond, and with a sickening thud her heart hit her stomach as she made her way across the room to that other door.

On the other side was a fully equipped hospital room that had been constructed for use in the event of emergencies like the one Leona found herself faced with now.

She could not see the old sheikh because the doctors and nurses were gathered around him. But she could see Hassan and Rafiq standing like two statues at the end of the bed. They were gripping the rail in front of them with a power to crush metal, and their faces were as white as the *gutrahs* that still covered their heads.

Anguish lurked in every corner, the wretched sound of the heart monitor pulsing out its frighteningly erratic story like a cold, ruthless taunt. It was dreadful, like viewing a scene from a horror movie. Someone held up a hypodermic needle, clear liquid sprayed into the air. The lights were bright and the room bare of everything but clinical-white efficiency.

No, she thought, no, they cannot do this to him. He needs his room, with his books and his divan and his favourite pile of cushions. He needed to be surrounded by love, his sons, gentle music, not that terrible beep that felt to her as if it was draining the very life out of him.

'Switch it off,' she said thickly, walking forward on legs that did not seem to belong to her. 'Switch if off!' she repeated. 'He doesn't want to hear that.'

'Leona…' Hassan spoke her name in a hoarse whisper.

She looked at him. He looked at her. Agony screamed in the space between them. 'Tell them to switch it off,' she pleaded with him.

His face caved in on a moment's loss of composure. Rafiq didn't even seem to know that she was there. 'Don't…' he said huskily.

He wanted her to accept it. Her throat became a ball of tears as she took those final few steps then looked, really looked down at the ghost-like figure lying so still in the bed.

No, she thought again, no, they can't do this to him. Not here, not now. Her hand reached out to catch hold of one of his, almost knocking the nurse who was trying to treat him.

He felt so cold he might have been dead already. The tears moved to her mouth and spilled over her trembling lips. 'Sheikh,' she sobbed out, 'you just can't do this!'

'Leona…'

The thin, frail fingers she held in her hand tried to move. Oh, dear God, she thought painfully. He knows what is happening to him! 'Switch that noise off—switch it off!'

The fingers tried their very best to move yet again. Panic erupted. Fear took charge of her mind. 'Don't you dare bail on us now, old man!' she told him forcefully.

'Leona!' Hassan warning voice came stronger this time. He was shocked. They were all shocked. She didn't care.

'Listen to me,' she urged, lifting that frighteningly cold hand up to her cheek. The fingers moved again. He was listening. He could hear her. She moved closer, pushing her way past the doctor—a nurse—someone. She leaned over the bed, taking that precious hand with her. Her hair streamed over the white pillows as she came as close to him as she could. 'Listen,' she repeated, 'I am going to have a baby, Sheikh. Your very first grandchild. Tell me that you understand!'

The fingers moved. She laughed, then sobbed and kissed those fingers. Hassan came to grasp her shoulder. 'What do you think you are doing?' he rasped.

He was furious. She couldn't speak, couldn't answer, because she didn't *know* what she was doing. It had all just come out as if it was meant to. *Inshallah*, she thought.

'He can hear.' She found her voice. 'He knows what I am telling him.' Tremulously she offered Hassan his father's hand. 'Talk to him,' she pleaded. 'Tell him about our baby.' Tears were running down her cheeks and Hassan had never looked so angry. 'Tell him. He needs to hear it from you. Tell him, Hassan, please…'

That was the point when the monitor suddenly went haywire. Medics lunged at the sheikh, Hassan dropped his father's hand so he could grab hold of Leona and forcibly drag her aside. As the medical team went down in a huddle

Hassan was no longer just white, he was a colour that had never been given a name. 'You had better be telling him the truth or I will never forgive you for doing this,' he sliced at her.

Leona looked at the monitor, listened to its wild, palpitating sound. She looked at Rafiq, at what felt like a wall of horrified and disbelieving faces, and on a choked sob she broke free from Hassan and ran from the room.

Back down the corridor, up the stairs, barely aware that she was passing by lines of waiting, anxious servants. Gaining entrance to their apartments, she sped across the floor to the bedside cabinet. Snatching up Evie's testing kit, trembling and shaking, she dropped the packet twice in her attempt to remove the Cellophane wrapping to get the packet inside. She was sobbing by the time she had reached the contents. Then she unfolded the instruction leaflet and tried to read through a bank of hot tears, what it was she was supposed to do.

She was right; she was sure she was right. Nothing—nothing in her whole life had ever felt as right as this! Five minutes later she was racing downstairs again, running down the corridor in between the two lines of anxious faces, through doors and into the sheikh's room and over to her husband.

'See!' she said. 'See!' There were tears and triumph and sheer, shrill agony in her voice as she held out the narrow bit of plastic towards Hassan. 'Now tell him! *Please…!*' she begged him.

'Leona…' Hassan murmured very gently.

Then she heard it. The silence. The dreadful, agonising, empty silence. She spun around to look at the monitor. The screen was blank.

The screen was blank. 'No,' she breathed shakily. 'No.' Then she sank in a deep faint to the ground.

Hassan could not believe that any of this was really happening. He looked blankly at his father, then at his wife, then at the sea of frozen faces, and for a moment he actually thought he was going to join Leona and sink into a faint.

'Look after my son's wife.' A frail voice woke everyone up from their surprise. 'I think she has earned some attention.'

Before Hassan could move a team of experts had gone down over Leona and he was left standing there staring down at the bit of white plastic she had placed in his hand.

She was pregnant. She had just told him that this red mark in the window meant that she was pregnant. In the bed a mere step away his father was no longer fading away before his eyes.

Leona had done it. She'd brought him back from the brink, had put herself through the trauma of facing the answer on this small contraption, and she'd done both without his support.

'Courage,' he murmured. He had always known she possessed courage. 'And where was I when she needed my courage?'

'Here,' a level voice said. 'Sit down.' It was Rafiq, offering him a chair to sit upon. The room was beginning to look like a war zone.

He declined the chair. Leave me with some semblance of dignity, he thought. 'Excuse me,' he said, and stepped through the kneeling shapes round Leona, and bent and picked her up in his arms. 'But, sir, we should check she is...'

'Leave him be,' the old sheikh instructed. 'He is all she needs and he knows it.'

He did not take her far, only to his father's divan, where he laid her down, then sat beside her. She looked pale and delicate, and just too lovely for him to think straight. So he did what she had done with his father and took hold of her hand, then told her, 'Don't you dare bail out on us now, you little tyrant, even if you believe we deserve it.'

'We?' she mumbled.

'Okay, me,' he conceded. 'My father is alive and well, by

the way. I thought it best to tell you this before you begin to recall exactly why you fainted.'

'He's all right?' Her gold-tipped lashes flickered upwards, revealing eyes the colour of a sleepy lagoon.

I feel very poetic, Hassan thought whimsically. 'Whether due to the drugs or your bullying, no one is entirely certain. But he opened his eyes and asked me what you were talking about just a second after you flew out of the room.'

'He's all right.' Relief shivered through her, sending her eyes closed again. Feeling the shiver, Hassan reached out to draw one of his father's rugs over her reclining frame.

'Where am I?' she asked after a moment.

'You are lying on my father's divan, ' he informed her. 'With me, in all but effect, at your feet.'

She opened her eyes again, looked directly at him, and sent those major parts that kept him functioning into a steep decline.

'What made you do it?'

She frowned at the question, but only for a short moment, then she sighed, tried to sit up but was still too dizzy and had to relax back again. 'I didn't want him to go,' she explained simply. 'Or, if he had to go, I wanted him to do it knowing that he was leaving everything as he always wanted to leave it.'

'So you lied.'

It was a truth she merely grimaced at.

'If he had survived this latest attack, and you had been wrong about what you told him, would that have been a fair way to tug a man back from his destiny?'

'I'm pregnant,' she announced. 'Don't upset me with lectures.'

He laughed. What else was he supposed to do? 'I apologise for shouting at you,' he said soberly.

She was playing with his fingers where they pleated firmly with hers. 'You were in trauma enough without having a demented woman throwing a fit of hysterics.'

'You were right, though. He did hear you.'

She nodded. 'I know.'

'Here…' He offered her the stick of white plastic. Taking it back, she stared at it for a long time without saying a single word.

'It doesn't seem so important now,' she murmured eventually.

'The proof or the baby?'

She shrugged then pouted. 'Both, I suppose.'

In other words the delight she should be experiencing had been robbed from the moment. On a sigh, he scooped her up in his arms again and stood up.

'Where are you taking me now?' she questioned.

'Bed,' he answered bluntly. 'Preferably naked, so that I can hold you and our child so close to me you will never, ever manage to prise yourself free.'

'But your father—'

'Has Rafiq,' he inserted. 'And you have me.'

With that he pushed open the door to the main corridor, then stopped dead when he saw the sea of anxious faces waiting for news.

'My father has recovered,' he announced. 'And my wife is pregnant.'

There, he thought as he watched every single one fall to their knees and give thanks to Allah, that has killed two birds with one single stone. Now the phones could start buzzing and the news would go out to all corners of the state. By the time they arose in the morning there would not be a person who did not know what had taken place here tonight.

'You could have given me a chance to break the news to my own father.' Leona showed that her own thoughts were as usual not far from his own.

'He knows—or suspects. For I told him when I asked him to come here tonight. That was while we were still sailing the Red Sea, by the way,' he added as he walked them through the two lines of kneeling bodies. 'Raschid alerted me at Evie's instigation. And I am telling you all of this because I wish to get all my guilty machinations out of the way before we hit the bed.'

'You mean that Evie knew you suspected when I called her up yesterday and she didn't drop a hint of it to me?'

'They are sneaky, those Al-Kadahs,' he confided as he trod the stairs. 'Where do you think I get it from?'

'And your arrogance?'

'Al-Qadim through and through,' he answered. 'Our child will have it too, I must warn you. Plenty of it, since you have your own kind of arrogance too.'

'Maybe that's why I love you.'

He stopped halfway up the stairs to slash her a wide, white rakish grin. 'And maybe,' he said lazily, 'that is why I love you.'

She smiled, lifted herself up to touch his mouth with her own. He continued on his way while they were still kissing—with an audience of fifty watching them from the floor below.

Why not let them look? Sheikh Hassan thought. This was his woman, his wife, the mother of his coming child. He would kiss her wherever and whenever. It was his right. *Inshallah.*

Sharon Kendrick started story-telling at the age of eleven and has never really stopped. She likes to write fast-paced, feel-good romances with heroes who are so sexy they'll make your toes curl! Born in west London, she now lives in the beautiful city of Winchester – where she can see the cathedral from her window (but only if she stands on tip-toe). She is married to a medical professor – which may explain why her family get more colds than anyone else on the street – and they have two children, Celia and Patrick. Her passions include music, books, cooking and eating – and drifting off into wonderful daydreams while she works out new plots!

Look out for Sharon Kendrick's latest sexy
and compelling title:
EXPOSED: THE SHEIKH'S MISTRESS
On sale in September 2005, in
Modern Romance™!

SURRENDER TO THE SHEIKH

by
Sharon Kendrick

CHAPTER ONE

THERE was something about a wedding. Something magical which made everyday cynicism evaporate into thin air. Rose twisted the stem of her champagne glass thoughtfully as they waited for the best man to begin speaking.

She'd noticed it in the church, where even the most hardened pessimists in the congregation had been busy dabbing away at the corners of their eyes—well, the women, certainly. Women who would normally congregate in wine bars, denouncing the entire male sex as unthinking and uncaring, had been sitting through the entire service with wistful smiles softening their faces beneath the wide-brimmed hats.

Why Rose had even shed a tear herself, and *she* was not a woman given to a public display of emotion!

'In my country,' announced the best man, and his jet-black eyes glittered like ebony as they fixed themselves on the bride and groom, 'we always *begin* the wedding feast with a toast. That their mutual joy shall never be diminished. And so I ask you to raise your glasses and drink to Sabrina and Guy.'

'Sabrina and Guy,' echoed the glittering crowd, and obediently raised their glasses.

Not for the first time, Rose found herself surveying the best man over the top of her glass, along with just about every other female in the room, but then it was hard not to.

He was certainly spectacular—and spectacular in the true sense of the word. But, there again, not many men were fortunate enough to have a real live *prince* acting as their steward!

His name was Prince Khalim, as Sabrina had informed her excitedly when she'd begun to plan the wedding. A real-life

5

prince with a real-life country of his own—the beautiful Maraban—over which he would one day rule, as his forebears had ruled for centuries. He was an old schoolfriend of Guy's, Sabrina had shyly confided to Rose—the two men being as close as two men who'd known each other since childhood could be.

Rose had been expecting the prince to be short and squat and rather ugly—but, for once, her expectations had been way off mark. Because Prince Khalim was quite the most perfect man she had ever set eyes on.

He was tall—though perhaps not quite as tall as the groom—and he wore the most amazing clothes that Rose had ever seen. Exotic clothes in sensual fabrics. An exquisite silken tunic coloured in a soft and creamy gold, with loose trousers worn beneath.

Such an outfit could, Rose reasoned, have made some men look as though they were on their way to a fancy-dress party—maybe even a little bit feminine. But the silk whispered tantalisingly against his flesh, and there was no disguising the lean, hard contours of the body which lay beneath. A body which seemed to exude a raw and vibrant masculinity from every pore.

Rose swallowed, the champagne tasting suddenly bitter in her throat. And then swallowed again as those onyx eyes were levelled in her direction and then narrowed, so that only a night-dark gleam could be seen through the thick, black lashes.

And with a slow and predatory smile, he began to move.

He's coming over, Rose thought, her hands beginning to shake with unfamiliar nerves. He's coming over *here!*

The gloriously dressed women and the morning-suited men parted like waves before him as he made an unhurried approach across the ballroom of the Granchester Hotel, his regal bearing evident with every fluid step that he took. There was a dangerous imperiousness about him which made him the focal point of every eye in the ballroom.

Rose felt her throat constrict with a sudden sense of fear coupled with an even more debilitating desire, and for one mad moment she was tempted to turn around and run from the room. An escape to the powder room! But her legs didn't feel strong enough to carry her, and what would she be running from? she wondered ruefully. Or whom?

And then there was time to think of nothing more, because he had come to a halt in front of her and stood looking down at her, his proud, dark face concealing every emotion other than the one he made no attempt whatsoever to conceal.

Attraction.

Sexual attraction, Rose reminded herself, with a fast-beating heart.

It seemed to emanate from him in almost tangible waves of dark, erotic heat. He wanted to take her to his bed, she recognised faintly, the cruel curve of his mouth and the glint in his black eyes telling her so in no uncertain terms.

'So,' he said softly, in a rich, deep voice. 'Are you aware that you are quite the most beautiful woman at the wedding?'

He sounded so English and it made such an unexpected contrast to those dark, exotic looks, thought Rose. She forced herself to remain steady beneath the dark fire of his stare and shook her head. 'I disagree,' she answered coolly—unbelievably coolly, considering that her heart was racing like a speed-train. 'Don't you know that the bride is always the most beautiful woman at any wedding?'

He turned his head slightly to look at Sabrina in all her wedding finery, so that Rose was given an unrestricted view of the magnificent jut of his jaw and the aquiline curve of his nose.

The voice softened unexpectedly. 'Sabrina?' he murmured. 'Yes, she *is* very beautiful.'

And Rose was unprepared for the sudden vicious wave of jealousy which washed over her. Jealous of *Sabrina*? One of her very best friends? She sucked in a shocked breath.

He turned his head again and once again Rose was caught

full-on in the ebony blaze from his eyes. 'But then so are you—very, very beautiful.' The mouth quirked very slightly as he registered her unsmiling reaction. 'What is the matter? Do you not like compliments?'

'Not from people I barely know!' Rose heard herself saying, with uncharacteristic abruptness.

Only the merest elevation of a jet eyebrow which matched the thick abundance of his black hair gave any indication that he considered her reply offhand. It was clear that people did not speak to him in this way, as a rule.

He gave an almost regretful smile. 'Then you should not dress so fetchingly, should you? You should have covered yourself in something which concealed you from head to foot,' he told her softly, jet eyes moving slowly from the top of her head to the tip of her pink-painted toenails. 'It is all your own fault.'

Even more uncharacteristically, Rose felt colour begin to seep heatedly into her cheeks. She rarely blushed! In her job she dealt with high-powered strangers every single day of her working life, and none of them had had the power to have her standing like this. Like some starstruck adolescent.

'Isn't it?' he prompted, on a sultry murmur.

Rose blinked. She *had* dressed up, yes—but it was a wedding, wasn't it? And every single other woman in the room had gone to town today, just as she had.

A floaty little slip-dress made of sapphire silk-chiffon. The same colour as her eyes, or so the cooing sales assistant had told her. And flirty little sandals with tiny kitten heels. She'd bought those in a stinging pink colour, deliberately *not* matching her dress. But then matching accessories were so passé—even the saleswoman had agreed with that. No hat. She hated confining her thick blonde hair beneath a hat— particularly on a day as hot as this one. Instead, she had ordered a dewy and flamboyant orchid from the nearby florists, in a paler-colour version of the shoes she wore. She'd pinned it into her hair, but she suspected that very soon it would start wilting.

Just as *she* would, if this exotic man continued to subject her to such a calculating, yet lazy look of appraisal.

She decided to put a stop to it right then and there, extending her hand and giving him a friendly-but-slightly-distant smile. 'Rose Thomas,' she said.

He took the hand in his and then looked down at it, and Rose found her eyes hypnotically drawn in the same direction, shocked by her reaction to what she saw. Her skin looked so very white against the dark olive of his and there seemed to be something compellingly erotic about such a distinctive contrast of flesh.

She tried to pull her hand away, but he held tight onto it, and as she drew her indignant gaze upwards it was to find the black eyes fixed on her mockingly.

'And do you know who I am, Rose Thomas?' he questioned silkily.

It was a moment of truth. She could feign ignorance, it was true. But wouldn't a man like this have been up against pretence and insincerity for most of his life?

'Of course I know who you are!' she told him crisply. 'This is the only wedding I've ever been to where a real-life prince has been acting as best man—and I imagine it's the same for most of the other people here, too!'

He smiled, and as she saw the slight relaxation of his body Rose took the opportunity to remove her hand from his.

Khalim felt the stealthy beat of desire as she resisted him. 'What's the matter?' He gave her an expression of mock-reproach. 'Don't you like me touching you, Rose Thomas?'

'Do you *normally* go around touching women you've only just met?' she demanded incredulously. 'Is that a favour which your title confers on you?'

The beat increased as he acknowledged her fire. Resistance was so rarely put in the way of his wishes that it had the effect of increasing them tenfold. He saw the clear blue brilliance of her eyes. No, a hundredfold, he thought and felt his throat thicken.

He gave a shrug. A little-boy look—the black eyes briefly appealing. It was a look that had always worked very well at his English boarding-school, especially with women. 'You took my hand,' he protested. 'You know you did!'

Rose forced a laugh. This was ridiculous! They were sparring over nothing more than a handshake! And Khalim was Guy's friend. Sabrina's friend. She owed it to them to show him a little more courtesy than this. 'Sorry.' She smiled. 'I'm a little overwrought.'

'Is it a man?' he shot out, and before she had time to think about the implications she shook her head.

'What an extraordinary conclusion to jump to!' she protested, but the admonishment made no difference.

'What, then?' he persisted.

'Work, actually,' she said.

'Work?' he demanded, as though she had just said a foreign word.

But then maybe to him it *was* a foreign word. A man like Prince Khalim had probably never had to lift his hand in work. 'Just a busy week.' She shrugged. 'A busy month—a busy year!' She sipped the last of her champagne and gave him a look of question. 'I'm getting myself another one of these—how about you?'

Khalim sucked in a breath of disapproval. How he hated the liberated way of women sometimes! It was not a woman's place to offer a man drinks, and he very nearly told her so, but the fire in her eyes told him that she would simply stalk off if he dared to. And he wanted her far too much to risk that...

'I rarely drink,' he said coolly.

'Good heavens!' said Rose flippantly. 'How does your body get hydrated, then? By intravenous infusion?'

The black eyes narrowed. People didn't make fun of *him*. Women never teased him unless invited to, by him. And never outside the setting of the bedroom. For a moment, he considered stalking away from *her*. But only for a moment. The bright lure of her flaxen hair made him waver as he imagined unpicking it, having it tumble down over his chest—its contrast as marked as when he had pressed his fingers against her soft white skin, just minutes ago.

'Alcohol,' he elaborated tersely.

'Well, I'm sure they run to a few soft drinks,' said Rose. 'But it doesn't matter. I'm going to, anyway. It was nice talking to you, Pr—'

'No!' He caught hold of her wrist, enjoying the purely instinctive dilating of her blue eyes in response to his action, the way her lips fell open into an inviting little 'O'. He imagined the sweet pleasures a mouth like that could work on a man, and had to suppress a shudder of desire. 'Not Prince anything,' he corrected softly. 'I am Khalim. To you.'

She opened her mouth to say something sarcastic, like, Am I supposed to be flattered?—but the ridiculous thing was that she *was* flattered. Absurdly flattered to be told to use his first name. She told herself not to be so stupid, but it didn't seem to work.

'Let me go,' she said breathlessly, but she thrilled at the touch of his skin once more.

'Very well.' He smiled, but this time it was the smile of a man who knew that he had the ability to enslave a woman. 'But only if you agree to come and find me once the music starts, and then we shall dance.'

'Sorry. I never run after a man.'

He could feel the rapid thundering of her pulse beneath his fingertips. 'So you won't?'

The silky voice was nearly as mesmeric as the silky question. 'You'll have to come and find *me*!' she told him recklessly.

He let her go, taking care to conceal his giddy sense of elation. 'Oh, I will,' he said quietly. 'Be very sure of that.' And he watched her go, an idea forming in his mind.

He would make her wait. Make her think that he had changed his mind about dancing. For he knew enough of women to know that his supposed indifference would fan the desire she undoubtedly felt for him. He would tease her with it. Play with her. He knew only too well that anticipation increased the appetite, and thus satisfied the hunger all the more. And Rose Thomas would sigh with thankful pleasure in his arms afterwards.

On still-shaking legs, Rose headed for the bar, hoping that the bewilderment she felt did not show on her face. She did not fall for men like Khalim. She liked subtle, sophisticated and complex men. And while she recognised that he had a keen intelligence—there was also something fundamentally *dangerous* about this black-eyed stranger in his exotic robes.

Inside, she was jelly. *Jelly.* Her hands were trembling by the time she reached the corner of the ballroom where a white-jacketed man tended an assortment of cocktails and champagne.

She could see Sabrina at the far end of the room, a vision in white as she giggled with one of her bridesmaids—Guy's youngest niece.

'Champagne, madam?' smiled the bartender. 'Or a Sea Breeze, perhaps?'

Rose opened her mouth to agree to the former, but changed her mind at the last minute. Because something told her she would need her all her wits about her. And alcohol might just weaken an already weakened guard.

'Just a fizzy water, please,' she said softly.

'Too much of a good thing?' came a voice of dry amusement, and she looked up to find Guy Masters smiling down at her.

Rose liked Sabrina's new husband enormously. He was outrageously handsome, outrageously rich and he loved Sabrina with an intensity which made Rose wistful, and determined that she would never settle for second-best.

Rose had met Sabrina when she had gone in search of a

rare book, and Sabrina had helpfully scoured all the index-files until Rose had found what she'd been looking for. It had been the day after Sabrina had become engaged to Guy, and she had excitedly shown off her ring to Rose—a plain and simple but utterly magnificent diamond.

Sabrina hadn't really known anyone in London, other than Guy's friends, and the two women had been of similar age and similar interests.

'Or are you driving?' questioned Guy, still looking at her glass of mineral water.

'Er, no,' she said, in a faint voice. 'I just want to keep a clear head about me.'

'Quite wise,' remarked Guy, and he lowered his voice by a fraction. 'Since my old friend Khalim seems to have set his sights on you.'

'He…he does?' And then thought how obscenely *star-struck* that sounded. She cleared her throat and fixed a smile onto her lips. 'Not really. We just had a chat, that's all.'

'A *chat*?' asked Guy, now sounding even more amused. 'Khalim exchanging small talk? Now, that'll be a first!'

'Wonderful wedding!' said Rose valiantly, with an urgent need to change the subject. 'Sabrina looks absolutely stunning.

At the mention of his new wife's name, Guy's face softened into a look of tenderness, the intentions of his schoolfriend instantly forgotten. 'Doesn't she?' he asked indulgently, and then a slight note of impatience entered his voice. 'Between you and me, I just wish we could forget the damned dancing and just *leave*!'

Rose smiled. 'And deny your wife her wedding day! I think you can wait a little longer, don't you, Guy? After all, you've been living together for well over a year now!'

'Yeah,' sighed Guy. 'But this is the first time it will have been, well, legal…' He looked down into Rose's face. 'Why, you're *blushing*!' he observed incredulously. 'I'm sorry, Rose—I certainly didn't mean to embarrass you—'

'No, you weren't. Honestly,' Rose assured him hastily. She wasn't going to point out that it was a pair of glittering jet eyes being lanced provocatively in her direction which had the heat singing remorselessly in her veins. In a way, she wished that maybe Guy and Sabrina *would* leave. And then she could leave, too. And she wouldn't have to dance with Khalim and put herself in what was clearly becoming apparent would be a very vulnerable position indeed.

You don't *have* to dance with him, she reminded herself sternly. It wasn't a royal command. Well, of course it *was*, she realised with a slight edge of disbelief. But even if it was, she was not one of Khalim's subjects and London was not part of his kingdom! She could just give him a small, tight smile and tell him that she wasn't really in the mood for dancing.

Couldn't she?

But in the event she didn't have to. Because Khalim came nowhere near her. She found herself observing him obsessively, while doing her level best not to appear to be doing so.

He stood out from the crowd of fabulously dressed guests, and not by virtue of his own glorious and unconventional attire. No, it went much deeper than that. Rose had never met anyone of royal blood before, and of course she had heard the expression of regal bearing—but up until now she realised that she hadn't really known what it had meant.

There was some innate grace about the way he carried himself. Some fundamental and rare elegance in the way he moved. She had never seen anything like it. People noiselessly slipped from his path. Women stared at him with looks of undisguised and rapacious hunger on their faces.

Did he notice? Rose wondered. His proud, handsome face did not seem to register any emotion at all. But maybe he was used to it. Why, he had only had to lay his hand autocratically on *her* wrist to have her virtually melting at his feet.

The meal was served and Rose found herself seated with a banker on one side of her, and an oceanographer on the other. Both men seemed amusing and intelligent and the oceanographer was handsome in the rugged kind of way which denoted a healthy, outdoor lifestyle. He flirted outrageously with Rose, and even an hour ago she might have been receptive enough to respond.

But the only man who burnt a searing image on her subconscious sat at the top table, picking at his food with the kind of indifference which suggested that conventional hunger was not uppermost in his mind.

At that moment, Khalim looked up and glittered a black look in her direction—a look which sent a shiver tiptoeing down her spine. Quickly, she put her fork down and pushed the plate away.

'So what do you do, Rose?' asked the oceanographer.

She turned to look at him with a smile. 'I'm a headhunter.'

'Really?' He grinned. 'I guess you earn lots of money, then!'

Which was what people *always* said! 'I wish I did!'

The waitress leaned over, a look of concern on her face. 'Is everything all right with the salmon, miss?'

Rose nodded, looking guiltily at the untouched plate. 'It's fine! I'm just not very hungry, that's all!'

The waitress had the kind of build which suggested that no plate of hers was ever returned unless completely clean. 'Someone in the kitchen just said that we shouldn't bother offering the top table any pudding—so much food has come back from there as well! Maybe you should be sitting with *them*!' she joked.

'Maybe!' laughed Rose politely, half of her thankful that she was nowhere near Khalim, while the other part of her wished desperately to be within his exciting and yet dangerous proximity. She risked another look, seeing how the diamond lights of the chandeliers emphasised the creamy-gold silk of the robes he wore and the raven gleam of his black hair.

Valiantly she forced a few raspberries down her throat, but even the plump and succulent fruit failed to tempt her. And then at last it was time for the cutting of the cake, and the speeches.

Rose could barely take in a word of the best man's speech—she was so mesmerised by his dark, proud face. Her eyes feasted on his features—the hard, bright eyes and the stern expression which made her feel she'd won the lottery when it softened into affection. His mouth was a contrast of lush, sensual curves, but the upper lip had a hard, almost cruel streak. She shivered. Be warned, she thought.

Guy's speech had every woman in the room all misty-eyed with emotion as he gazed down in open adoration at Sabrina and spoke of his love for her.

And then the band struck up and people drifted onto the dance-floor and Rose's heart was in her mouth as she remembered Khalim's intention to dance with her.

But he did not come near her, just returned to his seat and sat there imperiously, his gaze drifting over her from time to time, the black eyes luminous with sensual promise.

Rose allowed herself to dance with whoever asked her, but her heart wasn't in it. She moved mechanically as the oceanographer took her in his arms, stiffening with rejection when he tried to pull her a little closer.

She sat down and was just beginning to seriously hope that Guy and Sabrina would depart for their honeymoon, so that she could leave as well, when Khalim appeared in front of her, the black eyes narrowed in mocking question.

'So,' he said softly. 'I have taken you at your word and come to find you.' The black eyes glittered. 'Though you made yourself very easy to find, Rose—you sweet, blushing flower. Now—' his voice dipped in sultry question '—shall we dance?'

Her cheeks *were* stinging at the implication that she had just been sitting there, waiting for him—but then, *hadn't* she?

'Is that supposed to be an invitation I can't resist?' she shot back at him.

A smile hovered at the edges of his mouth. 'No, Rose,' he purred. 'It is a royal command.'

She opened her mouth to object, but by then it was too late, because he had taken her hand with arrogant assurance and was leading her onto the dance-floor.

'Come,' he said quietly.

She moved into his arms as though her whole life had been a dress rehearsal for that moment. He placed his hands at the slim indentation of her waist, and Rose's fingers drifted with a kind of irresistible inevitability to his shoulders. She breathed in the faint scent of sandalwood about him, its soft muskiness invading her senses with its sweet perfume.

Rose considered herself a modern, independent woman, but a minute in Khalim's embrace was enough to transform her into a woman who felt as helpless as a kitten.

Khalim felt the slow unfurling of desire as he moved his hands down to rest on the slender swell of her hips. 'You dance beautifully, Rose,' he murmured.

'S-so do you,' she managed breathlessly, gloriously aware of the hard, lean body which moved with such innate grace beneath the silken robes. 'L-lovely wedding, wasn't it?' she commented, and said a silent prayer that her sanity would return. And soon!

He didn't reply for a moment. 'All women like weddings,' he mused eventually.

She thought she heard deliberate provocation and lifted her head to stare him straight in the eyes, the bright sapphire of her gaze clashing irrevocably with glittering jet. 'Meaning that men don't, I suppose?'

He raised a mocking brow and thought how bright her hair, and how white her soft skin, against which the soft curves of her lips were a deep, rich pink. Like the roses which bloomed in the gardens of his father's palace and scented the night air with their perfume. His pulse quickened. 'Do you always jump to conclusions, I wonder?'

'But you meant me to,' she parried. 'It was a remark designed to inflame, wasn't it?'

He shook his head, his desire increased by her feisty opposition. 'It was simply an observation,' he demurred. 'Not a...how-do-you-say?' He frowned, as if in deep concentration. 'Ah, yes—a sexist comment!'

Rose leaned away from him a little, and felt the almost imperceptible tightening of his hands on her hips, as though he couldn't bear to let her go. 'You can't pretend to be stumbling over the language with *me*, Khalim!' she said crisply, trying to ignore the thundering of her heart beneath her breast, 'when I happen to know that you went to school in England and are as fluent as I am!'

She was *very* fiery, he thought with a sudden longing. 'And what else do you know about me, Rose Thomas?' he mused.

Briefly she considered affecting total ignorance. This was a man with an ego, that was for sure! Yet how often did people speak their minds to a man with his power and his presence?

'I know that you are the heir to a mountain kingdom—'

'Maraban,' he elaborated softly, and his voice deepened with affectionate pride.

Something imprecise shimmered over her skin at the way he said that single word and a sense of hazy recognition made her shiver. 'Maraban,' she repeated wonderingly, until she realised that she was in danger of sounding starstruck again.

'What else?' he prompted, intrigued by that dreamy look which had softened her features when she had said the name of the land of his birth. And then his mouth hardened. Maraban was an oil-rich country—and didn't fabulous wealth always produce enthusiasm in the greedy hearts of most Westerners?

She wondered what had caused the fleetingly judgemental

look which had hardened his face into a stern mask. She snapped out of her reverie to deliver a few home truths.

'I've heard that you have something of a reputation where women are concerned,' she told him crisply.

'A reputation?' It sounded too close to unaccustomed criticism for Khalim not to experience a sudden flicker of irritation. 'Do elaborate, Rose.'

'Do I need to? You like women, don't you?'

His smile grew cynical. 'And is it wrong to enjoy the many pleasures which the opposite sex can offer?'

His words were accompanied by the splaying of his fingers over her back, and Rose found herself wondering what it would be like if her skin were bare. And his... She swallowed. 'You make women sound like an amusement arcade!'

He smiled. 'It is an interesting analogy,' he remarked, and resisted the urge to move his fingertips to lie just below the jut of her breasts. He wanted her, and he never had to try very hard, not where women were concerned. There had only ever been one woman who had turned him down, and that had been Sabrina.

He moved his head slightly as the bride and groom passed by, and saw Sabrina gazing up into the face of her new husband. Khalim had instantly forgiven and understood her rejection, because she had been in love with his best friend.

Resisting the urge to explore Rose's breasts, he kept his hands right where they were. For while his seduction of Rose Thomas was a certainty, he suspected that he would have to take things slowly...

'So,' he said huskily. 'You are at an advantage, are you not? Since you know something of me, while I know nothing of you, Rose—other than the fact that you are the most beautiful woman in the room.'

'So you said earlier,' answered Rose sweetly, pleased to see the fleeting look of irritation which hardened the dark face. She teased him a little more—just for the hell of it. 'I can't see why women fall for your charms if you keep coming out with the same old compliment!'

'Oh, can't you?' he questioned silkily, and with a fluid movement of grace caught her closer still, so that their bodies melded together with shocking intimacy. He noted with satisfaction the instant darkening of her eyes, the two high spots of colour to her cheeks. Through the thin layers of silk which covered him, and her, he could feel the tiny tight buds of her breasts as they flowered against his chest and he felt another sharp pull of desire.

'D-don't,' protested Rose weakly, shaken by a sweet flood of need, stronger and more powerful than anything she had ever experienced before.

Triumphantly, Khalim felt her tremble against him and pressed his lips close to where the bright, flaxen hair gleamed against her ear. 'Don't what?' he whispered.

'Don't.' But her voice shook so that the word was unrecognisable and she had to try again. 'Don't stand so close to me.'

With the instinctive mastery of the conqueror, he did exactly as she asked, moving a little away from her, and he heard her unmistakable little of gasp of protest. 'Is that better?' he questioned silkily.

Better? Rose felt as bereft as if someone had just shorn off her long hair and left her neck bare and cold. She found herself wanting to beg him to pull her back into that warm, enticing circle, until common sense began to reassert itself. She was not the kind of woman to beg a man to do *anything*. 'Much better,' she agreed levelly.

He didn't believe her for a moment. Khalim smiled, acknowledging what he knew to be a universal truth—that the chase was often the most exciting part of the conquest. 'So why don't you tell me something about yourself?' he murmured.

She turned her face upwards, her eyes sparking a challenge. 'What would you like to know?'

'Everything. Absolutely everything.'

Rose's mouth curved into a smile. 'You'll have to be a *little* more specific than that, I'm afraid!'

He wondered what she would say if he told her the only thing he really wanted to know was what her naked body would look like. Stretched out in rapturous abandon on the slippery-soft sheets of his enormous bed. 'So tell me what you do,' he murmured.

'You mean, work-wise?'

He nodded, thinking that she had no need at all to work. She could easily be a rich man's mistress, he thought. His. Why had he never met her before? 'Or shall I guess what kind of work you do, Rose?'

'You can try!'

'Simple. A model?' he mused.

'I'm not tall enough,' she objected, hating herself for the warm glow which his compliment produced. 'Or thin enough.'

Irresistibly, his eyes were drawn to the luscious swell of breast and hip. 'You are perfect,' he said huskily. 'Quite perfect.'

Within the circle of his arms, Rose shivered. She wasn't *used* to men saying things like that, and certainly not within minutes of meeting her! Mostly, she mixed with lofty intellectuals who might occasionally pay her a clever-clever compliment. Not men who made no attempt to hide a primitive and compelling kind of desire. 'That's outrageous flattery!' she protested.

'Flattery, yes. Outrageous, no!' He turned her round in time with the music, admiring her natural and subtle grace.

He really was the most wonderful dancer, thought Rose. She rarely danced properly like this—and never with a prince! It was heavenly to glide around the dance-floor in the arms of a man. Instead of everyone jigging about doing their own thing and usually managing to connect with her on the way!

He was staring down at her in a thoughtful way, and she immediately wiped the look of dreamy bliss off her face. 'So you've given up, have you? You're not very good at guessing, are you?' she challenged.

'Maybe not, but there are many things I am *extremely* good at, Rose,' he boasted silkily, and chose just that moment to move a silken thigh between hers, immediately losing himself in an erotic dream of making love to her.

In time with the sexual boast, Rose felt the pressure of his leg, and the unmistakable iron of the steely muscle which lay beneath the delicate fabric. An unfamiliar hunger shot through her as she felt her heart-rate soar and something deep inside her began to slowly dissolve. She had to stop this. Now.

'I'm a head-hunter,' she said quickly.

Khalim's dream was shattered by her words. 'Head-hunter?' he questioned, and frowned, his mind firing up with savage imagery.

'Yes, you know—I find people for jobs!'

'I know what a head-hunter is! And you are successful in your line of work?'

'Yes, I am.'

'Then, you must be a very intuitive woman, Rose.' The tip of his finger rippled slowly over the curve of her waist and he felt her shiver in response. 'Ve-ry intuitive.'

Warning bells began ringing in her mind. 'I-I think I've had enough dancing,' she said breathlessly, feeling ridiculously disappointed when he took her at her word and let her go.

'I agree.' The tug of desire had become persistent and uncomfortable. It made him want to take her. To... Khalim found himself having to fight for the rigid self-control which had been a fundamental part of his upbringing. And it was many years since he had had to fight for anything. He took a step backwards, steadying his suddenly shallow breathing.

Missing the feel of silk and the scent of sandalwood, Rose

placed her hands over her flushed cheeks and could feel pulses fluttering absolutely everywhere. And it was only then she noticed that the floor was completely empty and that everyone was standing watching them.

'Oh, my God!' she moaned. 'Look!'

'It seems that we have inadvertently been providing the floor show,' said Khalim, in some amusement, as he followed the direction of her gaze.

Rose's distress grew even more intense, especially as Guy had chosen that moment to approach them and had clearly overheard Khalim's remark.

'A very *erotic* floor show,' he teased.

Rose suppressed a groan. They had been acting like a couple of irresponsible teenagers!

'We were simply dancing.' Khalim shrugged, his black eyes sending out a conspiratorial gleam to Rose.

'Is that what you call it?' joked Guy. 'Anyway, Sabrina and I are planning to leave now.' His grey eyes crinkled as he looked at his best man. 'And thanks for the honeymoon, Khalim.'

Silken shoulders were raised in a careless shrug. 'It is nothing other than my pleasure to give,' he drawled.

'Sabrina told me the destination was a secret,' said Rose.

The two men exchanged glances.

'And so it is. Traditionally, a secret shared between the groom and best man. But do not fear, I will tell you later, beautiful Rose,' promised Khalim softly.

'Later?' she asked, with a quick glance at her wrist-watch. Who had said anything about later?

'But of course. You and I are going for a drink together afterwards.'

Guy smiled. 'Are you?'

Rose saw the black eyes being levelled at her consideringly, saw the arrogant expectation that she would simply fall in with his regal wishes! And who really could blame him, after her shameless display on the dance-floor?

'But you told me you rarely drink, Khalim,' she reminded him innocently. 'So wouldn't that be an awful waste of your time?'

He opened his mouth to object, and then shut it again. Somewhere deep in his groin, Khalim felt a pulse begin to beat with slow insistence. He felt the sweet, sharp tang of desire and yet he instantly recognised her determination to oppose him. It flashed in sapphire sparks from her beautiful blue eyes. No matter what he said, Rose Thomas was not planning on going anywhere with him tonight. 'You don't want to?'

The note of incredulity in his voice was unmistakable, and Rose was very tempted to smile. But something in the cold glitter of his gaze made her decide that smiling maybe wasn't the best idea. 'It's been a long day,' she told him apologetically. 'And I'm bushed! Some other time, perhaps?'

Khalim's face grew distant; indeed, he barely noticed Guy slipping away to find Sabrina. 'I never issue an invitation more than once,' he told her coldly.

Rose was aware of a lurching sense of regret. You've missed your chance, girl, she thought—even while the sane part of her rejoiced. This man was different, she recognised. Different and dangerous. He had the power to make her vulnerable, and he was the last person she wanted to be vulnerable around. Why, a man like that would chew her up and spit her out in little pieces!

'What a pity,' she said lightly.

His black eyes lingered on the lushness of her lips, the creaminess of her skin. 'A pity indeed,' he agreed, briefly bowing his dark head before sweeping away from her across the ballroom.

And she watched him go with a thundering heart.

'They're leaving!' called someone, and Rose looked across the room to see that Sabrina had changed out of her bridal gown into a silvery-blue suit and was carrying her bouquet, Guy in an impressive dark suit at her side.

Everyone began to surge out of the ballroom to wave them off, but Rose hung back. She could see Khalim talking to Guy and she found herself unwilling to face him, aware of a dull sense of an opportunity lost, an opportunity never to be repeated.

She saw Sabrina turn and teasingly hold her bouquet of lilies above her head while every female present lifted their arms in hope of catching it. Even Rose eagerly raised her arms to catch the waxy blooms as they came flying in her direction, but the redhead beside her was more eager still.

'Gotcha!' she shouted as she leapt into the air and pounced triumphantly on the bouquet.

It's only a tradition, Rose told herself dully as she watched the girl ecstatically smelling the flowers. Why would catching a bunch of flowers guarantee that you would be the next to be married? And it wasn't as if she even *wanted* to get married, was it? These days lots and lots of women in their late twenties were electing to stay single.

But when she looked up again, it was to find herself caught in the lancing gaze of a pair of glittering black eyes.

I have to get out of here, she thought, with a sudden sense of panic.

CHAPTER TWO

In a daze, Rose left the Granchester and found herself a taxi, but afterwards she couldn't recollect a single moment of the journey. Not until the cab drew up outside the flat she shared in Notting Hill did reality begin to seep back into her consciousness as she tried to rid herself of the memory of the dark prince, with his proud, sensual face.

She let herself in through the front door and put her handbag on the hall table, relieved to be home. And safe.

She loved her flat—it was her very first property and occupied the first floor of a grand old high-ceilinged house. But it was an ambitious project for a first-time buyer and the repayments on her loan were high, which was why she had taken on a flatmate—Lara.

Lara was a struggling actress who described herself as Rose's lodger, but Rose never did. Equality was something she strove for in every area of her life. 'No, we're flatmates,' she always insisted.

It was a typical bachelor girls' home—full of colour in the shared areas and rather a lot of chaos in Lara's bedroom— because, much as she nagged, there didn't seem to be anything Rose could do to change Lara's chronic untidiness. So now she had given up trying.

There were brightly coloured scarves floating from a coatstand in the hall, and vases of cheap flowers from the market dotted around the sitting room. And the bathroom was so well stocked with various lotions and potions that it resembled the cosmetics counter of a large department store!

'Anyone at home?' she called.

'I'm in the kitchen!' came the muffled reply, and Rose walked into the kitchen to find Lara busy crunching a choc-

26

olate biscuit and pouring coffee into a mug. Her staple diet and *my* coffee, thought Rose ruefully as Lara looked up with a smile and held a second mug up. 'Coffee?'

Rose shook her head. 'No, thanks. I think I need a drink.'

Lara raised her eyebrows in surprise. 'But you've just been to a wedding!'

'And I barely touched a drop all day,' said Rose grimly. She had deliberately avoided liquor so that she would have all her wits about her, and then just look at the way she had behaved on the dance-floor! She sighed as she poured herself a glass of wine from the cask in the fridge.

'Are you okay?' asked Lara curiously.

'Why shouldn't I be?'

'You just seem a little…I don't know…tense.'

Tense? Rose sipped at her wine without enjoyment. She could see her reflection in the pig-shaped mirror which hung on the kitchen wall. Her face was *unbelievably* pale. She looked as if she'd seen a ghost. Or a vision maybe… 'I guess I am,' she said slowly.

'So why? What was the wedding like? Awful?'

'No, beautiful,' said Rose reflectively. 'The most beautiful wedding I've ever been to.'

'Then why the long face?'

Rose sat down at the kitchen table and put her wineglass down heavily. 'It's stupid, really—' She looked up into Lara's frankly interested brown eyes. 'Did I ever tell you that Sabrina's new husband is best friends with a prince?'

Lara's eyes grew larger. 'You're winding me up, right?'

Rose shook her head and bit back a half-smile. It did sound a bit far-fetched. 'No, I'm not. It's the truth. He's prince of a country—more a principality, really—called Maraban—it's in the Middle East.'

'And next, I suppose you'll be telling me that he's outrageously good-looking and rich, to boot!'

Rose sighed. 'Yes! He's exactly that. Just about the most

perfect man you've ever seen. Tall, and dark and handsome—'

'Oh, ha, ha, ha!'

'No, he *is*! Honestly. He's divine. I danced with him...' Her voice tailed off as she remembered how it felt to have his body so tantalisingly close to hers. 'Danced with him, and—'

'And what?'

'And—' No need to point out that she had got a little carried away on the dance-floor. She squirmed with remembered pleasure and glanced up to see Lara's open-mouthed expression.

'Oh, Rose, you *didn't*?'

Rose blinked as the implication behind Lara's question squeaked its way home. 'No, of course I didn't! You surely don't imagine that I'd meet a man at a wedding and hours later leap into bed with him, do you?' she questioned indignantly.

But you did it in thought if not in deed, didn't you? mocked the guilty voice of her conscience.

Lara was looking at her patiently. 'So what happened?'

'He, well, he asked me to go for a drink with him once the bride and groom had left,' explained Rose.

'What's the problem with that? You said yes, of course?'

'Actually,' said Rose, in a high, forced voice, not quite believing that she had had the strength of will to go through with it, 'I said no.'

Lara was blinking at her in bemusement. 'You've lost me! He's gorgeous, he's royal and you *turned him down*! *Why*, for heaven's sake?'

'I don't know.' Rose sighed again. 'Well, maybe that's not true, I suppose I do, really. He's so utterly irresistible—'

'That's usually considered a plus where men are concerned, isn't it?'

'But he would never commit, I know he wouldn't—it's written all over his face!'

Lara stared at her incredulously. 'Never *commit*?' she echoed. 'I can't believe I'm hearing this! Rose, you've danced
with the guy once and already you're talking commitment?
And this from the woman who has always vowed never to
get married—'

'Until I'm at least thirty-five,' said Rose with a look of
fierce determination. 'I'll have achieved something by then,
so I'll be ready! And people live longer these days—it makes
sense to put off getting married for as long as possible.'

'Very romantic,' said Lara.

'Very realistic,' commented Rose drily.

'So why the talk of commitment—or, rather, the lack of
it?'

Rose took a thoughtful sip of wine. She wasn't really sure
herself. Maybe because she didn't want to be just another
woman in a long line of discarded women.

But wouldn't it just sound fanciful if she told Lara that
Khalim had a dangerous power about him which both attracted and yet repelled her? And wouldn't it sound weak if
she expressed the very real fear that he could break her heart
into smithereens? Lara would quite rightly say that she didn't
know him—but Rose was intuitive, more so than usual where
Khalim was concerned. She knew that with a bone-deep certainty—she just didn't know why.

She had been 'in love' just twice in her life. A university
affair which had occupied her middle year there and then, in
her early days in advertising recruitment—she'd dated an ac-
count executive for nine fairly blissful months. Until she had
discovered one evening that he wasn't really into monogamy.

She wasn't sure whether it was her pride which had been
hurt more than anything else, but from that day on she had
been sensible and circumspect where men were concerned.
She could take them or leave them. And mostly she could
leave them…

'Do you fancy going to see a film?' asked Lara, with a
glance at the kitchen clock. 'There's still time.'

Rose shook her head. What would be the point of going to a film if you knew for a fact that you wouldn't be able to concentrate on anything other than the most enigmatic face you had ever set eyes on? 'No, thanks. I think I'll take a shower,' she said with a yawn.

Aware that he was being closely watched by his emissary, Khalim paced up and down the penthouse suite with all the stealth and power of a sleek jungle cat. Outside the lights of the city glittered like some fabulous galaxy, but Khalim was impervious to its beauty.

Whenever he was in London on business, which he usually arranged to coincide with Maraban's most inhospitable weather—Khalim always stayed at the Granchester Hotel. He kept the luxurious rooms permanently booked in his name, though for much of the year they lay empty. They had been decorated according to his taste in a way which was as unlike his home in Maraban as it was possible to imagine. Lots of pale, wooden furniture and abstract modern paintings. But that was how he liked to live his life—the contrast between the East and the West each feeding two very different sides of his nature.

Once again, black eyes stared unseeingly out at the blaze of lights which pierced the night sky of London.

Eventually, he turned to Philip Caprice and held the palms of his hands out in a gesture which was a mixture of frustration and disbelief. He'd been bewitched by a pair of dazzling eyes so blue and hair so pale and blonde that he couldn't shake her image from his mind. He had wanted her here with him tonight—on his bed and beneath his body. And he would fill her. Fill her and fill her and…he gave a groan and Philip Caprice looked at him in concern.

'Sir?' he murmured. 'Is something the matter?'

'I cannot believe it!' Khalim stated bluntly and gave a low laugh. 'I must be losing my touch!'

Philip smiled, but said nothing. It was not his place to offer an opinion. His role was to act as a sounding-board for the prince—unless specifically invited to do otherwise.

Khalim turned hectic black eyes towards his emissary, trying to forget her pale enchantment. He could feel the fever of desire heating his blood, making it sing like a siren as it coursed its way around his veins. 'You are not saying anything, Philip!'

'You wish me to?'

Khalim drew a deep breath, swamping down the unfamiliar feeling of having been thwarted. 'Of course,' he said coolly, and then saw Philip's look of indecision. 'By the mane of Akhal-Teke, Philip!' he swore softly. 'Do you think my arrogance so great, my ego so mighty, that I cannot bear to hear the truth from you?'

Philip raised his dark eyebrows. 'Or my interpretation of the truth, sir? Every man's truth is different.'

Khalim smiled. 'Indeed it is. You sound like a true Marabanesh, when you speak like that! Give me your interpretation, Philip. Why have I failed with this woman, where never I have failed before?'

Philip intertwined his long fingers and spoke thoughtfully. 'All your life you have had your every wish pandered to, sir.'

'Not all.' Khalim's eyes narrowed dangerously as he mouthed the soft denial. 'I learnt the rigours of life through an English boarding-school!'

'Yes,' said Philip patiently. 'But ever since you reached manhood, little has been denied to you, sir, you know that very well.' He paused. 'Particularly where women are concerned.'

Khalim expelled a long, slow breath. Was he simply tantalised because for once something had eluded him? Why, some of the most beautiful women in the world had offered themselves to him, but his appetite had always been jaded by what came too easily. 'Only one other woman has ever turned me down before,' he mused.

'Sabrina?' said Philip softly.

Khalim nodded, remembering his easy acceptance of *that*. He tried to work out what was different this time. 'But that was understandable—because she was in love with Guy, and Guy is my friend whom I respect. But this woman…this woman…'

And the attraction had been mutual. She had been fighting her own needs and her own desires, he knew that without a doubt. When he'd taken her in his arms, she'd wanted him with a fire which had matched his own. He'd been certain that he would make love to her tonight, and the unfamiliar taste of disappointment made his mouth taste bitter.

'What is her name?' asked Philip.

'Rose.' The word came out as if it were an integral line of the poetry he had learnt as a child. It sounded as scented-sweet and as petal-soft as the flower itself. But the rose also had a thorn which could draw blood, Khalim reminded himself on a shudder.

'Maybe *she's* in love with someone else?' suggested Philip.

'No.' Khalim shook his head. 'There is no man in her life.'

'She told you that?'

Khalim nodded.

'Maybe she just didn't…' Philip hesitated before saying '…find you attractive?'

Khalim gave an arrogant smile. 'Oh, she did.' He placed his hand over his fast-beating heart. 'She most certainly did,' he murmured, remembering the way she had melted so responsively against his body. And her reaction had not just been about chemistry—undeniable though that had been. No, hers had been a hunger sharpened and defined by the exquisite torture of abstinence.

As his had been. How long since a woman had excited him in this way? Since his father's illness when much of the burden of responsibility for running the country had fallen onto his shoulders, there had been little time to pursue pleasure. And no woman, he realised, had ever excited him in *quite* this way.

Khalim swallowed. Her scent was still clinging to the silk of his robes. Unendurable.

'I must take a bath,' he ground out.

He had a servant draw him up a bath scented with oil of bergamot, and, once alone, he slipped off the silken robes, totally at ease in his nakedness. His body was the colour of deeply polished wood—the muscles honed so that they rippled with true power and strength.

It was a taut and lean body, though he had never stepped inside a gym in his life—that would have been far too narcissistic an occupation for a man like Khalim. But the long, muscular shaft of his thighs bore testimony to hard physical exercise.

Horse-riding was his particular passion, and one of his greatest sources of relaxation. He felt at his most free when riding his beloved Akhal-Teke horse across the salt flats of Maraban with the warm air rushing through his dark hair and the powerful haunches of the stallion clasped tightly between his thighs.

He lay back among the bubbles and let some of the tension soak from his skin, but not all—not by a long way. Rose Thomas and her pale blonde beauty were uppermost in his mind, and thoughts of her brought their own, different kind of tension. He felt the hardening of his body in response to his thoughts, and only through sheer determination of will did he suppress his carnal longing. But then, he had never once lost control over his body…

Should he woo her? he thought carelessly. Besiege her with flowers? Or with jewels perhaps? He rubbed thoughtfully at the darkened shadow of his chin. There wasn't a woman alive who could resist the glittering lure of gems.

He smiled as he stepped from the circular bath and tiny droplets of water gleamed like diamonds on the burnished perfection of his skin.

He had no appetite. Tonight he would work on some of the outstanding government papers he had brought back with him from Maraban.

He slipped on a silken robe in deepest, richest claret and walked barefoot back through the vast sitting room and into the adjoining study, where Philip was busy tapping away at the word processor.

He looked up as Khalim came in.

'Sir?'

'Leave that, now,' ordered Khalim pleasantly. 'I have something else for you.'

'Sir?'

'Find out where Rose Thomas lives. And where she works.'

CHAPTER THREE

EVEN after an hour-long bath and drinking chamomile tea, Rose slept surprisingly little that night. Especially considering that she had had a long and heavy week at work the previous week and then gone out with Sabrina on her 'hennight' a couple of nights before the wedding.

She tossed and turned for most of the night as an aching sense of regret kept sleep at bay.

And a pair of black eyes kept swimming into her troubled thoughts. Eyes which glittered untold promise, and a body which promised untold pleasure.

She rose late, and was just getting dressed when she heard Lara's voice calling her name excitedly.

'Rose! Quickly!'

'I'll be there in a minute!'

She pulled on an old pair of jeans and a simple pale blue T-shirt and walked into the sitting room, where Lara was clutching excitedly at the most enormous bouquet of flowers she had ever seen.

There were massed blooms of yellow roses, studded with tiny blue cornflowers, and the heady fragrance hit her as soon as she entered the room.

'Wow!' said Rose admiringly. 'Lucky girl! Who's the secret admirer?'

'They aren't for *me*, silly!' choked Lara jealously. 'It's your name on the card—see.'

Her fingers trembling, Rose took the proffered card with a dawning sense of inevitability. She stared down at the envelope, and the distinctive handwriting which spelt out her name.

'Well, aren't you going to open it?' demanded Lara. 'Don't you want to know who they're from?'

'I know exactly who they're from,' said Rose slowly. 'Khalim sent them.'

'You can't know that!'

'Oh, yes, I can.' She gave a wry smile. 'I may have had a few sweet and charming boyfriends, but not one who would spend this much on a bunch of flowers.' But curiosity got the better of her, and she ripped the envelope open to find her hopes and her fears confirmed.

The message was beautifully and arrogantly stark.

'The yellow is for your hair; the blue for the sapphire of your eyes. I will collect you at noon. Khalim.'

'Oh, my *goodness*! How utterly, utterly romantic!' squeaked Lara, who was busy looking over her shoulder.

'You think so?' asked Rose tonelessly.

'Well, I'd be in absolute heaven if I got flowers like these from a man! And what a masterful message! You'd better get a move on!'

But Rose wasn't listening. 'What a *cheek*!' she exploded as her eyes roved over the message again. 'How dare he just *assume* that he can tell me a time and I'll be meekly sitting here waiting, like a lamb to the slaughter?'

'But you aren't going out anywhere else today, are you?' asked Lara in a puzzled voice.

'That isn't the point!'

'Well, what *is* the point?'

'The point is that I don't *want* to go out with him!'

'Don't you? Honestly?'

Honesty was a bit more difficult. Rose had worked hard on her independence and her sense of self-possession—both qualities which she suspected Khalim could vanquish with the ease of a man who had sensual power untold at his fingertips.

'A tiny bit of me does,' she admitted, and saw Lara's face

go all mushy. 'But the rest of me is quite adamant that he would be nothing but bad news!'

Lara sighed. 'So what are you going to do? Tell him that to his face? Or just pretend to be out when he calls?' She brightened a little. '*I* could go instead, if you like!'

Rose was unprepared for the shaft of jealousy which whipped through her with lightning speed. She shook her head. 'I'm a realist,' she said proudly. 'Not a coward. If I turn Khalim down again, then he'll just up the ante—and I am not prepared to be bombarded with charm and expensive trinkets.'

And wouldn't he just wear her down anyway?

'He's the kind of man who thrives on the chase,' she said slowly. 'The kind of man who isn't used to being rejected— it's probably a first for him!'

'So what, then?'

Little shivers of excitement rippled down Rose's spine as a decision formed in her mind. 'I'll go,' she said, in a voice which wasn't quite steady. 'And I'll convince him that I'm not the sort of woman he wants.'

'What sort of woman is that?' asked Lara, mystified.

'A temporary concubine!' said Rose, and then, seeing Lara's expression of mystification grow even deeper, added, 'Someone who will live with him as his wife, until he tires of her, and then on to the next!'

'You don't sound as though you like him very much,' said Lara thoughtfully.

And that was just the trouble. She didn't. And yet she did. Though how could she form *any* kind of opinion about the man, when she didn't really know him at all? She was simply sexually captivated by a man who exuded an animal magnetism which was completely foreign to her.

'I'm going to go and get ready,' she said, looking down at her faded jeans.

'What shall I do with the flowers?'

At the door, Rose turned and smiled. 'I'll forgo the obvious suggestion! You keep them, Lara,' she added kindly, and went back into her bedroom to change.

At least her wardrobe was adequate enough to cope with most things—even something like this. Her job meant that she had to look smart or glamorous whenever the occasion beckoned. Though an outing with a prince was so far outside her experience!

Still, a midday assignation was unlikely to call for much in the way of glitter, and she deliberately chose her most expensive and understated outfit. A demure shirt-dress in chalky-blue linen. It looked very English, she decided, and not in the least bit exotic. As she slid the final button into its hole she wondered whether that was why she had chosen it. To emphasise the differences between her pale restraint and his dark, striking beauty.

She swept her hair back and deftly knotted it into a French plait, and had put on only the barest touch of make-up before she heard the pealing of the front door bell. Drawing in a deep breath for courage and hoping that it might calm the frantic beat of her heart, Rose went out into the hall to answer it.

She pulled open the front door and saw that it was not Khalim who stood there, but a very tall dark-haired man dressed in an immaculate suit, his green eyes glittering with something akin to amusement as he looked down at her belligerent expression.

'Miss Thomas?' he asked smoothly.

He had a cool and rather beautiful face and was the kind of man who might, under normal circumstances, have made her heart beat a little faster. But these were not normal circumstances, Rose reminded herself.

'That's me,' she said inelegantly.

'The Prince Khalim is downstairs waiting for you in the car,' he said quietly. 'Are you ready?'

Rose frowned. 'And you are?'

'My name is Philip Caprice. I am his emissary.'

'Really?' Rose drew her shoulders back. 'And did Prince Khalim not think it *polite* to come and call for me himself?'

Philip Caprice hid a smile. 'It is quite normal for him to send me to collect you.'

'Well, it is not *normal* for me!' said Rose heatedly. 'If he can't even be bothered to get out of the car, then perhaps you would be so kind as to tell him that *I* can't be bothered going downstairs!'

Philip Caprice frowned. 'Look—'

But Rose shook her head. 'I'm sorry,' she said firmly. 'I know you're only doing your job—but your boss's... *invitation*—' she bit the word out sarcastically '—leaves a great deal to be desired. It might have been more polite if he'd actually phoned me to arrange a time, instead of calmly announcing it the way he did! Either he comes up here, or I'm staying put.'

Philip Caprice nodded, his green eyes narrowing, as if recognising determination when he saw it. As if recognising that, on this, she would not be budged.

'I'll go and tell him,' he said. 'Perhaps you could leave the door open?'

'Having to ring the doorbell would be too much of an indignity, I suppose?' she hazarded, but she did as he asked.

She stood for a moment and watched him go, before stalking back into the sitting room where Lara, who had been listening to the entire conversation, was see-sawing between fascination and horror.

'Oh, Rose,' she whispered admiringly. 'You've done it now! Bet you anything he just drives away!'

'I sincerely hope he does,' said Rose coolly.

'Do you really?' came a deep, velvety voice from behind her, and Rose whirled round to see Khalim standing there, with such a glint in his black eyes that she was unable to tell whether he was amused or outraged.

'Y-yes! Yes, I d-do,' she said breathlessly, her heart clenching tightly in her chest as she saw how different he looked today. The eyes glittered with the same predatory promise, but there was not a flowing robe in sight.

Instead he was wearing an exquisitely cut suit in deep charcoal-grey—a modern suit with a mandarin collar which set off the exotic perfection of his face. And where the flowing silk had only hinted at the hard, lean body which lay beneath—the suit left absolutely nothing to the imagination and Rose just couldn't stop looking at him.

His shoulders were broader than she had realised, much broader, while the narrow hips were those of a natural athlete. And the legs…good heavens, those legs seemed to go on forever. Such powerful legs.

Rose opened her mouth to say something, but words just failed her.

'You want me to go away?' he prompted silkily.

Did she? 'It would probably be for the best,' she answered truthfully.

'But you've dressed for lunch,' he observed, his eyes sweeping over the elegance of the pale linen dress.

'Yes, I have.'

'So why waste all that effort?'

'It wasn't much effort.' She shrugged. 'It only took me a few minutes to change!'

'I'm flattered,' he said drily.

She fixed him with a reproving stare. 'I'm used to men being courteous enough to collect their date, and not sending a *servant* to collect them!'

His eyes grew flinty. 'Philip is no servant,' he said coldly. 'He is my emissary.'

'Let's not quibble about terminology!' she returned. 'Why didn't you come yourself?'

Khalim sighed. What would her reaction be if he told her that he had never had to? That all his life he had only had to metaphorically click his fingers and whichever woman he'd wanted would come—if not running, then walking pretty quickly.

'But I am here now,' he said, in as humble an admission as he had ever made. Because he suspected that Rose Thomas was not playing games with him, and that if he pushed her too far then she would simply refuse to come. And he wanted her far too much to even countenance that.

He turned to where a tousled-headed brunette was gazing at him in wonder from the other side of the crimson-painted room, and gave her a slow smile.

'Khalim,' he said, with a slight nod of his head.

Rose was infuriated to see Lara virtually dissolve into a puddle on the carpet—but who could really blame her? It was something outside both their experiences, having a man of this calibre here, exuding vibrancy and sheer physical magnetism.

'L-Lara Black,' she stumbled. 'And I'm very pleased to meet you…K-Khalim.'

Any minute now and her flatmate would start prostrating herself in front of him, thought Rose despairingly. She turned to find those impenetrable dark eyes now fixed on her.

'Shall we go?' he questioned quietly.

She knew that it would be impossible to backtrack, even if she had wanted to—and to her horror she discovered that there was no way she wanted to. She wanted one lunch with this magnificent man. One lunch to show him that she was his equal. That she wouldn't crumble and capitulate in the face of all his undoubted charms.

One lunch, that was all.

'Very well,' she answered, in a quiet tone which matched his.

Khalim very nearly allowed a small smile of triumph to creep onto his lips, until he drew himself up short. There was no victory to be gained from that coolly dispassionate acceptance! he reminded himself. But instead of feeling irritation at her unwillingness to co-operate, he found that his senses were clamouring to life, making his blood sing out that heated, relentless rhythm once more.

'Come, then, Rose,' he said, and gestured for her to precede him.

In the hallway, however, he halted, and Rose's mouth
dried as she turned to see why. He was too close. The hall
was too small. If she reached out her hand she could touch
that proud, beautiful face. Could run her fingertips along his
sculpted chin, and meet the faint rasp of shadowed growth
there. She swallowed.

Khalim's eyes gleamed. So. He had not been mistaken. It
was for her just as it was for him. She wanted him. He noted
the coiled-up tension of repressed desire in her rigid frame.
He could read it in the dark helplessness of her eyes, and in
the fulsome pout of her soft lips.

'So,' he said unsteadily. 'Where would you like to go?'

'Haven't you booked anywhere?' asked Rose in surprise.
She had assumed that he would want the best table in one of
the best restaurants—and Sunday was traditionally a very
busy day for eating out.

'No.' He shook his head.

'That will limit our choice somewhat.'

'I don't think so.' He saw the frown which had creased
the milky-white space of skin between two exceptionally fine
eyebrows. 'I never have to book,' he explained, and for the
first time in his life he realised that he sounded almost apologetic.

And then Rose began to get her first glimmer of the implications of dating this man. She tried to make light of it
and smiled. 'One of the perks of being a prince, I suppose?'

'That's right.' He found himself smiling back, unable to
resist that sunny and unsettling curve of her mouth. 'Where
would you like to go?'

Rose wasn't a head-hunter for nothing. Her 'people skills'
were what kept her going in a competitive industry. She
guessed that luxury would be second nature to Khalim—so
wouldn't he be a little bored with luxury?

'There's a local Italian restaurant called Pronto! on Sutton

Street,' she said. 'Simple food—but good. And you can usually get a table there!'

He was pleasantly surprised, expecting her to plump for somewhere much more up-market than her local restaurant. 'Then let's go and find it,' he murmured.

On the way downstairs, Khalim was hypnotised by the proud set of her shoulders and the plaited hair of brightest gold which had captivated him from the moment he had first seen her.

Outside sat the most luxurious car Rose had ever seen—a great black gleaming monster of a car, with tinted windows and a liveried chauffeur who was standing beside it, and who immediately sprang to open the door.

'Take us to Pronto!,' said Khalim. 'On Sutton Street.' And the chauffeur inclined his head respectfully.

Rose climbed into the back seat, noting that Philip was seated at the front, next to the chauffeur. And next to him, a dark-suited and burly individual. A bodyguard? she wondered nervously. Probably.

The car cruised slowly through the traffic-snarled streets, until it drew up outside a restaurant whose exterior was adorned with a giant picture of the Italian flag.

'Vibrant,' observed Khalim softly as the chauffeur opened the door for them and they both climbed out onto the pavement.

'Isn't Philip joining us?' asked Rose.

Khalim suppressed a feeling very close to frustration, but even closer to jealousy. *Jealousy?* So she wanted his cool and handsome emissary to join them, did she? Was she attracted to him, he wondered in disbelief, or did she simply want a chaperon?

His mouth hardened. 'No, he is not.'

Now, what had put *that* look there? puzzled Rose, shocked by the sudden surge of relief which washed over her. She *wanted* to be on her own with him, she realised sinkingly, her growing attraction to him becoming all too apparent by the moment. But with an effort she managed to shrug it away. 'Fine by me,' she said easily.

Inside the restaurant it was even more vibrant—with Italian music playing gently in the background.

The waitress gave Khalim an appreciative glance. 'Have you booked?' she asked him.

Khalim shook his head. 'Can you fit us in?'

'Sure can!' The waitress grinned, and winked at him.

Rose glanced at Khalim rather nervously. Obviously the woman had no idea that she was being so familiar with a member of Maraban's royal family—but would Khalim be forgiving, or outraged? I don't *care*, she thought fiercely. *I'm* going to enjoy my lunch!

But, strangely, Khalim found that he was enjoying the un-accustomed pleasure of anonymity. Normally he would not sanction such an intimacy—and particularly not from a wait-ress in a rather basic restaurant.

And yet Rose looked incredibly relaxed—even in the cool linen dress which gave her the outward appearance of an ice-maiden—and he wanted to relax *with* her. Not to pull rank.

'Thank you,' he murmured.

Something about the way he spoke made the waitress nar-row her eyes at him, for she suddenly looked rather flustered and led them to what was undoubtedly the best table in the room.

The only one, thought Rose rather wryly, which was not sitting right on top of its neighbours!

He waited until they were seated opposite one another and had been given their menus, before he leaned forward.

'So was this some kind of test, sweet Rose?' he wondered aloud.

She caught the tantalising drift of sandalwood and fought down the desire to let it tug at her senses. 'Test?'

'Mmm.' He looked around. 'Did you think I would baulk at being brought to such spartan surroundings?'

She raised her eyebrows and gave him a considering look.

'Oh, dear me,' she murmured back. 'You may be a prince, but must I also classify you as a snob, Khalim?'

A rebuke was almost unheard of. He could not think of a single other person he would have tolerated it from. But coming from Rose with that quietly mocking tone, it was somehow different. And to Khalim's astonishment, he found himself tacitly accepting it as fair comment.

'You haven't answered my question,' he returned smoothly. '*Was* it some kind of test?'

Why not be honest? Wouldn't a man like this spend his life being told what he *wanted* to hear, rather than the unadulterated truth?

'I thought that you might have had your fill of fancy restaurants,' she observed. 'I mean, surely luxury must grow a little *wearing* if it's relentless? I thought of bringing you to a place you would be least likely to eat in, had the choice of venue been yours. And so I brought you here,' she finished, and lifted her shoulders in a gesture of conciliation.

Guileless! he thought, with unwilling admiration. 'How very perceptive of you, Rose.'

The compliment warmed her far more than it had any right to. 'That's me,' she said flippantly, picking up her menu and beginning to study it, only to glance up and find him studying *her*. 'Shall we order?'

Khalim's black eyes narrowed. He had never had a woman treat him like this! Did she not realise that she should always defer to him? He felt a renewed tension in his body. Strange how such insubordination could fuel his hunger for her even more.

They both ran their eyes over the menus uninterestedly and ordered salads and fish.

'Wine?' questioned Khalim. 'Or would you prefer champagne?'

'But you rarely drink alcohol,' pointed out Rose. She crinkled a smile up at the waitress. 'Just fizzy water, please.'

'Or a fruit punch?' suggested the waitress.

Rose opened her mouth to reply, but Khalim glittered a glance across the table at her, and she shut it obediently.

'Fruit punch,' he agreed, and he began to imagine what it would be like to subdue her in bed.

When they'd been left on their own once more, Rose felt distinctly uncomfortable under his lazy scrutiny.

'Do you *have* to stare at me like that?'

'Like what?' he teased.

As if he would like to slowly remove her dress and run his hands and his lips and his tongue over every centimetre of her body. Rose shivered with excitement. 'You don't need me to spell it out for you. It's insolent.'

'To admire a ravishing woman? Rose, Rose, Rose,' he cajoled softly. 'What kind of men must you have known before me if they did not feast their eyes on such exquisite beauty?'

'Polite ones,' she gritted.

'How very unfortunate for you.' He saw the threat of a glare, and retreated. 'Are we going to spend the whole lunch arguing?'

Arguing seemed a safer bet than feasting her eyes on *him*, though maybe not. Didn't this kind of sparring add yet another frisson to the rapidly building tension between them? Rose felt a slight touch of desperation. Where were her 'people-skills' now, when she most needed them? 'Of course not,' she said, pinning a bright smile to her lips. 'What would you like to talk about?'

She sounded as though she was conducting an interview with him, thought Khalim, with increasing disbelief. By now she should have been eating out of his hand. 'Are you always so...' he chose his word carefully '...*arch* with men?'

'Arch?' Rose took the question seriously. 'You think I'm superior?' Her eyes glinted with amusement. 'Or is it just that you aren't used to women who don't just meekly lie on their backs like a puppy, where you're concerned?'

'Not the best analogy you could have chosen, sweet Rose,' he murmured mockingly. 'Was it?'

And to her horror, Rose started blushing.

He saw the blush. 'My, you *are* very sensitive, aren't you?'

Only with him! 'No.' She shook her head. 'I'm a big girl. I live in the real world. I have a demanding job. If I can't cope with a teasing little comment like that, then I must be losing the plot.' And that was exactly what it felt like. *Losing the plot.* 'Perhaps I *was* being a little arch. Maybe it's a reaction. I just imagine that most women allow you to take the lead, just because of your position.'

'Again, very perceptive,' he mused. 'It makes a refreshing change to have a woman who—'

'Answers back?'

He had been about to say *have a conversation with*, but he allowed Rose her interpretation instead. His own, he realised, would surely have sounded like an omission. What kind of relationships had he had in the past, he wondered, if talking had never been high on the agenda? He nodded. 'If you like.'

The waitress chose that moment to deposit their fruit punches in front of them, and they both took a swift, almost obligatory sip, before putting the glasses down on the table, as if they couldn't wait to be rid of them.

Rose leant forward. 'So where were we?'

Confronted by the pure blue light of her eyes, Khalim felt dazed. He wasn't sure. With an effort, he struggled to regain his thoughts. 'I suspect that it's time to find out a little about one another. One of us asks the questions, while the other provides the answers.'

'Okay.' She nodded, thinking *this* should be interesting. 'Who goes first?' she asked.

By rights, he did. He always did. It was one of the privileges of power. But, perversely, he discovered that he wanted to accede to *her*. 'You do.'

Rose leaned back in her chair. She spent her whole life interviewing people and she knew that the question most often asked was the one which elicited the least imaginative response. So she resisted the desire to ask him what it was *really* like to be a prince. She was beginning to get a pretty good idea for herself. Instead she said, 'Tell me about Maraban.'

Khalim's eyes narrowed. If she had wanted to drive a stake through the very heart of him, she could not have asked a more prescient question. For the land of his birth and his heritage meant more to Khalim than anything else in the world.

'Maraban,' he said, and his voice took on a deep, rich timbre of affection. He smiled almost wistfully. 'If I told you that it was the most beautiful country in the world, would you believe me, Rose?'

When he smiled at her like that, she thought she would have believed just about anything. 'I think I would,' she said slowly, because she could read both passion and possession in his face. 'Tell me about it.'

When he was distracted by the intuitive sapphire sparkle of her eyes, even Maraban seemed like a distant dream, Khalim thought. Did she cast her spell on all men like this?

'It lies at the very heart of the Middle East,' he began slowly, but something in the soft pucker of her lips made the words begin to flow like honey.

Rose listened, mesmerised. His words painted a picture of a magical, faraway place. A land where fig trees and wild walnut trees grew, its mountain slopes covered with forests of juniper and pistachio trees and where dense thickets grew along the riverbanks. He spoke of jackals and wild boar, and the rare pink deer. A place with icy winters and boiling summers. A land of contrasts and rich, stark beauty.

Just like the man sitting opposite her, Rose realised with a start as he stopped speaking. Dazedly she stared down at the table and realised that their meals had been placed in front of them, and had grown cold. She lifted her eyes to meet his, saw the question there.

'It sounds quite beautiful,' she said simply.

He heard the tremor of genuine admiration in her voice. Had he really spoken so frankly to a woman he barely knew? With a sudden air of resolve he gestured towards the untouched food.

'We must eat, if only a little,' he said. 'Or the chef will be offended.'

Rose picked up her fork. She had never felt less like eating in her life—for how could she concentrate on food when this beautiful man with his dark, mobile face made her hungry for something far more basic than food?

'Yes, we must,' she agreed half-heartedly.

They pushed the delicious food around their plates mechanically.

'Tell me about yourself now, Rose,' he instructed softly.

'Essex will sound a little dull after Maraban,' she objected, but he shook his head.

'Tell me.'

She told him all about growing up in a small village, about catching tadpoles in jam-jars and tree-houses and the hammock strung between the two apple trees at the bottom of the garden. About the life-size dolls' house her father had built beside the apple trees for her eighth birthday. 'Just an ordinary life,' she finished.

'Don't ever knock it,' he said drily.

'No.' She looked at him, realising with a sudden rush of insight that an ordinary life would be something always denied to him. And wasn't it human nature to want what you had never had? 'No, I won't.'

'You have brothers and sisters?' Khalim asked suddenly.

She put her fork down, glad for the excuse to. He really *did* seem interested. 'One older brother,' she said. 'No sisters. And you?'

'Two sisters.' He smiled. 'All younger.'

'And a brother?'

'No,' he said flatly. 'No brother.'

'So one day you will inherit Maraban?' she asked, and saw his eyes grew wary.

'Some far-distant day, I pray,' he answered harshly, aware that her question had touched a raw nerve. Reminded him of things he would prefer to forget. Things which simmered irrevocably beneath the surface of his life. His father's health was declining, and the physicians had told him that he would be unlikely to see the year out. The pressure was on to find Khalim a wife.

He stared at the blonde vision sitting opposite him and his mouth hardened. And once he married, then sexual trysts with women such as Rose Thomas would have to stop.

Rose saw the sudden hardening of his features, the new steeliness in his eyes. She shifted back in her seat, knowing that the atmosphere had changed, but not knowing why.

Khalim's breath caught in his throat. Her movement had drawn his attention to the soft swell of her breasts beneath the armoury of her linen dress. She could not have worn anything better designed to conceal her body, he thought, with a hot and mounting frustration—and yet the effect on him was more potent than if she had been clad in clinging Lycra.

In Maraban, the women dressed modestly; it had always been so. Khalim was used to Western women revealing themselves in short skirts or plunging necklines, or jeans which looked as though they had been sprayed on.

But Rose, he realised, had somehow cut a perfectly acceptable middle path. She was decently attired, yet not in the least bit frumpy. Contemporary and chic, and so very, very sexy…

He felt another swift jerk of desire. He must rid himself of this need before it sent him half mad. The sooner he had her, the sooner he could forget her. 'Shall we go?' he asked huskily.

Rose stared at him. The black eyes seemed even blacker, if that was possible, and she knew exactly why. The waves of desire emanating from his sleek physique were almost palpable. Her mouth felt suddenly dry; she knew instinctively what would be next on the agenda. She must resist him. She *must*. He was far too potent. Too attractive by far. Did she want to be just another woman who had fallen into Khalim's bed after a brief glimmer of that imperious smile?

No!

'Why, certainly.' She smiled. 'I have a lot of work back at the flat which needs catching up on.'

He ignored that, even though her offhand attitude inflamed him as much as infuriated him. She would be much more co-operative in a moment or two. He had not misread the signs, of that he was certain.

And Rose Thomas wanted him just as much as he wanted her…

He stood up, and Philip appeared at the door of the restaurant almost immediately.

'Come,' said Khalim.

'Aren't you going to pay the bill?'

'Philip will settle it.'

Rose walked out to the car, where the chauffeur was already opening the door. It was *unbelievable*! Did none of life's tedious little chores ever trouble him? 'I suppose you have someone to do everything for you, do you, Khalim?' she offered drily, then wished she hadn't. For in order to answer her question he had barred her way, and she could see the light of some glorious sexual battle in his eyes.

'I have never exercised my right to have someone bathe me,' he returned softly.

'Your *right*?' she questioned in disbelief. 'To *bathe* you?'

'Why, of course. All princes of Maraban have a master…or mistress of the bathchamber.' He shrugged, enjoying the spontaneous darkening of her eyes, the way her lips were automatically parting. As if waiting for the first thrust of his tongue. Yes, now, he thought. *Now!*

'So where do you want to go from here, Rose?' He dipped his voice into a sultry caress, allowed his mouth to curve with sensual promise. 'Back home to work? Or back to my suite at the Granchester for…coffee?'

His deliberate hesitation left her in no doubt what he *really* had in mind, and as she met the hard glitter of his eyes Rose couldn't deny she was tempted. Well, who wouldn't be? When every pore of that magnificent body just screamed out that Khalim would know everything there was to know about the art of making love and a little bit more besides.

But self-preservation saved her. That, and a sense of pride. One lunch and one arrogant invitation! Did he imagine that would be enough to make her fall eagerly into his bed? She stared into a face which had 'heartbreaker' written all over it.

'Home, please,' she said, and saw a moment of frozen disbelief. 'I have a mountain of work to do.'

CHAPTER FOUR

THE intercom on her desk buzzed and startled Rose out of yet another daydream involving a black-haired man in silken clothes, throwing her down onto a bed and...

'Hel-lo?' she said uncertainly.

'Rose?' came the voice of Rose's boss, Kerry MacColl. 'It's Kerry.'

'Oh, hi, Kerry!'

'Look, something rather exciting has come up and I need to talk to you. Can you come in here for a moment, please?'

'Sure I can.' Trying to project an enthusiasm she definitely wasn't feeling, Rose pushed away the feedback form she had been completing and went out into the corridor towards Kerry's room, which was situated on the other side of the passage.

Headliners was one of London's most successful small head-hunting agencies, and Rose had worked there for two years. It specialised in placing people in jobs within the advertising industry and was famous for its youth, its dynamism and eclectic approach—all highly valued qualities when it came to dealing with their talented, but often temperamental clients!

Their offices were based in Maida Vale, in a charmingly converted mews cottage. It had been deliberately designed so that their workplace seemed more like a home from home, and was the envy of the industry! The theory was that relaxed surroundings helped people do their job better and, so far, the practice was bearing out the theory very nicely.

Rose could see Kerry working at her desk and walked straight in without knocking, since she had always operated an open-door policy. And although, strictly speaking, Kerry *was* her boss—she was only a couple of years older than Rose—she had never found the need to pull rank. Headliners eight employees all worked as a team, and not a hierarchy.

She looked up as Rose came in, pushed her tinted glasses back up her nose, and smiled. 'Hi!'

Rose smiled back. 'You wanted to see me?'

Kerry nodded and fixed her with a penetrating look. 'How are you doing, Rose?'

Rose forced herself to widen her smile. 'Fine.' She nodded. And she was, of course she was. Just because she had spent the week since her lunch with Khalim thinking about him during every waking moment—it didn't mean there was anything wrong with her. And even if when she went to bed there was no let-up—well, so what? Maybe sleep *didn't* come easily, and maybe all her dreams *were* invaded by that same man—but that did not mean she was not fine. She wasn't sick, or broke, or worried, was she?

She had tried displacement therapy, and thrown herself into a week of feverish activity. She had spring-cleaned her bedroom—even though it was almost autumn!—and had gone to the cinema and the theatre. She had attended the opening of an avant-garde art exhibition and visited her parents in their rambling old farmhouse.

And still felt as though there was a great, gaping hole in her life.

'I'm fine,' she said again, wondering if her smile looked genuine.

Kerry frowned. 'You're quite sure?' she asked gently. 'You've seemed a little off colour this week. A bit pale, too. And haven't you lost weight?'

For a moment, Rose was tempted to tell her, but she never bought her problems into work with her. And, anyway, she didn't *have* a problem! she reminded herself. 'Oh, come on! Who *isn't* always trying to lose weight?' she joked.

'True.' Kerry indicated the chair opposite her. 'Sit down.'

'Thanks.' Rose wondered what all this was about, and

started to feel the first stirrings of curiosity. Kerry seemed terribly excited about something. And it must be something big because Kerry was the kind of seen-it-all and done-it-all person who wasn't easy to impress.

'What if I told you I'd just had lunch with a client—'

'I'd say lucky you—I just had a boring old sandwich at my desk!' And no need to mention that most of it had ended up in the bin.

'A client.' Kerry sucked in a deep and excited breath and then Rose really *was* surprised. Why, her sophisticated and sometimes cynical boss was looking almost *coquettish*! 'The most surprising and unbelievable client you can imagine.'

'Oh?'

'What would you say if I told you that we are being hired by a—' Kerry gulped the word out as if she couldn't quite believe she was saying it '—*prince*?' Kerry sat back in her chair and looked at Rose, her face a mixture of triumph and curiosity.

Rose felt as though she were taking part in a play. As though someone else had written the script for this scene which was now taking place. It was surely far too much of a coincidence to suppose that…that… Her heart was pounding unevenly in her chest. 'A prince?' she asked weakly, playing for time.

Kerry completely misinterpreted her strangulated words. 'I know,' she confided. 'It took me a little while before I could believe it myself! I mean, there isn't much that surprises *me*, but when a Lawrence-of-Arabia-type character walks into one of London's top restaurants and every woman in the room sat staring at him, open-mouthed. Well, suffice it to say that I was momentarily speechless!'

'That *must* be a first,' said Rose drily, and forced herself to ask the kind of questions she would normally ask if her brain weren't spinning round like a carousel inside her head. 'What did he want?'

'That's the funny thing.' Kerry picked up a pencil and twirled it thoughtfully around in her fingers. 'He wanted *you*.'

Disbelief and a lurching kind of excitement created an unfamiliar cocktail of emotion somewhere deep inside her. *'Me?'* squeaked Rose. 'What do you mean, he wanted me?'

Kerry frowned. 'Calm down, Rose—I'm not talking in the biblical sense!'

No, but you could be sure that *he* was, thought Rose, and her heart-rate rocketed even further.

Kerry smiled encouragingly. 'He—'

'What's his name?' put in Rose quickly, thinking that maybe, just maybe—there *was* another prince in London with dark, exotic looks.

'Khalim,' said Kerry, and her face took on an unusually soft expression. 'Prince Khalim. It's a lovely name, isn't it?'

'Lovely,' echoed Rose faintly. 'Wh-what did you say he wanted?'

'He wants to employ our agency to head-hunt for him! More specifically,' added Kerry, 'he asked especially for *you*.'

'D-do you know why?'

'Oh, yes,' said Kerry happily. 'He told me. Said he'd heard that you were probably the best head-hunter in the city, and that he only ever uses the best!'

The word *uses* swam uncomfortably into her mind and refused to shift. Rose frowned in genuine confusion. 'You mean he's in advertising?'

Kerry shook her head. 'Oh, no—it's nothing to do with advertising. He wants you to find someone to be in charge of his country's oil refinery. The man who has been there since the year dot is taking early retirement, apparently.'

Rose stared across the table in disbelief. 'But we don't *do* oilfields!' she protested. 'Our speciality is advertising.'

'That's exactly what I told him,' said Kerry smugly. 'I felt it was only professional to point that out. I said that my advice would be to consult someone who was familiar with that particular field.'

'And what did he say?' asked Rose, knowing that the question was in many ways redundant, and that she had a good idea of what was coming next.

She had.

'Oh, he said that the principles for finding the right person for the job were the same, no matter what the particular job,' Kerry explained airily. 'Matching skills with needs.'

'I'll bet he did,' said Rose dully. What Khalim wanted, Khalim had to have. And he wanted her, she knew that. The only trouble was that she wanted him, too—and she was only just beginning to discover how much...

Kerry gave her a piercing stare. 'This wasn't the kind of reaction I was expecting, Rose. I thought you'd be leaping up and down with excitement,' she said, and leaned forwards over the desk. 'When someone of this man's stature hears that one of your staff is about the best there is, and decides that no one else will possibly do. Well—' she shrugged, but there was no disguising her disappointment '—*most* people would be absolutely delighted! Is there something you're not telling me?'

Rose was a naturally truthful person, but this was her *boss*. And, anyway, even if she told the truth—how weak and pathetic would she sound if she came straight out with it? Kerry, I've met him and he desires me and I desire him too, but I'm reluctant to start anything that I suspect is only going to end in tears.

'No,' she said quickly. 'There's nothing of any relevance to the job.' And that much was true. If any of her ex-boyfriends had come to the agency requesting that she found someone to work for them—she wouldn't have had a problem doing it. Wasn't she in danger of letting Khalim tangle her life up into knots?

'Think of the opportunities this presents!' enthused Kerry. 'This could give us the chance to branch out into a completely different field. The world could be our oyster—and just think of our profile!'

Kerry spoke sense; the professional in Rose acknowledged that. There was no way she could turn down such a golden opportunity, even if she *had* been railroaded by the coolly manipulative Khalim into doing so. She put as much enthusiasm as she possibly could into her reply. 'I'd love to do it, Kerry.'

Kerry beamed. 'Good! He wants to see you first thing in the morning. Well, ten o'clock, to be precise.'

'Where?' But Rose knew the answer to this, too.

'At his suite. The *penthouse* suite! At the Granchester Hotel.' Kerry winked. '*Very* posh! Just make sure you wear something nice!'

Rose opted for the cover-up. A silk trouser suit in a sugar-almond pink. And the complete opposite of a come-and-get-me look, with her hair caught back in a stark pony-tail and her make-up so sparing that it was virtually non-existent.

She arrived at the Granchester at precisely five to ten and the first person she saw standing at the other end of the vast foyer was Philip Caprice. As expected.

She saw his hand move to the breast pocket of his suit, and then, with a slightly wary smile, he walked across the foyer towards her.

'Hello, Rose.' He smiled.

It wasn't *his* fault that he worked for a man who used his untold influence to control events, she supposed, and she gave him a returning smile.

'Hello, Philip. Khalim sent you down to collect me, I suppose?'

'No, Khalim has come down to fetch you himself,' came a smooth, velvety voice from just behind her, and Rose turned round to find Khalim standing there, the black eyes glittering with some unspoken message. Was that triumph she read there? She supposed it was. He had got exactly what he wanted. Or so he thought...

'And I suppose I should be flattered, should I?' she asked spikily.

Khalim gave a hard smile. 'Actually, yes, perhaps you should. After all, most women find it a pleasure to be in my company.'

'But, presumably, they haven't been manipulated into it, like I have?'

Khalim stilled. 'Are you intending to make a scene in the middle of the foyer?'

'You classify giving a legitimate opinion as making a scene?' Rose smiled. 'What spineless women you must have known in the past, Khalim!'

And looking at the feisty sparkle which was making her blue eyes shine like sapphires, Khalim was inclined to agree with her. 'Shall we go upstairs?' he asked pleasantly.

The words came blurting out before she could stop them. 'Why, so that you can seduce me?'

The black eyes narrowed, but then his mouth curved in a slow, speculative smile. 'Is that what you would like, then, sweet Rose?'

And, to Rose's horror, that smile had the most extraordinary effect on her. She found her skin warming under that unmistakable look of approbation, as if she had found herself beneath the gentle heat of a spring sun. Her heart began to patter out an erratic little dance and little shivers of sensation skittered all the way down her spine.

With a supreme effort, she said firmly, 'No, what I would *like* is to have been given some choice in taking this job!'

'I'm sure you were perfectly free to turn it down.' His shrug was disarming, but the steely intent behind his words remained intact.

'Yes, that would have gone down very well with my boss, wouldn't it? Sorry, but I don't want to take this highly lucrative contract, because...'

'Because?' he questioned so silkily that the hairs on the back of her neck began to prickle, and she stared at him indignantly.

'Because a man who is capable of such underhand—'

But her words were waylaid by long, olive-coloured fingers being placed on her arm. She could feel their gentle caress through the thin silk of her suit jacket, and at that moment felt as helpless as a rabbit caught in the glaring headlights of an oncoming car.

'Let us continue this discussion upstairs,' he instructed smoothly. 'I am not certain that I am going to like what I am about to hear—and, if that is the case, then I most assuredly do not wish for all the staff and guests of the Granchester to be privy to it.'

Rose opened her mouth to protest, then closed it again. What was the point? She was here to do business, after all. 'Will Philip be accompanying us?'

Dark eyebrows were raised in mocking query. 'Ah! Once again you have need of a chaperon do you, Rose?'

Her own look mocked him back. 'Of course not! I'm a professional—and our business will be conducted on just that footing. I know that I can rely on you to abide by that, can't I, Khalim?'

Her attempt to dominate made him ache unbearably, and Khalim felt the slow pull of sexual excitement. What untold pleasure it would give him to subjugate her fiery insurrection!

'A word of warning, Rose,' he murmured. 'A Marabanesh is master of his own destiny. Rely on nothing and you shall not be disappointed.' He turned his dark head. 'Come, Philip,' he drawled. 'The lady requests your company.'

Philip Caprice seemed slightly bemused by the interchange. 'I'm honoured,' he replied.

But Rose could barely think straight. All the way up in the lift, Khalim's words kept swimming seductively around in her head. *Master of his own destiny.* Why should that thrill her so unspeakably? Because the quiet Englishmen of her acquaintance would never have come out with such a passionate and poetic phrase?

His suite was something outside Rose's experience, even though her work had taken her to plenty of glamorous places in her time. But this was something else! She looked around in wonder. It was absolutely vast—why, she could imagine two football teams feeling perfectly at home here! And it was furnished with sumptuous understatement.

She didn't know quite what she had expected—Middle-Eastern opulence, she supposed, with golden swathes of material, and mosaics and richly embroidered cushions scattered on the floor, perhaps even a water-pipe or two!

And she couldn't have got it more wrong, because Khalim's suite was so very English. Comfort, with a slight modern edge to it; it was thickly carpeted in soft pale cream with three enormous sofas coloured blood-red. On the wall hung some magnificent modern paintings—huge canvases whose abstract shapes took the mind on surprising journeys.

But it was the view which was the most stunning thing the suite had to offer—because along the entire length of the room ran floor-to-ceiling windows overlooking London's most famous park. She gazed down, thinking that it was so unexpected to see a great sward of green right bang in the middle of a bustling city.

And when she looked up again, it was to find Khalim watching her.

'You like it,' he observed, and the pleasure in his voice was unmistakable.

'It's beautiful,' she said simply. 'Absolutely beautiful.'

And so was she, he thought. So was she. Quite the most beautiful woman he had ever seen, with her pale blonde hair and milky-white skin, and a pert little nose offset by the most sinful pair of lips imaginable. Again, he felt the irresistible pull of desire, but he quashed it ruthlessly.

At his English boarding-school, he had sometimes liked to fish—the calm and the quiet and the splendid isolation had soothed his homesick soul during the times he had been missing his homeland quite desperately. And early on he had learnt that the most prized fish were those which proved the most difficult to catch.

And so it was with Rose. He acknowledged that she wanted him, too, and he suspected that she was perceptive enough to have recognised it herself. But she was not like other women, he knew that with a blinding certainty. She would not fall easily into his arms, no matter how much she wanted him.

He smiled, not oblivious to the impact of that smile. 'Please sit down, Rose. Shall we have coffee?'

His tone was so courteous and his manner so charming that Rose was momentarily captivated. She completely forgot about giving him a piece of her mind. Why, for a moment, she felt almost *flustered*.

'Er, thank you,' she said, and slid down onto one of the blood-red sofas, astonished when a middle-aged woman, who was obviously a Marabanesh herself, carried in a tray of fragrant-smelling coffee.

Had someone been listening for his command? she wondered rather helplessly, before realising that *yes*, they probably had! He *was* a prince, after all, with people hanging onto his every word.

And then she remembered. He might be a prince, but he was also a devious manipulator who had used his money and position and power to get her here today!

With a smile, she took one of the tiny cups from the woman, and put it down on the floor so that she could delve into her briefcase.

She extracted a sheaf of papers and fixed him with a bright, professional smile. 'Right, then. Let's get started!'

'Drink your coffee first.' He frowned.

She gave another brisk smile. 'You're not paying me to drink coffee, Khalim!'

His frown deepened. 'What do you want to know?' he asked sulkily.

Rose almost smiled again. Why, right then, she got a fleeting glimpse of the little boy he must once have been! And a very handsome little boy, too! 'You went to school with Guy, didn't you?' she asked suddenly.

Satisfied that she had fallen in with his wishes, and was postponing the start of the meeting in deference to him, Khalim nodded. 'A very English boarding-school,' he said and sipped his own coffee.

'How old were you?'

His face suddenly tensed. 'Seven.'

The way he shot that single word out told her it had hurt. And why brush those feelings under the carpet? Wouldn't a prince be 'protected' from so-called prying questions such as those. And if you bottled things up, didn't that mean you would never be able to let them go? 'That must have been very difficult for you,' she ventured cautiously.

Khalim regarded her thoughtfully. Brave, he reasoned. Few would dare to ask him such a personal question, and there were few to whom he would give an answer. But on her angelic face was an expression of genuine concern, not just mere inquisitiveness.

'It wasn't…' He hesitated. A Marabanesh man of his stature would never admit to human frailty. 'Easy,' was all he would allow.

Understatement of the year, thought Rose wryly.

He saw her take her pen out of her briefcase, and suddenly found that he didn't want to talk business. 'It was the tradition,' he said abruptly.

She glanced up. 'The tradition?'

'For princes of Maraban to be educated in England.'

'Why?'

He gave a rather speculative smile and Rose was suddenly alerted to the fact that this man could be ruthless indeed. *Remember* that, she told herself fiercely.

'So that it is possible to blend into both Eastern and Western cultures,' he replied.

And sitting there, with his immaculately cut suit and his handmade Italian shoes, he did indeed look the personification of Western elegance. But the deep olive skin and the glittering black eyes and the decidedly regal bearing bore testament to the fact that his roots were in a hot, scented land which was worlds away from this.

And remember that, *too*, thought Rose.

'Maraban sells oil all over the world,' he continued. 'And wherever I go, I am aware that I am my country's ambassador. It has always been to my advantage that I am able to merge into whichever culture I am with at the time.'

'So you're a chameleon?' asked Rose thoughtfully.

He gave a slow smile. 'I prefer to describe myself as a man of contrasts.'

Hadn't she thought exactly that, the very first time she had met him? Rose shifted uncomfortably. It felt slightly disconcerting, alarming even—to be echoing Khalim's thoughts.

She took a sip from her coffee, then put the cup back down on the floor.

'So, to business. And I need you to tell me, Khalim— exactly what is it you want?' she asked him crisply.

For once it was difficult to focus on business—he couldn't seem to kick-start his mind into gear. He wondered what she would say if he told her that what he *wanted* was to make love to her in such a way that every man who ever followed him would be like a dim memory of the real thing. He felt the powerful thundering of his heart in response to his thoughts.

'Let me give you a little background first,' he began softly. 'Maraban has substantial reserves of oil in—'

'The Asmaln desert,' she put in quickly. 'And other natural resources include deposits of coal, sulphur, magnesium, and salt.'

Khalim looked at her in astonishment. 'And how, for an

Englishwoman, do you know so much about my country?' he demanded.

Rose's mouth pleated with disapproval. 'Oh, *really*, Khalim! Once I knew that I had to take the wretched job, I approached it in exactly the same way as I would any other! Information is power, and I spent until late last night finding out everything I could about Maraban!'

His eyes narrowed with unwilling admiration. 'What else do you know?'

'That only four per cent of the country is cultivated, nearly all of which is irrigated. I also know,' she added, 'that Marabanesh pistachio nuts are considered to be the finest in the world!'

'And do you like pistachio nuts?' he asked seriously.

Her mouth lifted at the corners. 'Oh, I wouldn't dream of having a gin and tonic without one!'

Such flippancy was something he was unused to as well— at least from anyone outside his inner circle. Yet his mouth curved in response to that frankly mischievous smile. 'Then I must arrange to have some sent to you, Rose,' he murmured. 'A whole sackload of Maraban pistachios!'

It was distracting when his hard face softened like that. It started making her imagine all kinds of things. She tried to picture him doing ordinary things. Going to the supermarket. Queuing up at the petrol station. And she couldn't. She tried to picture him on holiday, swimming…

Oddly enough, that was an image which imprinted itself far more clearly and Rose saw glorious dark limbs, all strength and muscle as they submerged themselves in warm and silken waters. With almost painful clarity, she recalled just how it had felt to move within the sandalwood-scented circle of his arms at the wedding reception.

Khalim saw the sudden tension around her shoulders. 'Something is wrong?'

Had he noticed the hectic flush which was burning its way along her cheekbones? She stared fixedly at the pristine papers on her lap, unable to meet his gaze, terrified that his slicing black stare would be able to read the unmistakable longing in her eyes.

'No,' she said, with slow emphasis, until she had composed herself enough to meet that challenging look head-on. 'Nothing is wrong, Khalim. But I'm still waiting for you to tell me what it is you're looking for.'

Khalim recognised her determination, and a will almost as forceful as his own. It was a heady discovery, he thought as he began to speak.

'Maraban has one of the world's most well-run oil refineries and the man who heads it up is taking early retirement.'

'And you want someone to replace him?'

Khalim shook his dark head. 'No one could ever replace Murad,' he said thoughtfully. 'He has been there for many years, and there have been many changes in the industry during that time. No, I need someone to take oil production into the first third of this century and there are two likely candidates working there at present. I need a man with vision to head it up—'

'Or a woman, of course?'

Jet sparks heated the onyx eyes, bathing her in an intensely black light.

'No,' he contradicted resolutely. 'Not a woman. Not in Maraban.'

Rose bristled; she couldn't help herself. She thought about all she had striven to achieve in her life. 'So women aren't equal in Maraban?'

'I think you are intelligent enough to know the answer to that for yourself, without me having to tell you, Rose,' he remonstrated quietly.

'It's disgraceful!' she stormed.

'You think so?' His voice was dangerously soft.

'I know so! Women in this country died to have the right to vote and to call themselves equal!'

'And you think that makes them happy?'

Her eyebrows shot up. 'I can't believe you could even ask me a question like that!'

He smiled, savouring the rare flavour of opposition and conflict. 'I just did.'

Rose very nearly threw her pen across the room in a fit of pique, before remembering herself. Since when had she taken to hurling missiles? She steadied her voice with a deep breath instead. 'Of course equality makes women happy! What woman worth her salt wants to spend her life living in a man's shadow?'

The woman he would marry would be only too glad to. His mind skipped to the women currently being vetted as eligible wife material, then thought how unlike them this woman was. Their very antithesis. He felt the thrill of the forbidden, the lure of the unsuitable, and it heated his blood unbearably. 'You should not judge without all the facts available to you, Rose,' he remonstrated softly. 'Women in Maraban are very highly respected and they are treated with the utmost reverence—because they are seen as the givers of life. Come and see for yourself whether the women of Maraban are happy.'

She stared at him, furiously aware that wild hope was vying with indignation. 'What do you mean?'

In that moment, he had never rejoiced in his position quite so much. How perfect that whatever he desired should be granted to him without effort. And he desired Rose Thomas more than anything in his life to date. He gave a cool and glittering smile. 'You will accompany me to Maraban,' he purred.

CHAPTER FIVE

'YOU *are* kidding, Rose?'

Rose stared at her flatmate, still slightly reeling from Khalim's unarguable statement. 'I wish I was!'

Lara cocked her head to one side and grinned. 'Oh, no, you don't! What other woman do you know who wouldn't want to be whisked off in a private jet with a prince—a *prince*, no less, who looks like Khalim does? And acts like Khalim does!'

'High-handed!' grumbled Rose.

'Masterful,' sighed Lara.

Of course, Lara wasn't entirely wrong—not about Khalim, nor Rose's attitude to being whisked off in such an extraordinary fashion. Because if she examined her feelings honestly, wasn't there a part of her—and quite a large part of her—which was feeling almost sick with excitement at the thought of being taken to Maraban by its overwhelmingly attractive prince and heir? Any minute now she would wake up and find that the alarm had just gone off!

'So tell me why you're going again,' said Lara, screwing her face up, as if she hadn't understood the first explanation, which Rose had blurted out. 'Just to find out about how women in Maraban live, compared to their Western counterparts? Is that it?'

Rose shook her head. 'No. That was just the provocative way he phrased it.' Along with the even more provocative look which had gleamed with such dazzling promise from those inky eyes. 'But the fact is that I'll probably be recruiting from within Maraban itself, or the surrounding countries if that fails. There are two possible candidates there already, so I really do *need* to go.'

'Oh, you poor thing!'

She'd phoned Kerry to broach the subject of her journey, and her boss had sounded bemused.

'Of course you must go, Rose. You're in charge of the job, aren't you?' Kerry had said, her voice sounding slightly puzzled. 'Go where you need to go; the prince is paying.'

Oh, yes, the prince was paying all right, and in paying the prince was also managing to demonstrate just how wide-reaching were his influence and power.

And power was, Rose had to concede with a guilty shiver, a very potent aphrodisiac indeed. She must remember that. Khalim would not be blind to that fact either, which meant that she would have to be very, very careful not to let it all go to her head. She thought back to how she had greeted his suggestion.

'Where will I be staying?' she demanded, not caring that Philip had sucked in a horrified breath at the tone she was using. 'In a hotel, I hope?'

Khalim stilled. She really could be most insolent! If she were not quite so beautiful, he really would not have tolerated such disrespect. 'Maraban has internationally acclaimed hotels,' he told her smoothly. 'But as my guest you will naturally stay in my father's…'

Rose looked up as she picked up on his hesitation—the last man she would have expected being stuck for words. 'Your father's what?'

'Palace,' he said reluctantly.

Rose widened her eyes. His father's palace, no less! Well, of *course* he would have a palace, wouldn't he? Royal families did not generally live in trailer parks! She looked at him with interest, her indignation dissolving by the second.

Had his reluctance to speak been motivated by the fact that palaces were what really drew the line in the sand? Palaces were what emphasised the unbreachable differences between Khalim and ordinary people like her. And, if that was the case, then didn't that mean that there was a thoughtful streak running through him? Despite her reservations, she smiled.

'And is it a beautiful palace?' she asked him softly.

An answering smile curved the edges of Khalim's hard mouth. Most people rushed onto another subject—seeing his home simply as some kind of status symbol, forgetting that palaces tended to be designed with beauty in mind. But then Rose, he suspected, had a very real sense of the beautiful.

'Very.' His reply was equally soft. 'Would you like me to describe it to you, or will you wait and see for yourself?'

Rose swallowed down temptation. The very last thing she needed was that deep, sexy voice painting lyrical pictures for her. A voice like that could suck you in and transport you away to a magical place and make you have foolish wishes which could never come true. And Rose needed her feet set very firmly on the ground.

'No, I think I'll wait and see for myself, thank you,' she said primly, tucking her still pristine papers back into her briefcase. Khalim had promised to fill her in about the oil refinery on the plane and she was glad to agree. At least it would give them something to talk about, other than the kind of irritating questions which kept popping to the forefront of her mind, such as, Khalim, why are your lips so beautiful? Or, Khalim, did anyone ever tell you that you have a body to die for?

'Rose!'

Rose blinked out of her reverie to find Lara staring at her as if she were an alien who had just landed from the planet Mars. 'Wh-what is it?' she stumbled.

'You looked miles away!'

'I was.' In Maraban and in Khalim's arms again, to be precise. Wondering if the land he had described could ever possibly live up to the richness of his description of it. I hope not, she thought distractedly. I really do.

'When are you going?' asked Lara.

'The day after tomorrow.' Khalim had wanted to fly out

first thing the next morning, but Rose had put her foot down. She might have a wardrobe which could cope with almost any eventuality, but a trip such as this required a dash round London's biggest department stores! And hadn't it been immensely pleasurable to see his incredulous expression when she had opposed his wishes to leave when *he* wanted? She'd heard Philip's disbelieving snort as she'd refused to back down!

Who knew? Khalim was a man used to always getting his own way, and thwarting his wishes occasionally might just be good for him! Why, he might even thank her for it one day!

'Very well,' he had agreed coldly. 'The day after tomorrow.'

She spent the next day shopping and on impulse bought a new evening gown far more glittering and ostentatious than any of her normal purchases. But once she'd packed she felt almost sick with nerves, and realised that she'd better tell her parents she was going abroad. She rang and rang their old farmhouse, but there was no reply, and so she phoned her brother instead.

'Jamie? It's me, Rose!'

'Well, hi! How much do you want to borrow?' came back the dry comment.

'Very funny!'

'But you never seem to ring me these days, sister dearest—'

'You've lost the use of your dialling finger, have you? Men are notoriously bad at communication and I don't see why it should always be the women who stay in touch!'

Jamie sounded indulgent. 'Fair! So is this just a friendly chat with your favourite brother?'

'My only brother.' Rose smiled, and then grimaced at her reflection in the mirror. 'Well, actually, no—I've been trying to ring Mum and Dad—but there's no reply.'

'That's because they're up in the Lake District—'

'They're *always* going somewhere!'

'But it's good, isn't it? That they're enjoying their retire-ment—I hope *I'm* still having such a good time, at their age!'

'Yes,' said Rose thoughtfully. 'I wanted to tell them that I'm going abroad for a couple of days.'

'Oh? Anywhere nice?'

Rose removed a speck of dust from the mirror with her fingernail. 'Have you heard of a place called Maraban?'

There was a pause. 'Isn't it in the Middle East?'

'That's right.'

'So is it work? Or a holiday?'

'Oh, work. I've, er, been asked to find someone to head up their oil refinery.'

She could hear the frown in Jamie's voice. 'Really? But I thought you only worked in advertising?'

'Usually I do.' She scowled in the mirror again as if Khalim's reflection was mocking back at her. 'But this is special, or rather the client is. He's a…um…he's a prince.'

'Sorry? Must be a bad line—I thought you said he was a prince.'

How far-fetched it sounded! Her voice sounded almost apologetic. 'I did. He's Prince Khalim of Maraban.'

There was a moment of astounded silence before she could hear Jamie expelling air from between pursed lips—an ex-pression of bemusement he had had since he was a little boy. Then he said, 'Wow! Lucky girl!'

'Aren't I?' she agreed, just hoping that it sounded con-vincing, because most women *would* be thrilled and excited by the idea, wouldn't they? 'You can tell all your friends I'm going to stay in a palace!'

'Heck,' he said softly, still sounding slightly stunned.

'And the other thing—'

'Mmm?'

'It's just that Lara's going to be away filming, and I just wondered whether you would pop your head into the flat on your way home from work—just check that there aren't any free newspapers or letters making it look like the flat is empty?'

'Course I will,' he replied cheerfully. 'You should try living somewhere that doesn't have such a high quota of burglars!'

'I know.' Rose let out a small sigh. 'Listen, thanks, Jamie.'

'Sure.' There was another pause. 'Rose, this trip—it *is* all perfectly above board, isn't it?'

'Of course it is! What else would it be? It's business, Jamie, strictly business.'

But as she replaced the receiver, Rose wondered if she had been entirely honest with her brother...

The following morning, she opened the door and her mouth fell open when she discovered that it was Khalim himself who stood there.

He saw the pink pout of her lips and smiled a predatory smile. 'Surprised?' he murmured. 'Were you expecting Philip?'

Well, yes, she was surprised, but not because he hadn't sent his emissary to collect her. Mainly because he had switched roles again. Gone was the exotic-looking businessman in the beautifully cut suit. Instead, he was dressed in a variation of the outfit he'd been wearing at the wedding—a flowing, silken top with loose trousers of the same material worn underneath. But today the robes were more silvery than gold. A colder colour altogether, providing an austere backdrop to the dark, proud features. Oh, but he looked magnificent!

'You've ch-changed,' was all she could breathlessly manage.

'Of course I have. I'm going home,' came the simple reply. 'Are you ready?'

She'd packed just one suitcase, and it stood in readiness in the hall. She gestured to it and then *was* surprised when he picked it up.

He saw the look and correctly interpreted it. 'You imagined that I would send someone up to collect it? That I should never carry anyone else's bags?'

'I suppose I did.'

Astonishingly, he found that he wanted to enlighten her—to show her that he was not just a man who had been cosseted by servants from the moment of his birth.

'There were reasons behind me being sent to boarding-school other than to learn to blend into both societies,' he told her softly. 'Like cold showers and rigorous sport and the discipline of learning to stand on my own two feet.'

She stared at him, all too aware of the dark luminosity of his eyes. 'And was it hard?' she questioned. 'To adapt to a new culture and all that went with it?'

Her direct questions went straight to the very heart of the matter; impossible to ignore or to brush aside. He shrugged. 'Little boys can be cruel.'

'Yes, I know.' She wondered if he was conscious that remembered pain had clouded the amazing black eyes. 'And how did you cope with that?'

He pulled the door open and motioned for her to precede him. 'You have to appear not to care. Only then will you cease to become the butt of playground mockery.'

She saw a picture of a beautiful young boy with hair as black as his eyes. Outstanding in more than just looks and an easy target for boys who had not had so many of life's gifts conferred on them.

'Khalim—'

She was close enough for him to feel the sweet warmth of her breath. Close enough for him to have coiled his fingers around the narrow indentation of her waist and to have pulled her to him, and kissed her.

Would she have resisted? He doubted it. No woman who had ever been kissed by him had failed to follow it up by tumbling into bed with him. But the timing was wrong. Why begin something only to have it end unsatisfactorily? If he made love to her now, then it would be a swift coupling in her bedroom—with no guarantee that the flatmate would not suddenly return. And Philip and the chauffeur sitting waiting downstairs in the car. That would do her reputation no good at all, he realised—shocked that it should matter to him.

'Let's go,' he said, and moved away from her before his body picked up any more of her enticing signals.

The long black car soon picked up speed once they were out of the clutches of the city itself and heading towards Heathrow Airport.

Khalim, rather surprisingly, took out a laptop computer and sat tapping away at it for the entire journey, leaving Rose with little to do other than to pull out a book to read, which was at least a distraction from the unnerving presence of the man by her side.

She was reading *Maraban—Land of Dreams and Contrasts*, by Robert Cantle, a weighty book and, apparently, the definitive work on the country, which she'd bought on yesterday afternoon's shopping trip. She'd expected to have to wade through it, but she couldn't have been more wrong. It was, she thought to herself dreamily, absolutely *fascinating*.

Khalim glanced over at where she sat engrossed, and raised his dark brows.

'Not exactly what you'd call light reading,' he observed.

She heard the surprise in his voice. 'You expected me to sit flicking through magazines, I suppose?'

'Never suppose, Rose,' he returned softly. 'Never with me.'

In the confines of the luxurious car, his proximity overwhelmed her and she found herself edging a little further up the leather seat away from him. 'I'm enjoying it,' she told him solidly.

'You *do* take your work seriously, don't you?' he commented drily.

She looked up and treated him to a cool stare. 'Please don't patronise me, Khalim. The more I know about Maraban, the better I am able to do my job.'

He smiled, and settled back to his screen, thinking that Rose Thomas was proving to be much, much more than a pretty face. A *very* pretty face.

His eyes flickered to where one shapely thigh was outlined beneath an ankle-length skirt in a filmy, pale blue material which matched the simple cashmere sweater she wore. She'd dressed appropriately, he thought with pleasure.

He'd had many Western lovers, but none who seemed to have such a genuine interest in his country. Plenty who had *pretended* to, he remembered. His mouth hardened. But they had been the matrimonally ambitious ones, and as easy to spot as the glittering sapphire—as big as a swan's egg— which dominated the crown he would one day inherit.

He glanced out of the window, knowing that he would soon have to face the reality of his destiny. For that very morning had come news from Maraban that his father was frailer than before. Pain etched little lines on his brow as he acknowledged that the mantle of responsibility had slipped a little closer to his shoulders.

Would this be his last, delicious fling before it descended completely? he wondered.

Rose had never been on a private jet before and the interior of the Lear matched up to her wildest expectations. Most of the seats had been removed to provide a spacious interior, and two stewardesses were in attendance.

Very much in attendance, thought Rose grimly, suspecting that both had been chosen for their decorative qualities as much as for their undoubted efficiency. And both, like herself, were blonde—though these blondes had not had their colouring bestowed on them by nature.

Khalim introduced her to the pilot, who was obviously a fellow Marabanesh, and once they had effected a smooth take-off he turned to her, studying her mutinous expression with amusement.

'Does something displease you, Rose? Is something wrong?'

She certainly wasn't going to tell him that in her opinion the stewardesses could have done with wearing something which resembled a skirt, instead of a pelmet. She met his eyes, and once again her heart thundered in her ears. 'Wrong?' she managed, as smoothly as she could. 'What on earth could be wrong, Khalim?'

He had hoped that she was jealous; he wanted her to be jealous.

In fact, he had slept with neither of the attendants, even though it would have taken nothing more than a careless snap of the fingers to do so. He suspected that the two women would have been game for almost anything—and that even a *ménage à trois* would have been greeted with delight, instead of derision. But he would never have sullied himself with such a dalliance, even though he knew that many of his cousins enjoyed such debauchery.

'Shall we eat something?' he questioned as the taller of the stewardesses approached them.

She remembered what he had said to her in the restaurant. She'd never felt less like eating in her life, but to refuse would surely be an insult to his chef? 'Yes, please.'

'And we will drink mint tea,' he instructed.

'Sir.' The stewardess inclined her blonde head respectfully.

The two attendants began laying out a feast on the low, circular table. Rose looked down at the engraved bronze plates, enjoying the colour and variety of the different foods which they held—tiny portions which pleased the eye and tempted the palate.

'You like these things?' asked Khalim as he offered her a tiny pancake stuffed with cheese and doused with syrup, resisting the urge to feed her, morsel by morsel, then have her lick his fingers clean.

'I've never tried food like this before.' She bit into it. 'Mmm! It's yummy!'

'Yummy?' He smiled as he observed her, enjoying the unconscious sensuality of watching her eat. 'Then you have many pleasures in store, Rose,' he told her, his voice deepening as he thought of the ultimate pleasure she would enjoy with him.

Something in his voice drove all thoughts of food clean out of her mind, and she lifted her head to find herself imprisoned in the black gleam of his eyes. She put the half-eaten pancake down with fingers which were threatening to shake.

He hadn't touched a thing himself, she thought, as he chose just that moment to languidly stretch his long legs out, and the brush of the silk as it defined the muscular thrust of his thighs was positively *indecent*.

'Something is troubling you, Rose?' he murmured.

'Nothing,' she lied and directed her gaze to his chest instead, but that wasn't much better. She found herself imagining what his torso would be like without its silken covering—hard and dark, she guessed, with the skin lightly gleaming like oiled satin. 'N-nothing at all.'

He saw the swift rise of colour to her cheeks and the sudden darkening of her eyes. He could order everyone to clear the main salon now, he thought heatedly. And take her quickly before this hunger became much more intense.

But what if she cried aloud with pleasure? Sobbed her fulfilment in his arms as women inevitably did? Did he really want the two attendants exchanging glances as they listened at the door while he made hard, passionate love to her?

'Eat some more,' he urged huskily.

'I...I'm full.'

He glanced at his watch. 'Then I shall order for these plates to be removed—'

'And then you'll tell me all about Maraban's oil refinery?'

she put in quickly, because at least that would take her mind off things. Him.

The oil refinery? He threw her a look of mocking bemusement as he leaned back against the cushions. Never had a woman surprised him quite so much as Rose Thomas and surprise was rare enough to be a novelty! 'That is what you would like?' he questioned gravely.

'More than anything in the world!' she agreed fervently, but the gleam of discernment in the black eyes told her that they both knew she was lying.

He spoke knowledgeably for almost an hour, while Rose butted in with intelligent questions. The first time she asked him something, he raised his eyebrows in a look which would have made most people freeze and then retreat.

'I need to *ask* you these things,' explained Rose patiently, reminding herself that maybe it wasn't *his* fault that people usually hung on adoringly to every word he said.

'Such pertinent questions,' he conceded in a murmur.

'There you go again, patronising me!' she chided.

'That was not my intention, I can assure you.'

She paused, unsure whether to frame the question she *really* wanted to ask, and then remonstrating with herself for an uncharacteristic lack of courage. 'Khalim?'

His eyes narrowed, some instinct telling him that this was not another query about Maraban's oil output. 'Rose?' he returned softly.

'Just why *did* you want me to act as your head-hunter?'

He curved her a slow, almost cruel smile. 'I had to have you.'

Rose froze. 'You mean—'

He shook his head. 'I was informed that you were the best head-hunter in town—I already told you that.'

'Thank you.'

Her blue eyes shone a challenge at him and he found himself smiling in response. 'You also asked me whether I had employed you so that I could seduce you.'

Some of her customary grit returned and she didn't flinch beneath his mocking gaze. 'But you neatly avoided answering me, didn't you, Khalim?'

'Did I?'

'You know you did.'

He narrowed her a speculative glance, then shrugged. 'I can't deny that I find you beautiful, or that I want you in my bed, but—'

She sucked in a breath which was both shocked and yet profoundly excited. The men she knew just didn't *say* things like that! 'But what?'

'Sleeping with me isn't a prerequisite for landing the contract.'

'But will I get a bonus if I *do* succumb to your charms?' she asked flippantly.

Khalim's face darkened and he very nearly pulled her to him to punish her with a kiss which would dare her to ever mock him so again. But he stopped himself in time; instead, he forced himself to imagine how sweet the victory would be after such a protracted battle!

'Put it this way,' he warned her silkily, 'that as a man I will attempt to seduce you—no red-blooded Marabanesh would do otherwise.' A slow, glittering look. 'But you are perfectly within your rights to turn me down.'

Rose stared at him as she felt the irrevocable unfurling of desire, knowing that his words were iced with an implicit boast. That no woman Khalim attempted to lure to bed would ever be able to resist him.

And Rose had spent her life resisting men who saw her as just a trophy girlfriend, with her blonde hair and her bright blue eyes. Just you wait and see, Prince Khalim! she thought.

He was intrigued by the defiant little tilt of her chin, and his need for her grew. He controlled his desire with an effort and distracted himself by flicking another glance at his watch.

'Do you want to look out of the window?' he asked unsteadily. 'We're coming into Maraban.'

CHAPTER SIX

SUNLIGHT danced and shimmered across a wide expanse of water, and Rose was spellbound—enough to be impervious to the sudden build-up of tension which his silken words had produced.

'Water!' she exclaimed as the beauty of the scene below momentarily drove all her newly learned facts about the country straight out of her head. 'But I thought—'

'That you would be coming to a barren and desolate land with not a drop of water in sight?' he chided. 'That is the Caspian Sea, Rose, and the borders of Maraban lie on its Western shores.'

'Oh, but it's beautiful!'

'You seem to think everything *about* Maraban is beautiful,' he commented indulgently.

'But it is!'

He thought how wonderfully uninhibited her appreciation was, and how her eyes sparkled like the blue waters of the Caspian itself.

'Fasten your seat belt,' he murmured gently. 'The heat can sometimes make the landing turbulent.

But, in the event, their descent to Maraban was as smooth as honey, and as the plane taxied down the runway Rose could see a large number of men standing in line, all in flowing robes which fluttered in the small breeze created by the aircraft.

'Gosh, it's a deputation,' she observed.

Khalim leaned across her and glanced out of the window, and her senses were invaded by the subtle persuasion of sandalwood.

'I shall go out alone,' he told her. 'If you want to go and freshen up.'

'So you don't want to risk being seen with me, Khalim?' she asked wryly. 'Are you planning to smuggle me off the plane with a blanket over my head?

He wondered if she had any idea how privileged she was to accompany him in this way! If it had been anyone else, he would have flown them over separately. But he had not wanted to take the risk of her refusing to come…

'I don't imagine that you would wish to be subjected to the wild conjecture which your appearance would inevitably provoke.' His tone was dry. 'The less we announce your presence, the less tongues in the city will gossip.'

She got some idea then of how public his life had to be, and how rare the opportunity to play any of it out in private, and, in spite of everything, she felt her heart soften.

'Yes, of course. I understand.' She nodded. 'I'll go and freshen up as you suggested.'

He laughed. 'Why, Rose—that's the most docile I've ever heard you be!'

She put on a suitably meek expression. 'And you like my docility do you, Oh, Prince?'

The breath caught in his throat and dried it to sawdust and his heart clenched inside his chest. 'No. I like you fiery,' he told her honestly. 'You make a worthy combatant.'

Which pleased her far more than remarks about the colour of her hair or the sapphire glitter of her eyes. Her looks she'd been born with and were just the luck of the draw—her personality was a different matter. And if Khalim approved of certain facets of her nature…now, that really *was* a compliment!

Just don't get carried away by compliments, she reminded herself.

She enjoyed the luxury of the aircraft's bathroom, which contained the most heavenly sandalwood soap. Rose picked it up and sniffed it, her eyes closing for a moment. It smelt of *him*. She washed her hands and her face with it, and it was as though the essence of Khalim had seeped into her skin itself.

Stop it, she told herself as she brushed her hair and slicked on a little lipstick. You're walking straight into his honeytrap.

She stepped back to survey the results in the mirror, thinking that at least she *looked* cool and unflappable. Only the slightly hectic glitter of her eyes betrayed the fact that inside she was churned up by conflicting emotions—and the most disturbing one of all was the fact that Khalim was beginning to grow on her.

Grow on her? Who did she think she was kidding? Why, it was as if he had taken up root inside her mind and managed to invade most of her waking thoughts. Whatever had she thought about before Khalim had entered her life?

After twenty minutes, he returned to the aircraft, by which time Philip had joined her in the main salon.

'Rose and I will go in the second car with the bodyguard,' said Khalim imperturbably. 'Will you take the first car and prepare them at the palace for my arrival?'

'Of course.' Philip gave Rose a curious glance, before bowing to the prince.

'Why does he look at me that way?' asked Rose, after he had gone.

For a second he experienced a rare moment of indulgence. 'What way is that, sweet Rose?'

'You saw.'

Khalim sighed. Would the truth go to her head? Fool her into believing that her presence here had an ultra-special significance? Or a future?

'Because you are the first woman I have ever brought here to Maraban,' he admitted, on a growl.

She didn't react. 'Should I be flattered by that?' she questioned drily.

He found her coolness utterly irresistible. Even though it *was* rather galling to be shown nothing in the way of gratitude! 'I would not dare to presume it—not of you,' he murmured. 'Come, Rose—enough of this sparring—let me show you my country.'

The hot air hit her with a heated jolt, even though it was now September and Khalim informed her that the temperatures were already cooling down towards the icy winter which followed.

And the drive to the palace was a feast to the senses! Rose stared out of the limousine window with fascination at the scenes which unfolded before her. Maraban's capital was absolutely heaving with people and there were cars and carts and camels all vying for space along the congested roads of the city. She could see dusty boxes of oranges, and live chickens in a cage.

The main thoroughfare had obviously been cleared for Khalim's arrival, and she could see crowds jostling to catch a glimpse of the enigmatic profile through the smoked-glass window.

The palace was some way out from the main drag of the city, and Rose's first sight of it was unforgettable. In the distance, tall mountains reared up in jagged peaks, and against the cloudless blue cobalt of the sky stood the palace itself—gleaming purest gold in the honeyed light of the afternoon sun.

Rose was silent and Khalim looked at her, taken aback by the rapture which had softened her features into dreamy wonder.

'You like my home?' he asked, knowing deep down that such a question was redundant.

It seemed unbelievable that such an extraordinary building could ever be described by the comfortable word 'home'.

'How could I not like it?' she questioned simply.

Khalim's mouth hardened. Was she really as guileless as she seemed? Or was she cynically aware that her eyes were like dazzling blue saucers when she spoke with such emotion, their light lancing straight to his very heart?

He shook his head slightly in negation. He wanted her body, that was all.

That was all.

'Tell me what to expect when we arrive,' said Rose, wondering why he was scowling when all she had done was tell him she liked his home.

Sometimes, he reflected ruefully, she sounded as if *she* were the one expressing a royal command! 'My mother and sisters have their own section of the palace—we will join them for dinner and you will meet them then. You will have your own suite of rooms, and a girl will be assigned to look after your needs.'

'And your father?'

'My father lives in a different section of the building.'

She hesitated. 'Because he's sick, you mean?'

Khalim frowned. 'You are very persistent, Rose! No, not simply because he is sick—it is our royal custom. Princes of Maraban do not sleep with their women, not even their wives.'

Rose looked at him in disbelief. 'You mean that they just go and have *sex* with them, and then go back to their own apartments?'

'*Sometimes* they remain there for the night,' he informed her benignly, though he could not imagine leaving *her* alone for one precious second of the night.

'Lucky old them!' said Rose sarcastically.

'Actually,' he iced back, 'they *would* show gratitude, yes!'

'For being downtrodden, you mean?'

'I think you forget yourself, Rose!' he snapped.

'I think not! I am not your royal subject, Khalim! And if I have an opinion which happens to differ from yours—well, that's just *tough*!'

He had never felt so turned on by a woman in his life and the desire to kiss her was overwhelming. But by then the car was driving slowly into the inner courtyard where trees provided a welcome shade—the sunlight dappling through broad, verdant leaves. Khalim clicked his tongue with irritation as the chauffeur opened the door for her.

But when Rose alighted from the car, she was hit with the most unforgettable and heady fragrance, so powerful that it halted her in her tracks.

'What is that amazing scent?' she whispered, their disagreement forgotten.

A sense of destiny whispered disturbing fingers over his flesh. 'It is the fragrance of the roses which bloom in the palace gardens,' he murmured, watching as the sun turned her hair into a gold just a shade lighter than the palace itself. 'The sweetest scent in the world—but you must wait until the evening time, when the perfume is increased by a hundredfold.'

But as they walked side by side towards a pair of vast, ornate doors, he thought that no scent could be sweeter than the subtle perfume which drifted from her skin, more beguiling than any siren.

Robed figures awaited them, and Rose was introduced, certain that she would never be able to remember all these new and unusual names. The men all bowed courteously but she could detect flashes of curiosity on their hard, dark faces. I wonder if they approve of me, she thought, but then found Khalim's gaze on her face, more encouraging than she could have believed it would be, and she felt the warmth of his protection.

And all the while she felt that they were surrounded by other watchers, by unseen eyes. She caught a brief glimpse of a young woman, spectacularly clad in crimson silk, but when she turned her head to get a better look the woman had disappeared again.

Khalim followed the direction of her gaze. 'Fatima!' he called, and the young woman reappeared, only her eyes visible above a scarlet yashmak.

She performed an elaborate sort of bow, and Khalim said,

'This is Rose Thomas. I have brought her here to do a job for me. I want you to make sure that she has everything she needs. Say hello now, Fatima.'

'Good afternoon,' said Fatima, in a soft, halting English accent. 'I am pleased to meet you.'

Khalim laughed. 'Fatima is learning English!'

'I'm impressed,' said Rose gravely. 'And rather ashamed that my Marabanese only amounts to about five words.'

Khalim glimmered her an onyx gaze. 'I will teach you,' he promised softly. Oh, yes. He would teach her the many words of love. She would learn to please him in his own language. 'Now Fatima will show you to your rooms—and you shall bathe and change—then later I will come for you.'

She wanted to ask him exactly what he meant by such a masterful and yet ambiguous expression as that—*I will come for you*—but it didn't really seem appropriate, not with Fatima hanging onto every word. He probably meant that he would come to take her down for dinner. So why did that make her heart crash against her ribcage in disappointment?

'Come, please,' said Fatima, with a shy smile.

Rose followed her through a maze of silent marble corridors, thinking that unless she had a guide she would get hopelessly lost.

At last Fatima opened a set of double-doors leading into a large, cool room and Rose looked around her, her eyes feasting themselves on the richly embroidered cushions which were scattered over a wide, low bed covered in a throw of embroidered gold. A carved wooden chest stood in one corner, and the room smelt faintly of incense—though a bronze vase which was crammed full of crimson roses only added to the perfumed atmosphere.

One wall contained bookshelves and closer inspection showed a variety of novels and textbooks, some in Marabanese, but mostly in English. Well, at least she would not be bored!

The shutters were closed but Fatima went over to the window and opened them, and outside Rose could see a profusion of blooms of every hue and their scent drifted in to bewitch her.

The rose garden!

Had Khalim deliberately put her in here, to enchant her with their fragrance? To remind her of the flower she had been named after?

She shivered as a sense of the irrevocable washed cool temptation over her skin.

'You will bathe?' asked Fatima, and gestured towards a door leading off the enormous room.

'Yes, yes, please—I will.'

'And you wish me to assist you?'

Rose shook her head, and smiled, thinking how different Maraban hospitality was! 'No, thanks, Fatima—I'm used to managing on my own,' she answered gravely.

Fatima nodded and gave another shy smile. 'I will bring mint tea in an hour.'

'That will be wonderful. Thank you.'

After the girl had left, Rose went into the bathroom to find a deep circular bath, inlaid with exquisite mosaics in every conceivable shade of blue. There were fragrances and essences from Paris, and fluffy towels as big as sheets. East meets West, she thought with approval, and turned the taps on.

It was the best bath she had ever had. Lying submerged in scented bubbles in the high, cool splendour of the vaulted bathroom, she felt that the real Rose Thomas was a very long way away indeed. So why did she suddenly feel more *alive* than she had ever felt before?

By the time she had dried her hair, it was getting on for seven o'clock. When would Khalim come, and what should she wear for dinner? Would her gorgeous new evening gown make her look like some kind of houri?

In the end, she decided on a simple silk dress which brushed the floor when she walked. The sleeves were long and loose and it was the soft, intense colour of bluebells. Her hair she left loose and shining, and as she stared at herself in the long mirror she thought that she could not possibly offend anyone's sensibilities in such a modest gown.

Fatima came, bearing a bronze tray of mint tea. In true Eastern style, Rose settled herself on an embroidered cushion on the floor, and had just poured herself a cup when there was an authoritative rap on the door. Her heart began to thunder.

'Come in,' she called.

The door opened and there stood Khalim. He, too, had changed, and he must also have bathed, for his black hair was still damp and glittered with a halo of stray drops of water. His robes were coloured deepest claret—like rich, old wine—but his face looked hard, his expression forbidding as he quietly shut the door behind him.

'Do you always invite men so freely into your bedroom, Rose?' he questioned softly.

She put the cup down and looked up at him, knowing that she was not prepared to tolerate his insulting implication. Nor prepared to admit that she had known it was him, simply from the assertive way he had knocked on the door! She shrugged her shoulders in a devil-may-care gesture. 'Oh, they usually come in two at a time! At least!'

'Please do not be flippant with me, Rose!' he exploded.

'Well, what do you expect?' she demanded. 'I *presumed* that no one would come here, except for you! And I *presumed* that while I was here I would be under your protection, but maybe I was wrong!'

'No.' His voice was heavy. He was used to obedience, not passionate logic from his women. 'No, you were not wrong.'

'Well, then—don't imply that I am loose with my favours—'

'Rose—'

'And don't you *dare* make a value judgement about me, when you barely know me, Khalim!'

Barely *know* her? Why, his conversations with Rose Thomas had been more intimate than those he'd had with any other woman before! He felt he knew her *very* well, and he had certainly told her more about himself than was probably wise. His voice gentled as he slid onto a cushion opposite her. 'Do you want me to know you better, Rose?'

Shockingly, she did—she wanted him to know her as intimately as any man could. She wanted to see the contrast of his long-limbed dark body entwined with the milky curves of her own. She wanted to feel the primitive thrust of his passion, the honeyed wonder of his kiss. She stared down at the clear chartreuse colour of her mint tea, afraid that he would see the hunger in her eyes.

'Rose?'

His voice was beguiling, but she resisted it. 'What?'

'Look at me.'

Compelled to obey by the command in his voice, she slowly lifted her head to find herself dazzled by a gaze of deepest ebony.

The pink flush which had gilded her pale skin pleased him, as did the darkened widening of those beautiful blue eyes. 'Do you want me to know you better?' he repeated on a sultry whisper.

The question was laced with erotic expectation, and a passive side she never knew existed wanted to gasp out, Oh, yes. Yes, *please!* But such capitulation must be par for the course for a man like Khalim. She would never win his respect if she fell like a ripe plum into those tempting arms. And his respect, she realised with a start, was what she wanted more than anything.

His body he would give her freely; his deference would be a far more elusive prize.

'Obviously—' she forced a breezy smile '—we will get to know each other better during my stay here. I have no objection to that, Khalim.'

It was such a deliberate misunderstanding that, instead of

feeling indignant, he began to laugh softly. 'You wilfully misunderstand me, Rose,' he murmured. 'You are quite outrageous.'

How rare the sound of his laughter, thought Rose with a sudden pang of compassion. How often could a man like this really let himself go?

She smiled and lifted up one of the china cups. 'Tea, Khalim?' she enquired.

He was still laughing when they went down to dinner.

As he guided her through the maze of marble corridors towards the dining hall, Rose wondered how he had spent his afternoon. Would it seem prying if she asked? 'Have you seen your father yet?' she asked softly.

His face tightened with pain and if she could have wished the words unsaid, she would have done so.

'I'm sorry, I didn't mean to—'

'No.' He shook his dark head. 'We cannot ignore reality, however painful it is. Yes, I saw him.' He paused. He could not talk freely to his mother or his sisters about his father's failing health, for they would begin to weep inconsolably. Nor Philip either. Philip was a man, and men discussed feelings only with discomfort. But Khalim had a sudden need to express himself—to articulate his fears. This was death which he was soon to encounter and he had known no close deaths other than his grandparents' when he had been away at school in England.

'He is fading.' He forced himself to say the brutal words, as if saying them would give life to them. Or death to them, he thought bleakly.

'I'm so sorry.' For one brief moment he looked so vulnerable that she longed to take him in her arms and lay his proud, beautiful face down on her shoulder and to hug him and comfort him. But surely such a gesture would be misinterpreted—even if it *was* her place to offer him solace, which it certainly wasn't.

But then the moment was gone anyway, for the face had resumed its proud and haughty demeanour as he inclined his head in wordless thanks for her commiseration.

'Let us go and eat,' he said.

Dinner was a curious affair, made even more so by the fact that Rose felt as though she was on show—which she guessed she was. But even more curious was Khalim's mother's initial reaction to her.

Khalim ushered Rose into the room where a very elegant woman aged about sixty sat with her two daughters at the long, rectangular table.

The three women wore lavishly embroidered robes, and Rose noticed that Khalim's mother's sloe-shaped black eyes narrowed and her shoulders stiffened with a kind of disbelief as Rose walked rather nervously into the ornate salon. She said something very quickly to her son in Marabanese, and Khalim nodded, his eyes narrowing thoughtfully.

But once Khalim had introduced them, she relaxed with a graciousness which disarmed her and shook Rose's hand and bid her welcome.

'What should I call you?' asked Rose nervously.

'You should call me Princess Arksoltan.' His mother gave her a surprisingly warm smile. 'My son must respect your work very much if he has accompanied you to Maraban.'

Khalim scanned his mother's face, but it bore no trace of disapproval. And why should it? She knew him well, and, yes, he *did* respect Rose's professional skills. His mother also read voraciously and that had, in its way, made her outlook unusually unfettered by tradition.

Perhaps she suspected that he would consummate his relationship with Rose while she was here. But that would not worry her either—she was as aware as he was that he must marry a woman of Maraban blood. She would turn a blind eye to any dalliances which occurred before that marriage would take place. As soon it must, he reminded himself, remembering the prospective brides who had been paraded before him just before he had flown out for Guy's wedding.

A host of dark-eyed virgins, their faces concealed by their yashmaks. Young and exquisitely beautiful, not one had dared meet his eye. He had asked himself whether he found any of them attractive, and the answer had been yes, of course he did. A man would have to have been made of stone not to. But their inexperience and respect for his position would make them merely hostages to his desires. By definition, it would be a submissive and unequal marriage.

He looked at Rose, at the proud way she bore herself and the confidence with which she returned his stare. He felt the muffled acceleration of his heart and cursed it.

'And these are my two sisters,' he said huskily. 'Caiusine and Enegul.'

His two sisters were impossibly beautiful with black eyes and the thickest falls of ebony hair imaginable. And none of the women wore yashmaks, Rose noted in surprise as she took her place at the table, with Khalim on one side, his mother on the other.

Soundless servants brought platter upon platter of food, while candles guttered on the table, blown by the scented breeze which drifted in through the open windows.

'Will you drink wine, Rose?' Khalim asked her softly, watching the rise and fall of her breathing and the way it elevated her magnificent breasts.

She shook her head. 'I won't, thank you. I'll have what everyone else is having.'

Khalim poured her juice, silently applauding her for her diplomacy, while Rose chatted about the purpose of her trip in answer to his sisters' interested questions.

'Tomorrow we're going to the oil refinery,' she told them.

'And Khalim is letting *you* choose Murad's successor?' asked Enegul in astonishment.

Black eyes glittered at her through the candlelight and his

sister's question only crystallised what Rose had suspected all along.

'I think that Khalim has already decided who he wants to replace Murad,' said Rose slowly as the absurdity of the situation dawned on her. As if a man of Khalim's power would rely solely on *her* judgement! 'And I'm just here to confirm his decision.'

He felt the dry beat of desire. Obviously, she was nothing but a witch—well schooled in the art of sorcery! 'How very perceptive of you, Rose.'

'That's my job,' she answered sweetly.

'And what if you and Khalim disagree?' asked Arksoltan. Black clashed with blue in visual duel.

'Then it's whoever argues the case for their choice best, I guess,' said Rose.

'Khalim, then!' put in the younger sister loyally.

'Do not underestimate the power of Rose's debating skills,' came his dry response.

He accompanied her back to her room, and the corridors were echoing and silent, empty save for the ever-constant presence of his bodyguard who followed at a discreet distance behind them.

Her senses were full of him as they walked side by side. The whisper of the silk as it clung and fluttered around the hard, lean body and the faint drift of sandalwood from the warmth of his skin. But there was an unmistakable tension about him, and it had transmitted itself to her so that her breathing had become unsteady, her heart rate erratic as she thought of what *could* lie ahead.

Would he try to kiss her tonight? And didn't she, if she was being honest—and she spent her life trying to be honest—didn't she want that more than anything else?

'You have enjoyed your evening with my family, Rose?'

She nodded. 'I thought it very good of your mother to entertain me when she must be so worried about your father.'

'To be royal means to learn to hide your feelings.' He

shrugged. 'And it would be unforgivable not to show hospitality.'

She nodded, and thought of his mother's initial reaction to her. 'When I walked into the dining room, your mother looked…'

He stilled. 'What?'

'I don't know—shocked—surprised.' She shrugged. 'Something, anyway.'

'Is there anything which escapes those perceptive eyes of yours?' he demanded.

'And she said something to you, too—something in Marabanese which I couldn't understand.'

He nodded.

'What was it, Khalim?'

He gave a painful sigh, knowing that he could not be evasive with her, could not resist the sapphire appeal in her eyes. Was this destiny he was about to recount, or simply history? Coincidence, even? 'You bear a strong resemblance to a woman my great-great-grandfather knew.'

She stared at him, wondering what he wasn't telling her.

He seemed to make his mind up about something. 'Come with me,' he said, and changed the direction in which they were walking.

Intrigued, Rose quickened her step to match his. 'Where are you taking me?' she whispered.

'You will see.'

The chamber he took her to was so carefully hidden that no one could have found it, certainly not unless they were intended to. A small, almost secret chamber containing nothing other than books and a desk, with a carved wooden stool.

And a portrait.

'Look,' said Khalim, very softly, and pointed to the painting. 'Look, Rose. Do you see the resemblance now?'

The air left her lungs of its own accord, and Rose sucked in a shuddering gasp of astonishment.

A portrait of a woman, whose flaxen hair was contrasted

against a gown of crimson silk, her blue eyes capturing the viewer—mesmerising, bright blue eyes which seemed to see into your very soul. Her face was pale, almost as pale as Rose's own skin and she knew without a doubt that this was no Marabanesh woman.

'Wh-who *is* it?' she whispered, and she only just prevented herself from saying, Is it *me*?

'A woman that Malik loved,' he told her tonelessly.

'And lost?' she guessed.

He shook his head sadly. 'She was never his to be had, Rose,' he said. 'The cultural differences between them were too great. And they discovered that love, in this particular case, could not conquer all. She returned to America and they never saw one another again.'

'Oh, but that's terrible!' she breathed.

'You think so? It was the only solution open to them, my sweet, romantic Rose.'

She discerned in his voice the emphatic acceptance of his own destiny, and she didn't say another word as he ushered her out of the room and back towards her own apartments.

'We are here.' He stopped outside her door and stared down at her for one long moment. 'And now...' he was aware of the sudden rapidity of his breathing, the erratic thundering of his heart '...you must sleep, or...'

'Or what?' she asked breathlessly.

He didn't answer at first, just raised his dark hand to lift a strand of the blonde hair which rippled down over her shoulders. 'So pale. Pale as the moon itself,' he whispered.

She stared up at him, too excited to be able to say a single word, other than his name. 'Khalim?' And it came out like a prayer.

He looked down into her eyes, read the unmistakable invitation in them and felt a heady rush of triumph wash over him, knowing that she wanted him, that he could pin her up against the wall and make her his.

He felt himself grow exquisitely hard in anticipation, until he drew himself up short and reminded himself that this was no ordinary woman. She was more beautiful than most, for a start. And a woman like this would surely spend her life warding off advances from men. Not that she would ever reject *him*, of course—but how many times would she have been made to wait for something she wanted? To simmer with desire? Until the slow heat of need became unbearable and boiled over into a heated fire?

And hadn't he become curiously *intimate* with this Rose? Confided in her in a way which was unknown to him? He had heard men say that sex combined with intimacy was the most mind-blowing experience of all. Could he not taste that pleasure once, just once, before his inevitable marriage?

He curved his mouth into a slow, almost cruel smile as he bent his head and briefly touched his lips to hers, feeling her instinctive shudder of elation being quickly replaced by one of disappointment as he swiftly lifted his head away from hers.

'Goodnight, sweet Rose,' he said softly, resisting the soft, blue temptation of her eyes. And he turned back along the wide, marbled corridor, the shadowy figure of his bodyguard immediately echoing his movements, and she watched him go with a sense of disbelief.

Had she been mistaken, then? Imagining that Khalim's not-so-hidden agenda had been to seduce her? And she had actually *accused* him of that? Oh, Lord! She leaned her forehead against the cool of the wall, recognising that she had just succeeded in making a complete and utter fool of herself.

CHAPTER SEVEN

BUT by the time she was dressed the following morning, Rose had recovered most of her equilibrium. The morning sun always had a habit of putting things into perspective. Okay, so Khalim hadn't made a pass at her—why, she should be celebrating, not moping around the place! Falling into his arms—which she had been all too ready and willing to do last night—was a sure-fire recipe for a broken heart. Her head had already told her that in no uncertain terms.

His authoritative rap sounded just after nine, but she went through the pantomime of asking, 'Who is it?' and hearing the reluctant trace of amusement in his voice as he replied. 'Khalim.'

She opened the door to find the ebony eyes mocking her. 'Good morning, Khalim,' she said innocently.

'I see you learn your lessons well,' he told her softly as he scanned her face for the tell-tale signs of crying. But there were none, and he was taken aback by a sense of disappointment that she had not wept in the night for his embrace.

And Rose knew exactly what he was thinking! Had he hoped to find her despondent? she wondered wryly. 'That depends on whether or not I have a good teacher!' she murmured.

'And am I?' he purred. 'A good teacher?'

She walked past him, knowing how dangerous this kind of conversation could be if she allowed it to continue. The seductive tilt to his question made her want to melt into his arms, and that was *not* on his agenda—he had made that *quite* clear. 'It doesn't require a lot of skill to tell someone not to open the door without first finding out who's there!'

Khalim's mouth hardened. Such impudence! So—today

she was refusing to play the game, was she? He wondered anew why had he not tasted the pleasures she had been all too willing to offer him last night, tasted them over and over again until he had grown bored with them?

'Let us go and eat breakfast!' he growled.

'Lovely,' she murmured.

They broke bread and ate fruit on a terrace which overlooked the tiered rose-gardens and the scent and sight of the flowers were almost too distracting. Just as Khalim was. And where had her appetite gone? Rose picked undisinterestedly at a pomegranate and drank juice instead.

'You aren't hungry?' he demanded irritatedly, because of his restless night racked with frustrated dreams.

'It's too hot.'

Too *something*, he thought, shifting slightly in his chair as if mere movement could dispel the rapidly building ache of longing deep inside him. 'We shall drink some coffee, and then leave.' He glanced down her long legs which were modestly covered in sage-green linen, matching the short-sleeved safari shirt which gave no emphasis to the curve of her bosom beneath. 'I see you have worn trousers.'

'I knew you would not want me showing any flesh.'

He bit back his instinctive comment that she could show him as much flesh as she wanted, and whenever she wanted.

'And I didn't know if I would have to climb stairs at the refinery,' she continued animatedly. 'So I played safe.'

'Yes.' His pulse hammered as he imagined her walking upstairs, worrying about her modesty. Affording him the occasional tantalising view of lace panties. A pulse began to hammer at his temple. She *would* wear lace, he was certain of that. And once they were lovers he would buy her a tiny little skirt and she would wear no panties at all, and he would demand that she climb the stairs in front of him...

'Khalim? Is something wrong?'

Her face was an enchanting picture of genuine concern, and Khalim glared. 'Nothing is wrong!' he snapped as his erotic daydream didn't *quite* do the decent thing of leaving him alone. 'But the sooner we get out to the refinery, the better!'

They drank their coffee in uncomfortable silence and then walked around to the front of the palace, where two gleaming four-wheel drives sat awaiting them.

Khalim went to the first and opened the passenger door for her and Rose looked over her shoulder to see that the second vehicle had a burly and shadowy figure at the driving seat.

'Who's in the other car?' she asked as he climbed in and turned the key in the ignition and the second vehicle started its engine in synchrony.

'My bodyguard,' he said shortly.

The ubiquitous bodyguard! 'Doesn't your bodyguard have a name?'

He gave a thin smile. 'I am monitored twenty-four hours a day, three hundred and sixty-five days a year, Rose,' he said. 'There are a team of them—faceless, nameless and invisible to all intents and purposes. It is better that way—if I build a relationship with any of them then it makes me...' He had been about to say vulnerable, but changed his mind. Khalim *vulnerable*? Never! 'Familiarity makes them more accessible to bribery,' he compromised.

She tried to imagine being watched all the time. 'And don't you ever feel trapped?'

'Trapped?' He considered the question as he turned right onto a wide, dusty road surrounded by sand which was the pale silvery colour of salt. 'I have never known any different,' he explained slowly. 'Even at school, I had someone there, a figure always in the background.'

'But don't you ever want to break free?' she asked wistfully.

Her voice held a trace of disquiet, and something in the way her face had softened made Khalim feel a sudden overwhelming sense of regret for what could never be. 'This is freedom of a kind,' he said simply. 'To be alone in a car with a beautiful woman, here in Maraban.'

She thought about this as the car effortlessly negotiated the pock-marked road. 'Why have you never brought a woman here before? There must have been...' She tried to be sophisticated but, stupidly, her voice threatened to crack. 'Lovers.'

There had been women, yes—many lovers in his thirty-five years. So why was it that he could not picture a single one of their faces? Nor recall one conversation which had enthralled him enough to stay locked in his memory?

'My family and my people would disapprove if I flaunted Western permissiveness in their faces.'

Rose flinched at his choice of phrase, but his attention was on the dusty horizon ahead of them, and he did not notice. Did he classify *her* as a permissive Westerner, then?

He tried to give her a brief picture of his existence. 'I live two types of life, Rose. The man who jets around the world and wears suits and stays in all the major cities—he is not the same man who dwells here in Maraban.'

'A man of contrasts,' she said slowly. 'From a land of contrasts.'

He was unable to resist a slow smile of delight. 'A few hours in my country and already you are an expert!'

That smile tore at her heart. Wasn't he aware of its devastating impact? Didn't he know he could ask for the moon with a smile like that—and very probably be given it on a shining golden platter? It just wasn't fair, thought Rose as she stared sightlessly out at the unforgiving desert. 'That's another part of my job,' she said. 'I learn very quickly.'

He wondered what had made her renew that flippant tone, or to sit so rigidly in her seat, but at that moment he saw the gleam of reflected light which heralded the first view of the refinery.

'Look, Rose,' he urged softly.

She forced herself to look interested, forcing herself to put thoughts of Khalim out of her mind. He wasn't hers. He never *could* be hers. What would Kerry say if she knew that her finest head hunter was sitting staring dismally ahead like a lovesick schoolgirl?

But the smile she had pinned onto her face became genuine as she stared at the maze of silver towers and pipes which appeared on the stark horizon.

'It's so modern!' she exclaimed. 'Like a space-age city!'

'You imagined camels, did you?' he questioned drily. 'Robed figures rolling barrels of crude oil around?'

'Maybe a bit,' she admitted.

'Maraban's refinery is one of the world's finest,' he told her, with a quiet pride. 'It takes billions to build a refinery and millions to maintain. Cost-cutting inevitably leads to breakdowns in the system, and we must be one hundred per cent reliable if we are to stay ahead of our competitors.'

There was a tough, uncompromising note to his voice, and in that moment she realised that he was far more than just a figurehead. He was *involved*. Caring. Passionate. About his country and its industry, if nothing else.

The guards at the heavily barred security gates, who had obviously been alerted to their arrival, bowed and ushered them through and Khalim drew up outside the simple but beautifully designed main entrance. Huge tubs of fleshy-leaved shrubs gave a welcoming flash of green.

He turned to look at her, thinking how wonderfully cool she looked with her hair caught back in that sophisticate pleat. Almost aloof—like some exquisite ice maiden. An ice maiden he would one day make take fire, he vowed silently, and then cursed the answering kick of excitement in his loins.

'I have arranged for you to interview both men in the director's office.'

She nodded as she picked up her briefcase from the floor of the car. 'Good. I'll meet you afterwards.'

His smile was bland. 'I don't think you understand, Rose. I will, of course, be present during the interviews—'

'You will not.'

His eyes narrowed with displeasure. 'Quite apart from the fact that I am not used to having my wishes so flagrantly flouted—my family *own* this refinery. Any decisions will ultimately come back to haunt me. I should like to observe each man's interaction with you.'

'Fine.' Rose flashed him a fake-pleasant smile and put her briefcase back down on the floor just as Khalim jumped out of the vehicle and pulled her door open.

'Come on,' he said, seeing that she sat there, so still that she could have been carved from marble.

'I'm not going anywhere.'

Frustration and recognition of that stubborn streak of hers very nearly made him lose his temper. 'Oh, yes, you are,' he contradicted softly. 'I happen to be paying you to—'

'You're paying me to do a job!' she snapped. 'And I cannot do it properly if you happen to be sitting in the room like some great big spectre!'

'Spectre?' he repeated faintly. So she was openly insulting him now, was she?

'You're not just the boss—so to speak—you're their *ruler*, for goodness' sake! How can I expect them to answer me honestly, when all they'll be concerned about is saying what they think *you* want to hear?'

He glowered at her, because he knew she was right—and the only conclusion he could draw from that was that *he* was wrong. And he was never wrong! 'Are you getting out?' he asked dangerously.

'Not unless you agree to my terms,' she answered sweetly.

There was a short, tense silence. He wondered what would happen if he exercised his royal prerogative and picked her up and carried her to the director's private dining room and ravished her there and then? And then shook his head in disbelief at the answering throb of need his thoughts had produced.

Was she going to drive him *insane*, this Rose Thomas?

'Very well,' he agreed tightly. 'It shall be as you wish.'

'Thank you,' she said, but as she slid from the car he caught her wrist, bringing her up close so that black eyes dominated her vision, burning like coals brought up from the depths of hell. And she shivered in response to his touch, even though the temperature was soaring.

'You may find me a far more daunting adversary than you imagine, Rose,' he warned her softly.

Something in his face told her they weren't talking oil refineries now and excitement and fear fused in the pit of her stomach. 'But we aren't fighting any more,' she protested.

'Now you've got your own way, you mean?' he mocked. 'Oh, yes, we are. We've been fighting one way or another since the moment we first met.' And maybe there was only one way to get this confounded conflict out of his system once and for all. He felt another heated tug of desire, provoked by the irresistible darkening of her eyes.

She stared at him. And the stupid thing was that all she wanted right then was for him to kiss her. To kiss her and never stop kissing her. 'K-Khalim?' she said falteringly, shaken by the depths of his anger—an anger which was surely disproportionate to the crime of having the courage to stand up to him? Especially when her professionalism was at stake.

'Come inside,' he said with silky menace as he steeled his heart to the appeal in her eyes, 'and I'll introduce you.'

He showed her into the director's office, which looked like any other high-ranking executive's hidey-hole, with the exception of the pictures on the wall which were both exotic and vaguely erotic. And the desk looked like something out of a museum, with its dark, old wood inlaid with gold.

'Murad Ovezov, the present incumbent, has agreed to speak to you first. He should be able to give you a good idea of what the job entails.'

She hated this new coldness in his eyes, the new *distance* in his attitude towards her. Well, tough! He had hired her to do a job, and do it she would—to the very best of her ability. And that definitely did not include having his powerful and disapproving person present at the interviews!

She gave him a cool smile. 'Thank you, Khalim—you can send him in now.'

It was *unbelievable*, he fumed as he went off to find Murad. She was dismissing him like a servant! She answered him back! Well, she would not be answering him back for much longer. Soon she would be agreeing to everything he said! He would satisfy her as no other man had, and she would be enchained to him for ever!

Murad Ovezov was a man of sixty years, and, although age had painted its inevitable lines around his black eyes, he still exuded a certain *power*. He had worked at the Areeku refinery since it had opened, gradually working his way up until he held the highest position within the factory.

'It's very good of you to see me,' said Rose politely.

He gave a wary bow. 'I was not expecting intervention,' he said, in faultless English.

'I think that you and Khalim have probably decided for yourselves who you wish to replace you.' She smiled, noticing him start when she used the prince's first name. 'I'm here as the fail-safe mechanism—a third party often sees different qualities. Or failures.'

He nodded in comprehension. 'Where would you like to begin?'

She spent half an hour with Murad and then Serdar Kulnuradov was brought in. He was aged forty, confident and knew the refinery inside out. He quoted figures and projections with such fluidity that Rose was left reeling with the breadth of his knowledge.

'Thank you for your time,' she said as he stood up to leave.

Serdar gave a short bow. 'It is my pleasure.' He paused. 'Though it is not usual in Maraban to be interviewed by a woman.'

'Especially a foreign woman?' suggested Rose, with a wry smile. 'I can imagine.'

Oraz Odekov was ushered in next—and a different breed of man entirely. For a start he was aged just thirty and Rose's line of questioning produced quite different answers from those of Serdar.

'And how do you see the future of Areeku?' she asked him at the end of the interview.

And where Serdar had basically said that he wanted more of the same, Oraz was concerned with minimising the effects of pollution.

'You think that's important?' enquired Rose.

'I know so,' he answered simply. 'That is the way of the world today. Countries who do not fight to keep the planet clean will ultimately be discriminated against.'

'Thank you,' she said, and scribbled it down.

He hesitated by the door, and his handsome young face gave a small smile. 'May I be so bold as to say how refreshing it is to have a woman involved in the selection procedure? This, too, is the way forward.'

Go and tell Khalim that, thought Rose irreverently as she smiled back.

Khalim appeared just seconds later. Had he been waiting out in the corridor? thought Rose in wonder. Like a boy waiting outside the headmaster's study.

'Made your mind up?' he asked.

Well, he was certainly to the point when it came to business, thought Rose with some admiration.

'Yes.'

'And?'

'It has to be Oraz.'

There was silence. 'Because he's young and good-looking, I suppose?'

'Please don't insult me, Khalim!'

He sighed. 'Because Serdar is set in older ways than yours and because you are a feminist, is that it, Rose?'

She looked at him steadily. 'I never bring my own personality or prejudices into the selection process—whether or not *I* think I could get on with them is irrelevant. I'm not going to be here, am I? And please don't start calling me a "feminist", Khalim, especially in that derogatory tone.'

'Oh?' His eyes held a mocking challenge. 'You're saying you're not?'

'I'm saying that I don't like labels! Of any kind! I'm just a woman, who believes in equality, that's all.'

The very *last* kind of woman he should be attracted to! And yet he was intelligent enough to realise that her unsuitability was part of what *made* her attractive to him. Her lively mind and keen wit and her refusal to be cowed were qualities he was unused to. Qualities which were proving more aphrodisiac than plump oysters!

'So you're in a dilemma now, aren't you, Khalim?'

He looked at her from between narrowed eyes. Had the minx now managed to read his mind? 'A dilemma?' he stalled.

'Of course. You clearly want Serdar to be the next director, while my advice to you is to appoint Oraz.'

'Because?'

'You want my reasons?'

His smile was coolly assessing. 'That *is* what I'm paying you for.'

She didn't react, but why should she? He spoke nothing but the truth. She *was* here on a professional basis—solely on a professional basis, she reminded herself—and he *was* paying.

'Okay. Serdar has the greater experience, I grant you that, but Oraz has vision. A vision to carry the Areeka well into the middle of this century, and to make it a refinery to be reckoned with.'

He smiled again. 'My very sentiments.'

She stared at him a moment before the gleam in his black

eyes told her exactly what he meant. 'You mean…that you *agree* with me?'

He sighed, almost wishing that she had chosen contrary to his own instincts. 'Yes, Rose. I am entirely in accordance with your wishes.' He glanced at his watch. 'Now let me take you back to the palace for lunch, and afterwards…'

His words tailed off in a silken caress and Rose's heart began to pound uncomfortably in her chest.

'Afterwards?' she asked, relieved that her voice didn't sound *too* eager.

'Afterwards I shall take you riding.'

'I don't ride.'

There was something sensual and uncompromising in his answer.

'But I do,' he said.

CHAPTER EIGHT

THE stables were almost like palaces themselves—huge and cavernous and completely spick and span. Rose knew little of horses, but she knew enough to realise that these bright-eyed animals were well cared for. And that the black stallion whose ear Khalim was tickling—surprisingly gently—was like no other horse she had ever seen, with its fine, narrow body, long legs and slender neck.

'What an unusual creature,' she breathed.

He paused mid-stroke, and Rose found herself wondering what it would be like to have those long, sensuous fingers stroking *her* with such a light caress.

He had changed from his silk robes into close-fitting jodh-purs and a gauzey white shirt, and had borrowed a similar outfit from one of his sisters for Rose. She thought that now he looked like some tousled buccaneer—wild and carefree. Contrasts again, she thought as she watched him.

'This is an Akhal-Teke,' he purred. 'One of the oldest breeds in the world—bred and raced for almost three thousand years. These horses are prized for their desert hardi-ness—with their remarkable endurance and resistance to heat.'

A sense of history and longevity wrapped dreamy arms around her, and her voice was dreamy as she asked, 'And is this *your* horse?'

'Yes, indeed.' His voice deepened with pleasure. 'This is Purr-Mahl. The name means literally, "Full Moon"—'

'And he was born by the light of it, I presume?'

'You presume correctly, Rose.' He smiled. 'I sat and watched the birth, saw the contrast between the silvery-pale

gleam of the moon and the night-dark colour of the foal, and
I named him there and then. Come, let me sit you upon him.'

'But I don't ride, I told—'

Her protest was already lost on the warm, sultry breeze as
he swung her up into his arms, and she wished that he could
carry on holding her like that for ever, but he carefully placed
her in the saddle instead.

'Press your thighs hard against his body,' he urged and
felt a renewed awakening of need. 'Let him know you are
there.'

She did as he instructed while he took the reins and led
the horse out into the yard where a bodyguard stood, his face
inscrutable in the glaring heat of the sun.

Khalim led her round and round the yard for a while and
then he murmured something in his own language to the
bodyguard, who gave a small bow in response.

Picking up a small leather bag, which he slung over his
shoulder, he led her out through the gates to where the stark,
shimmering vista of the desert awaited them, with the vast
mountains dominating the skyline.

'What did you say to the bodyguard?' she asked him curiously.

'Just that you did not ride, and that I wanted to show you
the view from the gate. He is new,' he added casually.

He led the horse a little way into the silvery-white sand,
and then suddenly, without warning, he sprang up behind her,
and pulled her close into his body at the same time as he
seized the reins to urge the horse forward with a murmured
word of command and a light slap to the shank.

And they were off!

'Khalim!' Her startled word streamed out like the wind
which whipped through her hair.

'Do not be frightened, sweet Rose,' he murmured against
her windswept hair.

But it was not fear she felt, it was something far closer to
exhilaration. He held her tightly against the hard, lean column

of his body, and he handled the horse with such control and mastery that Rose instinctively felt safe.

Safe? Was she mad? Galloping full-pelt across an unforgiving landscape towards the mountains with this dark, enigmatic prince who was taking her who knew where?

Yes, safe. As if this was somehow meant to be. As though all along this had been meant to happen.

As the mountains grew closer, time and distance lost all meaning for her, she had no idea how far they had ridden, or for how long, when, just as suddenly as he'd begun, he steered the horse to a halt in some kind of valley.

Rose could see fig plants and forests of wild walnut trees. And surely down there was the silver glimmer of water?

He jumped down from Purr-Mahl and held his arms up to her and there was a moment of suspended silence while she stared into the enticing glitter of those ebony eyes before sliding down into his arms.

'Sweet Rose,' he said softly.

Had she thought he would kiss her then? Because she was wrong. Instead he took her by the hand and led her towards where she thought she had seen water, and indeed it was, with dense dark thickets of green growing alongside.

He sat down where it looked most hospitable, and patted the ground beside him.

This is a dream, thought Rose. *This is a dream.* And why not? Was Maraban not the land of dreams as well as contrasts?

He pointed to the distant peak of one of the towering mountains.

'When I was a boy,' he said, and his voice softened with memory, 'my father and I used to wait for the first thaw of spring to melt the snow on those mountain peaks, and to flow down to swell the icy river. And we would ride here and drink the crystal waters from a goblet—'

'Why?'

He turned and smiled, and she had never thought that he

could look so impossibly carefree. 'Just for the hell of it.'
He shrugged, sounding as English as it was possible to be.
He took the leather bag from his shoulder and drew out a
small golden goblet, studded with rubies as wine-dark as the
robes he had been wearing the other night. 'Always from this
goblet.' He smiled.

Rose took it from him and studied it, turning it round in
her hands. 'It's very beautiful.'

'Isn't it? Thousands of years ago my ancestors carried it
along with many other treasures, when they trekked to this
fabled mountain oasis to establish their kingdom.'

But even as he painted beauty with his words, he also
painted sadness. For in that moment Rose gleaned some
sense of his tradition, his history. He was not as other men.
He could not make the same promises as other men. She'd
been right from the very first when she had said to Lara that
he was not able to offer commitment. And as long as she
could accept that…

He put his hand inside the bag again, and drew out a flask
in the same gold and claret-coloured jewels as the cup.
'When I was seventeen, he brought me here as usual, only
this time we did not drink water; we drank wine.' He smiled.
'Rich, Maraban wine, made from the wild grapevines which
grow in the mountain valleys.' His eyes grew soft. 'Will you
drink some wine with me, Rose?'

She knew a little then how Eve must have felt when the
serpent had offered her the apple, for the question he asked
was many-layered. 'I'd love to.'

He tipped some of the ruby liquid into the cup and held it
up to her lips. 'Not too much,' he urged gently. 'For Maraban
wine is as strong as her men.'

She closed her eyes as she sipped and felt its warm richness invade every pore of her body, and when she opened
them again it was to find Khalim staring at her with such a
transparent look of hunger on his face that she started, and a

droplet of wine trickled from her lips and fell with a splash onto her wrist.

It lay there, a tiny crimson-dark star against the whiteness of her skin and they both stared at it.

'Like blood,' said Khalim slowly. 'The rose has a thorn which draws blood.'

She raised her head and so did he and the look they shared asked and answered the same question, and the goblet fell unnoticed to the ground as he bent his head to kiss her.

Her lips fell open to his velvet touch and she heard herself making a little sound of astonished delight, because she had wanted this for so long. Oh, too long. Much, much too long.

He tangled his fingers in the silken stream of her hair and deepened the kiss. 'Rose,' he groaned against his sweet plunder of her mouth and they fell back against the coarse, desert grass. 'Beautiful, beautiful Rose.'

Her fingers greedily explored the magnificent musculature of his torso through the thin, billowing shirt he wore, kneading her hands against his back as though he were the most delicious kind of dough.

Khalim felt that he might explode with wanting. But more than that—he knew that this woman above all others deserved his honesty. And that had to come now, before it was too late.

He lifted his head from hers and gazed down at her, feeling the heated flush of desire as it snaked its way across his cheekbones. Saw her matching response and the longing which darkened her eyes into twin eclipses.

He drew a long, shuddering breath. 'I have to tell you something,' he began unsteadily.

But Rose was proud. And she was also perceptive—they both knew that. She shook her head. 'I know.'

'You can't know!' he protested.

She wanted to say it *her* way—because she suspected that his words could wound her more deeply than any dagger. 'There can't be any future for us; I know that. This is this, and nothing more than this, and I mustn't read anything else into it.' She actually smiled at his expression of perplexity, recognising that this was a man who was used to calling the shots! 'Don't worry, Khalim,' she finished huskily. 'I won't.'

He shook his head and made a silent curse. By withdrawing emotionally, as she had just done so neatly, she had succeeded in making him want her even more! Impossible! And his need was made all the more poignant by knowing that he could never really have her!

She saw the look of pain etched on his features, and lifted a wondering hand to smooth it down over the hard jut of his jaw. 'Khalim?' she questioned softly. 'What is it?'

He gave a muffled groan as he bent to kiss her neck, his fingers moving to swiftly unbutton her thin shirt, his groan deepening as his hands found and cupped the curved perfection of silk-and-lace-covered breasts.

He peeled the shirt open and levered himself up to stare down at her, his eyes as wild and as black as the stallion they had just ridden. He didn't speak another word until he had slithered down the jodhpurs past her ankles and impatiently removed each sock, until she was lying there in just her bra and panties.

'Lace.' He swallowed as his gaze raked from her face, down over her bosom, and down further still until it came to rest with rapt fascination at the flimsy little triangle of silk and lace which was all that kept him from her greatest treasure. 'I always knew you would wear lace, Rose.'

'And you?' She turned the tables as she reached her hand up and scraped her fingernails against his nipples through the white voile of the billowing shirt. 'What about you, Khalim?'

He was used to complete mastery. 'Me?' he questioned unsteadily, an unmistakable note of surprise in his voice. 'What about me, Rose?'

'Take it off,' she ordered softly.

Her words sent the blood coursing heatedly around his veins. 'Is that a…command?' he demanded unsteadily.

She revelled in the sense that something here was different for him. 'It most certainly is.'

The sight of her head pillowed on the flaxen satin of her hair, and her big blue eyes and soft pouting mouth, was almost as much of a turn-on as her near-naked body. Khalim began to unbutton his shirt with fingers which threatened to tremble.

'You have me in your thrall, sweet Rose—see how my hands shake,' he murmured as the shirt was flung onto the desert scrub. 'Now name your next command.'

'Take it off,' she instructed, revelling in the heady sensation of having such power over this man. *This* man.

'What?' But the attempted tease came out in a kind of strangled plea.

'Everything.'

His long black riding boots were kicked off, and then he fingered the button of his jodhpurs, seeing from the automatic thrusting of her breasts that she was hurtling towards a stage of almost unbearable excitement. You and me both, he thought, with a helpless kind of rapture.

He made his undressing as slow and as deliberate as he could, and Rose was shocked, startled and unbearably aroused to see that he wore nothing beneath the jodhpurs, absolutely nothing. Nothing to disguise the awesome power of his erection. She swallowed, wondering whether... whether...

He read the expression in her eyes as the jodhpurs joined the shirt. 'You worry that I am too much of a man for you?'

She laughed in soft delight at the arrogant boast. 'Maybe you worry that I am too much of a woman for you!'

For answer he pulled her panties down with more speed than grace, and then his hand reached behind her to unclip her bra with one deft movement, freeing the tumultuous splendour of her breasts.

He took one breathless look at her nakedness, before coming to lie on top of her, dipping his head to suckle greedily at her breasts, his fingers moving between her thighs to flick at her slick heat.

Rose's head fell back. 'Oh! Khalim!'

'You want me to stop?' he suggested, lifting his head away from her nipple so that she almost fainted with disappointment.

'Yes! No!'

'What, then?'

'I want to savour it. Savour you.' She wanted this feeling to go on and on and on and never stop. Khalim *hers*, in her arms, as she had dreamed of him being since the moment she had first seen him.

'Next time,' he promised. 'This has been too long in the waiting. Now we will satisfy our hunger—later we will attend to the feast.'

She felt the caress of his fingers and shuddered. 'This is feast enough, Khalim.' She sighed. 'Feast enough.'

'Oh, Rose.' He smiled as her body responded instinctively to his touch. 'Sweet, beautiful Rose.'

But he could wait no longer, his desire for her too intense to bear. In that moment just before the communion of their bodies, he felt as though he were about to embrace life in a way in which he had never embraced it before.

He parted her thighs with eager hands and she felt the unbelievable power of him moving against her. Surely it was too soon? Surely she was not ready? But she dissolved into honeyed heat at just that first touch, and her thighs parted wider of their own accord and as he took one long, sweet thrust he made a low moan.

He filled her in every way he could—physically, mentally, emotionally. Joined in a fundamental flow, while the hot desert sun beat down on them, he was no longer Prince Khalim and she no longer Rose Thomas, the woman of his employ. Now he was just a man, and she was just a woman, locked in the most basic rhythm of all.

She couldn't remember the kisses, or the murmured things

he whispered in her ear—some in English and some in a far more thrilling foreign tongue which she recognised as Marabanese. She only knew that the stars were beckoning her, that her world was about to explode.

And his.

He lifted his head to stare down at her, as helpless at that moment as he had ever been, sensing her release in conjunction with his own.

And then it happened, on and on and on, until their cries were replaced by the soft sound of the desert wind, their stricken breathing calming at last and their sweat-sheened bodies glued together.

Rose felt her eyelids drifting downwards, but he shook her awake.

'No, Rose,' he murmured. 'You must not sleep.'

'*Must* not?' she questioned automatically, even as a lazy yawn escaped her.

He smiled, but it was a rueful smile. Even in the midst of their mutual pleasure—still she challenged him! He kissed his finger and placed it over her lips to silence her. 'They will come for us very soon,' he said.

That had her sitting up immediately, and she saw his eyes darken at the unfettered movement of her bare breasts. 'Who will? When?'

'My bodyguards.' He shrugged, leaning over to rescue her discarded panties and bra.

She shook the stray grains of sand out of her underwear and turned to glare at him. 'And they'll know where to find you, of course?' she demanded crossly. 'This is the usual location for your little *trysts*, is it?'

'Rose, Rose, Rose,' he murmured. 'Fiery, beautiful, argumentative Rose! I have never brought a woman here before—'

No, of course he hadn't. No other Western woman had ever accompanied him to Maraban. And no Maraban woman would have cavorted with such abandon on the ground with the heir to the throne.

'How will they find us, then?' She stood up and pulled her panties all the way over her slender thighs, enjoying the brief look of frustration which clouded his eyes. 'Are they clairvoyant, or something?'

He zipped up his jodhpurs with difficulty. Impossible that she should have aroused him again so quickly, but somehow…somehow, she had. 'They will follow the trail of the horse,' he said shortly, and roughly pulled his shirt on.

Rose was struggling into her clothes. 'What must I look like?' she moaned. 'Won't they take one look at us and know exactly what we've been doing?'

He gave a rueful shrug. Rose cherished honesty, didn't she? Then honesty she would have. 'They would take one look at you and think that I was the worst kind of fool if we had *not* been doing what they suppose.'

'Oh!' Her cheeks were burning. 'And what will they think of me?'

He gave her a cool, steady look. 'Do you seek the approval of my bodyguards?' he questioned. 'Or my approval?'

'Neither!' she snapped. 'I'm thinking about my professional reputation!'

'But your job is done. You are here now as my guest. My *lover*.' He lingered on the last word with a sense of treasures to come, and then looked at her with a question glittering from his black eyes. Would she voice her objection to the term of possession without any promise of commitment?

But Rose simply stared back at him without regrets. She had given herself to him freely. Completely. In a way she had given herself to no man before. She had never known that love-making could be that intense, that profound, that…*fundamental*. She shivered with the memory.

And he had not told her lies. On the contrary, he had been totally open with her. Had told her before he'd made love to her that there could be no long-term future—and she had accepted that and given herself to him as he had given himself to her.

So why not enjoy these exotic fruits of temptation for as long as they were available? To treasure and store up memories which would see her into old age. For she knew without a doubt that no man could ever follow Khalim.

'Will you be my lover, Rose?' he asked softly.

She opened her mouth to speak just as she heard the dry beat of hooves on the sand, and looked up into the distance to see four horsemen on the horizon, galloping fast towards them.

And then she smiled, deliberately enticing him with a slanted look of remembered pleasure. 'Yes, Khalim. I will be your lover.'

CHAPTER NINE

ROSE felt as though she had been taken prisoner on the ride back to the Palace.

There had been a short, sharp exchange between Khalim and a man she had never seen before, a formidable-looking man in rich robes, whose bearing immediately distinguished him as someone of substance. Rose couldn't understand a word of what they were saying, but she guessed that the man's quietly restrained anger was an admonishment to Khalim for breaching security.

Khalim lifted her gently onto his mount and she held on tightly to his waist, longing to turn her head and to steal a glance at him, but she resisted, relieved when the golden gleam of the palace came into view.

Khalim dismounted and lifted her down, and in one single, suspended moment their eyes met and in his she read, what…?

Longing. Yes. And surely a brief dazzle of tenderness. But something else, too—something which stirred a wistful fear deep inside her—for wasn't that regret there? A regret which told as clearly as words would have done that she must accept the limitations of their affair. And never hope.

'I'll see you to your rooms,' he said in a low voice.

The man in the rich robes said something and Khalim turned his head and made a snapped reply.

'Come!' he said to Rose, and led her through the courtyard and into the palace.

'Who was that man?' she asked him once they were out of earshot.

'My cousin, Raschid,' he said.

'He's angry with you?'

Khalim allowed himself a small smile. 'Furious,' he agreed. But making love to Rose had been worth any amount of fury.

'And will you get into trouble?'

He raised his dark brows. 'I think not. I am the prince, after all,' he said autocratically.

He spoke with an arrogance that no other man could have got away with, thought Rose, guiltily acknowledging the thrill of pleasure that his mastery gave her. 'Of course you are,' she murmured.

They reached her rooms and he paused, reaching his hand out to cup her chin, wanting to kiss her above all else, and to lay her body bare once more. He bit down the dull ache of frustration.

'I will have food sent to you here for I cannot be with you this evening,' he told her shortly.

She opened her eyes very wide as her heart pounded with disappointment, but she was damned if she would let it show. 'That's a pity,' she said calmly.

A *pity*? Had he thought she would beg him to stay? Or interrogate him about where he was going? And didn't her lack of jealousy make him want her all the more? 'But I will come to you later, sweet Rose.'

'I might be asleep.'

'Then I will wake you,' he said on a silken promise, and he planted a sweet, hard kiss on her mouth before sweeping away.

Rose slowly got out of her rumpled clothes and took a long, scented bath before slipping into a pair of pure white trousers made out of finest cotton-lawn, and a little shirt of the same material.

Fatima appeared with a tempting array of food—a type of tomato stew with baby okra and lamb accompanied by a jewel-coloured rice dish. And a platter of pastries, glistening with syrup and stuffed with nuts and raisins. There was pomegranate juice and mint tea to drink.

But once she had gone, Rose only picked uninterestedly at the dishes on offer.

How could she concentrate on something as mundane as food, when her mind and her senses were filled with the memory of Khalim and his exquisite love-making? He had been everything. Tender and yet fierce. His kisses passionate and cajoling. He had moaned aloud in her arms, had not held back on showing her his pleasure—and that in itself felt like a small victory.

With disturbing clarity she recalled the vision of their limbs entwined, his so dark and so muscular, contrasting almost indecently with her own milky-white skin, and then she sighed, wondering if she would ever be able to concentrate on anything other than her Marabanesh prince ever again.

More as diversion therapy than anything else, she picked up Robert Cantle's book on Maraban, and read the chapter on Khalim's forefathers, and the establishment of the mountain kingdom.

There were richly painted portraits of his recent ancestors—and one in particular which had her scanning the page avidly. Malik the Magnificent, she read. It was him! Khalim's great-great-grandfather whose thwarted love had borne such a striking and uncanny resemblance to Rose herself.

She studied a face almost as proudly handsome as Khalim's with its hard, sculpted contours and those glittering black eyes and luscious lips, and she sighed again. Don't start getting all hopeful, Rose, she told herself fiercely. You could not have had it spelt out more explicitly that love affairs like this have no future.

At eleven, she put the book down, telling herself that he would not come tonight. She began pulling the brush through her hair, telling herself not to be angry, but she *was* angry. Was this a taste of things to come? How he thought he could treat his women? Keep them hanging around *at his convenience*?

She flung the hairbrush down just as the door slowly

opened, and there stood Khalim in robes of deepest sapphire, his eyes narrowing with undisguised hunger as he caught the unmistakable outline of her body through the thin material of her clothes.

Rose bristled. 'I didn't hear you knock.'

'That's because I didn't,' he said, shutting the door softly behind him.

'Why not?'

He stilled as he heard the reprimand in her voice, and he turned to meet the blue blaze of accusation which spat from her eyes. 'Because we are now lovers, Rose. This afternoon you gave yourself to me with an openness which suggested that we have no need for barriers between us. Do I need to knock on your door?'

The voice of reason in her head told her to back off, but she had missed him, wanted him, and felt hurt by his unexplained disappearance, and so she ignored it. 'Damned right you need to knock!' she retorted. 'I may be mature enough to realise that this is a very grown-up affair with no promises or expectations on either side—but that does not mean that I'm prepared to be trampled on like some sort of chattel!'

If he hadn't wanted her so much, he would have walked out there and then. No woman had ever spoken to him with such a flagrant lack of respect—especially when he had had her gasping and sighing in his arms on the desert grass!

'I do not treat you as a chattel,' he answered coldly.

'No? You just make love to me and then waltz off for the evening without bothering to tell me where you are going?'

He hid a smile. Ah! So she was *jealous*, was she? Good! 'But you just told me that neither of us have any expectations, Rose,' he demurred.

'That's not an expectation!' she declared wildly, wondering where all her powers of logic had flown to. 'That's just simple courtesy. Where were you?'

He had been foolish to imagine that he would not have to tell her. He had not wanted to hurt her, but now he saw that by not telling her he must have hurt her more. He was not used to analysing what effect his actions would have on a woman's feelings. Usually, he did what the hell he liked, and was allowed to get away with it. With anything.

'I had dinner with my mother and my father,' he said softly. 'My father is too frail to accommodate—' he very nearly said 'strangers' but bit the word back in time '—guests,' he finished heavily.

Rose stared at him. 'And that's all? Why didn't you tell me that?'

She would never be able to find out, and yet Khalim realised that if he was anything less than truthful with his fiery Rose, he would lose her.

'No, that isn't all.' He sighed. 'There was a young woman there, too.'

Rose froze as some new and unknown danger shimmered into her subconscious. 'I'm not sure that I understand what you mean.'

'My father is very frail—'

'I know that.'

'Soon he will die,' he said starkly, and there was a long, heavy pause. 'And I must take a bride when the year of mourning is complete.'

It was the most pain she had ever felt and she felt like smashing something—anything—but somehow, miraculously, she managed to keep her face composed. Why crumple when this was what her instincts and her common sense should have told her? 'And this—young woman—was, I presume, one of the *suitable* candidates being lined up for you?'

How preposterous it sounded coming from his beautiful, English Rose! 'Yes.' He thought back to the girl being brought in by her mother, her slim, young body swathed in the finest embroidered silks. Only her eyes had been visible, and very beautiful eyes they had been, too—huge, and doe-like, the deep rich colour of chocolate.

But she had been tongue-tied at first, and then so docile

and submissive—so adoring of her prince and heir. He had seen his mother's approving nod, and the sharp look of pleasure on the face of the girl's mother, and had tried to imagine being married to a woman such as this.

She would bear him fine Marabanesh sons and in time she would grow fat and he would grow bored. Had his mother and his father noticed his distraction with the idea? he wondered now.

'So is she going to be the lucky one?' asked Rose, only just preventing herself from snarling.

'No, she is not.'

'Oh? Did she discover how you'd spent your afternoon, then? Lying with me under the hot desert sun? Making love to *me*?'

The taunt triggered memory, fused and exploded in a fury of anger and almost unbearable passion. He pulled her roughly into his arms, though he saw from the instant dilation of her eyes that she was not objecting. Not objecting one bit, he thought as he drove his mouth down hard on hers.

And only when he had slaked a little of his hunger for her did he lift his head and gaze down into her dazed face as her eyelids fluttered open to stare up at him.

Her lips opened to frame his name, but no word came.

'Rose,' he said gently, his breath warm and soft on her face. 'How can we be lovers if you make such unreasonable demands on me?'

Her fingers bit into the hard strength of his shoulders beneath the sapphire silk. 'Most people wouldn't call them unreasonable!'

'Most people, most people,' he chided. 'Rose, Rose, my sweetest Rose—I am not most people. We both know that. I told you that right from the very beginning.'

She shook her head sadly. 'No, not right from the beginning, Khalim. You told me just before you made love to me, when making love had become as inevitable as night following day. You did everything in your not inconsiderable power to get me to arrive at that point. You played me as you would—' memory flashed into her subconscious as she recalled something he had told her about his schooldays, his love of fishing '—a *fish*! That's what you did! Yes, you did, and don't deny it! Teased me and tempted me, and—'

He cut short her protests with a forefinger placed softly on her lips, feeling them tremble beneath his touch, and he felt a surge of something far greater than mere desire. How well she knew him! How was this possible in so short a time?

'Yes, I plead guilty to your accusations,' he admitted slowly. 'Every one of them.'

Her anger was mollified by the triumph of knowing that she understood him a little too much for his liking, and her fingertips curled spontaneously into the nape of his neck, like a kitten's claws.

He felt her capitulation in the instinctive sway of her body, her hips folding into his, where fire and desire were building and burning, and he groaned.

'So can we not just enjoy this…now, my sweet, sweet Rose? To take what many pleasures are ours?'

It was, she recognised, an expression of need as much as lust, and the closest that Khalim would ever come to…not begging, exactly, because a man like Khalim would never, ever beg. But beseeching, certainly. She stared up into his face, and all her objections withered into dust.

'Yes, my darling,' she said shakily. 'We can.'

His hand was unsteady as he traced a slow line with his finger, from neck to navel, the filmy white material of her blouse moulding itself to the slim curves beneath.

'I want to see you naked,' he said huskily. 'Properly naked against satin, not sand.' He drew the cotton top over her head, his breath freezing with pleasure as he saw the unfettered lushness of her breasts and the flaxen hair which streamed down over them. He bent his head to kiss one puckered, rosy nipple.

'Oh!' she sighed, squirming her hips in helpless pleasure. 'You are a wicked, wicked man, Khalim.'

'You bring out the wickedness in me,' he murmured.

'The feeling is mutual,' she murmured back. 'So, so mutual.' Rose's hands slid underneath the sapphire silk of his gown, fingertips feasting on the feel of the satin skin which lay over the muscular definition of his torso. She felt him shudder beneath her touch and knew another moment of triumph, suspecting that once again he was close to the edge. And that was a heady feeling. This man of control and power—*hers*!

'I wanted to make this a long, slow undressing,' he said, bending his head to whisper in her ear.

'I sense a ''but'' coming.'

'Mmm. I think it will take many days before I can bear to prolong the pleasure in that way. Shall we…?' He paused, and trickled a finger down to rest possessively in the small dip of her navel. 'Shall we quickly remove these constraining garments, so that we can come together without barrier?'

But the word stirred an uncomfortable thought which had occurred to him over dinner that very night.

'And I have brought with me—' he scowled as he forced himself to say the abhorrent word, but only abhorrent when used in connection with Rose '—*condoms*! We were too reckless and too hungry for one another earlier.' When, for the first time in his life, he had made love without protection. It had also occurred to him that she might have become pregnant, and an intense and primitive yearning had swept over him. Only to be replaced by a fervent prayer that it should not be so.

For it would be impossible if Rose Thomas were carrying his child. Impossible!

Rose shrugged the slippery silk impatiently over his shoulders and let it flutter to the ground.

'You don't need them,' she told him.

Black eyes iced instantly at the implication. 'What don't I need?' he questioned softly.

She met his gaze without flinching. 'Condoms. We won't need them.' She hesitated. Surely she wouldn't have to spell it out for a man of the world such as this?

'Why not?'

Apparently she did.

'I'm on the pill,' she said bluntly.

'No!' His mouth formed the denial as if he had been stung.

'Yes,' she insisted quietly.

His heart pounding with an unendurable jealousy, he tightened his grip on her. 'So this is the way of Western women, is it?' he demanded. 'Always prepared, is that so? *Just in case?*'

'Don't be so hypocritical, Khalim,' she answered with dignity. 'I happen to be on the pill because my periods were heavy and irregular—'

'Your *periods*?' he demanded incredulously.

She guessed correctly that women did not speak of such matters with Khalim. So they were allowed certain intimacies with him such as sex, were they? But nothing in the way of *real* intimacy. Of women as they really were. Well, she had taken him on *his* terms; now let him take her on *hers*. She tried to make allowances for his upbringing and his culture. 'It's a very effective remedy,' she explained patiently.

'And also very convenient if you happen to just want to fall into bed with someone?' he scorned.

She wrenched herself away from him and fixed him with a withering stare. 'If you believe *that*, then you can get out of here right now, and don't bother coming back!'

He could see from the fire in her blue eyes that she meant it, and he forced himself to draw a steadying breath. 'I shouldn't have said that—'

'No, you're right—you shouldn't!' Her breathing came fast and rapid and indignant. 'How many lovers have you slept with in your life, Khalim?'

'You dare to ask me *that*?' he questioned dangerously.

'I'll bet it's a whole lot more than *I* have—which is precisely *two!*'

He flinched again and his mouth hardened. How dared there have been another before him? How *dared* there! '*Two!*'

'Yes, two. Actually not terribly shocking considering that I'm twenty-seven years old and have grown up in the kind of culture I have! I have *never* gone to bed with anyone indiscriminately! Can you look me in the eye and honestly say that *you* haven't, either?'

He stared at her, torn between fury and admiration. His beautiful, logical Rose! Applying the same rules of life for her as well as him! He bit down the pain of jealousy and a slow light began to glimmer at the back of the black eyes.

'You have never actually been to bed with *me* either, have you, sweet Rose?' he murmured, taking her unresisting hand and raising it to his lips to kiss it. 'And I think that is a situation which we should remedy now, with all seemly haste.'

How powerful he looked. How masterfully dark and virile and proud. Rose wondered half wildly whether she should have prevented him from scooping her up into his arms and carrying her over to the low mattress. A victor with his spoils, she thought weakly.

But then she was the victor, too. Because to have provoked that look of sensual promise coupled with a barely restrained impatience to make love to her was the most potent sensation she had ever encountered.

She let the last of her misgivings go as he laid her down on the embroidered coverlet, tugging at the silk cord which bound his loose trousers so they fell to the floor.

My heavens, but he was aroused! Darkly and magnificently aroused. Her mouth began to tremble as he slid her cotton trousers all the way down her legs and tossed them aside with an impatient disdain.

'Khalim,' she gasped as he came to lie beside her, his arms snaking possessively around her waist while his eyes burned down at her like smouldering coal.

'What is it, sweetest Rose? You want me to kiss you now?'

It was exactly what she wanted—the touch and the warmth and the security of his lips caressing hers. So that for one mad and crazy moment she could imagine that it was not lust which made this kiss such magic, but fool herself into thinking it was something as elusive and as precious as love.

CHAPTER TEN

KHALIM stayed with her for most of the night, but slipped out as dawn began to paint a pink and golden light on the horizon.

He swiftly dressed, then bent his head to kiss her, his lips lingering regretfully on her pouting mouth. 'The plane leaves at midday,' he murmured. 'Be ready to leave at ten.'

'Mmm?' she questioned groggily.

It had been the night of her life. His love-making had known no boundaries—nor hers, either. She'd given herself to him without inhibition. But with love, she realised with a sinking heart as she acknowledged the emotion which had first crept and then exploded deep inside her.

She loved him.

The realisation gave her no real pleasure—for what pleasure could ever be gained from a love which was doomed right from the start? But she *had* taken him on her terms, and she *did* want him, and because of that she pinned a sleepy smile onto her face.

'Mmm?' she questioned again, stalling for time, time to be able to react in the way expected of her, and not with the gnawing feeling of insecurity which had started to overwhelm her every time she thought about losing him.

'Be ready by ten,' he instructed softly, wishing that he could lie with her here until the morning sun filtered its way in precious golden shafts through the shutters.

She nodded and watched him go, all elegance and grace as he swished out of the room in the silken robes.

She ate the fruit and bread which Fatima brought to her room for breakfast and was ready by nine when there was a knock on the door and she opened it to find Khalim standing there, changed from his robes into one of his impeccably cut suits, ready for the flight back to London, and with an unusual expression on his face.

He looked perplexed.

'What is it?' she asked him quickly.

He shrugged. 'My father has requested that he meet you.'

Rose opened the door a little wider. 'You sound surprised.'

He was. Exceedingly. It was inconceivable—to *his* mind, in any case—that his father should express a wish to meet his Western blonde. But he would not tell Rose that.

'He is so frail,' he told her truthfully, 'that he sees few visitors.'

Except for prospective brides, thought Rose bitterly—bet he sees *loads* of those. 'Then I must be honoured,' she answered.

He nodded absently, his mind far away. 'I will arrange to have your bags taken out to the car,' he said. 'Now, come with me.'

She thought how distracted he seemed as he led her through the maze of marble corridors into a much larger and grander part of the palace. Past silent figures who watched them with black eyes which were unreadable, until at last an elaborately ornate door was flung open and they were ushered into a bedchamber.

At the far end of the room was a large and lavishly decorated bed, and, lying on it, a man whose unmoving rigidity proclaimed the severity of his illness.

'Come,' said Khalim softly.

By his father's bed sat his mother, her face troubled, and she nodded briefly at Khalim and then, not quite so briefly, at Rose.

'Father,' said Khalim. 'This is Rose Thomas.'

In a face worn thin by illness, only the eyes remained living and alert. Keen, black eyes, just like his son's. He gave a small smile and Rose was overwhelmed by the graciousness of that smile.

'So,' he said slowly. 'I believe that I must thank you for confirming Khalim's chosen successor for the oil refinery.' Another smile, this time rather more rueful. 'An opinion which differed from my own. And therefore Khalim said that we must bring in an independent arbitrator to decide.'

Rose looked up at Khalim in surprise, and met a mocking glance in return.

'Thank you. It is a great honour to meet you, sir,' she said quietly, and bowed her head.

The old man nodded and said something very rapid to Khalim, in Marabanese, and then Khalim tapped her arm. 'Come, Rose,' he said. 'Will you wait in the outer chamber while I bid my father farewell?'

Rose slipped silently from the room, her heart clenching as she read the pain in Khalim's face. Did every departure seem like the last time he would ever see his father? she wondered as she sat on a low couch outside the bedchamber.

It seemed a long time before Khalim came out again, and when he did his face was grave and Rose sprang to her feet.

'Is everything…okay?' she asked. It seemed a stupid question under the circumstances, but Khalim did not seem to notice.

'His physician is with him now,' he said slowly. 'Come, Rose—we must go to the airport, where the plane awaits us.'

They walked back along the corridor and he glanced down at her. 'The way you looked at me back there,' he mused.

Rose's eyes opened very wide. Had he seen the tell-tale signs of love? she worried. And wouldn't that be enough to send him fleeing in the opposite direction?

'When?'

'When my father told you that we had agreed to bring in an outsider to arbitrate, you looked surprised. What was the matter, Rose—did you imagine that I had invented the job as a ploy to get you out to Maraban?'

'It would sound insufferably arrogant of me to say yes,'

she answered slowly. 'But maybe just a little, then, yes—yes, perhaps I did.'

He admired her honesty—it would have been easy for her to have been evasive, and to lie. And, in truth, had not such a vacancy existed—then might he *not* have manufactured an excuse to bring her on such a trip? He smiled. 'You have fulfilled all my expectations, Rose. In every way and more.'

The limousine whisked them to the airport at Dar-gar and they were immediately escorted onto the plane, where Philip Caprice and the two glamorous air stewardesses were waiting for them.

And it wasn't until the plane had taken off into a cloudless blue sky and Khalim found his eyes wandering irresistibly to her pure, beautiful profile that he began to experience some of the misgivings which his father had already expressed so eloquently.

He had not wanted to leave her this morning, and now he felt like dismissing Philip and making love to her again. Rose Thomas was getting under his skin, he acknowledged—and he seemed to be hell-bent on breaking every single rule which mattered.

His mouth hardening, he deliberately picked up his brief-case and pulled a sheaf of papers out.

Rose interpreted the body language. The almost impercep-tible way he turned away from her. Oh, yes! He'd been vir-tually silent in the car on the way to the airport, and now she was getting the cold freeze. Was he having second thoughts? Had he thought more about the heinous crime of her being on the pill and decided that she was the worst kind of woman?

Was this the reality of being Khalim's temporary woman?

She got to her feet and met the hard, dark question in his eyes. 'I'm going to freshen up,' she said, and picked up the smaller of her two bags.

When she emerged a whole half an hour later, Khalim froze.

While in Maraban she had dressed most appropriately, in trousers or long skirts—clothes which modestly concealed her delectable shape. But now she had changed into a strappy little sundress in a golden colour which matched her hair, and which showed off far more brown and shapely leg than he was comfortable with.

He shifted in his seat. Not at *all* comfortable with. He waited until she had decorously taken her place beside him before challenging her.

'What is the meaning of this?'

She turned her head and raised her eyebrows. Now he was *talking* to her as though she were his concubine! 'The meaning of what?'

'This…this…vulgar *display* of your body,' he grated, realising that he did not want her body on show for anyone. Anyone but *him*!

'But this is exactly the kind of dress I was wearing when we first met,' she pointed out reasonably. 'You liked it well enough then, as I remember.'

'But now,' he said coolly, 'I do not.'

'Oh?'

He lowered his voice to a sultry whisper. 'I do not want other men looking at you in that way!'

'You mean the way *you're* looking at me?' she enquired innocently.

'That is *different!*'

'I fail to see how!' she answered wilfully.

He drummed his fingers impatiently against the arm rest. Well, short of marching her back into the bathroom and insisting that she put something decent on, there was little he could do.

He made a terse and impatient sound beneath his breath, feeling the uncharacteristic tug of frustration—and not solely sexual frustration, either. No, this was a frustration born out of the knowledge that he had finally met a woman who would not bend to his will! His match!

'Wear what you like!' he gritted.

'I intend to!'

The rest of the journey was completed in a stony silence, while Rose fumed and wondered how she could ever have thought herself in love with such a tyrant of a man.

Then she stole a glance at that beautiful, dark profile and thought of his tenderness and his passion during the night, and once again her heart pained her as though someone had driven a stiletto into it, then slowly twisted it round.

By the time they had disembarked into the waiting limousine at Heathrow Airport, Khalim was in the rare quandary of not knowing what to do. Or, rather, of knowing exactly what he *wanted* to do—which was to rush Miss Rose Thomas straight back to his suite at the Granchester Hotel and ravish her to within an inch of her life. So that for ever after she would comply with every demand he ever made!

He sighed. The trouble was—that he did not want that at all. Her fire and her independence inspired him almost as much as it frustrated him. What a hollow victory it would be to have Rose in the compliant position he usually expected of his women!

The car slowed as it approached the busy thoroughfares of London and he forced himself to look at her.

Forced, indeed! As if looking at her could give him nothing but untold pleasure!

'Would you like to come home with me?' he murmured.

For Khalim, he sounded almost biddable, Rose thought. But not quite.

'You mean to the Granchester?' she enquired coolly.

'Of course!'

She shook her head. She had had enough of his surroundings and their influence. 'Why don't you come back with me?' she questioned innocently.

To that flat she shared with the other girl? Unthinkable!

And then he thought of the alternative, which was even more unthinkable—that he went home without her!

'Very well,' he answered.

'There's no need to make it sound as though I'm leading you into the lion's cage!' said Rose crossly.

'Not a lion, no,' he agreed, a hint of humour lightening the night-dark eyes. 'More some beautiful and graceful cat!'

She wasn't sure whether it really *was* a compliment—but she found herself basking in it anyway.

But as the car began to approach her road, Rose began to wonder whether it had been such a good idea to invite him. What if Lara had a load of her out-of-work actor friends around, lying all over the place and drinking wine and smoking cigarettes?

Or what if Lara had had a heavy night, and had left the place in a state of disarray—a common enough occurrence when Rose wasn't around to tidy up after her.

They left the bodyguard sitting in the car outside and went upstairs to the flat.

It was rather better than Rose had anticipated, but not much. There weren't a *crowd* of Lara's friends—just her on-off boyfriend, Giles, whom Rose always thought of as *very* off.

Giles had been born into a wealthy family, imagining that the world owed him a living. He had fluked his way into drama school and then coasted through the course—only just managing not to be asked to leave by the skin of his teeth.

Unfortunately he had the kind of blond-haired, blue-eyed looks and carved aristocratic cheekbones which meant that he could get any woman that he wanted—and Lara wanted him far more than he wanted her.

Which meant, thought Rose grimly, that she waited on him as if he were an invalid. Cooking up various little treats for him and pouring him glasses of wine at all hours of the day.

Like now.

So why was he polishing off a glass of Chardonnay in the middle of the afternoon? And looking at Khalim with a kind of jealous incredulity.

But then, Rose decided with more than a little satisfaction, Giles rarely met men who transcended *his* good looks so completely!

She looked around at the plates and cups and wineglasses littered around the sitting room and saw Khalim's lips curve with undisguised displeasure. Well, *let* him judge her, she thought proudly as she bent to pick up an empty wine bottle which was in danger of tripping someone up!

'Lara, you've already met Khalim,' she said shortly. 'Khalim, I don't believe you've met Giles, who is Lara's—'

'Lover,' drawled Giles arrogantly.

Khalim's facial muscles didn't move an inch. 'It is my pleasure,' he said smoothly and looked at Rose with a question in his eyes.

Now what? thought Rose helplessly. Did she take him to her room? No, she couldn't—she just *couldn't*. Not with Giles smirking like that and Lara affecting that puppy-dog expression whenever she looked at Khalim.

'Would you like some coffee?' she asked weakly.

'Thank you,' he replied, without enthusiasm.

The kitchen looked as though someone had tried to start World War Three in there—with every surface covered in used crockery and glasses.

And Lara had used up all the real coffee, thought Rose in disbelief as she picked up a nearly-empty jar and held it up to him.

'Is instant okay?' she questioned.

'Instant?' he echoed, as though she had just started speaking in Marabanese.

'Coffee,' she elaborated.

'Do you have any tea?'

'Yes. Yes, I do.' She made them two cups of herb tea and then cleared the table so that they could sit down and drink it.

They sat facing one another warily across the rising steam from their cups.

Now what? thought Rose again, before getting back some of her customary spirit.

'You don't *have* to stay, you know,' she bristled.

'No, I don't,' he agreed calmly, thinking that Rose—*his* Rose—should not have to live amidst such outrageous chaos. 'But you will not come back with me to the Granchester either, will you?'

'No.'

'Do you mind telling me why?'

How to explain that his costly surroundings only emphasised their inequality, and that if she was to spend the tenure of their fragile relationship always on *his* territory, then it would always seem a little tainted.

'Can't we just be like a normal couple?' she demanded. 'I don't always want to be surrounded by your bodyguards and the awe in which people hold you. Everyone always defers to your status—it's always there. A barrier.' She nearly said, A barrier towards getting to know you, and then stopped herself. Maybe he didn't *want* to get to know her on the level she craved to discover him.

He stared across the table at her. 'Then we seem to have reached some kind of stalemate, don't we, Rose? What do you suggest?'

The idea hit her like a thunderclap. If only they *could* be an 'ordinary' couple. The idea grew. 'Why don't you rent a flat of your own?' she suggested. 'A flat where we can meet as equals?'

'A *flat*?' he repeated.

'Why, yes.' Of course, they would never be *quite* the same as a normal couple. Khalim would never have to go begging to the bank manager for a loan, for example. But neutral territory would give them some kind of equality, surely?

'There are loads of—' she forced herself to say the hateful word '—short-let flats on the market in London. Furnished or unfurnished—suit yourself. Wouldn't it be…nice…' she gave him a kind of feline smile '…to have a place where we

were free to be ourselves? Within reason, of course,' she
added hastily. 'Obviously there would have to be some pro-
vision for your bodyguard.'

He raised his eyebrows. Good of her! And then he thought
about it. And thought some more. Didn't her words have
more than a kernel of truth in them? Wouldn't a rented flat
give him a fleeting kind of freedom? The kind of freedom
which most men of his age took for granted? The freedom...and he swallowed as he imagined a whole place of
their own. Where Rose could wander around wearing what
she wanted.

Where they could watch a video and eat their supper loll-
ing around on a sofa, as he had seen his friend Guy do with
Sabrina on so many occasions.

'Very well.' He nodded, and his mind started ticking over.
'I can see the wisdom behind your idea. I will get Philip to
start looking immediately—'

'No, Khalim!' she said, interrupting him. 'You have to do
it like other people do! *You* go and look at flats. You find
the one you want and *you* do all the transactions. Do it yourself for once! Forget Philip!'

Her feisty challenge drove the blood heatedly around his
veins and in that moment his desire to possess her made him
feel almost dizzy. But he would have to wait. He would not
bed her here with the feckless actor and her sweet but rather
untidy flatmate listening to them.

'I most certainly will, Rose,' he promised. 'And with
haste.' He lowered his voice into a sensual whisper. 'Because
believe me when I tell you that I cannot bear to wait for you
much longer.'

CHAPTER ELEVEN

IT WAS not a flat, of course. It was a magnificent, four-storey house in Chelsea.

'A flat would have caused too many problems for my security,' explained Khalim as he showed her through a wealth of magnificent, high-ceilinged rooms. And his Head of Security still had not forgiven him his breach when he had galloped off across the desert sand with Rose locked tightly against him! 'So what do you think?' he murmured. 'Does my Rose approve?'

How could she do anything but? Rose let her gaze travel slowly around the main drawing room. Everywhere she looked she could see yellow and blue flowers—saffron roses and lemon freesias, and the splayed indigo fingers of iris—and she was reminded of the bouquet he had sent her, when he'd first been trying to…

To what? To seduce her? She turned her head, so that he could not see her eyes. Had that been his only intention? Maybe it had, she acknowledged, but something else had grown from that intent. You didn't share a house with a woman if sex was the only thing on your mind.

Oh, *stop* it, Rose, she remonstrated with herself. Stop playing Little Miss Wistful.

'I love it. It's beautiful,' she said, and hoped that her voice didn't *sound* too wistful. Because they were *playing* house, not setting up house together, and she must never let herself forget that. But at times like this it wasn't easy.

She stared in slight awe at the two white sofas with their jade-green cushions, and the low bleached oak coffee-table. 'It all looks brand-new,' she commented with approval.

'That's because it is.'

Rose raised her eyebrows. Heaven only knew how much he would be paying per month for a place like this. She asked the question she had been dreading asking. 'How long is the let for?'

There was a momentary pause. 'I am not renting it,' he said quietly. 'I bought it.'

'You *bought* it? What, just like that?' she asked incredulously, until she realised how preposterous she must have sounded. A place like this would be nothing to a man of Khalim's wealth.

He saw her look of discomfiture. 'And for security reasons, all the furniture had to be brand-new—'

'What, in case there was an explosive device stashed behind the sofa?' she joked, then wished she hadn't.

'Something like that,' he agreed wryly.

'Sorry. That was a stupid thing for me to say!'

He smiled. 'How very magnanimous of you, Rose.'

When he smiled like that she was utterly lost. 'So you've bought a house,' she observed slowly.

'Well, to be honest—nothing I looked at to rent—' he remembered the bemusement of house-owners when he'd turned up with his bodyguard in tow '—came up to—'

She met his glittering black gaze. 'Palace standards?' she questioned drily.

How he loved it when she teased him that way! 'Mmm.' He swallowed down the desire which had been bubbling over all week. 'Anyway,' he finished, 'it will be a good investment.'

A good investment. Of course. That was how the rich made themselves richer, wasn't it? They invested.

Trying not to feel a little like a commodity herself, Rose wandered over to one of the huge picture windows which overlooked an intensely green square surrounded by iron railings and looked out.

'A very good investment, I'm sure,' she echoed.

'My bodyguard will have the self-contained unit downstairs,' he explained, watching the sudden stiffening of her shoulders and wondering what had caused it. 'And the upper three storeys will be entirely for you...and for me.'

Rose swallowed down the excitement that his words had produced. For the past week—was it only a *week*? It had seemed like a century in passing—she had thought of nothing else. Tried to imagine the reality of sharing a flat with Khalim, and every time she had failed to make that final leap of faith. To think that they actually would. That he would arrange it all himself. And then bring her here to live with him. Because when she had suggested that she simply visit him on occasional evenings and stay the night, he had swiftly censured her suggestion with arrogant assertion.

'No!'

'No?'

His black eyes gleamed. She could fight him on this, but she would not win. Oh, no. 'I do not want you to bring cases of clothes here, or have one toothbrush here, and another at your flat. You will live here, Rose, with me.'

For how long? her heart wanted her to cry out, but she steeled herself against its plea. She probably only thought she loved him. Wanted him because he was so completely unattainable. She must not place emotional demands on him which he couldn't possibly meet, because in time it would wear down whatever it was they had between them.

And what was that?

'Rose?' He broke into her reverie with a silky question.

Well, now was the time of reckoning, she told herself as he drew her into his arms and lowered his dark, beautiful head to hers. Now they would be able to see what they had between them.

His kiss was fierce and hard and long, whipping her up into a frenzy of need which matched his.

He found himself wanting to rip the little sundress from her body, to lay her down on the floor and impale her there. But there had been little restraint in his physical dealings with her so far. Little desire to show her the mastery of which he was proud.

For he had learned his sexual skills well. His eighteenth birthday present from his cousin had been a trip to Paris, to a hotel which had been the last word in luxury. And there, awaiting him, had been his 'present'—a stunning redhead in her forties, with a body which most men only dreamed of. A woman of the world, of a certain age. And in the three days and nights which had followed, she had taught him everything there was to know about the act of love.

The most important being, she had purred with satisfaction, the ability to give a woman pleasure.

He looked down into Rose's milky-pale face, where her sapphire eyes shone out at him like bright stars, and he felt an unrecognisable kick of emotion. He wanted to pleasure his Rose, he realised. To give her more pleasure than she had ever dreamed of. He smiled with the heady anticipation of it.

'Come and let me show you the bedroom now.'

She took his proffered hand, feeling oddly shy as he took her into a white and blue bedroom which was dominated by a vast bed.

He was watching her carefully. 'Rose,' he said, almost gently. 'Why do you blush?'

She certainly wasn't going to tell him that his smile had made her feel almost like... She shook her head at the ridiculousness of it all. Like a virgin bride on her wedding night. Who the hell was she kidding?

Oh, I *wish*, she thought helplessly as he drew her into the circle of his arms. How I wish.

'Now.' His voice deepened as he ran his ebony gaze over her. 'At last.'

He undressed her slowly, and with infinite care, his fingers teasing and tantalising her as they unbuttoned the sundress and then peeled it from her body. And then, as though he had all the time in the world—off came her lacy brassière.

And finally, with his fingertips flicking light and teasing movements which thrilled her to the very core—he slowly removed her little lace panties.

'Now let me look at you,' he commanded softly.

She should have felt shy in her nakedness, when he still stood so formidably clad in his dark grey suit—but how could she feel anything but pride under that warm look of approval? Instinctively, she lifted her shoulders back and the movement emphasised the lush thrust of her breasts.

He felt the unmistakable wrench of desire. 'Get into bed,' he commanded softly. 'You're shivering.'

Shivering, yes—but her tremble had nothing whatsoever to do with the cold, but with the tingling sense of expectation which washed over her as he began to unknot his tie.

He unhurriedly slipped his jacket off, and hung it over the back of the chair.

Come on, she thought. Come *on*!

But if he read the hunger in her eyes he chose to ignore it, his dark gaze not leaving her face as he slowly began to unbutton his shirt.

The shirt joined the jacket on the chair, and he unbuckled his belt before unzipping his trousers.

'You could strip for a living,' she told him throatily, unable to keep her thoughts to herself any longer.

He smiled. 'So could you. What say we make a living of it together?'

It was an outrageous fantasy, tinged with a poignancy produced by that elusive word 'together'. But she lost the sadness as he climbed into bed to join her, and pulled her into his arms, his warm, living flesh making her feel on fire where they touched.

'Just you and me,' he murmured, and cupped her breast in his hand, feeling the nipple thrust and jut against his palm in instant reaction. 'How do you like that?'

'What—*that*?' She jerked her head jokingly towards her

breast, where his hand looked so shockingly dark against the whiteness of her skin.

But he shook his head, a rare kind of tenderness filling his voice. 'No,' he demurred. 'I meant the you and me bit.'

'Oh, that!' She was about to make a flippant comment, the kind of comment which would keep her safe from hurt. But she read in his eyes an elemental truth—that right at that moment he was holding nothing back from her. And didn't such a truth deserve another? 'Oh, that is a prize beyond rubies,' she told him huskily.

He groaned as his mouth replaced his hand, locking his lips hungrily against the rosy nub which sustained all life. He wondered if these breasts would ever suckle a child.

A child that could never be his!

'Rose,' he groaned again, and the slick lick of his tongue made her feel almost weak with longing, so weak that she gave into her most primitive desire and slid her hand down between the muscular thighs until she had found what she was looking for.

'Rose!'

Her wanton capture of him made him feel as weak as water in her hands. And so did the way she was touching him, her hands lightly caressing the rock-hard shaft of him. His eyes closed and his head fell back against the pillow. Never, since that first induction to the pleasures of the flesh, had he allowed a woman such freedom with his body.

'Stop, Rose,' he begged.

'You don't like it?' she asked him innocently.

'I like it.' He said a single word in Marabanese he hadn't realised he knew, and then gently closed his hand over hers to stop her. 'Too much.'

She realised how much she had enjoyed seeing him look as dreamily helpless as that. To see him fighting for control. It made her feel strong. *Equal.* 'Well, then?' she whispered close to his mouth, so close that he touched his lips to hers.

'This is intended to be traditional love-making, Rose,' he told her sternly.

'And no demonstration that I have a certain amount of experience—and that you aren't my first lover?'

There was no flippancy in her voice now, Khalim recognised—with a flash of insight which dispelled the black clouds of his jealousy. Nothing but a wistful trace of insecurity, as though he would be judging her and finding her wanting. He tipped her chin upwards, so that their eyes locked on a collision course.

'You push me far, Rose,' he told her. 'Sometimes too far, I think.'

'You went mad when you found out I was on the pill!'

He had to force himself to stay calm and drew a deep breath. 'My harsh words on the subject in Maraban were based on...jealousy,' he grated, spitting out the unfamiliar word. 'Jealousy that I was not your first lover—'

'And I was jealous that you weren't mine,' she said softly, filled with a sudden boldness—because what was to be gained by hiding the truth from him?

Khalim expelled a long, low breath, remembering the newness, the vitality and sheer power of their first encounter, and he sought to honour it in some way. 'I felt like your first,' he said.

'And I yours,' she whispered back.

'You are more my equal than any woman I have ever met, Rose. You live by different rules to the women in my country, and the life you have lived makes you the person you are today. And I like the person you are today.'

A person who could get him running halfway around London to find a place for them to live, much to Philip Caprice's bemusement and his bodyguard's outrage!

'So don't you like your women to be subservient?' she asked him teasingly, wondering what she had said that was so wrong, because his face darkened with a simmering look of bitterness.

He thought of the unknown woman who would one day become his wife. And his eyes flickered down to where Rose lay—so pale and so beautiful—her hair spread like a moonlit fan across his pillow.

He shook his head. 'I never want subservience from you, Rose,' he whispered. 'Never from you.'

And all her thoughts and doubts and questions were driven from her mind as he began to stroke her, as if she were some pampered feline, and she wrapped her arms around him, kissing his neck and the bare warm flesh of his shoulders.

Khalim found that he wanted to touch her for ever, to run his fingertips over the creamy satin of her skin, to explore her body until he knew every curve and every dip of it. It was a new sensation for him—the wish to prolong the waiting, until it reached such a fever-pitch that neither of them would be able to resist it.

'Khalim!' gasped Rose, as his skilful touch took her down erotic pathways she had never encountered before, so close to the edge that if he didn't… 'Khalim!'

'Mmm?' What exquisite pleasure it gave him to see his Rose lying there, her hips in frantic grind, powerless to resist him. The sight of a woman yielding to him had never before had the power to make his heart thunder as though it really *were* the very first time. He knew then that he could make her beg for him, and knew also that it would leave a bitter taste in his mouth. For he was as much in her thrall as she was in his. 'It is time,' he whispered against her hair.

He moved to lie above her, dark and dominant and utterly, utterly in control as he parted her thighs, smiling as he felt her honeyed moistness.

And he entered her not with the powerful thrust of that first time in the desert—as though he would die if he didn't join with her as swiftly as possible. No, this, thought Rose as an unstoppable warmth began to unfurl deep within her— this was a long, slow movement which seemed to pierce at the very heart of her.

They moved in conjunction, in perfect synchrony, her pale, curving flesh complementing the hard, lean lines of his. Each lingering thrust set her trembling, until her whole body seemed to shimmer with some unexpected light.

Khalim felt as though he were enveloped in some dark, erotic enchantment, and he had to use every once of self-restraint he possessed to hold back. Until he saw the sudden arching of her back, the inevitable stiffening and then indolent splaying of her limbs as rapture caught her in its silken net.

And only then did he let go, with a moan which seemed to be torn from his soul itself.

Only then did he shudder with the pleasure of fulfilment, until he came to a perfect stillness—and allowed his head to fall upon the cushioned splendour of her breast.

They dozed on and off for most of the afternoon, and then he made love to her again. And again. Until she sat up in bed with her blonde hair all tousled and falling in disarray around her shoulders, while he sucked erotically on her forefinger.

'Khalim?'

'Mmm?' He loved the salty-sweet taste of her skin.

'I'm hungry.'

'Hungry?' The thought of food had not occurred to him, not with such a feast here in his arms, but then he had taught himself to transcend hunger. When reaching puberty he had been sent into the desert with his tutor and taught to go without food for days. Existing on a little water and what few berries were available. It was the simple code of the desert: that you should learn to do without, because you never knew when you might need to.

'Yes, starving, actually!' complained Rose.

He released her finger and lay back on the pillow, the sheet rumpled by his ankles, his dark body gloriously and proudly naked. 'You want that we should ring out for some food?'

She opened her mouth to say yes, when she remembered,

and shut it again. They were trying to be ordinary, weren't they? And if they were an ordinary couple who had just moved into their first home, then they would certainly not have an excess of cash to throw about.

'No. Let's have something here,' she said and tossed her hair back over her shoulder. 'I brought a load of groceries with me, remember?'

Khalim shrugged, and gave a satisfied smile. 'Whatever you wish to prepare will taste like manna, Rose.'

She was about to get out of bed when she frowned at his easy assumption that *she* would cook. 'Why don't *you* make us something to eat, Khalim?'

'*Me?*' he questioned. '*Me?*'

'Yes, you! I'm not asking you to run naked up and down Park Lane—just make us a cup of tea and a sandwich!'

'A cup of tea and a sandwich,' he repeated, on a low growl, damned if he was going to admit to her that he hadn't ever had to prepare a meal for himself in his adult life! He swung his long legs out of bed and stood naked in front of her, a mocking question in the dark eyes as he saw her unconscious little pout. He put his hands low on his hips, in a gesture of pure provocation.

'Sure?'

Rose licked her lips. So he was trying to use his sexuality to get out of making her a sandwich, was he? What place equality now? 'Quite sure,' she answered primly, but immediately turned over to lie on her stomach so that he wouldn't see the sudden tightening of her breasts.

He returned after so long that Rose was certain he must have fallen asleep in the kitchen, carrying a loaded tray with him. And he still hadn't bothered to get dressed!

But to her surprise, the sandwich was creditable.

'That looks really good, Khalim!' she exclaimed.

He sizzled a look at her. 'Don't patronise me, Rose,' he warned.

'I wasn't!'

'Oh, yes, you were!' His eyes glittered. 'Just because I haven't had to fend for myself doesn't mean I don't know what to do, if I need to—and you wouldn't need to be a culinary genius to be able to cut off two slices of bread and wedge a little salad between them.'

Round one to Khalim, thought Rose with unwilling admiration as she bit into the most delicious sandwich she had ever eaten.

CHAPTER TWELVE

LIVING with a prince wasn't a bit as Rose had expected—though, when she stopped to think about it, what *had* she expected? It wasn't exactly the kind of situation where you could rummage through your life's memory box and come up with a comparable experience, was it?

But there was only one word she could use to describe it. Bliss. Sheer and utter bliss.

She had never lived with a man before—had never felt any desire to make such a commitment to anyone before Khalim—and she was amazed at the way they just kind of slotted together as though this had always been meant to happen.

To her astonishment, the same things made them laugh—though for all the wrong reasons. Television game shows and badly made sitcoms, for example. And corny jokes which Khalim had apparently never grown out of since his schooldays.

'It is enjoyable to have someone to share them with,' he murmured to her one morning, when she was about to leave for work.

She heard the trace of wistfulness in the deep timbre of his voice. 'What an isolated life you have led, Khalim!'

He shrugged. 'Of course. It goes with the territory.'

And the territory in his case was real, not imagined.

And the other aspect of their life which was as close to perfection as Rose could imagine was their love-life. Their *sex*-life, she corrected herself automatically.

Just because Khalim sometimes astonished her with amazing tenderness during the act of love, didn't mean that he actually *felt* love. Sex *was* sometimes tender, just as sometimes it was fast and furious, or deliciously drawn-out. In fact, it had a hundred different expressions, and Khalim seemed intent on exploring each and every one with her.

On the downside, there was no doubt that Khalim had been spoiled—both physically and spiritually. There was often a tussle as to who got their own way, with Khalim often expecting her to accede to *his* wishes, simply out of habit.

'No!' she protested one evening, when she walked into the kitchen to find that the breakfast cups and plates still hadn't been stacked in the dishwasher. 'It's *your* turn to sort out the kitchen, Khalim!'

Khalim's eyes narrowed. This was fast turning into the farce of a camping trip he had been forced to endure at school at the age of thirteen! 'Haven't we taken this living a normal life to the extreme?' he demanded fiercely. 'Surely even normal couples get someone in to do the housework!'

'Yes, they do,' said Rose patiently. 'But that doesn't include general tidying up, does it? And anyway—' she looked up at him in appeal '—isn't that more of the same of what you're used to? People waiting on you, so that you don't live in the real world at all?'

Khalim gave an impatient little snort. Didn't she realise that when she opened those great big baby-blue eyes at him like that, he would agree to almost anything? He walked over to where she stood, like some bright and glorious vision in a short white skirt and a clinging scarlet T-shirt, and pulled her into his arms.

'Khalim, no!'

'Say that like you mean it!'

'I do!' she said, half-heartedly.

He shook his head as he lifted her face to his. 'Oh, no, you don't, my beauty,' he murmured, and bent his lips to hers.

She responded to him the way she always responded— with complete and utter capitulation, opening her mouth greedily to the seeking warmth of his, and tangling her fingers luxuriantly in the thick, black hair.

He gave a groan as he cupped her T-shirted breast, thinking how he had longed to hold her in his arms like this all day. She was like a fever in his blood, a fever he must purge before too long. He *must*. 'Let's go to bed,' he demanded heatedly.

'No!'

'No?' His black eyes glittered. Why was she saying one thing, while her body was saying the precise opposite? 'You mean you want me to do it to you here, standing up?'

Rose felt the instant pooling of need. He was outrageous! Irrepressible! She loved him—oh, how she loved him. 'No,' she said again, and with an effort disentangled herself from his arms, knowing in her heart of hearts that she was going a little bit over the top about this. But for heaven's sake— there was a *principle* at stake here! 'Well, really I mean yes— but *not until after you've stacked the dishwasher*!'

'If you think I'm going to allow domesticity to start dominating the *important* things in life, then you have made a very poor judgement, Rose,' he'd said, with a silky and sexual threat, and kissed her again, very soundly.

She lost that particular battle—but the crazy thing was that she didn't particularly care. She didn't care about anything, she realised.

Except for her dark lover with the soul of a poet, who would never truly be hers.

They went out—of course they did—just like any other couple. Except that they were not—and excursions into the outside world brought that fact crashing home. For trips to restaurants or the theatre were always shadowed by the discreet but ever vigilant bodyguard, who was never more than a few steps away from Khalim. Several times they ate with Sabrina and Guy, and Rose found herself glancing at Sabrina's shiny new wedding band with more than a little envy.

And each morning they both left for work, just like any other couple.

'Do you *have* to go to work?' Khalim demanded sleepily from their bed one morning, when the thought of having her in his arms for the rest of the day was just too much to resist. Philip could deal with all the most urgent matters, he thought hungrily. He threw her a sizzling look. 'I mean, *really*?'

'I most certainly do!' she replied crisply, steeling herself against the promise in those night-dark eyes. 'Why, are you offering to ''support'' me from now on, Khalim?'

He smiled, knowing that her challenge was an empty one. That his feisty, independent Rose would sooner sweep the streets than accept money from him! 'Any time you like,' he mocked. 'Any time at all.'

And it said a lot about her emotional state for Rose to realise that the offer actually *tempted* her for a moment. She spent one heady moment thinking how wonderful it would be to be 'kept' by Khalim, before swiftly taking herself out of the flat and heading off for her offices in Maida Vale.

Each day, Khalim went to his suite at the Granchester to join Philip Caprice where he locked himself into matters of state affecting Maraban, settling down to study the papers which had been sent for his attention.

And lately there were more and more of them, he acknowledged as he began to accept that the burden of his inheritance began to creep ever closer.

The heady, pleasure-filled weeks crept stealthily by. Each night he received reports on his father's health, and the physicians assured him that he was weak, but stable.

But one evening he replaced the telephone receiver with a heavy hand, tension etching deep lines on the dark, beautiful face, and Rose's heart went out to him, even as a cold feeling of the inevitable crept over her. 'Don't you want to go out to see him?' she asked softly. 'Shouldn't you be there, with him?'

He met her troubled gaze, her foreboding echoed in his

own eyes as he saw their fantasy life coming to an end. He nodded. 'I shall go at the weekend,' he told her. 'Once I have concluded the American oil deal.'

Her heart began to pound as she heard something new in his voice. Something she would have preferred not to have heard. Distance. She had heard it once before in Maraban and it had frightened her then.

Distance.

She stumbled over the words. 'And you may…you may stay there, I suppose?'

There was a long pause. 'That depends—'

'Please be *honest* with me, Khalim! Otherwise what good will this whole…' she couldn't think of a single word which would sum up the magic of their weeks together, and so she plumped for the prosaic '…*affair* have been, if the truth deserts us when it really counts?'

'Affair?' he echoed thoughtfully and then nodded slowly. 'Yes. I may have to stay. And I won't be able to take you with me, you know, Rose.'

'I know that. I never expected you to.'

'No.' She had placed no demands on him whatsoever, apart from a stubborn determination for him to do his share of the household chores. Would it have made him happier if she had broken down? Wept? Begged him not to go, or to smuggle her back to some anonymous house in Maraban? Because that at least might have given him some indication of her true feelings for him.

Never before had he encountered a woman who didn't demand words of love and commitment—particularly in the aftermath of love-making. But Rose had not. Did she not want emotional reassurance from him, then? Or was her eminently practical side simply telling her that such words meant nothing. That actions were what counted—and that soon he would have to leave.

'Then we'd better make the last of these two days,' she said unhappily.

He nodded, wishing that he could take the sadness from her eyes. 'Let's start right now.' And he pulled her into his arms and kissed her, dazed by the emotional effect of that sad, sweet kiss. 'A kiss like there was no tomorrow,' he murmured.

I wish tomorrow never *would* come, thought Rose as she kissed him back with a hunger which verged on desperation, a desperation which grew into a storm of passion which left them shaking and helpless in its wake.

They were slavish in their attention to detail, to try to make their last hours together as perfect as possible. The meals they cooked were their favourite meals; the music they played the most poignant.

And their love-making took on an extra dimension—the sense of inevitable loss they both felt making it seem more profound than it had ever done before.

She played with his body as she would a violin, fine-tuning every single one of his senses until he would moan with helpless pleasure beneath her hands and her lips.

The night before he was due to leave, they ate a sensual supper in bed and she was just licking off the strawberry yogurt which she had trickled on the dark matt of hair which sprinkled his chest when the phone rang.

'Leave it to the machine,' he instructed, his eyes tight shut with the pleasure of what she had been doing with her tongue.

She shook her head and sat back on her heels, wearing nothing but an exquisite wisp of scarlet silk he had bought her and then fought to make her accept. 'It might be Maraban,' she whispered. 'It might be news of your father.'

Guilt evaporated his pleasure instantly and Khalim reached his hand out and snatched up the phone.

'Khalim!' he said.

As soon as he started speaking in rapid Marabanese, Rose knew that something was very wrong—even if the dark look of pain which contorted his features hadn't already warned her.

He spoke in an unfamiliar, fractured voice and nodded several times, and when he put the phone back down Rose knew without being told that the worst had happened.

'He is dead?' she asked, in a shaking voice.

He didn't answer for a moment, shaking his head instead. The inevitable. The expected. And yet no less hard to bear because of that.

'Yes, he is dead,' he answered, in a flat, toneless voice. 'He died unexpectedly an hour ago.'

'Khalim—' she went to put her hand out to him, but he had already swung his long, dark legs over the bed and begun to dress. 'Can I *do* anything? Do you want me to phone Philip?'

'Philip is already on his way over,' he said, still in that strange, flat voice. 'The plane is being fuelled—and we will leave for Maraban immediately.'

Rose bit her lip. 'I'm so sorry, Khalim.'

He turned then and she was shaken by the bleak look of emptiness on his face.

'Yes. Thank you.'

He looked forbidding, a stranger almost, but Rose didn't care. She couldn't stop herself from moving across the room and putting her arms around him in a warm gesture of comfort. His body felt stiff, as if it was trying to reject the reality of what he had just heard, but she hugged him all the tighter.

'I should have been there,' he told her brokenly. 'I should have *been* there!'

'You couldn't have known! You were planning to leave first thing! It was unexpected, Khalim. Fate!'

'Fate,' he echoed, and tightened his arms around her waist.

Let it go, she urged him silently. Let it *go*.

And maybe her unspoken plea communicated itself to him in some inexplicable way, for she heard him expel a long, tortured breath and then his arms came round her, his head falling onto her shoulder, and she felt his long, drawn-out shudder.

They stood like that for moments—minutes, aeons, perhaps—until the insistent jangling of the doorbell could be heard.

He raised his head to look at her, and there was the unmistakable glimmer of tears in the black eyes.

'Khalim?' she whispered.

The great black cloud of grief which was enveloping him lifted just for a moment as he met the soft sympathy in her eyes, and grief became momentarily guilt.

This was the moment, he realised. The moment of truth. He would have to let her go.

And he didn't want to.

'May the gods forgive me for saying this at such a time,' he whispered, knowing that there would never be another moment to say it, 'but I do not wish to lose you, Rose.'

Oh, the pain! The spearing, unremitting pain of imagining life without Khalim. 'It has to be.' How rehearsed the words sounded, but that was because they were. She had been practising a long time for this very moment. 'It *has* to be.'

The doorbell rang again.

He lifted her chin, sapphire light blinding from her eyes. 'I must be in Maraban,' he told her, and then he said very deliberately, 'but I can come back.'

She stared at him as hope stirred deep within her, even while logic told her that any hopes she harboured would be futile. 'How?' she whispered.

'When things are settled.' He shrugged his shoulders. 'I will be able to visit you from time to time. It won't be the same, but...' His words tailed off as he saw the frozen expression on her face.

'What, and become your English mistress, while you take a bride back in Maraban?'

'I have no bride in Maraban!' he grated.

'Not yet! But soon you will!' She let out a deep sigh.

'Having to be content with little bits of you, when I've had…had…' Only now her words tailed off, too. She had been about to say that she had had all of him, but that hadn't been true, had it?

She had had his company and his laughter and his body, but there had never been any mention from Khalim of the most important thing of all.

Love.

She shook her head, fighting to keep her dignity. He would remember her as his proud, independent Rose, not a snivelling wreck of a woman. 'No, Khalim,' she said firmly. 'It won't work.' She pictured a life where she would always be waiting. Waiting for the infrequent phone call. Waiting for news that he had taken a wife at last. News of his wedding. Or of his baby, perhaps… She shook her head as the pain lanced through her again.

'Better we end it now, Khalim. Cleanly and completely. At least that way we'll be left with our memories, instead of destroying what we once had.'

Had he really imagined that she would agree to his outrageous suggestion? Could he honestly see Rose resigning herself to a lifetime of playing the understudy? And yet he did not want to let her go. Damn her! He knew that she still wanted him, just as much as he wanted her—so why could she not just agree to his proposition?

His mouth tightened, and he removed her hands from where they lay locked upon his shoulders.

'And that is your last word on the subject?'

She met the anger in his eyes and she turned away rather than face it. She did not want her last memory of Khalim to be one of smouldering rage. 'Yes,' she said.

'So be it,' he said, with chilling finality. 'Philip is waiting.'

She heard him leave the room and go to answer the door, heard him speaking in an undertone to Philip, and then suddenly he was back and she whirled round to find him looking remote and frozen, and she guessed that reality really was beginning to kick in. She wanted to go up and comfort him again, but there was something so forbidding about the icy set of his features that she didn't dare.

She wondered if her face showed that inside her heart was breaking. 'Goodbye, Khalim.'

He thought how detached she looked, as if nothing could touch her. And perhaps nothing could—for *he* certainly could not. She wanted no part of him, unless she could have everything of him. She wanted too much! 'You will continue to live here?' he questioned.

'How can I?' She meant—how could she possibly stay in a place which had been filled with his presence if he was no longer there? How could she bear to face the empty space on the bed beside her? Or consign herself to being without his warm body enfolding hers night after night?

'The deeds of the house are in your name,' he said. 'I bought it for you.'

'And why did you do that?' she demanded. 'As a kind of insurance policy?'

'You have a way of reducing everything down to the lowest possible denominator, don't you, Rose?' he stormed. 'It was supposed to be an act of generosity—nothing more sinister than that!'

But suddenly she felt cheap. So this really *was* the pay-off, was it? An expensive house in Chelsea to compensate for the fact that her sheikh lover had left her!

'I don't want your charity, Khalim!'

His face grew cold. 'Then please accept it as my gift, for that was the only way it was intended. Goodbye, Rose.' His black eyes raked over her one last time, before he turned away and out of the room without a backward glance.

Rose waited until she had heard the front door slam shut behind them and then counted slowly to a hundred, before she allowed herself the comfort of tears.

CHAPTER THIRTEEN

'ROSE, are you *mad*?'

Rose calmly finished placing the last of her clothes into a suitcase, and clicked the locks into place before looking up at Sabrina—a particularly glowing-looking Sabrina, she thought, with a brief pang of envy. But that was what being newly married did for you, wasn't it?

'No, I am certainly not mad. Why should I be?'

'Because this house is beautiful, and if Khalim wants you to have it—'

'I can't live here without him, Sabrina!' Rose thought how strained her voice sounded. Well, at least it would match the strain on her face. 'Can't you understand that?'

'I guess so.' Sabrina sighed. 'Guy was worried that something like this might happen.'

'You mean that Khalim would inevitably leave me to go back to Maraban and find someone more suitable?'

'Well, yes.' Sabrina bit her lip. 'I wanted to warn you about his reputation, but Guy said—'

'No.' Rose shook her head to interrupt her friend. 'I don't want Khalim portrayed as some feelingless heartbreaker who used me and then dumped me. I went into this with my eyes open, Sabrina. I knew exactly what would happen, and now it has.' And the pain of his leaving was more intense than she had imagined in her worst nightmares.

Sabrina had come straight round soon after Khalim had left for the airport. 'Khalim has just rung me,' she announced to a red-eyed Rose when she opened the door to her. 'Oh, darling Rose—I'm so very sorry.'

'He told you about his father, I suppose?' Rose questioned dully.

'Yes.' Sabrina shut the front door behind her. 'He also told me to look after you. He's worried about you, you know.'

'I'm not an invalid, Sabrina,' said Rose stiffly.

But actually, maybe she *was* beginning to feel like an invalid.

In the two hours since Khalim had left for the airport, she had wandered around the flat like a robot, picking up all her possessions and placing them in neat piles, ready to go.

It was surprising really, just how much of a home they had made. In three months of living together, they had built up much more than she remembered. Lots of books. Vases. A coffee set. A beautiful backgammon set. Little things she had brought to their home. A lump formed in the back of her throat and she swallowed it down.

No point in thinking like that. No point at all.

'But where will you *go*?' asked Sabrina.

Rose looked at her with a calm, frozen face. 'I'll be fine. Don't forget—I've still been paying the mortgage on my flat, all the time I've been living here with Khalim.'

'But I thought you said that Lara had moved that ghastly boyfriend of hers in.'

'Yes, she has.' Rose gave a worried frown, before a little of her customary fire returned to reassure her that she hadn't become a *complete* walking piece of misery. 'And she can jolly well move him out again!'

'And you're really going to sell this place?'

'Yes, I am.'

'Don't you think it's a little soon to be making major decisions like that?'

Rose shook her head. In a world which now seemed to have all the security of quicksand, there was only one thing she knew for sure. 'I won't change my mind,' she said quietly. 'I just know I have to go.'

'So will you buy somewhere else with the proceeds, if it's just the fact that you can't bear to live here without Khalim?'

'It isn't. I just don't want to be beholden to him in any way.'

'Oh, Rose, he can *afford* it!'

'That's not the point! I *know* he can afford it! But it will make me feel like it's some kind of pay-off.'

'I'm sure it isn't.'

'So I'm going to give the money to charity instead!' she declared.

'Khalim wouldn't want you to do that. He'd want you to use it on yourself. Guy says he's genuinely concerned about you—'

'Well, he needn't be,' said Rose stubbornly, because concern made her stupid heart leap with excitement. He might be *concerned*, but he wasn't here, was he? And he never would be, either. 'He's always telling me how brave and how strong I am. I'll get over it.'

Maybe if she said it often enough, she just might convince herself.

She stared at Sabrina's worried face. 'Khalim asked you out once, didn't he, Sabrina?'

Sabrina's eyes widened. 'Who on earth told you that?'

Rose smiled. 'Khalim did. He said…' Her voice began to waver as she remembered the closeness they had shared the night he had made the admission. 'He said that he didn't want there to be any secrets between us…' Her eyes filled with tears and she turned a stricken face to Sabrina who instantly came over and put her arms around her.

'Oh, Rose,' she whispered. 'Poor, darling Rose.'

'Just tell me one thing, Sabrina!' sobbed Rose helplessly. 'Why the hell did he have to be a *prince*? Why couldn't he have just been a normal *man*?'

The death of Khalim's father was announced on the national news that evening, and Rose found herself watching the set obsessively, unable to turn the television off, even though her sanity pleaded with her to.

There was a short clip showing Khalim arriving at Dar-gar airport, with hordes of people clogging up the tarmac and paying homage to their new leader.

How stern he looked, in his pure white robes, she thought longingly. And how icily and perfectly remote. Looking at the footage of his arrival, it seemed hard to believe that just a few hours ago they had been making love in the room next door.

She swallowed, and as the news switched to other items she turned the set off.

She went home to her flat that same evening, to find the place almost unrecognisable and Giles snoring on the sofa.

Biting back her temper, she marched over and shook him by the shoulder.

'Whoa!' He opened bleary eyes and blinked at her. 'Whassa matter?' he slurred.

Rose took a steadying breath as she backed off from the stench of stale alcohol. 'Where's Lara?'

'She's away filming. What are you doing here?'

'I'm moving back here—in to *my* home. I know it's short notice, but would you be able to find somewhere else to live, please, Giles? And if it's at all possible I'd like you out tonight.'

Giles sat up and sneered. 'What's happened? Has he kicked you out? Has your pretty prince tired of you?'

'Khalim's father died this morning,' she said, in a voice which was threatening to break.

Giles narrowed his eyes. 'So he's in charge now, is he? Wow!'

It shamed her that he had not expressed one single sentiment of sorrow for Khalim's father—even for convention's sake.

'Just go, will you, Giles?' she said tiredly.

'Okay, okay—I'll go and stay with my brother.'

Once he had gone, she set to cleaning the flat, and at least it gave her something to do to occupy herself, so that by midnight, when everything was looking pretty much normal again, she was able to take a long bath and fall into bed.

But she couldn't sleep.

For too long she had been used to drifting off in the warm haven of Khalim's arms. Now she felt cold. And alone. She put on a baggy T-shirt for comfort, but there was still precious little warmth to be found.

She found a purchaser for the house almost immediately. That part of Chelsea had people just *queuing* up to buy homes there—and she was lucky enough to find a newly engaged merchant banker who was a first-time buyer.

'I want to complete the sale as quickly as possible, that's my only condition,' she told him and his horse-faced fiancée.

'Soon as you like,' he agreed smoothly, barely able to contain his glee as he examined the luxurious wealth of fixtures and fittings.

Rose tried to throw herself into her work, and when the money for the sale came through she went straight to the Maraban Embassy in Central London. It was difficult to keep a rein on her emotions as she spoke to the receptionist—a man whose glittering black eyes reminded her of Khalim, and made her feel such a deep sadness.

'Yes?' he asked.

Rose pulled the cheque out of her handbag, still finding it difficult to come to terms with just how much money the house had made. Khalim had been correct, she thought wryly—it *had* been a good investment.

'I'd like to make a donation to the Maraban Orphans' Fund,' she said.

The receptionist put his pen down and his look of surprise quickly became a smile of pleasure. 'How very kind,' he murmured. 'I will ask one of our attachés to come down and speak with you.'

'Can't I just leave the money, and go?'

He glanced down at the cheque, narrowed his eyes in shock and shook his head. 'I'm afraid that will not be possible. You are extremely generous, Miss…' he glanced down at the cheque again '…Thomas.'

Twenty minutes later, Rose was shaking hands with a courteous if somewhat bland attaché, who kept thanking her over and over for her generosity.

'You would like to sign the book of condolence before you leave?' he asked.

Rose hesitated. 'Yes, please,' she said quietly.

They left her alone in a room where a black-draped photograph of Khalim's father hung above a simple arrangement of lilies, alongside which a single candle burned. It was a photo which must have been taken when he was in his prime. How like his son he looked with those stern, handsome features and those fathomless black eyes, she thought.

Hot tears stung her eyes as she lifted the pen and stared at it as if seeking inspiration. What to write?

And then the words seemed to come pouring out all by themselves.

'You were a fine ruler,' she wrote, 'whose people loved and respected you. May you rest in peace, in the knowledge that your only son has inherited your strength and your wisdom to take Maraban into the future.'

Somehow she got out of there without bursting into tears, but at least there was a sense of a burden having been lifted. She'd cut her ties with Khalim, she realised—and, in so doing, had shown her own strength and wisdom. Now she must get on with rebuilding her life.

But this was easier said than done.

A job which had once enthralled her now became a number of hours in the day to be endured. I *must* snap out of it, she told herself fiercely—or I won't have a job as well as my man.

Yet, try as she might, she found herself gazing sightlessly out of the window time after time.

In the weeks which followed Khalim's departure, images

came back to burn themselves in her mind's eye—and to haunt her with their poignant perfection.

She remembered the first time she had shared a bathtub with him, and after the inevitable love-making they had washed each other's backs, giggling as bubbles frothed up and slid over the side and onto the floor.

He had looked at her with an expression of mock-horror. 'Now who is going to clean *that* up?'

'You are! You're the one who insisted on joining me in the bath!'

In that split-second of a moment Khalim had looked carefree—his rare and beautiful smile making her heart race. 'You'll have to make me, Rose!'

'I have my methods,' she had purred boastfully, her hands sliding underneath the water to capture him, and he had closed his eyes in helpless pleasure.

So what was she doing remembering *that*? Trying to torture herself? To remind herself of how unexpectedly *easy* it had been to adjust to a man like Khalim? And it had.

She hadn't expected to be able to sit enjoying such simple companionship with him in the evenings as they'd played backgammon or cooked a meal together. Oh, *why* had it been so easy? she asked herself in despair.

And then, two nights later, she had a visitor when she arrived back at the flat after work.

Philip Caprice was sitting in a long, dark limousine outside the flat and Rose's heart leapt when she saw the car, her eyes screwing up in an attempt to scan the smoky glass, in futile search for the one person she really wanted to see.

Philip must have seen her approaching, because by the time she came alongside the car he had got out and was standing waiting, a polite but slightly wary smile on his face.

'Hello, Rose,' he said.

She nodded in greeting. His eyes looked very green against his lightly tanned skin. Tanned by the glorious heat of the Maraban sun, she observed with a pang. 'Philip,' she gulped.

'May I come inside and talk to you?'

She wanted to say no, to ask him what was the point—but her curiosity got the better of her. And, besides, she wanted to hear news of Khalim.

'Yes, of course you can.'

'Thank you.'

Lara was still away filming and so the flat was empty and mercifully tidy and she found herself thinking about the time when she had turned up with Khalim to find total chaos. Remembered the rather fastidious look of horror which had darkened his handsome face, and the resulting decision for him to find them somewhere to live.

Just *stop* remembering, she told herself fiercely. Stop it!

'Would you like some coffee, Philip? Or tea, perhaps?'

He shook his dark head. 'Thank you, but no.'

He seemed, she thought, a trifle uncomfortable. What was the purpose of his visit? she wondered. 'What can I do for you, Philip?' she asked pleasantly.

'Khalim has sent me.'

She bit her lip. 'H-how is he?'

'He's sad, of course—but coping magnificently, just as you would expect.'

'Yes.' Of course he was. Swallowing down her pain, she said, 'So what is the purpose of your visit here today, Philip?'

Philip nodded thoughtfully, as if her reaction was not the one he would have anticipated. 'He asked me to bring you this.' He opened up his briefcase and withdrew a slim, dark leather box and handed it to her.

Rose stared down at it. 'What is it?'

'Why don't you open it, and see?'

Caution told her to give it straight back to him, but that old devil called curiosity seemed to be guiding her actions instead. With miraculously unshaking hands, she opened the clasp.

Inside was a necklace, although the word seemed oddly

inadequate for the magnificent piece of jewellery which dazzled at her from its navy-velveted backdrop.

A necklace of sapphires and diamonds which blazed with unmatchable brilliance, and, at the very centre of the piece, a single deeper blue sapphire, the size of a large walnut.

Rose lifted her eyes to his, her face pale and her voice now trembling. 'Wh-what is the p-purpose of this?'

'Isn't it obvious?'

'Not to me it isn't, no. Why is he sending his emissary with expensive baubles? To sweeten me up? Is that it? To induce me to fall in with his wishes?'

'He doesn't want it to be over, Rose.'

'Well, it *is* over,' she said stubbornly. 'It has to be. I thought I made that clear. I'm not prepared to become his part-time mistress, Philip—I told him that unequivocally. So perhaps you'd like to give this back to him, and tell him that pieces of jewellery, no matter how gorgeous, will not change my mind.' And she snapped back the clasp and handed it back to him.

Philip stared down at the proffered case for a long moment before he took it. 'You won't change your mind?' he asked slowly.

She shook her head, but with the pain again came the sense of liberation, and of dignity. 'I can't. Tell him that. And tell him not to contact me again—that's best for both our sakes.' She kept her voice steady. 'Tell him to make a happy life for himself in Maraban, and I will endeavour to do the same for myself in England.'

Philip nodded. 'He will not be pleased.'

'I didn't imagine for a moment that he would be. And please tell him not to mistake my resistance for enticement.' She gave a heavy sigh. 'I'm trying to be practical, Philip, for both our sakes.' And my heart is too fragile. If I stop it now, I will survive, she thought. And so will he. If I let it continue in the cloak-and-dagger way of being his foreign mistress, then I risk it breaking into a thousand pieces.

'Do you have any message for him?'

She longed to ask Philip to tell him that she loved him, and that she would never stop loving him—but wouldn't that give him the power to try and wear her down? And who knew how long she would be able to resist *that*?

She nodded. 'Just wish him luck, Philip. Tell him to make Maraban great.'

Philip looked as though he wanted to say something else, but clearly thought better of it. He dropped the case into his briefcase and gave a brief, courteous smile.

'That was never in any doubt,' he said. 'It is his personal happiness which is precarious.'

So he wanted it all. A wife in Maraban and a mistress in London. She remembered something that Khalim had once said to her, and shrugged. 'And that, I'm afraid, Philip—that goes with the territory.'

CHAPTER FOURTEEN

THERE were swathes of dark green holly leaves, their blood-coloured berries gleaming as Rose looped them through the bannister of the sweeping staircase which dominated the hall-way of her parents' farmhouse.

'There!' She stood back to admire her handiwork and turned to where her brother was standing holding all the pins and tacks. 'What do you think, Jamie?'

'Perfect,' smiled her brother.

'And you like the tree?'

He stared for a moment at the huge conifer which stood next to the hatstand. She had festooned it with silver and gold baubles and tied scarlet ribbons around the ends of all the branches. 'Perfect,' he said again, and narrowed his eyes thoughtfully at her. 'You seem happier these days, Rose.'

She hesitated for a moment. Did she? Then appearances could be very deceptive. Because even though most of the time she *did* feel, if not exactly happy, then certainly more contented than before—the pain of losing Khalim could still come back to haunt her and tear at her heart with an intensity which had the power to make her feel weak and shaking.

She shrugged. 'Well, it's been over a year now since...' Her voice tailed off. To say the words made it real, and so much of her wished that it were nothing but some cruel fantasy.

'Since lover-boy went back to Maraban?'

She frowned. 'There's no need to say it in quite that tone, Jamie.'

'What way is that? The disapproving way in which any brother would speak if their sister had had her heart broken by a man who should have known better?'

172

Rose sighed. 'I keep telling you—he didn't exactly have to kidnap me! I knew exactly what I was getting into, I just—'

'Expected that the end result might be different?' he prompted softly.

Well, no. Of course she hadn't, not really. She had *hoped*, of course she had—because hope was part of the human condition, even when deep down you knew that to hope was useless.

She shook her head. 'I gave up hoping a long time ago, Jamie. Let's leave it, shall we? What time are Mum and Dad getting back?'

'Their train gets in at three, and I said I'd go and collect them from the station. Though it beats me why anyone in their right mind should choose to go Christmas shopping in London, on Christmas *Eve*!'

Rose smiled. 'It's a family tradition, remember? And I like traditions! Now I think I'll go and hang some greenery round the fireplace. Want to help me?'

Jamie grinned. 'I think I'm all spent out where decorating activities are concerned! I might just go and put a light under that pot of soup. Going to have some with me, Rosie?'

'No, thanks. I had a late breakfast.'

'You are eating properly again now, aren't you?'

'I never stopped!'

'That's why when you turn sideways you could disappear?'

She forced a smile. 'I'm not *thin*, Jamie—just slimmer than I used to be.'

'Hmm. Well, Mum is planning to feed you up on Christmas pudding—be warned!'

'Can't wait!'

She went into the sitting room and sat down on the floor to begin tying together the greenery she had brought in from the garden.

Hard to believe that they would soon be into a new year,

but maybe the brand-new start would give her the impetus she needed to get on with her life. *Really* get on with her life.

She had made changes. Had switched from Headliners to another, smaller agency—where the different faces and different clients had forced her to concentrate on work, instead of dwelling on the darkly handsome face she missed with such an intensity.

And she had sold her flat in Notting Hill, too. She had bought somewhere slightly smaller and in a less fashionable area of London, which meant that she no longer needed to take in a lodger.

She didn't have to pretend to be feeling good in front of a flatmate now that she lived on her own. And if she felt like a quiet evening in, reading or watching television, then there was no one to nag her about going out and *meeting* people. She didn't want to meet people. Especially not men. She had known very early on that Khalim would be an impossible act to follow, and in that her instincts had not failed her.

Somewhere in the distance, she heard the chiming of the doorbell, and because she was up to her ears in stray bits of conifer she hoped that Jamie might answer it. She heard the door open, and then murmurings.

'Rose!'

She blinked at the rather urgent quality in Jamie's voice. 'What is it?'

'You have a visitor.'

She looked up to see Jamie framed in the doorway of the sitting room, his face white and tense, a look of something approaching anger hardening his mouth.

'What's the matter?' she asked.

'It's *him*!'

'What is?' she questioned stupidly.

'*Khalim!*' he whispered. 'He's here. Right now. Waiting in the hall.'

The world span out of control and she felt all the blood

drain from her face. 'What does he want?' she whispered back, in a voice which did not sound like her own.

'To see you, of course!' Jamie glowered. 'You don't *have* to see him, you know, Rose! I can send him away, if that's what you want.'

And wouldn't that be best?

She had done everything in her power to eradicate him from her memory in the intervening year since she had last seen him. She had been largely unsuccessful in this, it was true, but it hadn't been through a lack of trying. Wouldn't seeing him again just reopen all those old wounds, making the original injury even worse than before?

But how could she *not* see him—when her heart was banging fit to burst at the thought that he was here? Now.

She stood up and brushed some spray fronds of greenery from the front of her jeans. 'No, I'll see him, Jamie,' she said quietly. 'Will you send him in, please?'

In an effort to compose herself, she walked over to the window and looked out at the stark winter landscape which seemed to mirror the icy desolation of her emotional state.

She heard him enter the room. That unmistakable footfall.

'Rose?' came the deep and slightly stern entreaty from behind her.

Heart hammering, Rose forced herself to face him, and when she did her breath caught in her throat with longing.

He looked...

Oh, but he looked perfect—more perfect than any man had a right to look. And he was not wearing one of the immaculate suits he usually wore when he was in Europe—instead, he was dressed in the flowing, silken robes of Maraban. The ebony eyes were gleaming with some unspoken message and his face was as stern and as fierce as she had ever seen it.

Sabrina's heart turned over with love and longing as she stared into the unfathomable glitter of his eyes, but she prayed that her face didn't register her feelings.

Why was he here?

'Hello, Khalim,' she said, in a voice which she didn't quite recognise as her own.

He thought how pale her face was, so that the blue eyes seemed to dominate its heart-shaped frame with their unforgettable dazzle. And how fragile she looked, too—the jeans he remembered looking slightly loose on the waist, and around the swell of her bottom. 'Hello, Rose,' he said softly.

She drew a deep breath. 'How did you find me?'

He gave a brief, hard smile. It had been clear that she had not wanted him to find her. She had changed her job and changed her flat—no, the message to stay away had been quite clear. 'It was not difficult.' He shrugged.

Not for him, no—of course it wasn't. 'Did you get Philip to search for me?' she mocked.

'What did you expect me to do?' he retorted. 'Scour the pages of the telephone directory myself? Running a country takes up almost all of my waking hours, Rose.'

'Of course. I shouldn't have been so flippant.' Her voice trembled. 'H-how is Maraban?'

'Lonely,' he said with the brutal honesty which seemed to come so easily around her.

She quashed the foolish flare of hope which leapt in her heart. She had never allowed fantasy to get in the way of reality where he was concerned, and she wasn't about to start now. 'Oh? So no suitable bride been found for you yet?'

'No,' he agreed equably, because the waspish way she asked that question told him that maybe her message of wanting him to stay away had been ambivalent. That maybe she still cared. 'No wife.'

'But not through lack of trying, I imagine?'

He was not going to tell her lies, nor to play games with her. 'That's right.' He allowed his mind to briefly dwell on every available high-born Maraban woman who had been brought before his critical eye. And how every doe-eyed look of submission had only emphasised the equality he had shared with Rose.

'But none of them came up to your exacting standards, Khalim?'

'Not one.' He smiled. 'That's why I'm here today.'

She reminded herself of what his terms had been before he'd left, and they would not have changed—why should they when the circumstances were exactly the same as before?

'Would you mind making yourself a little clearer?'

He owed her this. The unadorned truth. The only words which would express the only thing which mattered.

'I love you, Rose.'

The words rang in her ears. Alien words. Secretly longed-for but inconceivable words…words from which she would never recover if they weren't true. She met the lancing black stare and her heart began to pound. Because it didn't matter what logic or common sense told her—Khalim would not use words like that if he didn't mean them. Why would he?

Khalim narrowed his eyes as he watched the wary assessment which had caused a frown to appear between the two delicate arches of her eyebrows. Had he imagined that she would fall straight into his arms the moment that those words were out of his mouth?

'Shall I say it again?' he questioned softly. 'That I love you, Rose. I have always loved you. I shall love you for the rest of my days, and maybe beyond that, too.'

She shook her head distractedly. It didn't matter—because fundamentally nothing had changed. 'I can't do it, Khalim,' she whispered. 'I just can't do it.'

Black brows knitted together. 'Do what?'

'I can't be your mistress—I just can't—because it will break my heart.' Maybe if she appealed to his innate sense of decency, he might go away and leave her alone. Stop tempting her into breaking every rule in the book. She sucked in a huge, shuddering breath. 'You see, I love you, too—I love you in a way I didn't think it was possible to love.'

'And that's a problem, is it?' he asked gently.

'Of course it's a problem! I can't say I'm not tempted to become your mistress—of course I am! I've ached and ached for you since you went back to Maraban, and just when I thought I might be getting over it—'

'*Are* you?' he questioned sternly. 'Getting over me?'

The truth was much more important than remembering not to pander to his ego. 'No, of course I'm not,' she admitted. And she didn't think she ever would. 'But what chance do I have if we become lovers again? I'll just get sucked in, deeper and deeper, and then sooner or later there *will* be a Maraban woman who you will want to make your wife—'

'Never!' he said flatly.

'You can't say that!'

'Oh, yes, I can,' he corrected resolutely. 'There is only one woman who I could ever imagine making my wife. One woman who I have every intention of making my wife, and that woman is you, Rose. It only ever *has* been you.'

She stared at him in disbelief, telling herself that she had not heard him properly. Words of love and commitment she had only ever listened to in her wildest dreams. And dreams didn't come true—everybody knew that. 'You can't mean that.'

He smiled then as he heard the loving tremble in her voice. 'Yes, I can, Rose. I have the agreement of my government to make you my bride just as soon as the wedding can be arranged.'

She longed to touch him, to run her fingertips with reverent wonder along the sculpted perfection of his face, but she was scared. 'But why the change of heart?'

He shook his head. 'No change of heart, my darling—that has remained constant since the first time I ever laid eyes on you. The difference is that my advisors have come to realise that a happy man makes a good ruler.' The stark, beautiful truth shone like ebony fire from his eyes. 'And I cannot ever be a happy man without you by my side. Come to me, Rose, come and kiss me, and make my world real once more.'

She didn't need to be asked twice—she was across the room and in his arms, and as he buried his lips in the flaxen satin of her hair she discovered that he was shaking as much as she was.

'Khalim,' she said brokenly.

'Sweet, sweet, beautiful Rose—my Rose, my only Rose,' he murmured against its scented sweetness, and she raised her face to his in wonder as she read the look of love on his face.

He bent his head to kiss her, and an intense feeling of emotion threatened to rock the very foundations of his world.

They were breathless when the kiss ended, and Rose lifted her hand up, traced the sensual outline of his lips with her finger.

'They don't mind? They honestly don't mind you taking a Western woman for your bride?'

His shrug was rueful. 'The more traditional element of the court were distinctly unimpressed, but the hand of my father guided events—even beyond his death.'

'I don't understand.'

'Do you remember he asked to meet you?'

'Yes, of course I do!'

'He had sensed my distraction since meeting you and wanted to know why. And when he met you, he understood perfectly.' He paused. 'Afterwards he commented on your similarity to my great-great-grandfather's true love.'

'Y-yes,' she said slowly as she waited for the rest of the story to unfold.

'And Malik was never the same man after she was sent away—'

'Is that Malik the Magnificent?' she asked tentatively.

Khalim narrowed his eyes. 'How on earth did you know that, Rose?'

'I read about it, of course—in the chapter about your ancestors.'

He smiled, thinking that she would make a wonderful

Princess of Maraban! 'His heart was not into ruling after that. He complied with convention and took a Marabanesh wife, but was left a bitter and empty shell of a man.' His eyes met hers with a candid light. 'My father did not want to see history repeating itself.'

'History or destiny?' she echoed softly, and her eyes lit up with a glorious sense of the inevitable. 'Or maybe even *pre*-destination, as though all this was somehow *supposed* to happen all along.'

'Predestination?' His deep voice lingered thoughtfully on the word, and he nodded. 'Yes. It exists. It's what drives us all. It's why I met you, Rose.'

The love from his eyes dazzled her, and she gazed up at him. 'What on earth can I say to something as beautiful as that?' she whispered.

He smiled. 'Say nothing, sweet Rose. Just kiss me instead.'

EPILOGUE

THE late afternoon air was warm and scented as Rose and Khalim alighted from the smoky-windowed car and made their way towards their apartments—situated in the grandest part of the palace. And where once she had been taken to see Khalim's father as he lay dying.

Rose was grateful to have met him, no matter that the visit had been brief. It pleased and warmed her to know that he had had the perception and the wisdom to override convention and to let their wedding take place.

And what a wedding!

The whole of Maraban had gone absolutely wild with excitement, happy that their leader should have found a woman to love at last, and proud of the pale, blonde beauty of his Rose.

Guy had been delighted to be best man, and Sabrina her maid of honour, and all of Rose's family had been flown out to Maraban in some style. They had feasted and celebrated for three enchanting days, crushing lavender and rose petals beneath their feet as they danced, and at the very end of the celebrations Rose and Khalim had ridden through Dar-gar on their Akhal-Teke horses. Rose's mount in a pure white—as white as the winter snows—and in such contrast to Khalim's Purr-Mahl.

For he had insisted that she learn to ride—had even insisted on teaching her himself. And what a hard taskmaster he had proved to be—not satisfied until she could gallop alongside him with a fearlessness which matched his own.

Never satisfied…and yet always satisfied.

It was the same in their marital bed on silken sheets which whispered and wrapped themselves around their entwined bodies. Would their passion for each other never abate? she sometimes asked herself in helpless wonder as she came back down to earth from some remote place of pleasure which Khalim had taken her to.

She hoped not.

He touched a light hand to her elbow as a golden shaft of sunlight turned her hair to pure spun gold. 'Tired?' he asked softly, thinking how all the people had warmed to her that afternoon. As they always warmed to her. For his Rose had a gentle understanding which made people instantly love her.

As he loved her, he thought fiercely—loved her more than he would have thought possible to love another person.

'Tired?' Rose smiled up at him dreamily. 'No, of course I'm not. It was a wonderful afternoon. Wasn't it?' she asked him, a touch anxiously.

'You know it was.' They had been to the opening of the newly refurbished Maraban Orphanage, now named after its princess. No announcement had ever been officially made, but word had got around on the grapevine of Rose's generous donation when she'd still been living in London, when she had believed her relationship with Khalim to be over.

'Such unselfishness,' his mother had cooed, totally in thrall with her daughter-in-law herself. As were his sisters. In fact, everyone. Well, almost everyone.

Khalim allowed a wistful smile to play at the corners of his mouth.

Except for Philip, of course. Philip had tendered his resignation a year after Rose had become Princess, even though both she and Khalim had asked him to reconsider.

But Philip had shaken his dark, handsome head, the green eyes enigmatic, giving little away.

'I cannot,' he had demurred.

'It isn't *me*, is it, Philip?' Rose had asked him.

He gave her a fond smile. 'Never you, Princess,' he had murmured. 'But I am part of the past, it is time for me to go. Your new emissary must be someone who will engage in your joint future. Think about it. You know that what I say is true.'

Yes, Khalim had known—Philip's insight had been one of the reasons he had made him his emissary. And even Rose had known that, too—though she was sad for a little time, because she herself had become fond of the cool Englishman and his connection with her old life.

The doors to their apartments were opened and they went inside, Khalim giving a swift shake of his dark head to the robed figure who looked enquiringly at him. He wanted to be alone with her.

Because Rose had seen very early on in her marriage that absolutely everyone wanted a piece of Khalim, and that unless she put her foot down their time together would be limited indeed. And so—to much outrage at first—she had insisted on having her own kitchen built inside their private apartments.

'I don't always want to be served food,' she had told Khalim stubbornly when he'd tried to oppose her plan. 'Sometimes I want to cook myself, for just the two of us, the way I used to when we lived together in London, remember?'

He'd smiled. 'How could I ever forget?'

'And, of course, for you to cook for *me*!' She had seen his look of outrage and slanted him a provocative smile. 'We don't want you forgetting how to fend for yourself, do we, my darling?'

'Oh, Rose,' he had moaned, helpless in the capture of that smile.

He watched her now as she moved with such elegant grace towards the kitchen, and followed her, wondering whether he should take her to bed now, or later. That was the trouble and also the joy of their relationship—he never stopped wanting her. But his powers of self-control had been sorely tested.

Today, her flaxen hair was complimented by the lavender silk of the gown she wore, and he looked at her with a slightly jealous pride. Too bad that they were now having to contend with hordes of foreign journalists eager to capture the beauty of the Marabanesh princess. His Rose was going international, while he wanted her all to himself! And yet deep in his heart he knew that she gave herself completely to him. And always would.

She turned to find him watching her and thought that right now was just the moment to make her gift to him. 'Khalim,' she said softly, in perfect Marabanese. 'Shall I make some mint tea for us to drink?' And she thought that she would never forget the look on his face as he stared at her with a kind of dawning wonder.

'Rose?'

She continued speaking in his native tongue. 'I've been having lessons,' she told him shyly. 'From Fatima. Whenever you've been dealing with affairs of state, I've been poring over my dictionary! And Fatima says I'm almost fluent and that I—'

But she couldn't say any more on the subject, because he had swiftly crossed the room, and had pulled her into his arms and was looking down at her with a fierce and tender love.

'Were the gods looking down on us the day I met you, Rose?' he demanded heatedly. 'And were they Jupiter and Venus?'

'I expect so,' she said demurely, because she knew just what he wanted when he looked at her like *that*. What *she* wanted, too, more than anything else.

She gave herself up to his kiss. Well, the mint tea could always wait.

Kate Walker was born in Nottinghamshire but as she grew up in Yorkshire she has always felt that her roots were there. She met her husband at university and she originally worked as a children's librarian but after the birth of her son she returned to her old childhood love of writing. When she's not working, she divides her time between her family, their three cats, and her interests of embroidery, antiques, film and theatre, and, of course, reading.

Watch out for Kate Walker's emotional and gripping read, on sale December 2005, in Modern Romance™!

DESERT AFFAIR
by
Kate Walker

CHAPTER ONE

'EXCUSE me, but is this seat taken?'

Lydia didn't even have to look up to know who had spoken. There was only one person in the whole of the airport lounge who could have a voice like that. The sort of voice that wrapped itself around her senses like a slither of warmed silk, its low, lyrically accented tones making her skin shiver in reaction to the sheer sensuality of their sound.

She had spotted him as soon as she had walked into the room. It had been impossible *not* to notice him. He was tall, dark and devastatingly imposing; it seemed as if he were the only person in the place. The sort of man who would draw any woman's gaze with the automatic ease of a powerful magnet and then lazily hold onto it without any sort of effort on his part.

And he had made no effort at all. Though he could not have been unaware of her attention, the overwhelming interest she hadn't even had the strength to hide, he had done nothing at all to sustain it or show that it mattered in the slightest to him. No trace of reaction had touched the carved male beauty of his tanned face, no flicker of a smile either of welcome or even disdain. But he had not been unaware of her.

'I said…'

'I know what you said!'

The faint rasp of an edge to the beautiful voice, the hint of angry reproof, had her lifting her head sharply, tossing back the soft brown curls that framed her heart-shaped face. Wide-set blue eyes fringed by long, curling lashes clashed abruptly with harder, glittering black, and for a second she felt as if her heart had actually stopped in stunned disbelief.

Dear God, but he was even more spectacular close up! The true beauty of that golden skin, the sculpted cheek-bones and wide, hard, sensual slash of a mouth was like a blow in the pit of her stomach. His nose was long and straight, his hair unredeemed black, cut in an uncompromisingly severe crop that emphasised the total perfection of the superb, clean-cut lines of his features.

And if he had seemed tall from a distance then standing over her like this, with those amazing eyes fixed searchingly on her face, his impact was positively earth-shattering.

'I know what you said...'

Hastily Lydia adjusted her tone a degree or two downwards, from the pitch to which shock and apprehension had pushed it, wishing she could erase the flaring wash of colour from her cheeks as easily.

'But I would have thought that it was obvious that no one was sitting there.'

And that no one had occupied the chair beside her for all of the—what? Almost three quarters of an hour since she had taken up her position here. After all, he had been watching her for almost all of that time.

She had tried to bury her face in the copy of the magazine she had bought to while away the time waiting for her flight to be called, but she had felt the burn of his brazen gaze fixed on her. And she had met its cold scrutiny head-on if she'd so much as glanced upwards from the page.

'I wondered if you might be waiting for someone.'

'Well, no, I'm not! I'm here on my own!'

'Then may I join you?'

'Why?'

She knew she sounded suspicious, as stiff as a cat being threatened by the approach of a stranger into its territory, but she couldn't help it. It was how she felt, wary and unsure of herself. If anything, *she* felt like the intruder into the luxurious, opulent surroundings of the VIP lounge. It was not the sort of place she normally frequented, not the sort of place she could ever have afforded to be in if it hadn't been for her new job, the generosity of her employers.

He, on the other hand, looked totally, supremely at home here. His long, lean body might be clothed in the same casual jeans and a jumper that she had chosen for practicality during a long flight, but there could be no doubt that his clothing was very definitely not from the chain store where she had bought hers. No, the lines of his clothing murmured of designer labels and expensive tailoring, and she was sure that the smoky grey sweater that hugged the firm lines of his chest and skimmed the narrow waist and hips could only be of the finest, softest cashmere available. Everything about him said Money, with a capital M.

And in spite of the supremely civilised nature of his appearance, something about him seemed to whisper of a wilder spirit, an untamed, elemental part of his character that didn't fit with the ultra-modern surroundings.

'Why?'

He shrugged indolent shoulders, unconsciously drawing attention to their width and strength.

'To while away a little time. To ease the boredom of waiting with some conversation.'

A tiny hint of a smile curled that devastating mouth up at one corner and the onyx eyes gleamed for a second with a hint of mocking amusement.

'Is that such a terrible idea?'

'N-no…'

This was even worse! Her tongue seemed to be tangling up on itself, refusing to get the words out in any coherent form, and she was stumbling over the simplest of answers. And it was not a sensation she was used to.

She didn't normally have this sort of trouble in talking to strangers. She was *trained* to talk to them, after all! Trained to handle almost any sort of eventuality or problem. So why did this one man affect her like this?

'I'm expecting my flight to be called at any minute.'

'I doubt it.'

His glance towards the huge plate-glass windows was wry, his mouth taking on an expressive twist as he surveyed the scene outside.

'The snow is definitely getting worse and the wind's picking up. It's blowing a blizzard out there. No pilot worth his salt is going to even think of taking off in conditions like this. You'll be lucky if you're only delayed by a couple of hours.'

'*Only* delayed,' Lydia echoed bleakly. 'As opposed to what?'

'To your flight being cancelled completely and the airport being shut down for today. I think you'd better consider that possibility…' he added, seeing the way her face fell. 'From what I can see, it can only get worse, not better.'

And what would she do then? Lydia was forced to wonder. If the airport closed, she had nowhere to go; nothing to go back to. Today was to have been the start of her new life, a whole new beginning.

'Would having a drink with me be such a bad thing?' The thread of irony was definitely darker now, making her shiver faintly just to hear it.

'No…'

But still she couldn't make herself say yes, please sit down, introduce herself. All the normal politeness and pleasantries seemed to have fled from her mind, leaving it shockingly blank as a wiped blackboard.

'Just what is it that you're afraid of?'

Silkily spoken though they were, she knew the words were meant to sting and they did. Sharply.

'Do you really think that I'm about to pounce on you in front of all these other passengers—not to mention the airport staff? Perhaps you fear that, driven mad by your stunning beauty, I will ravish you without mercy.'

'Oh, now you're just being ridiculous.'

She struggled to ignore the sudden twist of her heart, the judder in her pulse as the impact of that 'stunning beauty' hit home. His tone had been ironical but something deep in those spectacular eyes had told her that the words had been more seriously meant.

'Please don't be silly. It's just that…that I really don't see exactly why you should want to. What would you get from talking to a complete stranger who is due to head out of here on a plane at any minute? I mean…why me?' she ended on an uncharacteristically plaintive note.

The wordless sound he made with his tongue was sharp, impatient, speaking eloquently of the irritation and temper he was struggling to rein back. It was also totally un-English making her wonder just what his nationality might be. That accent certainly wasn't Italian or Spanish. It was far more exotic than that, in spite of impeccable pronunciation and a natural ease of grammar. There was an arrogance and pride in both his profile and his bearing that made her think fleetingly of long-ago kings or Bedouin warriors, but such fanciful thoughts flew from her head when he spoke again.

'You are clearly not a fool,' he declared with a sudden harshness that brought a gasp of shock to her lips. 'So why do you behave as if you were? You know very well what is between us—what has been there from the moment I first laid eyes on you and you on me.'

'No, I don't!'

Sitting down kept her too far beneath him, making her position too vulnerable for her liking. In a rush she started to her feet, only to find that instead of making things easier she had in fact made them much, much worse.

Face to face like this, on the same level at last, she was supremely conscious of the difference in their builds. At five feet ten inches, she had always considered herself overly tall for a woman, but this man had the rare ability to make her feel small.

His head and shoulders topped hers by several inches, and she found that unless she looked upwards at an awkward angle she was forced to focus on the dangerous sensuality of his mouth. His beautiful mouth and the smooth olive skin that surrounded it, faintly shadowed by several hours' growth of beard. Immediately her thoughts jumped to imagine just what it would feel like to have that mouth on hers, to press her own lips against the satin warmth of his face.

She was now so close to him that the clean, faintly musky scent of his body tantalised her senses. It was impossible not to inhale secretly, sparking a reaction like the internal prickle of pins and needles.

'I don't!' she repeated, less certainly this time. 'What do you mean what there is between us? I don't know what you are talking about.'

Black eyes flashed as he turned a look of pure scorn on her flushed face.

'You know only too well what I'm talking about,' he tossed back at her in a low, dangerous voice. 'We both know what is happening between us, even if you are too craven to admit to it and give it a name.'

Unexpectedly he leaned forwards, reaching out with one long, tanned hand. The tip of his finger touched her cheek very lightly and then moved slowly and caressingly downwards, etching a trail of fire along her skin.

'And it is a very simple word,' he murmured beguilingly. 'Short, to the point, and so easy to say if you only have the courage to trust in yourself.'

His eyes held her, keeping her transfixed, unable to move, unable to blink. And what she read in that steady, ebony gaze, the fierce flames that burned in the darkness of his pupils, gave her the answer she both wanted and dreaded.

Sex.

The word flared in Lydia's mind, etched in letters of white-hot flame, so that she was sure that this disturbing stranger must be able to look deep into her eyes and read it clearly there.

Sex.

Pure and undiluted. Primal. Powerful. Totally primitive. The sort of instinctive, unthinking response that couldn't be understood or explained. Human interaction at its most basic. It couldn't be denied and it couldn't be resisted.

That was what blazed between them. What had sparked in her senses in the first moment she had set eyes on this man when she had walked into the room.

And it was clear that he too had felt that same shock of carnal recognition, the body-blow to the soul that said, I *want* this person. I want them so much that I feel I will die if I never have them. It dried her throat and made her heart pound. Her clenched hands were damp with sweat, her lips parched, but she didn't dare do anything to ease either physical sensation. To do so would be to reveal to those watchful, hunting hawk's eyes that she was light years away from being as calm as she wanted to pretend.

'I...'

She opened her mouth to deny the accusation of cowardice, but the knowledge of the truth dried the protest on her tongue and turned it into a raw, embarrassing croak.

'You...?' he encouraged softly, the single, husky word a seduction in itself. And the spot where his fingertip still rested on her cheek was a burning focus, a concentration of all the sensations he aroused in her.

It seemed obscene to be at the mercy of such primitive feelings in such public, impersonal surroundings. All around her was the hushed murmur of voices in desultory conversation. Other passengers lounged in the comfortable chairs, turning the pages of newspapers and magazines, or frowned into laptop computers, occasionally leaning forward to touch a key. No one even spared them as much as a curious glance.

And yet Lydia had the feeling that the awareness that pulsed between her and this man—a man whose name she didn't even know—must have enclosed them in a glowing, burning haze that swirled in the air and coiled round them like smoke. Her heart was beating a frantic tattoo, and she was sure that the hard, strong finger must feel the race of the blood in her veins and know what had caused it.

'You…?' he prompted again, but her tongue seemed too thick, too frozen to speak, and she could only shake her head in numb confusion.

His reaction was brusque and startling, making her flinch in a moment of shocked panic. The long forefinger was snatched away with a swiftly muttered imprecation in some language she didn't know, the words too harsh and swift to catch. Then his hand came down in a violent, slashing movement between their two bodies as if he were cutting off all communication between them.

'Enough!' he declared in a voice that rang with cold anger. 'I do not have time for this…'

And before she could register exactly what he had in mind he had spun on his heel and was clearly about to march away from her, dismissing her totally from his mind.

'I…'

Lydia struggled with the tangle of feelings that had knotted high up in her throat, choking off speech.

'I…' she tried again, her voice croaking rawly. 'I… Oh, please! *Wait!*'

In her mind, the last word was a wild, desperate cry, one that would have brought confused, irritated, and just plain curious looks her way from every other waiting passenger. But what actually came out was a weak, uncertain whisper, one that broke in the middle.

And one that she was sure he couldn't have heard. It seemed that way at first because for the space of several jolting heartbeats he didn't seem to react. He certainly didn't pause, and the impetus of his anger was such that the force of his movement took him well away from her, almost into the middle of the room, before he came to an abrupt halt and slowly, very, very slowly, turned back to face her again.

'What did you say?'

'I said…'

Lydia swallowed hard because she wanted this to sound so very different from that first, frantic call.

'I said, please wait. Please don't go.'

One jet-black brow lifted in sardonic interrogation and his handsome head inclined slightly to one side in apparent thoughtful consideration of the situation.

'You've changed your mind?'

'I—changed my mind.'

Better to let him think that. Better to let him believe that she had had second thoughts than to let him know what *she* had known all along. That there was no way she could have let him just walk out of her life as suddenly as he had walked into it.

But it had been only when he had actually moved away from her and her heart had cried out in distress at being abandoned like this that she had realised how much she had wanted him to stay.

'You changed your mind—and you want—what?'

'I'd like you to stay. And talk…'

Still he didn't move.

'And perhaps have that drink you suggested. After all…'

She tried for an airy tone, waved a hand in the direction of the windows against which the snow now swirled in

wild, blustering eddies, the view of the runways, the waiting planes totally obliterated from sight.

'Clearly neither of us is going anywhere soon. We might
as well spend the time here together as apart. The hours
always drag so much when you're waiting.'

Her voice faltered, going up and down embarrassingly
as she stared into his stony, set face and met no response.

Was the man waiting for her to *beg*? She wouldn't! She
had more pride! And yet if he turned away again...

'Please won't you join me?'

Still he waited one more nicely calculated minute. Just
long enough to stretch out her screaming nerves even
more, to twist them into hard, painful knots of tension.
Then as suddenly as he had turned away he swung back,
covering the short distance between them in a few swift,
confident strides.

It was like seeing a sleek black panther coming towards
her, Lydia thought, struggling to push away uneasy visions
of herself as the prey and this man very definitely in the
role of predator.

But then he turned on her a smile of such supercharged
charm that it would have melted an iceberg. One that left
her feeling as if the weak, ineffectual barriers she had been
trying to build up against him had shattered into splinters,
falling hopelessly at her feet.

'I'm glad you changed your mind,' he said, the unexpected warmth of his tone so unlike the icy harshness of
moments before that it rocked her sense of reality, making
her wonder for a second if she was even talking to the
same man. 'I *hate* waiting. I have no patience at all.'

'Me too,' Lydia admitted. 'I was bored out of my head
already. And it looks as if we're in for a long delay. Do
you think any of those planes are going anywhere today?'

The glance he turned in the direction she indicated was
brief to the point of indifference and her heart jumped on

a thrill of delighted confusion as his ebony gaze came back to her face and fastened on it fixedly.

'I doubt it.'

His shrug dismissed the matter from his thoughts, his obvious lack of concern intensely gratifying to her uncertain self-esteem. After long, lonely months of feeling unwanted and rejected, the glow of appreciation that burned like fiery coals deep in the darkness of his eyes was a balm to her wounded pride.

'But it is no matter. We won't care how long we have to wait. We won't notice the time.'

'No…'

It was all she could manage because it was happening again. The warm sensuality of his tone had dried her throat, leaving her lips parched so that she had to slide her tongue over them to ease the discomfort. And as she saw that intent, black gaze drop to follow the small betraying movement she felt its force as if it were an actual touch on her skin, and shivered secretly in response.

The need for that touch to be a reality sent a wave of hunger through her that drained the strength from her legs so that she had to sink down suddenly onto the nearest chair. It was either that or give herself away completely by falling in a ridiculously weak heap right at his beautifully shod feet.

'Won't you sit down too?' she managed.

And it was as he came down beside her that a new feeling hit. A disturbing, scary sensation that made her feel as if something wet and icy had slowly slithered down the sensitive length of her spine.

She was suddenly totally and inexplicably convinced that her life would never be the same again. That the whole of her future was bound up with this man and there was no way she could break free at all.

CHAPTER TWO

'SO, WHAT shall we talk about?'

Lydia had to force herself to drag her thoughts back from the disturbing paths they were determined to follow. She had already let this man rattle her far too easily. It was time she got back in control of the situation! Seeing him as the ruler of her fate, indeed! He was just a new acquaintance. A stunning, fascinating, lethally good-looking one, admittedly, but just a man for all that.

But then her eyes met the dark, deep set ones of the man beside her and the description 'just a man' once more became totally inadequate.

'Where should we begin?'

'Names would be a good place to start.'

She aimed for crisp matter-of-factness and was pleased to note that she actually managed to come close.

'We haven't even introduced ourselves yet. I'm Lydia Ashton.'

She held out her hand as she spoke, feeling better now that things were back on a more regular footing.

'And you are?'

A worrying glint of something that looked like amusement gleamed in his eyes but he followed her lead impeccably.

'Amir Zaman,' he said in that beautiful voice, the slight accent deepening on the words.

'Amir…'

This was the normal path of things—meetings, introductions, getting to know someone… Then, and only then, did you start to harbour the sort of unexpurgated, X-rated

16

thoughts that had been running wild in her head from the moment she had first set eyes on this man.

But then he took her hand in his and immediately she lost her grip on herself, all her careful control shattering in the space of a second.

His hand was warm and firm, his grip strong, controlled, she suspected, to ensure that the full force of it didn't crush her slighter fingers. But it was the feel of his flesh against hers, the sensual caress of skin against skin that sent a sensation like a fierce electrical charge shooting through her body. She had the crazy feeling that this was the one touch she had been waiting for all her life, and her head swam with the impact of its effect on her.

'Amir...' she tried again, struggling to conceal from him the way she was feeling. 'Unusual—and very definitely not English.'

'It's Arabic.' There was a surprising edge to his voice. 'It means Prince.'

It suited him too. Suited the proud carriage, the beautifully carved features, the way that dark head was held so arrogantly high. She could just imagine him in the wild, flowing robes of the Bedouin warriors. He would look stunning, exotic and magnificent.

'At least it means something. I once looked up Lydia in a dictionary of names. All it means, apparently, is ''a woman from Lydia'' which is somewhere in Greece.'

He was still holding her hand, she realised, not having released it after that first greeting. For the life of her she couldn't think of a way of freeing herself without communicating the wrong message with her actions.

So she simply let it lie where it was. Which was, after all, what she really wanted to do.

'Arabic.' Backtracking hastily, she tried to keep the conversation going. 'Is that where you're going?'

'To the Gulf?' The dark head inclined in agreement. 'That's where I was supposed to be flying to today.'

'You have friends there?'

'Family.'

Something had changed. Without knowing how, she had blundered in on a subject he didn't want to talk about, innocently crashing through barriers that she hadn't realised were there. There was a new hardness in the brilliant eyes, tightness around his mouth and jaw that made her shiver faintly in unease.

Perhaps it was the fact of being in a VIP lounge for the first—and probably the only—time in her life. Or perhaps it had something to do with being in transit, so to speak, not actually belonging anywhere at all at the moment, but being partway between her old life and the new. That and the whirling snow outside, obliterating the safe, familiar world she knew, had given her a strange sense of unreality. It was as if this room, this space where she and Amir Zaman sat, had become a separate little enclosed universe, a bubble suspended out of time, where none of the rules by which she normally ran her life actually worked, or even mattered.

Suddenly his hold on her hand no longer seemed so comfortable or so welcome. With a slight tug she managed to loosen his grasp, ease herself free.

'I think I'd like something to drink,' she managed unevenly.

'Of course.'

In an instant the disturbingly distant mood had vanished and he was all attention, all concern, the jet eyes turning immediately in search of an attendant.

One look was all it took. He didn't even raise his hand, made no gesture at all that she could detect, and yet the girl in the airport uniform immediately headed in their direction, summoned by the silent command.

'Yes, sir? What can I get for you?'

'Lydia? What would you like? Coffee? Or perhaps some wine?'

'Just coffee, please,' Lydia responded hastily. She didn't dare risk anything alcoholic. She was intoxicated enough as it was.

'Coffee for two, then.'

'Yes, sir.'

Lydia would not have been surprised to see her actually bob a respectful curtsey. The tone of his voice was pitched just right. It was perfectly polite, even courteous, but there was a note in it that demanded instant and total obedience, and warned of the risk of possible repercussions if that compliance was not forthcoming.

Obviously this Amir Zaman was someone who was used to giving orders—and having those orders carried out, she thought, studying the handsome face even more closely. And Amir meant Prince…

'Lydia…?'

'I—I'm sorry… What was it you said?'

Did he suspect that her thoughts had been of him? Of course he did! He did more than suspect. He *knew*. And it pleased him. Because it was what he wanted.

'I asked where you were travelling to. Where did you plan on flying to today if the weather had not intervened?'

'Oh—I was going to America. To California.'

And America was in the opposite direction to the way he was going. Fate had brought them together like this, but only for the briefest moment. And before very long fate would take them even further apart than ever.

She was going to America. Amir was stunned to find how much that fact affected him. It seemed to have the kick of a mule right in his stomach.

And why? Because this woman was heading in the opposite direction to him? Because she was going to California while he had to be in Kuimar?

'What's in California? A man?'

He tried to keep the question light, to reveal nothing of

the knot that formed in his stomach and pulled tight at just the thought of her with someone else.

'No, not a man—a job! *The* job. The sort of position I've been looking for for years. A dream job. Have you heard of the Halgrave Group of hotels.'

'I know of them.'

Of course he knew of them, Lydia reflected. Anyone with the sort of money he obviously had would know of the worldwide chain of exclusive, sinfully expensive hotels that had its base in California and a branch in almost every capital of the world.

'Well, they actually head-hunted me. I was working as Hospitality Manager in a Leicester hotel and they—they heard of me! They rang me up and asked me to come to a specially arranged interview. They offered me a position right there and then.'

'In California?'

'In California to start with. I have to do a six-week course to learn more about the company—the way they do things. After that I could be sent anywhere—anywhere at all. The world's my oyster.'

And the offer of a job couldn't have come at a better time. With her relationship with Jonathon floundering on the rocks, her dreams of becoming Mrs Lydia Carey totally shattered, she had been in desperate need of something to put in their place. When Halgrave had asked if she was prepared to travel, she had practically bitten their hand off in her eagerness.

And she wouldn't be human if she hadn't found herself wishing that Jon had known about her new venture. He had always accused her of being too conservative, too cautious.

'You're so careful about everything it's downright boring, Lydia,' he had scorned. 'No one would believe you're not even twenty-five yet, you're such an old stick-in-the-mud!'

And clearly Jon hadn't wanted to be married to a stick-in-the-mud, she reflected bitterly.

The return of the waitress with their drinks provided a much-needed diversion, a chance for her to recollect her thoughts and bring them back into the present, pushing away the discomfort of her memories of the past.

'How do you like your coffee?' Amir asked, taking control of even this small matter.

'Lots of milk, no sugar.'

He took his exactly the opposite way, she noticed, totally black and sweet. But it was the swift, efficient movements of his hands that fascinated her, the stunning effect of dark, luxuriant eyelashes lying in sooty arcs above the slashing cheekbones as he looked down to focus on the simple task.

He couldn't be more opposite to Jonathon either, she couldn't help reflecting. The other man had such a very English complexion, combined with smooth blond hair and blue eyes. The sort of colouring that she would have said was much more her type. Which was why it was so surprising that Amir had had this shockingly powerful effect on her.

'So there's no one you're leaving behind?' Amir continued the conversation where they had left off at the waitress' arrival. 'No one you'll miss?'

'No. Not even my parents. My parents decided to take a redundancy package that Dad was offered and went out to live in Portugal—opening a bar there. So, as I'm an only child, there was nothing to keep me here. No one to stay for.'

'And what if I were to ask you to stay?'

'What?'

Hastily swallowing down the sip of coffee that now threatened to choke her, Lydia set her cup and saucer on the table with a distinct crash. Looking into his darkly handsome face, she searched for the look of irony, the hint of amusement that would tell her he had only been joking.

She found none. Instead, her disbelieving look was met with one of total composure. And every evidence of total sincerity.

'W-what did you say?'

That black-eyed gaze didn't falter but held her wide-eyed look with an intent force that dried her mouth and set her heart fluttering high up in her throat.

'You know only too well what I said. And, what's more, you know exactly why I said it.'

'No—I…'

She looked like a startled fawn when she stared at him like that, Amir found himself thinking. Or like one of the newborn foals that were such a delight to him as they stared around, huge, stunned eyes trying to make sense of this new world into which they had arrived.

'It's quite simple,' he told her softly, leaning forward so that the husky whisper would reach her ears—and her ears alone. 'I have this fantasy that you do not get on that plane to California this afternoon. That you do not fly off to America and this wonderful new job…'

Her head went back sharply, blue eyes widening even more, her lips parting on a faint gasp of shock. He let his smile soothe her as he reached out slowly and gently. He caught her chin, resting one long finger and a thumb on either side, holding her still with only the lightest of pressure.

'But instead, in my dream, you stay here with me, and we explore what we've discovered. See where this takes us.'

'We…'

Lydia couldn't force her tongue around another word. Her thoughts were a whirling mass of chaos, incapable of forming a single coherent thread. The only thing she knew or recognised was this man before her. This hard-boned, devastating face, the obsidian glitter of those deep eyes holding hers with hypnotic ease.

And because her gaze was fixed on him so intently she saw the tiny flicker of a change when it came. Saw it, and knew what it meant, but her mind was too numb to react or pull away. Besides, she knew that she didn't *want* to react. That she wouldn't have freed herself even if she could, for all that his hold on her chin was so gentle it could have been broken in a second.

So she stayed where she was. Stayed absolutely still and watched that dark head come closer. Watched the devastating mouth soften, and come down on her own lips with obvious intent.

And that was when she realised that the softness had been deceptive. That his kiss was not the light, enticing caress she had been anticipating. Instead it was firm and strong and forceful, a revelation of feeling and a statement of intent all in one. In the same moment that it seemed to cajole her soul out of her body, it also awoke every stinging sense with the burn of a promise that made her thoughts swim in a heady delirium of longing.

And all the time he hadn't touched her except with his mouth. That long, strong body was still held well away from her, even the hand under her chin releasing her and falling back to his side, the other still resting on the strong, muscular thigh under the denim jeans.

He didn't need to hold her, and he knew it. Lydia knew it too. Knew that it was as much the force of her own feelings as anything he did that kept her in her seat, unable to move. That the flickers of white hot flame along every nerve in her body seemed to melt her bones, leaving her unable to support herself if she so much as tried to stand up.

'Help me, Lydia,' Amir murmured against her lips. 'Tell me what I can do to make you stay. To keep you by my side for just a little while longer.'

'I...'

Could she be hearing right? Had this stunning man actually said that he wanted her to stay? And was it possible that she was actually considering saying yes? She hardly knew any more about him than his name. She had no idea if she could trust him in any way.

Bewildered, she could only shake her head in bemusement at her own reaction.

'No?'

Amir had mistaken the reason for her reaction.

'Then let me persuade you...'

This time his kiss was pure enticement. Gently he edged her lips open, let the tip of his tongue play along their sensitised surface, making her sigh aloud in response. And now at last he moved, powerful fingers tangling in the soft fall of her hair, closing over the fine bones of her skull, holding her still so that he could deepen and prolong the caress.

Lydia's whole being was awash with a golden heat. Her heart was racing, pounding the blood through her veins and making her thoughts swim in sensuous reaction. She was lost, she knew, drowning in sensation, a wild need uncoiling deep inside her, centring hotly at the point between her thighs.

'Amir...'

'Ladies and gentlemen...'

A new sound intruded on the delirious yearning that hazed her mind. A man's voice, crisp and matter-of-fact and hatefully jarring in the way it broke into her sense of isolation, jolting her back to reality with a suddenness that shattered her sensual mood.

'Ladies and gentlemen, your attention please. We regret to inform you...'

The rest of the words passed totally over Lydia's head. Her brain seemed to have blown a fuse and she was incapable of taking anything in. Even the simplest words failed to make the slightest sense and when the announcement was over she could only stare blankly at Amir, her light brown brows drawing together in dazed confusion.

'What was all that about? What did they mean all services are cancelled?'

'I did warn you.' Amir's tone was dry. 'The weather has been getting worse all day. The blizzard's closed in and no planes can take off or land tonight. There'll be no flights out of here at least until tomorrow morning—if then.'

'No flights!' Lydia echoed, horror etched into her face. 'But why—how? Did you…?'

For a second she actually believed he might have been able to arrange it.

Amir's laughter should have reassured her, but somehow it had exactly the opposite result.

'My sweet Lydia, do you really think that I am capable of that? To organise such a thing I would have had to enter into a pact with the Almighty—or perhaps the Devil.'

Now *that* she could believe, Lydia admitted to herself. The wicked curl to his lips, the look of triumph in those eyes could only be described as fiendish. He might not have been able to arrange this situation, but it was quite clear that he fully intended to benefit from it. And his next words confirmed as much.

'But, no matter who created this, they have my undying gratitude. Now you'll have to stay.'

'But I can't stay here!'

Lydia's brain was working overtime, struggling to assess the situation, sort it out in her thoughts and come up with a solution.

'Where can I go? Where will I sleep?'

Oh, if only she hadn't given up her hotel room this morning! But she had left Leicester yesterday full of hope and excitement, looking forward to a totally fresh start. She had only booked for an overnight stay because she had always thought that by now she would be in her seat on board the plane, heading away from England and towards the new life she had dreamed of.

'What do I do now?'

'Don't panic,' Amir soothed. 'You can...'

Abruptly he caught himself up. What in hell's name was he doing? Had he really been intending to offer her the chance to stay in the apartment? Was he out of his mind?

It seemed he was. That was the only conclusion he could draw from the way he had behaved ever since he had first set eyes on this Lydia Ashton when she had walked into the room barely a couple of hours ago. His brain had to have been completely scrambled for him to have behaved as he had!

'...in my dream, you stay here with me, and we explore what we've discovered. See where this takes us.'

Had he really said that? Had he really been such a total, complete fool?

What was wrong with him?

Oh, he fancied this woman; there was no denying that. He most definitely had the hots for her—and how! But was he such a fool as to be led by his hormones into making what could possibly be the most dreadful mistake? Very likely the worst possible mistake of his life?

So this Lydia appealed to his most basic instincts. He had only to look at her to want her in his bed, that soft mouth opening under his, the fine curves of her body crushed close to his own frame, the bronze silk of her hair tangling around his fingers. Even now, just to think of it made him ache in such intensity that he wanted to groan out loud.

But how much was he prepared to pay for one night of passion—for the quick, urgent appeasement of his most masculine needs, the scratching of an itch, which was really all that this one-night stand would amount to?

Would this woman—any woman—be worth the sacrifice of all that he had worked towards for so long? Was any sexual gratification, however intense—and every instinct told him that with her it would be the most intense pleasure of his life—worth the loss of his lifetime's ambition? Could he really just abandon the goal towards which he had worked for the last twenty years, ever since the day of his eleventh birthday, when his mother had told him the truth about his father and his heritage?

No!

With an abruptness that jarred Lydia right to her soul, he suddenly released her and pushed himself sharply to his feet.

'You can find a hotel room to stay in overnight. The airline will have provided accommodation for everyone. If you come with me...'

He had already turned on his heel and marched off before Lydia had the time to collect her thoughts and gather up her magazine and her hand luggage. She could only stare bemusedly after him as she struggled to her feet, the sharp sting of distress adding to her mental confusion.

What had she done or said to make him react like this? Why had his mood changed so abruptly? Only moments before she had been sure that he had been about to offer her somewhere to stay the night with him.

And that if he had, she had been about to accept it.

But she had to have been deluding herself. She didn't even know if he lived in London, let alone close enough to get to tonight.

Face it, Lydia, she told herself in fierce reproof as she headed after Amir, you don't know enough about him to agree to *anything*. Coffee was okay. Letting him kiss you, bad enough. And as for 'in my dream, you stay here with me, and we explore what we've discovered'—you weren't really going to go along with that—*were you*?

'It's all sorted.'

Amir was heading back to her, making his way through the buzzing crowd with elegant ease.

'They're ringing round all the airport hotels now. You just have to wait and they'll let you know which one they're putting you in.'

'Great!'

She tried to make it enthusiastic and hoped it sounded better in his ears than it did in her own. She should be feeling relieved. Very possibly she had just had an extremely narrow escape.

But relieved didn't describe her mood at all. Instead she felt as limp as a pricked balloon.

'What about you?'

'Oh, I'll head back to my apartment. The snow may be bad but I should get there okay.'

One tanned hand lifted, revealing a slim, silver mobile phone.

'I just called my driver. He's bringing the car round right away.'

Was he really as keen to leave her as that? 'He's bringing the car round *right away*.' So much for 'you stay here with me'. He hadn't even waited to see her into a taxi, heading for her hotel. And as he spoke he was moving, drifting over to the huge windows, obviously intent on looking out to see if his car had arrived yet.

'So this is goodbye?' The words sounded bleak, desperately final.

'I guess it is.'

Another couple of minutes, Amir told himself. Just sixty—a hundred or so—seconds, and she would be gone. On her way to the hotel and out of his life. He could put her out of his mind, and maybe tomorrow when he woke up he'd be thankful that he hadn't given into the carnal temptation that had distorted his thinking so badly.

Just another sixty seconds…but they seemed to be ticking away far too slowly. And instead of feeling thankful, the only thoughts in his head were of just how lovely she looked standing there, with the soft bronze hair tumbled around her shoulders, her blue eyes wide and clear. The cream-coloured wool of her sweater clung in all the right places, the tight denim of her jeans hugging the curving hips and neat bottom with sensual provocation.

Seeing how the fullness of her mouth had been kissed free of lipstick, he found it impossible not to recall that *he* had done that and he had enjoyed every second of the experience. He still had the taste of her on his lips and his tongue. If he was honest he wanted her mouth again, wanted the...

No! Furiously he drew himself up, ruthlessly reining in the hunger that threatened to escape even his determined control. Out of the corner of his eye he saw the sleek dark shape of the Jaguar on the road below, edging its way through the whirling snowflakes, towards the entrance. Nabil had wasted no time.

'It's been a pleasure meeting you.'

'And you,' Lydia managed, matching his stiff withdrawal tone for tone.

To her total consternation hot tears were burning in her eyes and she blinked them back desperately, refusing to let them fall. He had already left her, mentally at least. There was no point in hanging around, dragging this out painfully. Far better to get it over and done with. Short and sharp, like ripping a sticking plaster off a wound in the hope that that way it would hurt much less.

'Goodbye, then.'

'Goodbye, Lydia.'

Why was she still hanging about? Over on the other side of the room someone was making an announcement about the rooms that were being provided, reading out names from a long list. When the idea of listening and learning where she would be tonight slid into Amir's mind he crushed it down immediately, refusing to let it take root.

Lydia Ashton was a complication he could do without. He didn't have room for her—or for any other woman in his life right now. Dammit, he was as good as married, at least in his father's eyes, if not in his own.

Unfortunately his body was refusing to obey his mind. Just being near to this woman was enough to make his heart beat in double-quick time, his blood throb in his veins. Rationally he might accept that she was trouble, but the more basic instinctive response that tightened every nerve, fanned the embers of hunger into a blazing, roaring flame, declared that it was a trouble he would welcome into his life. Every second that she hesitated was wearing down his resistance, reducing his will to fight.

'See you...'

At last she was turning away. Just as he thought he was home and free, just as he foolishly let his guard down a second too early, she suddenly swung back. He saw what was coming and was powerless to prevent it.

Her lips were on his cheek, warm and soft and delicately caressing. The soft curves of her body were pressed against his, her breasts against the wall of his chest, his pelvis cradling the finer bones of hers. A delicate perfume of lily and rose seemed to envelop him in a cloud, and underneath it was the clean, subtle scent of her skin, sweet and potent in a way that made his head spin dangerously.

'Lydia...' he tried to protest, but his voice failed him.

And then as he turned his head her lips touched his and he knew that he was lost.

With a groan he gave up the fight that he had been losing anyway and hauled her up against him, crushing her hard, imprisoning her in the strength of his arms.

'Don't go, Lydia,' he muttered, the words rough and thick and raw. 'Don't go to the hotel. Come back with me to my apartment. Stay with me tonight.'

She should never have kissed him.

Lydia recognised her mistake in the second that she

made it, but she was powerless to stop herself, incapable of resisting the impulse. She had meant it to be just a quick peck on his cheek, the briefest touch, there and gone again in a moment, but it didn't quite work out like that.

The second she felt the warmth of his skin, tasted it against her mouth, she knew she was lost. Heat flooded her body, turning her brain to molten liquid and leaving her incapable of thought. Her breasts were crushed against the hardness of his chest, her hips clamped tight against his so that she could feel the hard, heated force of his desire for her before she heard the echo of it in his voice.

And when he turned his head and his lips took hers in hungry demand she knew she didn't have a prayer.

'Don't go, Lydia…' he said, but really they both knew she wasn't going anywhere at all.

There was no way she could stay in a hotel room tonight. No way she could endure the soulless emptiness of even the best five-star accommodation. Not without him.

'Stay with me tonight,' Amir muttered rawly against her mouth and on a deep, aching sigh of surrender she gave him the only answer she could think of.

'Yes,' she muttered, her voice every bit as rough and uneven as his had been. 'Yes, yes, *yes*! Of course I'll stay with you.'

CHAPTER THREE

'OH, WOW!'

Lydia didn't even try to hide her amazement as she turned in a slow, stunned circle, staring unreservedly at everything around her.

'This is just amazing! Is it really all yours?'

When Amir had spoken of his apartment, she had known from his clothes and the fact that he had been in the VIP lounge that he wouldn't live in a small, shabby couple of rooms like those she had just left behind in Leicester. And the sight of his car and the waiting uniformed driver who had leapt from his seat to open the door for them had increased that certainty one hundredfold. But she had never anticipated anything like *this*.

The huge penthouse apartment would have swallowed up her small flat twenty times or more and still had room to spare. The high ceilings and huge windows gave an impression of air and space, and beyond the plate glass the brilliant night skyline of London glittered even through the raging snowstorm. Rich furnishings, heavy silk brocaded curtains and thick, thick carpets in all the tones of gold from the palest clotted cream to a deep dark bronze meant that the room appeared warm and welcoming in spite of the unpleasantness of the night. And to add to the sense of comfort, a bright fire burned in the wide hearth.

'Actually it's my father's. His taste is rather more ornate than mine.'

The sweep of his hand indicated the enormous, brilliantly sparkling chandeliers, the marble fireplace.

'But I have the use of it when I'm in London.'

'And who is your father?' Lydia was intrigued.

The sudden change in his face told her that once more she'd overstepped those invisible barriers, an unnerving glint in his dark eyes warning her to back off—fast.

Behind them, a small, discreet cough alerted them to the silent, stocky figure of the chauffeur standing just inside the doorway, still holding Lydia's hand luggage, which he had carried up in the lift with them.

'Oh, thank you!' she said impulsively, moving to take it from him, but the man's attention was fixed on Amir.

'Will that be all, Highness?' he asked. 'Or is there anything more you will want tonight.'

'Nothing.' Amir's tone was dismissive. 'If the weather clears, I will need you to drive Miss Ashton back to the airport tomorrow, but I'll let you know about that. You can take the rest of the night off.'

Lydia watched in bemused disbelief as Nabil swept a low bow before backing towards the door. He had almost reached it when she suddenly thought of something.

'Oh, wait a moment, please…'

Hunting in her handbag, she pulled out her purse. But before she could open it, Amir's hand, swift and firm, had clamped down hard on hers, stilling her movement.

'You can leave, Nabil.'

Another bow and the man was gone. As the door swung to behind him, she turned to Amir, annoyance sparking in her sapphire eyes.

'I wanted to give him a tip!' she protested. 'He drove us here safely in the most appalling conditions. And he carried my bag up…'

The impetuous words faded from her lips as she saw Amir's dark, reproving frown, the obvious disapproval in his face.

'It is not appropriate,' he snapped, releasing her at last.

'Not appropriate…But why? Highness!' she recalled shakenly. 'He called you *Highness*!'

It sounded even more unbelievable spoken aloud in her own voice.

'And you…just who *is* your father? Who are *you*?'

Amir had moved to the opposite side of the room where an opened bottle of wine stood on a tray alongside a pair of the finest crystal wineglasses. Ignoring her questions, he poured a little into one of the goblets and tasted it carefully. Evidently it met with his approval because he swiftly filled both glasses and held one out to her, the ruby-coloured liquid glowing fiercely in the light of the fire.

'Would you like a drink?'

'What I'd *like* is an answer—preferably several!'

His irritated frown told her that her voice had been pitched too high. It had needed to be for her to hear it over the fearful pounding of her own heart. Her pulse was beating far too fast, making the blood sound like thunder inside her head.

'I want an explanation. For a start, just *who* is your father?'

His shrug dismissed her question as a minor irritation, much as he might have flicked away an annoyingly buzzing fly.

'My father's identity is not relevant to this situation.'

'Your father's identity is supremely *relevant*!' Lydia countered, her breath hissing in furiously through her teeth. 'Because, Your *Highness*…' she emphasised the word viciously '…if you don't give me an explanation of exactly who you are and what is happening, then I am out of here—fast.'

His smile was slow, mocking, filled with infuriating condescension.

'And where, exactly, would you go?' he drawled smoothly.

The truth was that she had no idea. She didn't even really know where in London they were. She had caught a glimpse of the wide flow of the Thames, the huge arc of

the London Eye, the Houses of Parliament on the opposite
bank, but apart from that she was lost. But she wasn't
going to let him see that that worried her.

'I don't know and I don't care! But I know one thing—
I won't stay here! Not unless you start telling me the truth.'

'The truth?'

Amir sipped his wine, savouring it appreciatively before
he swallowed.

'The truth is simple. It's just you and I—a man and a
woman who find each other attractive and want to be together. That is all there is to it. Are you sure you wouldn't
like some of this wine? It really is excellent.'

Warily Lydia eyed the glass he held out to her again, a
look of suspicion on her face.

'What is this, Amir? You wouldn't be trying to get me
drunk, would you?'

The response she expected was that look of reproof once
again, so she was thoroughly thrown off balance by the
soft, warm sound of his laughter.

'And why would I do that, my dear Lydia? So that I
can have my wicked way with you? I hardly think so. For
one thing, my tastes don't run to a comatose partner, and
for another, the way that you responded to me earlier, the
fact that you are here with me now, would appear to indicate that I would not have to resort to such underhand
methods to seduce you.'

'You might have other things in mind.'

'Such as?'

He looked deep into her stubbornly set face and his
smile grew, that infuriatingly appealing chuckle sounding
deep in his throat again.

'Oh, please—not the white slave trade as well! Lydia,
sweetheart, you really must not let your imagination run
away with you! I assure you, I have nothing but your comfort at heart. You have had a long, frustrating day stuck in
that airport lounge, waiting for a flight that never came. I

brought you here so that you could unwind and get some rest.'

'Fat chance of that…' Lydia began, but he ignored her furious interjection and continued imperturbably.

'I'm sure you must be hungry. Right now, my house-keeper will be preparing our meal. All you have to do is to have a drink and wait for it to be served.'

The mention of a housekeeper was unexpected and a relief. Simply knowing that she wasn't alone with him in the apartment eased some of the tension that had held Lydia so tight. The stiffness of her spine relaxed, her shoulders dropping slightly, her whole body loosening up.

'That's better.'

Amir smiled his approval.

'You no longer look as if you expect to be executed at any moment. Now, if you'll just have a drink…'

With an impatient sound in her throat, Lydia snatched at the glass. Perhaps the wine would relax her a little. Even if she wasn't as stiffly uptight as she had been before, her stomach was still twisting painfully.

'It is delicious,' she conceded ungraciously as she let a mouthful of the rich, mellow liquid slide down her disturbingly dry throat. 'But you needn't think I'm letting you get away with it. I still want some answers to my questions…'

Amir's sigh was a masterpiece, a perfect blend of irritation and resignation.

'And clearly you are not going to give me any peace until I answer them,' he drawled, lowering himself elegantly into one of the huge, soft armchairs and leaning back against the cushions, his long legs stretched out in front of him. 'All right, then, ask away—but at least make yourself comfortable first. You make me feel uneasy, hovering over me like an avenging angel.'

When Lydia was tempted to fling at him the comment that she didn't give a damn how she made him feel, she hastily thought the better of it. For one thing, she seriously doubted that anything she did would make this man uncomfortable. And for another, the brief, worryingly dangerous mood that Amir had displayed just moments ago now seemed to have passed. She didn't want to risk provoking him into letting it come to the surface again.

'All right,' she conceded grudgingly, coming to sit opposite him, on the other side of the fire.

The wine really was wonderful, she admitted to herself, taking another appreciative swallow. She had never tasted anything quite so delicious. It was clearly a million miles away from the sort of supermarket plonk that was all she could ever afford.

'So,' Amir prompted when, lulled by the alcohol and the warmth of the leaping flames in the deep hearth, she took her time about continuing the conversation, 'what exactly is it that you want to know?'

'You can start with explaining who your father is. He must be someone important. I mean, I've never met anyone at all who was given the title of "Highness".'

His sigh was less good-tempered this time. Clearly his patience was wearing thin again.

'Since you are so determined not to let the subject drop—my father's name is Sheikh Khalid bin Hamad Al Zaman, King of Kuimar.'

For once, something had shut her up, he thought wryly, watching the way her soft mouth fell slightly open on a gasp of surprise. She looked totally dumbfounded at the news, which was hardly surprising. He had had much the same response himself when he had first learned the truth. Though, being only eleven at the time, he had expressed his disbelief rather more forcefully.

'You're joking!'

'I'm totally serious, I assure you.'

'You're really the son of a sheikh?'

'Only just,' Amir returned obscurely.

'Oh!'

It was about all Lydia could manage. She was remembering how she had imagined him dressed in the dramatic robes of a desert warrior. The thought had her burying her nose in her wineglass and taking a hasty sip.

'So, should I be curtseying to you—calling you Highness, too?'

'Lydia!' Amir groaned reproachfully. 'That's not what I want from you.'

'What *do* you want?' The question wouldn't be held back.

The look he shot her from under hooded eyelids held a distinctly sexual challenge in it, polished ebony eyes gleaming behind luxuriantly curling lashes.

'You have to ask? I thought it was patently obvious. I thought we both understood where we stand...'

Lydia shifted uncomfortably under that wickedly taunting scrutiny, his gaze seeming to strip away a protective layer of skin, leaving her painfully vulnerable and exposed.

'I thought so too—at first.'

'So what has changed?'

Amir sipped at his wine again, his intent stare not moving from her flushed face.

'You don't need me to tell you that!' she protested furiously. 'You know what's changed! *You've* changed! Your father is a sheikh. And, correct me if I'm wrong, but doesn't that make you one too?'

The way that Amir's sensual mouth twisted sharply told her she had displeased him. For the space of an uncomfortable couple of heartbeats she was sure that he wasn't going to answer, but then abruptly he inclined his head in brusque agreement.

'If you want my full name it's Amir bin Khalid Al Zaman. *Sheikh* Amir bin Khalid Al Zaman,' he reiterated with an impenetrable intonation on the words. 'My father named me Crown Prince on my thirtieth birthday.'

'You see!' Lydia exclaimed. 'This changes everything. You're royalty! And I'm just a very ordinary girl who—'

She broke off sharply as, with a muttered curse, Amir suddenly slammed his glass down onto the table with such a distinct crash that she fully expected to see the delicate crystal shatter into a thousand glistening pieces. The next moment he was on his feet, covering the space between their chairs in two long, forceful strides.

'It doesn't matter!' he declared, his tone rough and hard. 'Can't you see? It doesn't matter a damn!'

Before Lydia could quite register what was happening, he had clamped hard fingers around the tops of her arms and hauled her up out of the chair with such force that she fell against him, her own hands going out frantically, desperately seeking support. Beneath her clutching fingers she felt the hard muscles bunch and tense as Amir took her weight.

'Who I am, or what I am, has no bearing on this situation.'

'No bearing...'

It was difficult to speak. Almost impossible to *think*. The strength of his arms was all that held her upright. The heat of his body seemed to reach out and enclose her, enfolding her in sensual warmth. And the clean, spicy scent of his skin coiled around her senses, tantalising her nostrils, reminding her of the burning kisses they had shared until she could almost taste him again on her tongue.

'But it has to! It has to change so much!'

'Lydia, listen to me.'

Amir gave her a small shake, not rough but just hard enough to break through the buzzing haze of response inside her head and draw her eyes to his face. The fierce emotions that she saw there transfixed her, holding her unable to look away, every ounce of her concentration centred on him.

'When I'm with you, there is just you and me. Nothing

else matters a damn. When I'm with you I'm just a man—as you are just a woman. We are simply male and female, Amir and Lydia. Money, position, our place in life, all become totally irrelevant. I don't think differently because I am the son of a sheikh. I don't act differently. I am just like any other man. When I do this…'

He bent his proud head and took her lips in a long, deep kiss that made her senses reel. The blood burned in her veins, melting away all resistance until she was pliant against him, every muscle weakening, her bones seeming to melt.

'I am a man kissing a woman—my woman. The woman I want to possess so much that I *ache* with it! The woman who has stolen my soul from me—my mind, leaving me incapable of thinking of anything beyond her.'

She was crushed even closer, pressed so hard up against him that she felt the burn of the swollen evidence of his desire and shivered in response. This Amir was no longer the civilised, controlled man she had met just hours before but a fierce, arrogant, Bedouin warrior, with the heat of the desert in his veins, the burn of the sun in his eyes.

'I shouldn't be here. We shouldn't be here. I…'

Abruptly he broke off as a light tap came at the door. Amir froze, muttered something roughly, then looked down into Lydia's stunned face, probing her eyes searchingly.

Apparently what he saw there satisfied whatever question was in his mind because he gave a swift, brusque nod and turned his head towards the door.

'Come!'

It was all command, pure autocrat, giving Lydia a swift insight into the other Amir, *Sheikh* Amir Al Zaman.

The middle-aged, dark-haired woman who came half-way across the threshold then paused, bobbing a hasty bow, clearly knew that man only too well. She kept her head bent, her eyes on the ground as Amir fired a question at her in a language Lydia could not understand. She answered in the same language, receiving a nod of approval for her pains, and was clearly thankful to be dismissed, almost scuttling away in her haste to be gone.

'Did you have to speak to her like that?' Lydia protested indignantly when they were alone again.

'Like what, precisely?' Amir enquired, looking down his long, straight nose at her.

'Ordering her about that way! She clearly couldn't wait to get out of here.'

'So you speak Arabic—and the Kuimar dialect?'

His mocking tone set her teeth on edge. He didn't have to tell her she had got things wrong. It was there in every inflexion, every word. Deciding discretion was the best policy, Lydia refused to let herself be provoked into rash speak and waited instead for him to explain, as she had no doubt that he was going to do.

'Jamila had come to tell us that the meal she has prepared is ready. Naturally, she was embarrassed at intruding on what she felt was a very private moment. I assured her that she was not to blame if my lady friend did not understand the conventions…'

Did he know how ambiguous he had made that 'lady friend' sound? Lydia wondered, irritation stinging sharply. She very much suspected that he did—and that it had been quite deliberate. Her teeth snapped shut as she bit off the angry retort she was tempted to make.

'I understand the conventions only too well,' she managed with a stiffly clenched jaw. The irony of the situation only added to her annoyance, Jonathon's accusation of being a stick-in-the-mud sounding sharply in her head.

'But not as Jamila sees them. In Kuimar, no respectable woman would be seen alone with a man in his home at night.'

'No respectable woman!' He was really intent on compounding the insulting effect of that 'lady friend.'

'We are not in Kuimar now.'

'No, we're not.'

The hint of a curl at the corners of Amir's carved mouth seemed to indicate that he was only too aware of the struggle she was having to keep her voice reasonable and that, infuriatingly, he found that distinctly amusing.

'Which is what I told Jamila before I gave her the rest of the night off. Are you hungry?'

'Am I...?'

Lydia found the question difficult to consider, and not just because of the speed with which Amir had jumped from one topic to another. The realisation that the housekeeper, whose presence had seemed such a comfort only a few minutes ago, had now been dismissed for the night put her into a distinctly uncomfortable state of mind. She would be alone with Amir after all, and alone with him in a way that 'no respectable woman' should ever be.

Shouldn't that be her cue to say that she'd changed her mind? That she couldn't stay here after all. That she found she actually preferred the thought of the hotel room so would he please send for Nabil, or a taxi, and she'd head straight back to the airport?

Except that, as she had just said, they weren't in Kuimar. And the truth was that, even if it was safer, more respectable—more *sensible*—she didn't want to go.

Jonathon would never recognise her in the woman who knew she wanted to throw caution to the winds and stay here, ignoring every warning, every scream of self-preservation from the cautious 'stick-in-the-mud' part of her.

'Hungry? Yes, I'm starving!'

To her consternation, Amir met her response with a faint frown. One long finger touched her cheek as his beautiful mouth tightened disturbingly.

'Not the right answer, my dear Lydia.'

The thought of what the *right* answer should have been made her toes curl tightly inside her shoes.

'Not the right one, maybe.' She tried for laughter only to find that it broke revealingly in the middle. 'But an honest one!'

Amir's thoughtful pause made her heart jolt uncomfortably as she waited for his reply.

'It was not the answer I hoped I'd hear,' he murmured silkily. 'But you are lucky that I am in an indulgent mood. Shall we go through to the dining room?'

He held out his hand and Lydia had no choice but to put hers into it.

If this was Amir in an *indulgent* mood, she couldn't help thinking, then she really didn't think she wanted to meet him in a less tolerant frame of mind. Just the thought of it made her nerves twist so much that she had to pray her trembling fingers didn't give away her feelings to the man at her side.

CHAPTER FOUR

'HAVE you had enough?'

There was no mistaking the ironical note in Amir's voice, and frankly Lydia was not at all surprised to hear it there.

'I'm—not hungry any more.'

The truth was that she hadn't been hungry from the moment she had sat down at the table. Her appetite had totally deserted her when Amir had slid into the chair directly opposite her, elbows resting on the fine white linen cloth, tanned hands linked, his chin resting on the top of them, deep-set eyes fixed intently on her face.

'Help yourself,' he'd told her softly.

He had watched everything she'd done. That dark gaze had followed each movement of her hands, flicking backwards and forwards as she'd taken a little from each serving dish, spooning it onto her plate, until she'd found herself shivering faintly under that eagle-eyed scrutiny.

'Don't you want anything?' she had managed unevenly as a result of the ragged beating of her heart.

Amir had shaken his dark head.

'Not hungry,' he'd murmured. 'At least, not for food.'

She knew exactly what he meant. It was there in the burn of his brilliant eyes, the undisguised sensuality of that searching gaze. Lydia risked a hasty glance into his stunning face and immediately regretted it as her heart lurched high up into her throat and the hand that held the knife shook betrayingly.

'It—it's very good. This chicken is delicious.'

'Jamila is an excellent cook.'

He couldn't have sounded less interested.

44

But he didn't rush her. Instead he seemed content to wait and watch as she picked at the food, trying vainly to make some pretence of enthusiasm, struggling to swallow with a throat that had dried in the heat of her response.

In the end she pushed away her plate, unable to cope any longer.

'You've barely eaten a thing.'

'I wasn't as hungry as I thought.'

He must know what he did to her. Must know that that fierce, unblinking gaze was tying her nerves into knots, making her heart race in double-quick time.

'Not even some fruit?'

She looked like a startled deer, Amir reflected inwardly. Not scared exactly, just wary and uncertain. If he made one false move she could be up and gone. But he wasn't going to make that mistake. He wasn't going to rush things. In the airport he had thought that he'd only had minutes to win her over, make his mark on her consciousness; now it seemed that he had all night.

He could wait.

He reckoned she'd be well worth waiting for.

'What about some of this?'

He reached out slowly, took a perfect peach from the large glass bowl. The contrast between the hard strength of his tanned hands and the velvety skin of the fruit was devastatingly sensual. She couldn't drag her gaze away from the long, strong fingers as they curved around the ripe fruit, smoothing it softly.

In just that way would he touch her, she found herself thinking on a shiver. She could imagine how the caress would feel, the strong yet delicate tips of his hands trailing over sensitive nerves, awakening a stinging desire.

He didn't even have to *touch* her! She could feel that reaction already. Her blood sang in her veins, her flesh so sensitised that even the soft brush of her clothes over it was a delicate agony. She knew what was in his mind. They both knew exactly where his thoughts were heading.

So why didn't he *say* something? Why didn't he *act*?

'Try it…'

He had sliced off a thin sliver of the fruit and now he held it out to her, leaning forward to hold it level with her mouth so that all she had to do was open her lips. Like a child she did so and Amir dropped the juicy morsel onto her tongue. It was so ripe that it hardly needed to be chewed but slid down her throat so easily.

'Like that?'

His smile did dangerous things to her heart, making it clench on a wave of response, her mouth drying instantly.

'It's—perfect,' she croaked. 'Wonderful.'

'Then have some more.'

This time he kept his hand closer to his own side of the table so that it was Lydia who had to lean towards him in order to receive the fruit. The movement brought her face level with his, meant that she could look nowhere but into the black depths of his eyes. And, having looked, she couldn't turn away but was held transfixed, hypnotised by the golden flare of desire that burned there.

'More?' Amir questioned softly.

'Mmm.'

She couldn't find the strength to answer him but simply nodded. Her mind was too full of the sexual tug of his closeness, drowning in the dark pools of his eyes, to be able to form any words.

There was still a trace of peach juice on her lips and unthinkingly she let her tongue slide out to lick it away. Immediately Amir's dark gaze dropped down to follow the small movement, then flicked back up again, deeper, blacker, more powerful than before.

It was like being bathed in a river of fire. Like sitting directly in the path of the midsummer sun and feeling its heat wash over her. Her blood was aflame, her skin crying out for his touch.

'Amir…' she tried, but he shook his head gently.

'Hush!' he murmured softly, leaning forward once again to rest one forefinger over her lips to silence her. 'There's no need to rush this, darling. We have all the time in the world.'

She wanted only to do as he said. But at the same time she ached to touch him in some way, to know the warmth of his caress, the feel of his skin against hers.

And so she couldn't stop herself from pressing her lips to that restraining finger, taking one, then two, then three soft, lingering kisses with deliberate care. He tasted of peach juice and the intensely personal flavour of his skin, and she thought she had never known anything more wonderful in all her life. And all the time she kept her gaze fixed on his face so that she saw the way he closed his eyes for a moment, the inner struggle he had for control.

'Lydia…'

This time it was Amir who had trouble speaking, the softly accented voice cracking slightly under the effort of control he imposed on it. And because of that she found the strength to smile straight into his eyes.

'I'd like some more, Amir,' she murmured, knowing exactly the effect the deliberate double meaning would have on him. 'Please don't stop now.'

Don't stop! Amir thought hazily. Surely she knew that was the last thing on his mind. His whole body was tight as a bowstring with the tension of wanting her and yet holding back. He ached with it, *hurt* with it, and yet he wouldn't have it any other way.

He could see the effect it was having on her and so, although he could hardly endure the agony of waiting, in the same moment he wanted to prolong it endlessly. To draw out this most delicate of seductions, this tantalising foreplay, until they could both bear it no longer.

'Your wish is my command, my lady.'

He was sure that she barely tasted the next morsel of peach. That she chewed and swallowed on an automatic instinct, unaware of what she was doing. Her eyes were so dark, the pupils dilated until they concealed all but the faintest rim of blue, that she looked as if she had been drugged or stunned by some sort of blow.

'You shall have more—as much as you want.'

There was a tiny trickle of peach juice left at the corner of her mouth, slipping slowly down towards her chin, and automatically he lifted his hand to brush against her skin to wipe it away, then froze. A moment later he had replaced his finger with the touch of his lips, letting his tongue lick away the faint stickiness and leave it clean.

It was the moment that finally broke his resolve. Having touched her in this way, he found that he was caught, trapped, unable to move away again. Instead he could only linger, turning the gesture into a caress, pressing a slow kiss on the delicate line of her jaw and then another, closer to her mouth.

'Amir...'

It was a choking cry low in her throat, one that told him how close she was to breaking too. And, hearing it, he abandoned all thought of any further restraint, giving in to the wild surge of passion that ripped through his body like a flood tide.

'Lady, you've been asking for this all night!' he muttered roughly before a swift, almost violent movement of his head brought their lips together in a hungry kiss.

It was like being thrown straight into the eye of a storm. Thunder crashed in his head, lightning flashing behind his eyes. He couldn't have enough of her lips, couldn't get close enough to her to kiss her properly.

The damn table was right in the way.

With a muttered curse against her mouth, he reached for

her, hauling her towards him, sending cutlery and china scattering, falling to the floor in a series of crashes.

Lydia heard the sounds of the devastation through the roaring haze inside her head. She was aware only of the hard crush of Amir's lips against her own, the grip of powerful hands on her arms, lifting her bodily from her chair and dragging her closer towards him.

She was half on and half off the table, perching awkwardly on the fine cloth, dependent on his strength to keep her from falling. She was blinded by the whirling mist inside her head, unable to see anything of her surroundings, aware only of the fierce intensity of his eyes as they burned down into her.

'Amir…'

Her hands reached for his shoulders, clutching, holding on, initially, for much-needed support. But then her fingers brushed against the warm strip of skin beyond the neckline of the soft cashmere sweater and immediately her touch gentled.

'Amir…' she breathed again, letting her fingers slide over the satin flesh she had longed to touch, for aeons it seemed.

She felt the powerful muscles bunch and clench under her caress, heard his breathing catch in his throat then start up again, raw and uneven, in time with the jagged race of her own heart.

And all the time his mouth plundered hers. First savage, almost cruelly demanding, then gentling, soothing the bruises his inflamed passion had inflicted, and finally tender, so, so tender that her heart melted to liquid inside her and her head swam with the heady delight of it.

'You have bewitched me,' Amir muttered against her cheek. 'Since the moment I first saw you I have been unable to function, unable to *think* of anything beyond this. Beyond the need to kiss you, hold you, touch you…'

His hands were urgent at her waist, tugging her sweater

clear of the band of her jeans. Long fingers pushed up along her ribcage, then down between the denim and her skin as if he couldn't make up his mind what he wanted most to touch. He pulled her even closer, making her slide over the tabletop, sending another plate, another glass hurtling to the floor.

'Amir...' she choked, her protest edged with a tremor of shaky laughter '...we have to stop this.'

'*Never*...' His voice was thick and rough with angry protest, the ferocity of his refusal sending sparks of excited response searing along every nerve.

'No...'

The laughter was more pronounced now, threatening to merge into something close to nervous hysteria.

'I mean, we have to stop this *here*. If we're not careful we're going to wreck the joint. Look...'

Somehow she managed to get her hand between her cheek and his, to turn his face to the side so that he could survey the devastation they had wreaked. For a long moment it seemed that he could not take it in, the jet eyes still glazed with desire, every muscle in his face taut with hunger.

But then, slowly, he blinked and seemed to return to himself, surveying the wreckage with a touch of ruefulness but no real conscience.

'I always hated that dinner service anyway,' he muttered roughly. 'But you're right. This isn't the place for this. We would be far more comfortable upstairs...'

And before Lydia had time to register what was in his mind, he had lifted her bodily from the table, swinging her up into his arms with an ease that revealed the true strength of the muscles underneath the softness of the cashmere. Kicking her chair out of his way, he carried her towards the door.

'Amir!' Lydia protested breathlessly. 'Stop it! You can't...'

But he ignored her, crossing the hall in a few swift strides and turning to mount the first couple of stairs.

The upward movement made Lydia draw in her breath sharply, her arms instinctively going round his neck for security in a way that drew her close against him.

'Amir!' she said again on a very different note.

'What's wrong?' he asked huskily. 'Don't you trust me?'

Trust. The word reverberated inside Lydia's head. Trust him?

Oh, she trusted him to get her safely up the stairs; she had no doubt about that. She could feel the power in the chest against which her head lay, the iron strength of the arms that held her. She knew that he wouldn't drop her, or fall. Physically, she was quite safe.

But emotionally, it was a very different matter.

Emotionally she had no idea how she was going to come out of this. She couldn't say if she would survive unscathed, or emerge with just a few faint scars. She had never known anything like it; never known anyone like Amir. And, that being so, she had no way of predicting how she would feel when one day this was over, as it must inevitably be over.

People like her and Amir lived in separate worlds. They didn't usually meet under normal circumstances. If it hadn't been for the chance of fate they would just have been like ships that passed in the night, never making contact, never even knowing each other's names.

And wouldn't that have been safer?

'Lydia?'

He'd lost her somewhere, Amir realised. He could feel the wild excitement of just moments before seeping away from them like air from a pricked balloon. If he wasn't careful, it would be gone for good, he told himself, his fiercely aroused body screaming in savage protest at just the thought.

On the half-landing he paused, looking deep into her eyes.

'What is it? Second thoughts?'

'No...' But it didn't sound at all convincing.

'Listen to me...'

Slowly he lowered her to the floor, setting her upright with her back against the wall. Taking her small chin in one strong hand, he tilted her face up so that her hyacinth-blue eyes were forced to meet the black intensity of his gaze.

'Beautiful Lydia, there's no need for doubts. I promise you that I will never harm you. That I will make this the best I can for you. You can trust me with your life.'

When he looked at her like that, she would trust him with her soul. And, oh, she wanted that trust!

She didn't want this distance that had suddenly come between them, wiping away the fizzing, burning excitement of just moments before as if it had just been chalk marks on a blackboard, erased with one wipe of a cloth.

She wanted that excitement back. Wanted it raging through her body like a forest fire, burning in her head, obliterating all doubt, all thought, leaving only feeling. The sort of feeling that broke over her head like a tidal wave, swamping her completely.

And there was a simple, easy way to get it back.

'Kiss me, Amir,' she whispered pleadingly. 'Kiss me and show me how it can be...'

'Willingly...'

It was a rough, harsh mutter as his dark head came down towards hers, his mouth taking her lips with a wild demand.

And in the space of a heartbeat it was as if that moment of hesitation and doubt had never been. The tidal wave of desire swept through her, hot and wild, picking her up and carrying her with it into a world of oblivion. A world where only her body and the fierce, demanding hunger that spiralled deep inside had any relevance at all.

On a cry of delight and surrender, she opened her mouth to him and felt the hot invasion of his tongue. His long, hard frame crushed hers against the wall, heat and steel enclosing her, holding her prisoner. Against the fine bones of her pelvis burned the heated, swollen evidence of his desire for her. Just the feel of it sent a stinging shaft of longing straight into the innermost heart of her femininity so that she moaned aloud in need.

'Yes...'

Amir took the cry into his own mouth and expelled it again as a raw sigh.

'I know exactly how you feel, sweetheart. It gets me that way as well.'

His hands touched her face, her hair, her neck, slid in at the top of her sweater, then down to cover one breast.

'*You* get me that way.'

Lydia moved restlessly against the hard support of the wall, returning each kiss with another, more passionate, less inhibited, her arms closing round his neck, fingers clutching at the black silken strands of his hair.

'I want...I want...'

It was all she could manage but he didn't need any more and his laughter was a dark, sexy sound in her ear.

'Don't worry, darling. I know exactly what you want. For a start, you want this...'

He was edging her along the wall as he spoke, moving her towards the next flight of stairs, the next floor. And as they moved his hands were tugging at the waist of her sweater, pulling it roughly upwards.

Adrift on a hot sea of passion, Lydia made no protest when he wrenched it up and over her head. Instead, she helped him all she could, twisting her arms to free them from the sleeves and tossing the discarded garment aside so that it fell in a crumpled heap on the landing at her feet.

'And you want this…'

Her tee shirt and bra soon followed, dropping onto the step behind her as Amir half walked, half carried her up the next flight of stairs, and she heard her shoes bounce and tumble downwards as she kicked them off impatiently. The sound of the second one thumping all the way to the hall below was the last thing she registered before Amir's hands closed over her exposed breasts and she lost all capability of thought.

His hands burned against her skin, sending blazing shafts of need shooting through her as he cupped and held their soft weight, lifting them gently to meet the caress of his mouth.

'And this…'

Lydia collapsed against the hard wall at her back, grateful for its firm support, for the imprisoning cage of Amir's powerful legs that crushed her thighs. Without them, she felt she would crumple into a boneless heap on the floor, all her strength evaporating in the moment that demanding mouth closed over the tip of one aching breast. Her head went back, her body arching to meet that potent source of pleasure as his tongue swirled sensually over the tightened bud of her nipple, drawing it into the warmth of his mouth.

'Oh, yes, Amir, yes…'

It was an incoherent litany of joy, every ounce of her being concentrated on that one stinging centre of delight. And when his lips closed tightly, to tug and suckle on the sensitive point, she could only give in to the most urgent, primitive part of her, the part that made her clutching fingers twist and tug at his hair, trying to pull him even closer, to prolong and intensify this most thrilling of pleasures.

Somehow they stumbled up the remaining stairs to the landing, and it was only as he lowered her to lie on the wide expanse of soft deep green carpet that Lydia realised that she was almost completely naked. Her jeans and the small sliver of pale blue satin that was her only remaining underwear had been pushed down from her hips, tumbling into a crumpled pool around her ankles so that all she had to do was kick her legs to be free of them.

She didn't have a moment to feel exposed or cold. Barely had the time to blink, certainly not to think about coming out of the haze of hunger that held her in its grip before Amir too had thrown off his clothing and come down on the floor beside her, gloriously naked and force-fully, totally aroused. Just the sight of him made her shud-der in nervous excitement.

'But most of all…'

He pulled her towards him, sliding down the soft pile of the carpet, and covered her trembling body with the strength of his.

'What you want is this…'

Capturing both her hands in one of his, he held them pinioned above her head while with his free fingers he subjected her body to the most concentrated sensual assault she had ever known. He stroked every inch of her, found pleasure spots and erotic buttons she hadn't known she possessed. He traced hot trails of excitement over her hy-persensitive skin, curved his palm around her breasts, tor-mented the aching tips with gentle touches and tiny, deli-cate pinches.

And then, when she thought her mind would explode with the non-stop, endless pleasure that he had given her, he finally took those tormenting caresses all the way down the length of her body, slid them through the damp, warm curls and into the most feminine centre of her body.

'Amir!' Lydia gasped her delight, her body convulsing underneath him.

With a strength that surprised her, she wrenched her hands free, pushing them into his hair. Dragging his head

down, she crushed her lips passionately to his, putting all
her hunger, all the need that gripped her into the kiss.

'Now,' she muttered against his mouth. 'Oh, please,
please, now! Take me *now*!'

The words had barely left her tongue when he thrust
into her, wild and hard and so fiercely welcome that her
control shattered completely. When he began to move, she
went with him, driven by pagan, primitive desires that
were more powerful, more irresistible than anything she
had ever known.

Each movement of his powerful body brought a new
and heightened sensation. Each kiss, each caress took her
nearer and nearer to the edge.

'Lydia!' Amir choked, his voice rough and heavy, his
eyes blazing with passion, the hot colour streaking his
cheeks underlining the ruthless desire that gripped him.
'Lady, you are so *good*. Spectacular! I've never known
anyone like you.'

She opened her mouth to tell him that she felt the same
but even as she did he drove into her harder than ever
before, shattering her thoughts and reducing her to nothing
but a raging wildfire, totally beyond management, beyond
restraint.

The pulsing inside her head mounted higher and higher,
matched by the throbbing, spiralling heat between her legs.
She was climbing, soaring, flying, out in the sky, away
from the confines of the earth, until at last, with one wild,
abandoned cry, she felt herself splinter and the world cas-
caded around her in a myriad glowing lights.

CHAPTER FIVE

IT WAS something odd about the light, and a quality to the faint sounds of the day that she was unused to, that woke Lydia late the following morning.

For a couple of seconds she lay still, her mind blank and confused, not knowing where she was or how she had got there.

She *should* be in California, she knew. Should be waking up on the first morning of her new life, far away from everything she had wanted to leave behind, ready to start again.

But she wasn't. She was...

Amir!

The name, and with it the realisation, the memories, rushed into her mind with the force of a blow to her head. Her eyes flew open, staring unfocused round her, not knowing whether she was hoping or dreading to see the man who had brought her here.

'So you're awake at last.'

The low husky tones, agonisingly familiar even after so short an acquaintance, brought her head swinging round in shock.

He was sitting in a chair beside the bed, lounging back against the cushions, long legs stretched out on the carpet, arms folded firmly in front of him. He had pulled on jeans but that was all, and the broad, hair-hazed chest was completely naked. His feet were bare, and the lean cheeks, the strong bones of his jaw were shadowed with the dark stubble of a night's growth of beard.

But it was his eyes that drew her the most. Deep and dark and narrowed under heavily hooded lids, they were fixed on her face, watchful and alert to every faint flicker of emotion across her sleep-clouded features. And there was no emotion in them. No warmth. Nothing to give her any clue to the way he was feeling.

Lydia cleared her throat nervously.

'G-good morning.'

It was all she could think of to say. What *did* one say to the man who had effectively picked her up at the airport and brought her here for what was nothing more than a one-night stand?

One night. But *what* a night!

Hot colour flooded into her cheeks at the memory of the hours before she had finally fallen into the sleep of total exhaustion. Her eyes slid away from the steady, searching stare of the man who had reduced her to that state.

It was too late to feel embarrassed. Too late to scrabble for the bedclothes and pull them up around her nakedness. There wasn't an inch of her body that he hadn't seen, touched, *kissed*, and yet here, in the very cold light of day, she knew she couldn't face him with any degree of composure unless she was covered from her chin to her toes.

'Good morning.' Amir responded gravely to her shaky greeting. 'I don't suppose I have to do my duty as your host and ask whether you slept well.'

'N-no…'

Lydia wished desperately that she could get control of her voice. The only way to handle this was to be as cool and collected as he obviously was. To behave as if torrid one-night stands were very much a part of her life and she was used to waking up next to men she had known for barely half a day.

But it was very difficult when the truth was quite the opposite. She had never had a one-night stand in her life. And as for 'experience', she doubted that the few, unfulfilling months she had had with Jonathon quite came into that category.

'I—we—I was worn out.'

The sensual mouth twitched into something that might have been the beginning of a smile, but which was clamped down on hard before it could actually develop.

'We wore each other out,' he acknowledged dryly. 'It was quite a night. One I won't forget in a long, long time.'

'Well, I'm glad that at least I'll prove memorable to you,' Lydia declared, hitching herself up on the pillows and tucking the sheet firmly around her so that it covered her from her breasts downwards. It still didn't conceal the fact that her skin had burned a fiery red at his comment, but it would have to do.

'You'll be more than memorable,' Amir drawled in sardonic reply. 'Unforgettable would be the word I would use.'

'Is that meant to be a compliment?'

His tone had made the description decidedly ambiguous. So she didn't know whether to trust the quick, sharp flare of delight at the thought that this devastating man would find her impossible to erase from his memory.

'You can take it whatever way you like.'

Right now, he wasn't exactly sure how he meant it himself. The events of the previous night had knocked him for six from the start and he had been trying to catch up with his feelings ever since.

He only knew that most of the time he hadn't been thinking with his mind—certainly not with his intelligence—but with a far more basic part of his make-up.

But one thing was certain. He would never, *ever* forget the experience he had had last night, though the truth was that most of the details were decidedly hazy. From the moment that he had kissed away the trickle of peach juice from the corner of her mouth he had been caught up in a sexual firestorm that had taken possession of him right to his very soul and he had been incapable of thinking as a result.

He had simply *felt*. By Allah, how he had felt! He had never known such a concentrated, non-stop, mind-blowing tornado of pleasure as the one that had had him in its grip. Even now, just to think of it made his body harden in pleasurable recollection combined with an aching demand, so intense it was close to pain, that he repeat the experience all over again. And seeing Lydia sitting there in the bed—in *his* bed—with the sheet pulled up so closely round her was doing nothing to help his self-control.

'Would you like a tee shirt or something?' he demanded abruptly, seeing her blink in stunned confusion. 'To wear, I mean,' he elucidated when she frowned her bewilderment.

'I'm quite warm enough, thank you.'

'It wasn't your warmth or the lack of it I was thinking of. I meant that perhaps we would both be better able to concentrate if you had some clothes on.'

She thought she was removing all temptation, he knew. She believed she was acting prim and proper, concealing the parts of her that were likely to inflame lustful thoughts and so reducing the possibility of him being distracted by the sight of her body. She couldn't be more wrong.

Didn't she know that the soft linen sheet clung to every curve of her body? That it undulated over the soft mounds of her breasts, flowed down over the flat stomach and long, slim legs? Wasn't she aware of the way that, because the material was so fine, he could see the faint dark shadow between her legs? With the memory of how it had felt to bury himself in those curls still so strong in his mind, it was all he could do not to lurch out of this chair, fling back the covers to expose her tantalising nakedness and make love to her all over again.

At least they would have the comfort of a bed this time. Last night it had taken them a long time to even reach the bedroom, never mind the bed itself. It was only after the first fire of hunger had ebbed a little, after they had appeased their urgent, aching need for each other, that he had been able even to think of carrying her in here and placing her on the bed.

And just that brief respite had been enough to stoke the embers once again. The feel of her slim, soft body in his arms had been more than he'd been able to bear. He had no sooner lowered her onto the mattress than he had had to have her again. And she had responded every bit as hungrily to him.

No! Enough was enough! He couldn't think straight. He couldn't *think* at all.

Pushing himself out of the chair, he strode across to the cupboards, yanked open a drawer and snatched up the nearest tee shirt.

'Here!'

He almost flung it in her direction, refusing to let himself look while she struggled into the soft blue cotton without letting the sheet slip any lower.

'What do we have to concentrate on?' she asked, her voice still muffled by the enfolding garment.

'We have to talk.'

Amir couldn't bring himself to go back and sit down again. He found it much easier to give in to the restlessness he was feeling by pacing about the room, moving across the floor from one window to the other.

'Talk about what?'

Oh, Lydia, don't be a *fool*! Don't you know? Can't you guess? A one-night stand was all it was. He'd had his fun—he'd got what he wanted and now he wanted out.

'About us.'

'There is no—'

'I've been in touch with the airport.'

'Oh-h-h.'

It was a faint sigh. A sound of despondency that she couldn't hold back. Of course he'd been in touch with the airport. He wanted out—he wanted rid of her and he'd been determined to find out just how quickly it could be managed. What else had she expected?

'I rang them first thing.'

Naturally. She wished he would stand still, stop this restive pacing. He reminded her far too much of a hungry panther, prowling impatiently about its territory, looking for its next prey.

Well, she could make it easy for him.

'When does my flight leave? Luckily I don't have anything to get ready, because I never even unpacked. All I have to do is get my clothes…'

Her voice trailed off as she realised just what that would entail. She would have to go on a hunt for all the clothing she had discarded in stages on the way upstairs last night. Her shoes would probably have fallen into the hall. Her jumper would be on the half-landing, her bra beside it. And as for her jeans and panties…

'Here…'

Amir had picked something up from a chair and now he dumped the bundle on the end of the bed. Seeing what it was, Lydia coloured sharply, wishing the floor would open up and swallow her whole before she died of embarrassment and regret.

Her clothes. He had collected up all her clothes, even the shoes, folded them neatly and had them ready for her to put on. Was he so anxious for her to be gone?

'Thank you.' She forced herself to say it. 'I can be washed and dressed and out of your hair in five minutes flat. If you'll just…'

'No.'

It was flat and emotionless, bringing her head up in a shocked rush. His eyes were as unrevealing as his tone, impossible to read.

'No? No, what? No, I can't get dressed—or you don't believe I can get dressed in five minutes? No, you don't want me to use your bathroom?'

'I have no doubt that if you wanted to you could get dressed in much less than five minutes—much as I would prefer it if you didn't. But what I actually meant was, no, you can't leave.'

It was that 'can't' that did it. Thrown at her like a regal decree from the Crown Prince he was, it made her blood run cold, shivers slithering down her spine.

'And you can't make me stay!' she protested, sitting up sharply in bed. 'You're not in Kuimar now, *Highness*! You can't hold me against my will! There are laws against this sort of thing.'

At last Amir had stilled his restless movement. Standing between her and the door, he regarded her thoughtfully, with a definite wicked gleam in his dark eyes.

'I have no intention of holding you against your will, my dear Ms Ashton. And you won't need to invoke British or indeed international law against me. For one thing, I doubt if it would have any effect on the weather.'

'The weather?'

Lydia frowned her bewilderment.

'What has the weather got to do with this?'

'Everything. As I said, I phoned the airport first thing. The snow has been coming down all night, and fog has made matters even worse. They don't think they'll get the runways clear for three days at the least.'

'Is this the truth?'

Lydia eyed him suspiciously, frank disbelief shadowing her eyes.

'You wouldn't lie to me about it?'

'What benefit would there be for me in lying?' The look he turned on her was totally guileless—on the surface at least. 'What would it do for me?'

Why didn't he just say, I wouldn't go to the trouble of lying to keep *you* here? Lydia wondered grumpily, her mood aggravated by the unexpected pain in her heart at the thought.

'So I can't get away? There are no planes at all?'

'Not for three days—more if conditions worsen.'

'But what am I going to do?'

Now it was Lydia's turn to want to pace uneasily about the room. She made a move to fling back the covers and get out of bed in a way that expressed the unease and disturbance in her mind. But then, recalling the fact that the tee shirt she was wearing, although roomy enough, barely came down to the tops of her thighs, she hastily rethought. Instead she perched on the edge of the bed, with the sheets pulled over her legs.

'What about my job? Where can I stay?'

'There's plenty of room here.'

It was the last thing she had expected. Having convinced herself that he was anxious for her to leave, that he couldn't wait to see the back of her, she had never thought to hear him offer her any sort of help, let alone accommodation.

'You'd let me stay?'

'I'd like it,' he declared, shocking her even further with the note of sincerity that rang in his voice. 'Look, Lydia…'

He came back to the chair he had been sitting in, settled on the arm of it so that he was exactly level with her and could look her straight in the eyes, intent jet gaze meeting wary blue.

'I've already told you that last night was something I won't forget in a long time. It's also something I'd like to repeat—given the chance.'

He paused briefly, but just as Lydia was wondering whether she was supposed to be saying 'me, too', and speculating whether it would be wise or far too revealing, he went on in a more sombre tone.

'But right now…'

'Oh, I should have known there was bound to be a ''but''!'

Lydia was shocked by her own outburst, and the bitterness of the tone she used. She hadn't been prepared for the way that 'But right now…' had torn at her heart. And the realisation of exactly why that had hurt so much rocked her sense of reality dangerously.

How could she have let this man sneak into her heart after knowing him for such a short time? It wasn't even twenty-four hours since they had met! She knew almost nothing about him beyond his name and the fact that he was a wonderful lover. That was hardly a basis for coming to care about anyone!

'Well, it's all right, you don't have to spell it out. I can get the message as well as anyone. I'll even say it for you, shall I? It was great—I'll see you around. Thanks for everything. Or perhaps you were planning on adding, I'll give you a ring some time—like I'd be fool enough to believe that!'

The cool scrutiny of those deep eyes was disturbing, making her shift nervously on the bed, wondering just what was going on in that calculating mind.

'Don't you think you're rather rushing to conclusions?' he enquired softly, unsettling her even more.

'What other conclusion is there to come to? I'm not a child, Amir. Nor am I a silly schoolgirl brought up on comic-strip stories of love at first sight and happily ever after. I know that having sex—even the fantastic, mind-blowing sort of sex we shared—isn't any sort of guarantee of a deeper feeling. In fact it's usually not. It was probably the fact that we're complete strangers that made it that way.'

'But you agree that it was fantastic?' Amir inserted smoothly when she paused for breath.

Too late to back out now. She'd already opened her big mouth way too wide on that score.

'Well, yes.'

She tried desperately to sound offhand, as if thrilling,

mind-blowing sex with total strangers was something she experienced almost every second day.

'And that being so, it's something you'd like to repeat?'

'Might do. I don't know…'

What was she getting herself into here?

'Well, I do. I know I'd like to repeat the experience over and over again. But there's a problem.'

Of course. Now they were coming to it.

'For certain reasons—commitments I can't get out of— my life's not my own right now. I'm not a free agent. I certainly wasn't planning on starting any relationship with anyone, and, if that plane had left on time yesterday, I wouldn't be doing so now.'

He paused as if expecting some comment, but Lydia couldn't think of one to make. Added to that, her tongue seemed to have frozen in her mouth, and she couldn't have forced it to form a single word if she'd tried.

'But then, of course, I met you.'

And meeting Lydia had scrambled his thought patterns, driven all common sense from his head. For the space of a few crazy, heated hours last night he had forgotten all about his father and the conditions the stiff-necked old man had placed on his future. He'd forgotten all he'd fought for over the past years, the ambition that had driven him since his eleventh birthday.

But this morning a degree of sanity had returned. He wasn't going to throw over all he'd worked for. For years he'd got nowhere, feeling as if he were beating his head hard against a brick wall. Then, just as he had come close to deciding that it was time to give up, that the arrogant, cold-hearted old bastard just wasn't worth the effort, suddenly Sheikh Khalid had held out an olive branch. But an olive branch that had come with a price tag attached.

It was a price tag he could cope with. The end result would be well worth the small sacrifice he'd have to make. But that price tag meant that dalliance with other women, even women as appealing and enticing as Miss Lydia Ashton, was out.

And so he'd resolved that, no matter how much he might regret it, he had to make sure she was on the first plane out of London for California, heading for that dream job of hers and out of his life. Which was why he'd got onto the airport first thing.

Only to find that there would be no flights to anywhere for the foreseeable future.

'Another day, another time, it might have been different. We could have had some fun together for a while. But I don't have that while.'

'I see.'

Lydia's voice was flat, dreary, monotone. For a few wonderful moments there she had actually allowed herself to dream, to hope. To let a tiny chink of expectation slide into her mind and start to take root.

The hope that Amir might want more than the one-night stand.

Stupid! Foolish! Downright *naïve*!

Men like Amir didn't fall for women like her. They didn't lose their hearts to ordinary, everyday girls from ordinary, everyday families in ordinary, everyday towns.

Amir was a *sheikh*, for heaven's sake! A *Crown Prince*! He moved in elevated circles filled with wealthy, sophisticated women. Women who could embark on a casual affair without so much as a second thought and leave it again when the time came, without bothering to glance back.

Meeting her in the VIP lounge at the airport, he must have assumed that she belonged there. That she was as classy and urbane as the women he was used to mixing with. He'd had no way of knowing that the only thing that was classy about her was the job she had been heading off to.

'Well, it's all right, I'm not going to be difficult. I know a brush-off when I get one...'

'Dammit, Lydia, no!'

Once more Amir got to his feet in a swift fluid movement that expressed perfectly his impatience, the annoyance that sparked deep in his dark eyes.

'You're not listening to me! I'm not giving you the brush-off!'

'You're not?'

Try as she might, she couldn't stop her mouth from trembling in shock so that the words came out on a revealing quaver.

'Then what—?' she tried again but Amir cut across her swiftly.

'At least, not right now.'

Drawing in his breath on a sharp, resolute hiss, he raked both strong hands through the sleek gleaming silk of his hair before he fixed his eyes on her perturbed face once more.

'What I'm trying to say is that I can't offer anything with a future, anything more than a passing affair—and a brief one at that. Yesterday I thought we couldn't have more than that night, but this morning I discovered that fate has dealt us a very different hand of cards to the ones we originally had. The airports are closed; we can't go anywhere. We have an unexpected three days, Lydia. Three days we can spend together, if you want to.'

'If I...'

She couldn't finish the sentence, a rush of panicky self-preservation warring with the instinctive, yearning hunger in her mind. Her thoughts swung this way and that, whirling frantically, unable to come up with anything close to a decision.

Amir had taken her hands in his, enclosing her fingers and gripping them tight. His eyes burned as they held hers, willing her to do as he wanted.

'I can offer you three days, and the nights that go with them, Lydia. Nothing more. Three days together and then we go our separate ways. What do you say? Is it yes or no?'

CHAPTER SIX

THREE days!

He was offering her three days. Nothing more.

Three days. And the nights that went with them. Don't forget those nights.

How *could* she forget the nights?

Three days, three nights. It was nothing. It was everything.

When she'd been thinking this would only ever be a one-night stand, it was all she'd ever dreamed of. And it was so much less than she had truly dreamed of.

'Lydia?'

Amir gave her hand a little shake to bring her back to the present.

'What do you say?'

What *could* she say? Every sense of self-preservation warned her not even to consider it. All that was the old Lydia, calm, rational, cautious, declared loudly that she would be selling herself short, that there was no future in what he offered. At the end of the three days he would leave her, hurt and used, and go his own selfish way.

'Three days…'

'I know it isn't long, but it's all I have. All we have. It's that or nothing.'

'You certainly give it to me straight.'

Lydia hoped that her smile worked, that it hid the confusion and the hurt in her eyes.

'There's no other way to give it. I'm not offering any more, Lydia. There isn't anything more. But in those three days—and especially in the three nights we share—I promise you we'll have the affair of a lifetime.'

'Sounds tempting.'

Her words snapped off on a hasty intake of breath as he slid an arm around her waist and gently drew her close. Bending his head, he touched his lips to the soft fall of her hair then came even closer and laid his cheek against hers. The intensely personal scent of his skin filled her nostrils and the faint shadow of stubble rasped over her tender flesh.

'Then let me tempt you, sweetheart,' he murmured against her ear. 'Let me persuade you to stay and I promise you you'll never forget it. You can have anything you want. Everything you want.'

Everything except his love.

No!

Where had that crazy thought come from? She hadn't been considering the prospect of *love*. Love was something she had no place for in her life right now. It was the last thing she wanted. It would complicate things far too much.

'Everything?'

'Anything,' he confirmed deeply, his mouth moving gently against her skin, pressing on it slow, delicate kisses that stirred her senses to the depths of her soul. 'You only have to ask.'

Those kisses were stopping her from thinking. They were waking the deepest, most primitive longings in her. Hunger uncoiled between her legs, burning along her nerves like a forest fire. She couldn't stay passive any more and, with a swift twist of her neck, she turned her head so that her mouth was under his and she kissed him, hard and fierce.

For a second even Amir seemed taken aback. He stilled suddenly, dark head going back just an inch or two so that those ebony eyes could look straight into her wide blue ones.

'Lydia?' he questioned softly.

At the mercy of the clamouring demand of her body,

she had no time for hesitation, or fear. She met the searching demand of that concentrated stare head-on, not even
blinking in its power.

Taking his head in her hands, slender fingers lying along
the lean planes of his cheeks, shaping the hard bones, she
drew him closer, took his mouth in another kiss, slower
and more lingering this time.

'Lydia…' he said again, but in a very different tone.
'What is this?'

The faint unevenness of the question emboldened her,
gave her a new and intoxicating sense of power. Her smile
straight into those watchful eyes was confident, gleaming
with female triumph, holding a distinct edge of provocative challenge.

'You said I only had to ask.'

For the space of a single heartbeat he closed his eyes.
And when he opened them again the coal-dark depths were
lit from within by the golden flare of desire.

'And you're asking?'

Lydia nodded slowly, still holding his gaze with her
own.

'For everything?'

She nodded again, her mouth drying in the heat of her
need.

'For everything,' she croaked. 'And anything…'

'Then you'll have everything,' he told her huskily. 'Everything I can give you and more.'

His mouth took hers again as his arms came around her,
sliding under her legs, lifting her from the floor. He carried
her to the bed, laid her down, still with his lips plundering
hers, the erotic dance of his tongue making her senses
swim.

The skimpy tee shirt was no barrier to his urgent hands;
his jeans almost as easily dispensed with. His touch was
on her skin, her face, her breasts. And as she held out her
arms and welcomed him into her body once more Lydia

knew that she had made her decision and she had no intention of going back on it.

Three days. She had three days, and she was going to make the best of them.

When she had thought she would only have one night to remember, then three days seemed like a lifetime in comparison. Three days and three nights stretched ahead, seemingly endless, swollen with possibilities, an eternity of happiness.

Ruthlessly she squashed down the protests, the concerns of the other, the more cautious Lydia. She had been planning on a whole new beginning anyway. She had dreamed of breaking free of the constraints and the prudence that Jonathon had so scorned. The old Lydia might have feared the consequences. The new one embraced the experience willingly, opening her mind and her heart to it.

'I want everything!' she muttered against the heat of Amir's skin, matching her words to the rhythm of his powerfully thrusting body. 'I want everything—everything.'

'And you'll get it,' he promised thickly. 'Believe me, darling, you can have anything you want.'

Anything. Anything. It was like a litany of belief in her head, throbbing, pounding, rising to a crescendo in the moment that her control shattered and she cried out, clinging hard to his powerful shoulders, abandoning herself totally to him.

Anything.

Everything.

For three days.

But even the final reminder of reality that slid into her consciousness as her pulse finally slowed, her breathing eased, and she found herself able to think again had no effect on her decision.

So what if, after the three days, Amir left her without a second thought? What if he walked away and never looked back? Jonathon had done exactly that, and she had been so careful with Jonathon. She had taken things slowly, waited and held back before committing herself. And he had still walked out on her life, discarding her for someone else.

At least Amir had made no pretence of a future. He had been totally straight and upfront from the first. What she saw was what she got. And she was going to embrace that wholeheartedly, no holding back. Taking everything there was on offer.

Beside her Amir stirred lazily, drawing in a deep, contented sigh as he stretched like an indolent cat before a fire.

'Okay?' he asked, his breathing faintly uneven.

'Mmm.'

It was all Lydia could manage. Her heart was still pounding, as much from the significance of her decision as from the explosion of pleasure that had crashed through her.

A long, tanned arm snaked round her waist, whipcord strong muscles tautening to hold her tight as he came up on one elbow to kiss her arm, her cheek, her temple, and look down into her passion-sated face.

'You're sure?' he questioned softly. 'No regrets?'

Lifting her head, Lydia brushed her lips against his cheek, kissed his mouth, then dropped back on the pillow again.

'No,' she assured him confidently, her conviction blazing in her eyes. 'No regrets, none at all.'

'There's just one problem,' Lydia said an hour or so later when, having made love once again, they were finally forced by sheer hunger to think of leaving the bedroom at last. 'Something we hadn't thought of.'

'Oh?'

Amir had just come out of the shower in the *en suite* bathroom and was padding across the carpet, totally unselfconscious in his nudity, to pull open a couple of drawers and extract clothes from inside them.

'And what's that? Nothing important, I hope.'

'Could be quite important,' Lydia informed him, lounging back against the pillows in blissful laziness, her whole body limp and glowing from his attentions.

'What is it?'

Amir paused in his selection of clothing and swung round to face her.

He really had the most wonderful body, Lydia thought dreamily. Perfect. Tall and strong. Lean and muscular, without an ounce of excess weight anywhere on his powerful frame. The wide, strong wall of his chest was softly shaded with black silky hair that arrowed down to a narrow waist and hips and the long, long legs were as well built as the rest of him. And every glorious inch was covered in that smooth, tanned skin that made her fingers itch to touch it again, her mouth hunger to kiss it all over.

'What? *Lydia!*'

The sharpness of Amir's tone startled her out of her wanton daydream, forcing her to turn startled eyes on his exasperated face.

'Oh—sorry—what?'

'I said what is it? What's this problem you've just thought of?'

'It's nothing much…'

'Tell me.'

'Oh, all right. I suppose it might matter after all. I mean we do have to— Sorry!'

She broke off hastily as he gave a small growl of annoyance, rolling his eyes in a gesture of impatience.

'Sorry!' she said again. 'It's just that I don't happen to have any clothes. At least, nothing other than the ones I stood up in yesterday. If you remember, all my luggage was already checked in before the flight was cancelled and we—I—I never thought to go back and collect it before we came here.'

He hadn't thought of it either, Amir admitted privately. He hadn't thought of very much at all. If the truth were told, he hadn't been thinking at all, just acting purely on the sexual hunger that had overwhelmed them from the start and driven them blindly so that last night had been the only natural, inevitable conclusion of their meeting. Last night and the passion they had shared again this morning. A force as old as time, as primitive and powerful as life itself. Something too strong to be denied; too compelling to resist.

'So you see, I don't have anything to wear. Not if I'm going to stay here for three days and three…'

'And three nights,' Amir finished for her as the sentence faded away and hot colour washed over her whole body. 'Not that you have anything to worry about there. What you have on—or, rather, what you don't have on at this moment will be perfect for then.'

Lydia squirmed uncomfortably against the downy pillows, all her earlier ease evaporating like mist before the sun as he subjected her to a slow, lingeringly insolent survey from those burning dark eyes. She was suddenly a prey to a desperate need to snatch at the sheets and pull them up to cover her hastily, concealing every inch of her exposed body from him.

But she struggled to resist it. She could just imagine what Amir's response might be, the mocking gleam that would light in his eyes, the sardonic note that would colour his voice when he commented satirically that it was far, far too late for such thoughts of modesty now.

And he would be right. But that didn't change how she felt. She didn't know what was suddenly different; why she no longer felt totally comfortable in her nakedness when she had been so happy, so confident only moments before. But it was as if a chill wind had suddenly got up, feathering cold breezes over her exposed flesh and making her shiver.

'And as far as I'm concerned, you can stay like that for the whole three days,' Amir continued, pulling on his own clothes as he spoke. The gleam in his eyes had brightened, his appreciative smile turning into a wicked, sexy grin. 'I'd certainly have no objection to you wandering around the apartment stark naked...'

'Well I would!' Lydia snapped sharply, something in his tone making her skin prickle in unease. 'You're not going to play the sheikh with me, *Your Highness*.'

The barb hit home with more force than she had dreamed. She saw his long back stiffen, brilliant jet black eyes narrowing swiftly.

'And what,' he ground out harshly, 'is that supposed to mean?'

There was danger in his tone, a warning to be very careful, but Lydia determined to ignore it. He might be Crown Prince in his own country but he was only a man here in the privacy of his bedroom.

'Oh, you know—it smacks too much of the harem. Of the sheikh's favourite being brought out of purdah to be paraded in front of her master, dressed only in the seven veils...'

But she'd gone too far; his expression told her that. The stunning features had set into hard, cold lines, and the sensual mouth was no longer smiling, but clamped tight shut as if to hold back the rush of furious words he could barely keep in check.

'That is *not* what I meant!' he declared coldly. 'And you damn well know it.'

'Oh, do I?'

She no longer cared if he commented on her sudden modesty. She just knew she could no longer face him unless she covered herself and fast.

Snatching up the sheet, she coiled it round her, pulling

it tight into a sort of makeshift toga and tucking the ends in firmly. At least covered in some sort of way, she felt better able to face that angry gaze.

'It seems to me that it's exactly what you meant! That you wanted me here only for your pleasure and you weren't thinking of me… Are you *laughing*?'

He was too. And the worst thing was that all she could think of was the way that amusement warmed those stunning eyes. The smile on the beautiful mouth was wide and unrestrained, showing white, strong teeth. Aloof and distant and in pure Crown Prince mode, he had a masculine beauty that tore at her heart, but like this, easy and relaxed and oh, so human, he would be far too tempting to fall in love with.

No! Not that word again! Hastily she blanked it out, slamming the door shut in her mind.

She had to keep *love* out of this! There was no place for it in a three-day affair with no future.

'Lydia, *habibti*.' Infuriatingly, Amir was still smiling. 'If you'll get off your high horse, you'll see that you're wasting precious time. We only have three days, remember. We don't have time for arguments. And if you're truly worried about the clothes, then don't. We'll soon sort that out.'

'We will?'

She was still not sure she was ready to be appeased. Irritation prickled down her spine, and she had to bite back a hasty retort.

'How will we do that?'

'Leave it to me.'

He shrugged on a black long-sleeved polo shirt, tucking the base of it into the waist of his jeans and swiftly buckling the broad leather belt.

'But I'll make us something to eat first. I'm starving, and I'm sure you must feel the same.'

'I am hungry,' honesty forced Lydia to admit, struggling

against the feeling that she was being deliberately distracted, her thoughts diverted into other paths.

'Then have a shower and come downstairs. You'll have to wear your old clothes for now, but after breakfast we'll go shopping.'

'Shopping?'

Yes, that was guaranteed to soothe whatever had ruffled her feathers, Amir told himself cynically. The effect was instant, her head going back, eyes brightening. It was a trick that never failed. One hundred per cent success rate every time. Once a woman knew who he was—who his father was—it was only a matter of time before she started to work out just what his wealth could buy her.

He had to admit that this Lydia had lasted longer than most. Cleverly, she'd waited for him to come up with the idea, instead of suggesting it herself. But the end result was always the same. He was going to have to pay for the pleasure of her company in his bed.

'Can we go out in all this snow?'

'No problem. The airport may be closed because of ice and fog, but we can still get around town. At least we can go as far as necessary to buy you what you need.'

Lydia blinked in stunned confusion.

'You're going to *buy* me clothes?'

'I knew that would get your interest.'

On his way out the door, Amir had clearly not heard her properly and as a result he had interpreted her reaction as one of stunned delight, instead of which she was simply stunned—and not quite sure how she felt about this development.

'I never knew a woman yet who could resist the thought of going shopping for something new to wear. Yes, I'll buy you the clothes. But only if you hurry up and get dressed so that we can eat before I fade away completely.'

He was gone, running down the stairs, whistling softly, before Lydia could think of a suitable retort.

She was in the shower, washing her hair under the hot running water when realisation dawned. *Now* she knew why that change of mood had come over her. She knew exactly what had caused it. It was happening again now, just to think of it, the heat of the shower barely reaching her as she suddenly felt chilled to the bone.

'As far as I'm concerned, you can stay like that for the whole three days…'

Could he have spelled it out any more clearly?

She had been right to crush back those foolish, naïve thoughts that had kept sliding into her mind. Why had she ever even let herself allow the word 'love' to form at all? It was obvious that Amir had no such thing in his mind. Instead, he had made it plain that he saw her as only one thing—as a sex object, nothing more.

Lydia shivered as she forced herself to face facts. Could she really go through with this? Could she really accept the little he had to offer and not look for more, even for just three days? It was so alien to her way of thinking, her way of feeling, that wouldn't it destroy her?

But then she remembered the feel of Amir's hands on her body, the caress of his lips, the taste of his kisses, and the chill vanished, driven back by a flood of hungry, demanding heat. The heavy pounding of the water down onto her head was echoed in the pulse of need in her body.

If she closed her eyes she could relive those wild, passionate moments in Amir's arms, the sensual onslaught of his lovemaking, the blazing crescendo that had been her orgasm. She wanted *that* again—and again. Wouldn't she sacrifice feeling, emotion, sentiment for it, for the short time it was offered to her?

Yes, of course she would. But that didn't mean she had to sell herself short. Fired by a new determination, she switched off the shower and stepped out of the stall, reaching for a towel and rubbing herself briskly all over. She would show Amir that there was more to this affair than simply sex, she resolved. But he might take some careful handling while she did it.

CHAPTER SEVEN

'YOU took your time.'

Amir greeted Lydia casually when she finally appeared in the doorway of the huge, ultra-modern kitchen.

'The coffee's been ready for ages. So much for your boast that you could be dressed and ready in five minutes flat.'

'That was when I thought I was out of here for good.' Lydia hid the nervous thud of her heart behind a pretence of airy indifference. 'There wouldn't have been much point doing my hair or anything then.'

'But with the prospect of a little retail therapy on the cards, you thought you'd make the effort. The cards in question being my credit cards, of course.'

The cynicism in his tone made Lydia flinch, the resolve that had buoyed her up on her way downstairs receding fast, leaving her feeling limp and flat and desperately uncertain.

'You offered!' she protested.

'So I did. And don't worry, darling, I'll deliver—but after breakfast. I'll die if I don't have a coffee soon. Do you want to eat in here or—'

'Here,' Lydia broke in hastily.

She had peeped into the dining room on her way to the kitchen and had been subject to distinctly ambiguous feelings at the realisation that the chaos they had left behind on the previous night had been carefully tidied away. The remains of the meal had been removed, the disordered tablecloth, the damaged china swept up, presumably by Jamila or someone like her.

'It's warmer in here—more—friendly.'

She had been about to say 'more intimate' but had a hasty rethink. 'Intimate' was not a word she was comfortable with when used in the context of Amir.

The short journey downstairs from the bedroom to the kitchen had been a decidedly unsettling one. The realisation that she barely knew where any room in this house was, except for the bedroom, had brought home to her with shocking force just how little she knew about the man she had just spent the night with. The man she had been *intimate* with and with whom she had promised to spend every minute of the next three days.

Amir was a man who routinely flew first class, whose father owned this huge apartment, who had servants who appeared, silently and without needing any instruction, it seemed, to clear away any mess he might make.

What was she doing in the life of someone like that?

'So, what sort of clothes would you like?' Amir asked when, with the coffee poured, she had settled at the long wooden table with a plate of fluffy scrambled eggs and toast. 'What exactly did you have in mind?'

'I've been thinking about that...'

To her annoyance, Lydia found that her throat had suddenly dried, making her voice crack embarrassingly, and she reached for her coffee and drank some hastily to ease her discomfort.

'I'm not happy with the thought of you buying me anything. I mean, I won't need very much anyway—just something to change into—some clean underwear... Why are you looking at me like that?'

Amir lifted broad shoulders in a casual shrug.

'Because if you mean what you say, then I don't believe that you're actually real.'

'Why? Just because I don't want you to spend your money on me?'

'I can afford it.'

'I'm sure you can, but that doesn't mean I like the idea. That isn't what I want from you.'

'It isn't?'

In his experience, it was *exactly* what was wanted.

'Then what *do* you want?'

'I...'

How did she answer that? Stupid, impossible words like 'love' and 'commitment' and 'a future' rushed into her thoughts and she had to drive them away hastily, suddenly fearful that if she let them in, allowed them to take root in her mind, she might actually believe them.

'I don't know. I—I don't usually do this sort of thing. I...'

Suddenly inspiration struck and she seized on it thankfully, jumping to her feet in a rush.

'I know—wait a minute... Where did I leave my bag?'

When she came back into the kitchen a few moments later, clutching her hand luggage, Amir stared at her in frank bemusement as she scrabbled about in the flight bag, hunting for something.

'Lydia...'

'It's in here somewhere. Oh, yes!'

On an exclamation of triumph she pulled out a glossy magazine and dropped it onto the table.

'I don't usually buy this, but I wanted something to read on the plane and this...this caught my eye.'

She wasn't going to admit that she had also bought it because it was so totally unlike anything she normally read. That, filled with the spirit of adventure, the thought of a new start in life, she had picked this just because it was so different. That until now its mixture of celebrity gossip and articles on sex had never appealed in the slightest.

Amir regarded the brightly coloured cover, with its close-up photograph of a pouting, scantily clad model with an expression that was a blend of contempt and disbelief stamped onto his aristocratic features.

'And what, precisely, am I supposed to be looking at?'

'There's an article in here…'

Lydia forced herself to ignore the edge of amusement in his voice as she flicked through the pages hurriedly.

'I know, I was looking at it just before… There!'

She realised her mistake as soon as she had pushed the magazine across the table towards him. She couldn't have given herself away any more clearly if she had made up a placard that said, 'Totally unsophisticated. Never had an affair in her life,' and hung it round her neck.

As she watched Amir smooth down the pages of the magazine with long, elegant fingers she felt what little was left of her confidence seep out of her, leaving her feeling limp and completely stupid. He studied the article as if it were something strange and exotic that he'd never encountered before, a faint frown creasing the space between his black, arched brows.

'"The sensual stages of a super-sexy affair. From first kiss to yes, I do, or no, I don't,"' he drawled sardonically, lifting sceptical eyes to her pink-cheeked face. 'My dear Lydia, what *is* this?'

And have you gone completely out of your mind? He didn't actually put the question into words but it was there in his expression, in the tone of his voice.

'Are you suggesting that it's some sort of blueprint for our relationship?'

That carefully controlled patience in his words did more to express his mood than any less tolerant demand, and it set Lydia's heart fluttering in her throat.

'Well, yes—it could be that,' she improvised hastily. 'We have just three days together, and we want to make the most of it—yes?'

He was still regarding her as if he thought she had had some sort of dangerous brainstorm, but when she glanced at him questioningly he inclined his dark head in brusque agreement.

'Good, I thought you weren't with me then. We don't want to miss out any part of what makes—'

'A super-sexy affair…' Amir inserted ironically, almost destroying her ability to go on.

'I wouldn't put it quite that way myself.'

Jonathon would recognise that voice. Prim and proper, lips pulled tight like a purse-string, was what he had once called it. Remembering that she was supposed to be a very different person from the one Jonathon had known, Lydia made a determined effort to relax.

'But I did think it would be fun to try and fit in all these stages into the three days. Don't you agree?'

Pulling out a chair, she sat back down at the table and turned the magazine round so that she could read it properly. Concentrating hard on the text made it easier to forget that Amir was watching her, powerful black eyes fixed intently on her downbent head.

'Obviously we'll have to cram them up a bit. We can't wait—what's this one? Six months or so before we go on holiday together—we can hardly do that. But if we adapt and adjust here and there, I'm sure we could do them all— or come close to it. What do you think?'

'If that's what you'd like…'

He had to admit that she constantly surprised him, this Lydia Ashton. He never quite knew just what sort of a woman she would be next. From the moment she had frozen him out at their first meeting, to the wild, wanton creature she had been in his bed, she had had a dozen different faces and personalities, all of them intriguing and appealing in their own way.

And now she was someone else again. Suddenly the careful control of earlier that morning had slipped away, to be replaced with a youthful enthusiasm that was almost childlike in its bubbling excitement.

It was the distant opposite of the sort of sophisticated boredom and indifference he was accustomed to in many of the women he knew and in spite of himself he found it unexpectedly appealing. He also wanted it to continue, to keep Lydia with him for longer. And if playing along with her crazy idea of following this list did that, then he was prepared to do so.

'I'm sure we can manage something.'

'You'll go along with it? Great!'

She was painfully aware of the way that she was using enthusiasm to hide her inner insecurity.

'We don't have to do them in exactly this order, of course. For a start there are a couple of things we can cross off already.'

Pulling a pen from her handbag, she ticked off the first item on the list in the magazine.

'Meeting, for one, obviously. And first kiss…'

'And some of them we've rather jumped the gun on,' Amir put in dryly.

One long finger tapped an entry lower down the page, a devilish glint lighting his eyes as they looked up and into hers.

Seeing that the paragraph he had pointed to read, 'After a month to six weeks—you go to bed together', she coloured fierily.

'Yes, well, that's the way it's meant to be—we only have seventy-two hours, so we can't hang about.'

'And you can cross this one off too.'

Another gesture of his hand indicated the section on 'moving in together'.

'All right!' Lydia knew when she was beaten. 'So it was a silly idea! Go ahead; laugh at me if you want! I just thought that…'

She made to slam the magazine shut, only to have the movement stilled abruptly as Amir suddenly reached out, closing strong fingers over her hand.

'What makes you think I'm laughing at you?'

'Well, you have to be. You can't possibly be taking this seriously! I just wanted to put a bit of romance into this and you—'

'And I promised you the affair of a lifetime,' Amir inserted quietly, but with an ominous edge to his voice that froze her when she would have struggled, trying to throw off his imprisoning grip. 'Lydia, look at me…'

Stubbornly she kept her face averted, still unable to look into his eyes. She no longer knew which she feared most. That he would be laughing, finding her amusing, even ridiculous. Or that he wouldn't. And suddenly somehow the thought of Amir being deadly serious about this turned her blood to ice, freezing in her veins.

'Lydia, I said look at me.'

His chair scraped on the floor as he pushed it back and stood up, leaning across the table towards her.

His hand came under her chin, lifting it determinedly. For a second she thought about resisting, but even as the thought slid into her mind his grip tightened warningly. Rather than face an undignified struggle that she knew she must inevitably lose, she flung her head back sharply, looking him right in the face, defiant blue eyes clashing with ruthless black.

'Do I look as if I'm laughing?'

'Well, no,' Lydia had to admit.

He had never looked more stern—or appeared more awe-inspiring, she admitted to herself. He hadn't spoken loudly or harshly—he hadn't needed to. Just the sound of that clear, cold voice was enough to douse the tiny flame of rebellion even as it flared inside her mind. And none of the movements he had made had been fast or hard or even faintly cruel, but it had been enough to make her let any idea of struggle die unformed and submit to his determined control.

'You look deadly serious.'

'That's because I am. Because if this is what you want, then it's what I want too.'

It was shocking how much she wanted to believe him. How much she wanted every word to be meant, to be deeply sincere. But what was even more disturbing was the realisation that even if he didn't truly mean it, she didn't care.

For the three days she had, she was perfectly willing to suspend disbelief. She was quite prepared to accept that if he said something was so, then it *was* so, even if under other circumstances she would be totally sceptical of his assertion. Amir could claim that he adored her, that he worshipped at her feet, and for these seventy-two hours she would take his word as gospel. She didn't care if she was deceiving herself, if she was laying herself open to every sort of con trick it was possible to play. It was what she wanted right now.

After all, he was only doing it to keep her here and involved, to keep her sweet. And the frightening, the dangerous thing was that he didn't need to do any of it. She couldn't *be* any more sweet on him, any more involved. He'd swept her right off her feet in the first moment she'd seen him and she had had no chance at all of regaining her balance ever since.

'I just thought it would be fun.'

'And it could be. But I think what we have to do is to backtrack here a little bit, fit in the stages that we missed out by jumping straight in with our eyes closed. Things like…'

He considered the article, running his finger down the list of events.

'Like you taking my phone number and saying you'll call?' Lydia sounded sceptical. 'Don't you think we're past that?'

'Maybe, maybe not. What is your number anyway?'

'You don't—' she began, then broke off as he turned a gently reproving look on her.

'You wanted to do this,' he reminded her.

'Oh, okay.'

Automatically she recited the number of her mobile, though as he didn't note it down she didn't quite see the point.

'I'd like to do this again,' he said unexpectedly, looking deep into her eyes as he spoke. 'I'll give you a call, some time. Would you like that?'

Too much.

She was in danger of actually saying it. She even opened her mouth to let the words out when panic screamed at her not to be so stupid. Amir was only playing the game, going along with the fantasy she had created. She would be every kind of a fool to place any trust in what he did.

'You—you do that,' she managed unevenly. 'That number will get me any time.'

Just for a swift, anguished second, she suddenly had a vivid idea of how it might have been if things had been different, if she and Amir had met under other circumstances. Her heart kicked sharply on an echo of how she might have felt then at the thought that this devastating man actually wanted to see her again. It might have been weak-willed, naïve in the extreme, but she knew she would have spent every night on edge, just waiting, willing the phone to ring, longing to hear his voice.

She didn't like to consider how she would have felt if she'd never heard from him again.

'So now we've done that one.'

With a firm, decisive sweep of the pen, Amir ticked off the item on the list in the magazine.

'What can we do next? Oh, yes, we were going shopping.'

'No, we're not.'

If she had felt uncomfortable about it before, she felt a

hundred times worse now. Letting Amir buy her clothes, providing her with what amounted to a brand-new wardrobe, seemed to come with too many strings attached.

His sigh was a deliberate blend of annoyance and resigned patience.

'Do you ever do anything without arguing?' he demanded impatiently.

'I told you what I wanted.'

'So you did.'

His mouth twisted, the gleam of a dangerously explosive temper only just reined in burning in his eyes.

'But you can't just change the rules when it pleases you.'

'Rules? What rules? I...Oh-h-h!'

The words shrivelled on her tongue as Amir tapped the open magazine with an imperious finger.

'Stage Ten—you buy each other presents,' read the heading. 'You're crazy about each other and you want to show it. You feel totally extravagant and money is very definitely no object.'

'You see,' Amir put in silkily, murmuring the words against her ear, his cheek resting on her hair as she stared down at the words. 'I'm supposed to buy you presents. And the more extravagant, the better.'

But the extravagance of the presents was supposed to indicate the depth of his feelings for her. It was not just to compensate for the inadequacies of the clothing she had brought with her and ensure that she didn't have to wear the same sweater and jeans day in and day out for the next seventy-two hours.

'But I can't return the favour!'

What did one buy for a man who had everything? A man who was a Crown Prince, whose father was a *sheikh*?

'I can't buy you—'

'Lady, there's nothing you could buy me that I'd want any more than what you've already given me.'

Another day, another time, it might have been different. If he'd had another sort of future ahead of him, if his life had been at a different set of crossroads, then maybe there would have been something she could offer him. But not now.

'Lady, there's nothing you could buy me that I'd want…'

Cold and curt and stark, the words took her breath away. She had to bite down hard on her lower lip to drive back the cry of pain that almost escaped her. He had had what he wanted and there was nothing more she could give him.

'So, do we go out and choose some clothes?' Amir hadn't noticed her withdrawal, or if he had he was deliberately ignoring it.

'Okay.' She couldn't look him in the face, couldn't meet his eyes. 'I'll just clear up here.'

'Jamila can do that.'

'Amir, you may be used to having servants, but I'm not. I made the mess, I'll tidy it up!'

'Then I—' Amir began but out in the hallway the shrill ring of the telephone drew his attention.

'You get that,' Lydia told him. 'I'll finish in here.'

She wouldn't think about it, she told herself fiercely as she cleared the table, putting things in the dishwasher. She just wouldn't let herself brood on the fact that she had already given Amir the one, the only thing he wanted from her.

This wasn't a lifetime sort of thing. She had given herself three days out of reality just to enjoy this experience— to enjoy being with Amir. She wouldn't ask for anything else. She couldn't even let herself dream that there was the hope of anything else. To do so was to risk the total desolation of heartbreak when the end came.

She would accept this for what it was and nothing more. She was just drying her hands carefully when a sudden sound startled her. For a second she couldn't quite work out what it was, then it registered.

Her phone! Someone was calling her phone.

Hurrying to her bag, she picked it up and studied the number displayed. It wasn't one she recognised. In fact it was one she was absolutely certain she hadn't seen in her life before. Burning with curiosity, she thumbed the 'on' button.

'Hello?'

'Hi!'

It was Amir's voice, deep and husky, the faint trace of his accent highlighted and deepened by the receiver.

'I said I'd give you a call...'

'So you did.'

She was deeply thankful that he couldn't see her and so was unaware of the hot colour that rushed into her face, the sudden jerky beat of her heart, the way her eyes suddenly lit from within.

This was how it would have felt if this had been a real relationship. How she would have reacted if she'd waited around, dreaming of his call, willing him to phone. And then, like now, she would have tried to pay it cool, tried to pretend that it was no big deal, that she hadn't been waiting—not much anyway.

'What was it you wanted?'

'I wondered if you were free tonight? If you'd like to do something—a meal—a film maybe.'

'What is this, Amir?'

Lydia dropped all the pretence, unable to maintain it any longer.

'What are you doing?'

'Don't you know?'

Amusement threaded through the deep voice, enriching it with honey.

'Stage Five—comes after Stage Three— "He takes your

number and says he'll give you a call.'' And Stage Four—
''You wait in all week and he never phones.''''

Unable to resist a swift, stunned glance at the phone as
if were was actually Amir's face, Lydia bit her lip sharply.
How did he know? Had he actually been reading her mind?

'Stage Five,' Amir repeated. '''Just when you've given
up hope he finally rings and asks you for a date.''''

'And is that what you're doing? Asking me out on a
date?'

'Don't you think it's about time?' The amusement in
the husky voice had deepened. 'Like I said, it's time we
backtracked to Stage Five after rushing ahead to Stages
Twelve and Eighteen before we should. So—what about
tonight?'

'I—I don't know.'

What was the point? she wanted to ask. Why should
Amir bother to take her out on a date when he knew all
the time—they both knew—that at the end of the evening
she would be coming straight back here?

And weren't dates all about courtship, anticipation, enticement? Amir didn't have to bother with any of those.
He didn't need to wonder if she might end up in his bed.
He knew she had no choice. It was part of the bargain they
had made.

'I'm not sure…'

'Oh, I see,' Amir interrupted smoothly. 'You've moved
on to Six.'

The amusement was still there in his voice but this time
it was shaded with a darker note, one that made her nerves
twist to hear it.

'Playing hard to get?' Lydia's laugh was ragged at the
edges. 'I thought that was expected of me—if we're playing by the rules. But perhaps we'd better stop—'

'Lady, you started this.' Amir's voice was a low growl
down the phone. 'You can't back out now. We're not even

halfway through. You wanted that ''super-sexy affair'', so that's what you're going to get...'

But she'd been half joking, saying something only to cover up the nervousness she'd felt.

'You—you *mean* it?'

'I mean it,' Amir affirmed brusquely. 'Over the next three days you're going to get all of those ''sensual stages''. Every damn one of them.'

It was frankly scary how much he did mean it, he admitted to himself as he switched off his phone. He had started out meaning to convince her and had ended up convincing himself.

No, that wasn't strictly true. He hadn't taken that much convincing. In fact, he'd been up for it from the start. The whole silly, crazy idea had grabbed him in a way that nothing had done for a long, long time. It wasn't real, it was just play, pure fantasy, but fantasy was something his life had been missing for as long as he could remember. It had been nothing but hard work, determination and commitment. And the future that was planned out looked like going that way too.

Maybe now was time to play a little. He had this unexpected interval between one world, one life and another. Maybe he could snatch a little unplanned fun before the doors of reality closed again.

CHAPTER EIGHT

'But I don't need it!'

'Do you really think that matters?'

Amir's tone was one of resigned tolerance, but, sensitive to everything about him, Lydia caught the thread of impatience that warned of his temper fraying round the edges. It was almost frightening how well she knew him already, how easily she could judge his frame of mind, predict his changes of mood.

For most of the day he had been in a generous, expansive humour, spending money on her in a way that was almost shocking. She had very quickly learned not to pause to look at something, not to pick it up to admire, because if she did then Amir would have bought it for her before she could blink, adding yet another item to the growing collection of parcels that he wanted delivered back to the apartment.

But this dress was different. This dress was ridiculously expensive, even for the exclusive designer boutique they were in. It was also impossibly glamorous, the sort of dress she had never worn in her life, and one that she was never going to have a chance to wear in the future. Certainly not in the three days that she was to be with Amir.

'Do you like it?'

'How could anyone *not* like it?'

Turning round again, she contemplated her reflection in the full-length mirror, finding it impossible to believe that it was actually her.

In a lavender blue silk, the dress had a softly draped skirt and tight-fitting bodice, supported by thin, shoestring straps. Tiny beads of crystal were scattered across the delicate material, giving the impression that raindrops had just fallen onto it, pooling softly.

The colour did amazing things for her eyes, and the perfect fit and design made her look taller and slimmer than ever, the low-cut neckline framing the fine bone structure of her shoulders and neck, the soft curves of the tops of her breasts.

'I love it!'

'Then it's yours.'

'No!'

She swung back to where the man who had been at her side like a dark, sexy shadow all day now lounged indolently in the chair provided by the manageress, hands linked behind his head, black eyes lazily hooded.

'It's too expensive and I'll never wear it!'

'The cost is a pittance and you'll need it for number twenty-four.'

'Amir!'

Lydia actually stamped her foot in frustration at the way he wasn't listening, earning herself a quick, surprised glance from the saleswoman hovering nearby. The older woman obviously thought that she was quite, quite mad and had been of that opinion from the start. Why else would Lydia argue the toss at every turn, trying to dissuade this obviously indulgent lover from buying any more than the basics when he was clearly intent on lavishing a small fortune on her?

'Just *what* is number twenty-four?'

'Wouldn't you like to know?' he drawled teasingly, lightly touching one long-fingered hand to the inside pocket of his superbly cut jacket.

The faint rustle of paper under the soft, supple suede reminded Lydia of the way that, just before they had left the house, he had suddenly turned back, hurrying into the kitchen. Standing waiting by the door, she had heard the sound of tearing paper and as Amir had joined her once more he had been folding a couple of brightly coloured sheets into four.

'What's that?' she had asked in some surprise.

'The agenda for the next couple of days—the "Sensual Stages",' he'd elaborated when she'd frowned her incomprehension. 'We have to make sure we don't miss anything out.'

'Twenty-four?'

Now Lydia tried hard to recall just what other 'stages' she had seen, but number twenty-four eluded her, particularly when Amir lifted an autocratic hand, summoning the saleswoman to his side.

'We'll take this,' he said. 'And the rest…'

A casual gesture indicated other dresses, tops, skirts and trousers that Lydia had tried on earlier and which now hung on a rack on the other side of the room.

'Amir, no!' Lydia protested, horrified at the thought of the amount he had spent on her.

'Amir—yes!' he contradicted. 'Remember number ten—as extravagant as possible.'

She opened her mouth to argue further but one swift, reproving look from those brilliant dark eyes had her closing it again with a snap. It hadn't taken her long to learn that with Amir there was a line drawn very firmly to indicate just how far he would let her go. She could go right up to that line if she wanted, even put her toe on the outermost edge of it, and he would let her get away with it. But step over the line, by so much as an inch, and she was inviting instant and devastating retribution.

She'd learned that lesson earlier that day. They had stopped for a meal in an elegant restaurant and, lulled into a sense of false security by the relaxed ease Amir had shown until then, she had tried to satisfy her curiosity about him. She was involved so closely with this man in one way, had been totally intimate with him, known and touched every part of his body, let him kiss and caress hers in return, and yet she knew so little about him in others.

Over the meal he had asked her about her family, her life before she had won the job in California, and, inspired by his ability to listen, she had told him. He had a special way of making her feel that she were the only person in the room, so that it had all come pouring out without hesitation. She had told him about her parents, her first job as a trainee in the small, provincial hotel then, later, as Hospitality Manager in a four-star hotel in Leicester. With pride in her eyes, she'd recounted how she'd been headhunted for the California job, the stringent interviews she'd gone through to win it.

She'd told him everything about herself, even the uncomfortable story of Jonathon and his rejection of her. And so while they'd lingered over coffee, she'd felt that it had finally been his turn.

'And what about you?' she asked impulsively. 'What about your family? Isn't it time you told me about your father—the sheikh? If he's really your father, how come you speak such perfect English?'

Amir set his cup down on its saucer with a cold precision that later, looking back, she realised that she should have seen as the first hint of warning. But at the time, relaxed and content after a wonderful meal and a glass of wine, she didn't notice the immediate withdrawal, the storm brewing behind his dark eyes.

'My mother was English,' he said. 'And I was brought up in England.'

'Your mother didn't live with your father, then?'

'They separated when I was eighteen months old.'

'Oh, what a pity! Why?'

This time the danger signs were more overt; the tension in the strong jaw, the way his hand tightened over his teaspoon, were enough to make her realise she should proceed with caution.

'He believed that she had been unfaithful to her.'

It was still there, he realised with something of a shock. The pain, the sense of betrayal, wasn't locked away as securely as he had thought, but lingered just out of sight, easily revived again by a careless question.

'He didn't trust her enough. And he was too old-fashioned, too entrenched in the old ways of doing things that he couldn't see it was possible for a woman to have a male friend without something underhand going on.'

'Oh, how sad! But I'm surprised that he let you go with her. I would have thought that he would have wanted to keep his son...'

Amir dropped the teaspoon onto the table with a distinct clatter. He had thought that too, once. He had believed that his father wouldn't willingly have let him go or that, having had his hand forced, he would at least have been ready to welcome his son back with open arms.

He was uncomfortable with this line of conversation. He had promised himself this space between his two lives without the taint of the past darkening and spoiling it. His father had done that more than enough.

'Why—?'

'Lydia, that's enough!'

'But—'

'I said *that's enough*.'

'I just—'

She didn't even get a chance to form the sentence.

'I'm leaving,' he announced baldly. 'Are you coming or not?'

A tiny signal, so brief she hardly saw it, brought the waiter hovering nearby. With the bill paid, and without another word, Amir pushed back his chair and stood up. A moment later, he had turned his back on her and was marching across the room, heading for the exit. Not by so much as a gesture or a look did he give any indication of any interest in whether she followed him or not. It was only when she realised that he fully intended to walk away completely, leaving her behind without a second thought, that she saw she would have to hurry to catch him up if she was not to lose him for good.

'Wait for me!' she complained. 'Amir, I can't keep up with you at this pace!'

The burning look he shot at her from beneath the lush black lashes seemed to say that he didn't give a damn whether she kept up with him or not.

'What brought all this on? I only asked the same sort of questions you asked me. I didn't know it was a state secret! Nothing to start World War Three about.'

'Don't be silly!'

What *was* he doing? He hadn't wanted his father's malign influence to taint this brief idyll, and yet that was exactly what he was letting happen.

'I'm sorry,' he said stiffly. 'I don't want to talk about my family. They're not relevant to here and now—to you and me.'

To *you and me*.

He couldn't have said anything more calculated to stop her dead in her tracks. It even made her push aside the memory of that curt, 'I'm sorry', a response that had been tossed at her so harshly and so indifferently that it hardly merited the name of an apology at all.

And then he did something that made her forget the argument and all that had led up to it. After a swift glance at the clock, he reached into his pocket and pulled out a slim, gift-wrapped parcel.

'Now's the time to give you this. Happy anniversary.'

'Anniversary?'

'It's exactly twenty-four hours since we first spoke to each other—our first anniversary.'

His gift was on her wrist now. A slender gold watch that when she had opened it had been set to exactly the time of their meeting. Another present to add to the growing pile of things he had showered on her. Things she wasn't even sure she wanted.

But *you and me*. She wanted that. Oh, dear God, it was scary how *much* she wanted that! And the realisation of just what it meant to her stilled her impetuous tongue, and froze the angry protest on her lips.

They had so little time together. She didn't want to waste any of it arguing with him. She would only regret it later, when the three days he had allowed her were up, and she could no longer see or talk to him again.

And so she forced a smile onto her face, made herself meet those stunning eyes with a confidence she was far from feeling.

'Number ten it is, then.'

The smile became more genuine as she glanced into the saleslady's face, saw the stunned look in her eyes. By the time they had left the shop she couldn't hold back the giggles any longer.

'Did you see that woman's expression? Number ten, twenty-four indeed! She probably thought we were talking about positions in bed—that we were planning an orgy!'

'Then she was reading my mind,' Amir returned in a voice made husky by desire. The dark-eyed glance he shot her sizzled all the way from her head to her toes in a single, sweeping survey. 'Because that's exactly what I was thinking.'

And as soon as he said the words, that was exactly what she was thinking of too. Images that were positively indecent in a public street flooded her thoughts, heating her blood and making her pulse thud heavily in her veins. In spite of the fact that it had now begun to snow again and that the darkness of a freezing winter evening was already beginning to close in on them, she felt as if she were burning up with some raging fever, her clothes too rough against her suddenly sensitised skin.

'Me too,' she murmured, the sharp excitement of anticipation putting a shake into her voice.

'So...'

Amir snaked an arm around her waist, pulling her into the shelter of his tall, strong body as they moved off down the street.

'Do you have any more shopping to do?'

Lydia slanted a flirtatious, beguiling look up into his dark face.

'None at all.'

'So we can go home now?'

Home. It struck at her heart like a blow, driving all the air from her lungs in a shocked gasp. The apartment was home to Amir, but it would never be any such thing to her.

For the next three days it would be where she lived, where she ate, slept. Where she made love with Amir. But at the end of those three days she would pack her bags and leave and she would never see the apartment or Amir again.

'Amir...'

She choked out his name on a wave of distress, looking up into his shadowed face, seeing the way that the street lights, the glow from the shop windows illuminated those carved cheekbones, the brilliant eyes. And her heart clenched on a stab of pain as she suddenly realised just what was happening to her.

'Amir... This isn't working.'

It was obviously the last thing he had anticipated and she saw his proud head go back, saw the sudden flash of something raw, something unshielded in his eyes.

'What?' If his voice had been husky before, now it was hoarse with shock. 'What the hell's brought this on? *Why* isn't it working?'

There was no answer she could give. She couldn't even give herself one. Not unless she put into words the half-formed idea that had just exploded in her mind, shattering her thoughts and driving her into a numb sense of shock.

'Oh, don't ask me that, Amir!'

'And why not?'

To her consternation he came to a dead halt in the middle of the pavement, heedless of the mutters of disapproval from the other pedestrians who almost cannoned into him as he swung her round to face him.

'Don't ask!' he echoed savagely. 'Don't you think that at least you owe me some sort of explanation, not just "This isn't working"?'

Lydia flinched away from the ferocity of his question, shrinking into the upturned collar of her coat, hunching her shoulders against the force of his attack.

'*Why* is it not working? We had an arrangement—you agreed to it. Am I not fulfilling what you expected? What more is there you want?'

And there it was, Lydia thought drearily. There was the whole crux of the situation, the core of the problem. With the incisiveness of a brutally sharp knife, Amir had gone straight to the heart of what was troubling her—straight to *her heart*, which was where the problem lay.

'What more is there you want?'

He meant what more could he give her in the way of material things, and the real problem was that what she needed was *emotional* and that was something he was never going to give her.

'Amir,' she protested edgily. 'You're blocking the pavement; getting in people's way.'

His retort was short, succinct and extremely forceful, showing just how little he cared for the people who passed them by, heads turning in curiosity at the sight of the two of them standing still in the middle of what was now swiftly turning into a whirling blizzard.

'I want to know what's bugging you,' he insisted. 'Just what's going on in that lovely head of yours? And I don't intend to move from here until you tell me. So unless you plan on staying here all night, you'd better start talking— fast!'

Which was guaranteed to drive all coherent thought straight from her mind.

Except for one. And that was the realisation that had so shocked her only moments before that it had driven her into making that foolish declaration, and puzzling and infuriating Amir in equal measure, so that he had reacted as he had.

I think I'm falling in love with you.

It was the one thing she couldn't say. The one thing she *must not* say. It was the thing that Amir least wanted to hear; the fact that she absolutely did not want him to know.

Love was not part of their bargain. It had no place in the carefully defined and time-limited arrangement Amir had spelled out in the first place. And that arrangement was all he had to offer her; her part in it all he wanted from her.

'Lydia...'

Amir's tone warned that his patience was growing dangerously thin.

'Are you going to tell me, or do I have to drag it out of you? Two minutes ago you were as ready to go home as I was. You knew why—what I wanted, and it was what you wanted too. Wasn't it?—*Wasn't it?*' he demanded more sharply when she wouldn't meet the angry force of his eyes.

Lydia couldn't lie to him.

'Yes,' she admitted, shifting uneasily from one foot to another on the icy pavement.

'Then what changed your mind? Something I said or...'

The polished jet eyes went to the brightly lit window of the boutique they had just left. Behind the single display model in the window he could see the figure of the saleswoman busily packing away the clothes they had bought in layers of tissue paper before placing them in bronze-coloured cardboard boxes.

And suddenly he knew. He felt as if he had been kicked in the guts by the wild hind legs of a mule because it was so unexpected. He had been all sorts of a damn fool because for once he had actually been deceived. Somewhere along the line he had let down the powerful defences he normally kept carefully built up around his emotions and let this girl in.

He had forgotten about the lessons past experience had taught him and pushed aside the conviction that most women were only with him for what they could get. He had even allowed himself to believe that Lydia was different.

And now he had been proved wrong. And it hurt. It hurt badly.

'I see,' he said heavily. 'Oh, yes, lady. I see.'

'What?'

It was Lydia's turn to be bewildered, her eyes wide and stunned in the uneven light, the shadow patterns made by the whirling snow shifting and changing on her face.

'What do you see?'

Amir gave a nod of his dark head towards the shop they had just left.

'You have what you wanted, so now it "isn't working".'

The bitterness of his mimicry tore at her heart.

'You've got everything you thought there was on offer and now you're off.'

'No-o.'

It was finally beginning to dawn on Lydia just what he meant and her protest was a low moan of pain, barely audible above the wind.

'Yes,' Amir contradicted brutally. 'Yes, that's what you thought, my darling. What was going on in your scheming little mind. But let me tell you something, sweetheart...'

His tone turned the word into something that was light years away from any sort of endearment.

'You jumped too fast—made your play too early. Because that *wasn't* all I was going to give you. Not by a long way. You're going to kick yourself, darling, when you realise that if you'd just stuck around, stayed with me the three days we arranged—even one day more—then I would have—'

'*No!*'

Lydia couldn't bear it any longer. She couldn't listen to that brutal, cutting voice that lashed at her tender flesh like a whip, couldn't bear to see the bleak coldness of his eyes that looked straight through her as if she didn't really exist but was just a phantom, an image projected into the space in front of him.

'No, no, no! That isn't true! That isn't what it was like at all! Oh, Amir, *please*! You have to believe me!'

'No? Then what was it like, my lovely?'

The eyes he turned on her pale face were terrifyingly blank, all emotion drained out of them. Lydia had the sudden fearful thought that she would rather see something, anything at all, even if it was the burn of dangerous fury in those black depths. Anything, other than this opaque withdrawal.

But what could she say that didn't give her away and that he would believe?

'I—I just got frightened. It's all happened so fast. I've never experienced anything like this before.'

It was shocking how much he wanted to believe her. How he wanted to think that it was sincerity that burned in those pansy-dark eyes. That the pleading face she had turned up to his was genuine, and not just a play for his finer feelings. Either way it was working. He could feel the hurt anger start to ebb, leaving him bruised and wary.

The snow had soaked into her hair, flattening it around her finely shaped skull, and as he watched a tiny drop of water slipped from one dark strand and dropped onto her forehead. Slowly it slid over her skin, down towards her temple. Without thinking he put out a hand and caught it, wiping it away before it could fall into one of those bright blue eyes.

The tiny contact froze them both where they stood, eyes locking together, his breathing almost stopped.

'Amir!' Lydia murmured. 'Please...'

And suddenly he knew he didn't care. He didn't give a damn whether she was on the make or not. He'd promised himself three days and then she was leaving anyway. Just how much could she take from him in that short time?

And he wanted all of those three days. Wanted them more than he had ever wanted anything in the world. Even the need for his father's recognition hadn't been as fierce and strong as this, raging like a fire through his guts, twisting in every nerve.

'I got scare—' Lydia began but he didn't want her to talk any more.

The heavy pulse of desire was pounding through his veins, making it impossible to think. He was only aware of one thing, and that was the growing hunger, the insistent demand of his body. He didn't want *words*.

And so he laid one long forefinger across the softness of her lips, silencing her while his impenetrable gaze still held hers totally transfixed.

'Don't talk,' he said harshly. 'Not another word. We're wasting time with this. Time we don't have. All I want from you is two more days of your life. Two days and at the end of that we go our separate ways. You thought you could manage that this morning, so what's changed? Surely you can make it "work" for as long as that.'

It was that 'two more days' that did it. Just as it had when he had originally offered her the suggestion that they had just three days and three nights together when she had thought there would only be a one-night stand. So now the realisation that they only had two of those days left shocked her into knowing that she couldn't give them up, no matter what.

'Yes,' she whispered, shaken and low. 'Yes, I can manage that.'

'Then come here...'

He held his arms out to her and like a small, frightened animal seeking shelter she went into them willingly and eagerly. She felt his grip close around her, tight as steel bands, crushing her against the fine material of his overcoat, and it was like coming home.

One strong hand came under her chin, pushing her face up to meet his, and he took her mouth with a burning passion that made her head swim, a low moan of surrender escaping her immediately.

She wasn't aware of how long they stayed there, lips locked together, his tongue plundering the inner sweetness of her mouth, oblivious to the bitter fury of the weather or the amused glances of a dozen or more passers-by. She only knew that when he finally lifted his head, touched his lips to her forehead, and enveloped her in a fierce hug that crushed against the hard warmth of his body, she could find no strength to argue any further.

So when he said in a voice that was rough and thick with the passion that had them both in its grip, '*Now* we go home,' she could only nod in silent agreement. She couldn't think of any reason to object. Couldn't even recall why she had wanted to do such a crazy thing in the first place.

Managing the next two days with him, making that work, was the easy part.

It was the going their separate ways at the end of it that she couldn't bear to think about.

CHAPTER NINE

'So, what else is left on that crazy list of yours?'

Amir was lounging back in his chair in the sitting room, a mug of coffee in one hand and the morning paper open on his lap.

'How many more stages have we left undone?'

'Let's see...'

Lydia unfolded the pages from the magazine and smoothed them out. They were beginning to look rather worn now, crumpled and creased from being crushed inside Amir's pocket and then taken out again, and with many of the stages crossed off over the past day and a half.

'Meeting, phoning, first date...'

All of those had been checked off, and more.

Just for a moment she paused, her thoughts going back to the night before, after Amir had brought her back from the shops.

The short journey to the apartment had seemed impossibly long and unendurable. The atmosphere in the back of Amir's car, with Nabil silent and impervious in the driver's seat, had been so heated, so thick with desire, that she'd hardly been able to breathe. Under cover of the darkness, Amir had taken her into his arms and kissed her demandingly, crushing her mouth open under his, bending her head back against the iron support of his arm.

And when he had finished with her mouth he had trailed his lips along the burning line of her cheek, then up to the delicate curve of her ear. And there he'd lingered, whispering to her of the plans he'd had for when they got home, the things he'd wanted to do to her, with her, for her, until

110

she'd been writhing on the leather covered seat in an agony of excited anticipation, unable to bear the waiting until they'd been alone together again.

It had been every bit as electrifying as he had promised. From the moment that the door had slammed behind them and they'd been alone in the darkness of the hall, he had taken her into his arms again and subjected her to a sensual onslaught that had set her head spinning, her pulse thundering, and her breath coming in ragged, uneven gasps.

She'd been as hungry and impatient as she had been the first night, pulling at his clothes, wrenching his shirt open, pressing starving kisses against the hot satin of his skin. But Amir had been in a very different mood this time.

His seduction of her had been slow, enticing, totally sensual. He'd drawn out each kiss, each caress into long, agonising seconds, stroking and smoothing, tantalising until she'd been moaning under his touch, begging him to hurry.

'Hurry?'

The word was a husky laugh in her ear.

'Oh, no, my darling, not this time. Last night we couldn't wait. We didn't know how long we had and we had to cram as much as we possibly could into the space we had available. Tonight we have all the time in the world.'

This time their journey up the stairs was a slow, gentle progress. On each step he paused and kissed her, caressed her some more. And when they reached the landing he caught her up in his arms, carried her into the bedroom where he laid her softly on the bed and came down beside her. Pulling her close to him, he stroked her hair, smoothing it back from her face, following the touch of his hand with yet more burning kisses.

Her cheek rested against the fine material of his shirt, supported on the lean, hard wall of his chest, rising and falling with every deep, even breath that he took. Only the heavy pounding of his heart, beating as urgently as her own, gave away the fact that he was as aroused as she was, fighting as hard for control.

With a soft touch and even softer words he eased her clothes from her body, muttering thickly in the language of his father as he peeled away the tight jeans, the wisps of silk and lace that were her underwear.

'This is what works between us,' he told her between fierce, crushing kisses. 'We don't need to follow lists or magazine articles to ensure we've got this right.'

She welcomed the hard thrust of his forcefully aroused body into her, willing the pleasure it created to drive away all the doubts and fears that had bombarded her earlier that afternoon. This was what she wanted. This wild, blazing passion that erased thought, stopped worry and made her feel that there could be nothing better in the whole, wide world. With his arms tight around her, the strength of his body crushing her, she couldn't think of anything beyond him, and that was exactly how she wanted it to be.

'Some of these we're going to have to forget about,' she said now, frowning down at the magazine article in her hand.

'You think so?'

Amir stretched lazily, running both hands through the black silk of his hair. 'And why is that?'

'Well, it's hardly going to be possible to organise Christmas in February, is it? It's a little early for Valentine's Day, and my birthday isn't till the fourteenth of June.'

'Well, perhaps we'll find something to put in their place,' Amir told her, getting up in a single, elegantly fluid movement and strolling to the window to frown out at the scene in the street below. 'Though if this snow doesn't let up, we could well be stuck here until April, still waiting for the airports to open.'

A note in his voice caught Lydia very much on the raw.

'And that wouldn't please you, of course!'

Her retort had him swinging round to face her, earning her a reproving frown and an angry glare.

'What makes you say that?'

When he was in this mood, he was pure sheikh of the desert, Crown Prince of Kuimar from his head to his toes, Lydia told herself, tensing warily, preparing for the lash of his temper. It was easy to imagine him dressed, not in the Western clothes of casual jeans and loose shirt, but in the formal, flowing robes of his heritage. In her mind's eye she could picture him, tall and proud, striding across the desert of his homeland. Lord of all he surveyed.

'Why would it not please me?'

'Well, it would keep you from whatever you must get to in three—two now—days' time. It must be something very important.'

'It is.'

Well, she'd asked for that, Lydia admitted. In fact she'd gone down on her knees and begged for it, reminding him that his affair with her was strictly temporary. Not that he'd shown any sign of forgetting that fact, of course. His first action this morning had been to check with the airport again, even though a further fall of snow had made it highly unlikely that the planes were going to take off at any time today.

He couldn't have done anything more calculated to remind her that her time with him was strictly limited, and that he had no intention of changing his mind about that fact. And it hurt—terribly.

When he had slid from the bed and headed for the phone as soon as he had woken, she had stayed totally still, trying to pretend that she'd still been asleep so that she hadn't had to face him until she had gathered some degree of composure. At least keeping her eyes closed had held back the sting of tears that she'd refused to let herself shed. She hadn't felt that she'd been able to cope with the questions that would inevitably have followed.

'And you knew that before we started on this.' Amir's voice was harsh with angry reproof. 'So don't start telling me you're having second thoughts now.'

'Me? Second thoughts?'

The struggle to hide her pain made her voice high and brittle in a way that obviously displeased him. Another of those dark, disapproving frowns had her bringing it down an octave hastily.

'Not at all. But I was beginning to wonder if perhaps you had.'

'About ending this after three days?'

The look he turned on her made her heart shrink. It was just as well she hadn't been fool enough to mean that question the way he'd taken it. If she had even so much as entertained the hope that he was reconsidering his edict that after three days it was all over between them, then that fierce glare would have destroyed her dream in a second.

'No, not that! I was just thinking that perhaps you didn't even want to wait that long. You rang the airport last night and again first thing this morning.'

'I thought you had a job to go to.'

'Well, yes—I do…'

Clearly now was not the time to tell him that if he only said the word, if he asked her to stay, if he spoke one syllable of love she would reconsider her trip to California at once.

No, she didn't even need the word 'love'. Fool that she was, she was already in so deep that if he had simply said he wanted her to stick around, that he hadn't tired of her, she would have been tempted to stay.

But clearly Amir had no thoughts of saying any such thing.

'And I have commitments elsewhere.'

'What sort of commitments?'

No, Lydia! That was quite the wrong thing to ask. If he wanted you to know, then he would have said. He would have told you from the first!

But to her surprise Amir actually offered some sort of an answer.

'I'm travelling to Kuimar just as soon as the jet can leave.'

Somehow that didn't have quite the same ring in his mind as it had done forty-eight hours ago, Amir registered with a sense of shock. Two days ago he had been totally convinced, totally at ease with the decision he had made. Now he felt as if that certainty had been eroded from within. He no longer felt quite so comfortable with the plans his father had made for the future.

'My father is expecting me.'

He was more than expecting. The old man had sent out a royal decree and he had no doubt that it would be obeyed.

'And you have to go?'

'*Yes*, I have to go.'

He spoke with more force than he intended. Sometimes it seemed as if she came dangerously close to reading his mind. She had an uncanny knack of putting her finger right on the point that was fretting at his thoughts and aggravating the unease it was causing.

'More than that. I *want* to go. Kuimar is my country. I belong there even if I didn't grow up there as a child.'

'Why was that? Why didn't you grow up there?'

She wished the question back as soon as it slipped out. It was obvious that he'd said more than he'd ever intended and she was afraid that her impulsive query would drive him back behind the barriers he erected between her and the life he considered so private.

To her surprise he came prowling back across the room

to throw himself into the soft leather armchair he had left just moments before.

'When my father divorced my mother for being unfaithful, he also disowned me. He believed that I was not his son but the child of the man she had had an affair with. For years he would have nothing to do with either of us. That's why I grew up in England. As a matter of fact, my father only actually acknowledged me as his son two years ago.'

'I can't even begin to think how that must have felt. For both you and your mother.'

Amir's mouth twisted bitterly, his dark eyes staring broodingly down at a spot on the carpet.

'My mother died without ever being reconciled with my father. For years he totally ignored the fact that I existed—even when our paths were forced to cross.'

'How…?'

The twist to that sensual mouth grew more pronounced.

'I breed and train racehorses. My father's greatest obsession, after his country, is steeplechasing. But even if we were in the same paddock together he wouldn't even acknowledge my presence.'

'Oh, Amir!'

She wanted to go to him, to hold him, to say something, however inadequate, to show her sympathy. But the cold, set mask that was his face, the stiff, unyielding way he held his long body, all declared clearly, without words, that he would reject the gesture if she tried to make it. The barriers were firmly in place; the 'Keep out' signs ruthlessly displayed.

'What changed his mind?'

That jet-eyed gaze flicked up just once to sear her skin in a burning, savage flare of anger.

'His other wives did not provide him with the sons he wanted. Unfortunately for my father, all his other children have been female. In the end his hand was forced by the restlessness in the country because he didn't have an heir. He agreed to abide by the results of DNA testing.'

'He couldn't accept you without that!'

'My sweet Lydia—there was a throne and a country at stake. If I had been an impostor, it would have dishonoured his line for ever.'

'But didn't you…?'

'I did what had to be done,' Amir told her simply.

He didn't have to tell her what a blow to his pride it had been. It was there in his eyes, in the hard set of his jaw, the tension etched into the muscles of his face. She was beginning to see just why he was so determined to join his father in Kuimar as soon as he could. He had fought so hard for his place as the prince of that country, now that he had it he wasn't going to take any chances with losing it, whatever it took.

And that put her securely in her place, she told herself miserably. She was relegated to a position of no importance, no consequence in Amir's life, to be used for his pleasure and then discarded. After all, what did she have to set against the attractions of a whole country—a *kingdom* where one day he would rule as Sheikh?

She would do far better to end it now. It would hurt terribly, but sooner the anguish of a clean break than the slow death by letting the relationship fray and disintegrate into nothingness.

She had opened her mouth to declare as much, to tell Amir that she couldn't go on when a ring at the doorbell startled her.

'What's that?'

Unexpectedly Amir's cold expression had lightened. There was a new gleam in his eye, even the hint of a smile curving the corners of his mouth.

'Why don't you go and see?'

'But it won't be anyone for me. No one knows…'

'Go and see!'

It was a royal command, delivered in a tone that allowed for no thought of disobeying, so that Lydia got to her feet in a rush and hurried to the door without any further question.

'Miss Lydia Ashton? We have a delivery for you.'

'For me—but…'

Words failed her as she saw the huge bouquet of red, scented roses in the delivery man's hands. And behind him was another man carrying a matching bouquet…and another…and another…

Lydia fell back against the wall, unable to speak a word. Incapable of doing anything but waving them vaguely in the direction of the kitchen to deposit the flowers on the table. It was only when Amir appeared, providing a generous tip and ushering them out again, that she regained the use of her tongue.

'Did you do this?'

His grin was wide and wicked in its delight at her consternation.

'Number fourteen—appropriately enough,' he told her. 'Happy Valentine's Day, Lydia. *Our* Valentine's Day, anyway.'

It was the beginning of a day that blew Lydia's mind completely, leaving her incapable of thought, of reason, and eventually of any words at all.

She had said that in order to fit in all the 'sensual stages' mapped out in the magazine, she thought they would have to cram things up a bit, but she had never anticipated this! The day was a whirlwind of experiences, of sensations that came at her thick and fast until her mind was spinning dizzily.

Valentine's Day came first, with the roses, cards, a silk nightdress and negligée wrapped in silver paper. A couple of hours later, it was 'Easter'.

The biggest, most luxurious, Swiss chocolate egg she had ever seen was delivered to the door, along with armfuls of toys in the shape of fluffy yellow chicks and smooth white furry rabbits and finally baskets of primroses, daffodils, and tulips to fill every space where there wasn't already a huge bunch of roses.

'Amir!' she protested weakly, a shaken edge of laughter in her voice. 'This is crazy! You must have bought up a whole florist's shop—and a toyshop, come to that! And as for that Easter egg…'

'Are you telling me that you don't like chocolate?' Amir enquired, a teasing light dancing in his ebony eyes.

'No—I love it! But no one person could ever eat their way through a quarter of that.'

'Then you'll have to have some help.'

His smile grew wider, more vivid, deliberately enticing.

'I never intended that you should have it all to yourself. I did have plans to share it with you.'

They shared it in bed.

It started with Amir feeding her slivers of the sinfully rich confection as he had fed her the ripe peach on their first evening together. Later, Lydia found a childlike delight in tracing intricate patterns over Amir's golden skin using the deeper shade of the chocolate before she licked it off with a delicate care that had him groaning in erotic response. Later still they made love with the sweetness lingering on their lips, combining with the swirl of tongues, the intimate, intensely personal taste of each others' skin in a potently erotic cocktail.

And as they lay in bed afterwards, their breath gradually slowing, the slick sheen of sweat drying on their love weary bodies, Amir reached for the pages of the magazine that detailed the list he had been following.

'Valentine's. Easter…'

His rich deep voice was thick with satisfaction as he ticked them off.

'What's next?'

'Next?' Lydia groaned in disbelief. 'Amir, you can't be

serious! You've already spoiled me rotten. Any more would be too much.'

But Amir simply smiled and dropped a kiss on the top of her head.

'I promised you the affair of a lifetime,' he murmured against her hair. 'And that is what I intend to deliver. But not just yet.'

Briefly he glanced at his watch, nodding approval at what he saw.

'For now, it's still Easter,' he said huskily, turning her naked body in the bed so that she faced him once more, cupping the warm, silken weight of her breasts in both hands. 'Still spring. And you know what they say a man's mind turns to in spring.'

'Yours turns to that at any time!' Lydia retorted, her breath catching in her throat as he lifted her breasts to meet the heated demand of his mouth.

'Mmm,' Amir murmured against her skin, his breath feathering over the sensitivity of one tightened nipple, making her shiver in delicious anticipation. 'Spring and summer and autumn and winter…'

His tongue flicked out, encircled the aching bud, then he drew it softly into his mouth and suckled hard. And with a yearning cry of surrender, Lydia gave herself up to his lovemaking once again.

CHAPTER TEN

AT AROUND three in the morning Lydia finally gave up on any hope of falling asleep and slipped soundlessly from the bed. Leaving Amir deep in apparently dreamless oblivion, she tiptoed from the room and downstairs to the living room, pulling on her ivory silk robe as she went.

By rights, she too should have fallen asleep as easily as Amir, she reflected as she curled up beside the still-glowing embers of the fire he had lit earlier. But just as she had always done on special occasions as a child, she had found herself unable to relax, still too keyed up by the excitement and delight of the day.

And what a day it had been! There had been so many wonderful moments, so much to enjoy, making her feel as if she were fizzing inside, her blood actually sparkling in her veins. She had no longer seemed to be living in the real world, but as if she had been transported to some fantasy existence where every day was a holiday and she had only to wish for something for it to be granted her.

She had still been recovering from Amir's ardent love-making when he had slid from the bed and pulled on his jeans, snatching up his mobile phone and barking enquiries into it in incomprehensible Arabic. Obviously the answers had pleased him because he had been smiling in deep satisfaction when he had come back to the bed to rouse her from the half-sleep into which she had drifted.

'Come on, *habibti*,' he urged, shaking her gently. 'Time to wake up—we're going on holiday.'

That jolted her awake in a second.

'We're *what*? Amir...we can't!'

'We can. It's on the list. Number—'

'No, don't tell me, I remember. Number nineteen. Going on holiday. Sun, sea and sand. But this is London in the middle of a snowstorm in February. *How…?*'

'You'll see. Just come with me—trust me.'

Trust him! Lydia felt that if he had asked for her life she would have given it into his hands in the perfect confidence that he would take care of her and make sure that everything went right.

If there was a way to produce sun, sea and sand, then Amir would do it. She had no doubt of that.

But all the same she was stunned when the chauffeur-driven car took them to one of the largest, most luxurious gyms in the area. To a place where the swimming pool was not just the usual, clinically blue-tiled rectangle but an artificial idyllic beach in miniature, complete with sand, palm trees, and a special wave machine to make sure that the temperately heated water lapped against their feet in gentle movement.

Sunbeds reproduced the 'sun' part of the holiday, and Amir had even thought to provide a perfect, azure-blue bikini that he had ordered from the boutique they had visited the day before. To Lydia's amazement and delight, it not only fitted perfectly but also flattered and enhanced her figure wonderfully.

The mirror told her half the story on that, but the rest of it was there in Amir's eyes when he looked at her. In the flames of desire he didn't even try to conceal, the smouldering glance that sizzled all the way from the top of her shining bronze head, right down to the bare toes that curled on the water-splashed sand.

'As soon as I saw that, I knew it would be perfect for you,' he told her huskily. 'What I never guessed was just *how* perfect.'

And Lydia was only able to nod, her own voice having deserted her. She had been quite unprepared for the sight of Amir's sleek, bronze body as he emerged, dripping wet from the swimming pool as she appeared. With his black hair slicked back severely, every muscle toned and hard, the water drops sparkling against the darkness of his skin, he was pure Bedouin chieftain, powerful and untamed.

'In my country, water is like riches,' he told her, taking her hand and drawing her with him into the pool. 'Come with me, *habibti*, and let me bathe you in this most precious of elements. We have only the briefest of summers together, let's not waste a moment of it.'

The 'summer' Amir gave her lasted only a couple of hours, and she knew that, even as a child when she had wept at leaving the places where she had spent such a magical time, she had never packed away her bikini with so heavy a heart.

It wasn't just the end of the holiday he had created for her; it was the knowledge that with each hour that passed now, the length of their time together was diminishing fast. Already their second day would soon be over. So as she joined Amir in the luxurious limousine that was to take them back to his apartment her eyes burned with tears she did not dare to shed.

'Do we *have* to leave?' She sighed.

'Even the most wonderful holiday must come to an end, sweetheart.'

Amir had caught the betraying sheen in her eyes and he took her hand with an understanding that tore at her heart.

'But perhaps this will help lighten your spirits. Happy second anniversary, Lydia.'

'This' was a small, beautifully wrapped package that he produced from a pocket and slipped into her hand. Opening it, Lydia found that it contained a pair of the most beautiful diamond earrings.

'Oh, Amir!'

The gift was spectacular, the earrings exquisite, but what choked her up the most, tearing at her heart with bittersweet delight, was the realisation that once again he had remembered and marked the exact minute that they had met.

'Amir, they are *beautiful*. I really don't know how to thank you!'

'Don't you?'

His voice had deepened, grown husky, and the arm that lay lightly around her waist tightened, drawing her closer, his head coming down as he took her lips in a searing kiss of promise.

'I think you know only too well how you can thank me,' he murmured against her mouth. 'We both know.'

The rich, deep voice matched his kiss in a pledge of passion, the hungry demand in the lips that took hers making heat flood through her body so that she shifted restlessly against him, already aching with the hunger only he could appease. Once again, the journey back to Amir's apartment was going to be a long, long purgatory of waiting and anticipation.

'Yes,' she sighed, and it was a sound of surrender and delight in the same second. 'Yes. I know.'

She had thought—had hoped—that as soon as they reached the house he would take her straight to bed, but she was wrong. Instead, as soon as she entered the apartment, she stood stock-still, staring around her in stunned delight.

While they had been out, it seemed as if an army of skilled, industrious elves had been busy transforming the whole of the hallway and the living room beyond into a Christmas wonderland. An enormous tree, festooned with twinkling lights and baubles in silver and gold, stood in the corner, multicoloured parcels piled up at its feet. Beautiful garlands swathed the wooden banisters, the walls, the windows. Candles burned everywhere and even a bulging stocking hung from the wide mantelpiece of the huge fireplace.

'Happy Christmas, sweetheart,' Amir murmured in her

ear, but this time she could find no words to thank him. She was only able to stand transfixed, her hands up to her face, covering her mouth, tears of sheer delight tumbling down her cheeks.

And that hadn't been an end to it, Lydia recalled now, pulling the robe tighter round her and curling up on the edge of the hearth, hugging her knees, staring into the dying embers.

Somehow Amir had also provided a choir of carol singers, children with voices so beautiful they had brought tears to her eyes. Jamila had cooked and served a traditional dinner with all the trimmings. And, of course, the snow, still coming down in gentle flurries outside, had provided the perfect, Christmas card touch of beauty.

And then there had been the presents. A wonderful mixture of the wildly extravagant generosity she had come to expect from this man together with small, inexpensive gifts. But gifts that had been chosen with such understanding, such knowledge of her that they had made her head reel. They had only been together for a short while, but in that time Amir had listened and learned and his presents proved that he knew her almost as well as he knew himself.

But like the 'holiday' that afternoon, 'Christmas' could only last a few hours. They had made the magic stretch just a moment or two longer by staying up till midnight and toasting an imaginary New Year in vintage champagne. After that, Amir had made love to her right here, on the thick soft rug before the fire, his touch, his kisses, the final wild conflagration of her orgasm the perfect end to the perfect day.

But even the perfect day couldn't last for ever.

Lydia sighed, reaching for a log from the nearby basket and tossing it on the fire, watching as the flames flared suddenly and began licking greedily at its edges.

For ever was the one thing Amir could not provide.

The one thing he had no intention of providing.

For ever was not in Amir's vocabulary.

And that was why she was sitting here like this, unable to sleep.

A wave of misery swept over her, clouding her eyes, and the cheek that she laid against her silk-covered knees was once more damp with tears. But these were not the tears of joy she had shed earlier, or the sobs of ecstasy that had escaped her at the height of the lovemaking before this hearth. They were tears of desolation and regret at the thought that most of the three days that had seemed to stretch ahead so wonderfully, filled with all sorts of possibilities, were now in the past. Her time with Amir was almost over and she didn't know how she was going to face the future without him.

'Lydia…'

The soft sound of Amir's voice startled her, bringing her head up sharply, wide blue eyes going to the door. As always, her heart jolted wildly at the sight of him. Even with his black hair tousled, dark eyes still faintly blurred by sleep and the stubble of a daylong growth of beard shadowing his strong jaw, he was easily the most lethally attractive man she had ever seen.

'I'm sorry! Did I disturb you? I tried to leave as quietly as possible.'

'It wasn't anything you did. I was only sleeping lightly anyway.'

Well, it was half the truth, Amir told himself. He *had* found it hard to lose himself in the oblivion of sleep. But the real fact of the matter was that he had missed her. It had only taken a couple of seconds for the emptiness on her side of the bed to register, to penetrate the light doze into which he had drifted. She had barely closed the door behind her before he had been wide awake, staring at the ceiling.

At first he had fully intended to stay where he was and

wait for her to come back. She would only be a minute or two, he'd reasoned, and when she returned he could pretend that her getting back into bed had woken him. It would be the perfect excuse to put his arms round her, draw her close. They could make love again in the still, dark silence of the night. Already his body had been growing hard just at the thought.

But Lydia hadn't come back. And lying awake in the dark room had given him too much time to think. Because of the blackness, the stillness, he'd seemed so much more aware of everything, from the cooling space where Lydia's slender body had been to the faint ticking of the clock on the bedside table. That sound was suddenly too loud, too intrusive, reminding him of the way that time was ticking away, and with it this brief idyll of an affair with Lydia.

All too soon she would be gone, flying to America and that wonderful new job of hers.

And how would he feel then?

Suddenly too restless to stay still, he had flung back the bedclothes, pulling on a pair of black pyjama trousers and a matching silk robe, belting it tightly round his lean waist against the chill of the night as he went in search of Lydia.

'Couldn't you sleep?'

She shook her bright head, the tumbled waves flying round her face, and he had to struggle to control the instinctive kick of response low down in his body that made him want her all over again.

'No. Too much excitement for one day. My grandma always said it wasn't good for me. ''There will be tears before bedtime,'' she would tell my mother.'

'My grandmother used to say much the same thing.'

Amir came and sat on the couch near her, holding out his hands to the fire.

'Did she? But I thought…'

'My English grandmother—on my mother's side. I

never knew my father's mother. Would you like something
to drink—some tea perhaps?'

Once again Lydia shook her head and this time the immediate response was harder to take as he caught the faint,
sweet scent of her hair and her body.

'What I'd like to do is to talk.'

'Talk? About what? Anything in particular?'

'About you.'

Lydia knew her mistake as soon as she had spoken. She
saw his dark head go back, the swift narrowing of his eyes.
His long, relaxed body tensed up immediately, rejection of
what she had said stamped into every inch.

A couple of days before, his reaction would have silenced her, making her fear his possible response, the angry rejection of her enquiry that might follow. But now
she had little or nothing to lose. They only had one more
day together. And she couldn't leave knowing so little
about him, knowing that he had never really given her
anything of himself.

'Play fair, Amir!' she protested. 'You asked me enough
about myself. You know about my job, my family, my
friends. Now it's my turn.'

Talking wasn't what was on his mind right now. The
fire had caught more strongly, the flames flaring round the
log, lighting the darkness of the room. The golden flickers
came and went, creating subtle patterns on her upturned
face, gilding her skin and turning her hair to molten
bronze. His imagination was throwing wild, heated ideas
at him. Images of laying her down on the thick rug before
the fire, stripping the delicate silk of the robe from her
even softer body and making hot, passionate love to her
while the light of the fire played over her naked flesh.

But a second look at her face told him that even to try
it would be the wrong move. And perhaps she was right.

Talking would slow things down, increase the anticipation, prolong the pleasure of simply being with her,

knowing what was to come. The wild, heated pleasure of the first twenty-four hours had been amazing. Mind-blowing. The best sex he'd ever had. But he had also come to find a whole new sort of delight in the quieter moments. In simply sitting beside the water of the swimming pool, combing the tangles out of her hair, or joining in the 'New Year' ceremony she had insisted on following.

'We have to write down the things of the past year we want to put behind us and burn them up in the flames of a special candle,' she'd said. 'We record the good stuff as well, but that we put into an envelope and keep it for the coming year.'

And as he'd assumed that for the sake of this invented New Year, the 'past year' she'd referred to had simply been the time since they'd met, that had been easy to do. The one thing he'd had to regret was that they hadn't met earlier. Another day, another time, when he could have spent longer with her, getting to know her own unique individuality, enjoying more of the white-hot passion that blazed between them.

But perhaps it was better this way. At least, with the restrictions of the three days that was all the time they had together, there was no chance of the gloss ever fading, reality setting in—or, even worse, boredom.

So, 'Okay,' he said now. 'What do you want to know?'

Lydia couldn't believe her luck. Where she had expected an outright refusal, it was almost shocking that this had been so easy. Looking into his eyes in the light of the fire, she had seen the flare of a sensuality hotter than even the physical flames and had felt an immediate, answering shiver of response. If he had turned on his lethal, irresistible, seductive charm, she would have been lost. Unable to resist him, she would have responded at once, and this moment would have been lost.

But something had changed Amir's mood, and, terrified

of altering the atmosphere again, she hunted for a safe topic on which to begin.

'Tell me about the horses you breed.'

That was easy. Within a moment he was launched into describing the stud, the stallions he owned, the race winners he had bred. From there it was an easy step to his childhood on his uncle's farm, growing up as an English boy to all intents and purposes, but always knowing that there was something different about him.

'When did you find out the truth—that Sheikh Khalid was your father?'

'On my eleventh birthday.'

Amir turned his head to stare into the fire, the leaping golden flames reflected in miniature in his onyx eyes.

'My father had arranged a visit to a stud a couple of miles away, owned by the father of a friend of mine. As it was in the summer holidays, I was there, helping with the horses. I led out one of the stallions he was interested in. But it was me that he stared at; me that he watched. I never realised before then just how much I looked like my mother.'

Moving abruptly, he leaned forward to pick up another log and toss it deep into the heart of the fire.

'When I told her all about it, she decided that perhaps the time had come for me to know the truth.'

Lydia bit her lip hard, imagining how that must have felt. Reacting instinctively, she moved to sit closer to Amir, curled at his feet. When she laid a sympathetic hand on the hard curve of his knee he dropped his own to rest on top of it, strong fingers curving over hers.

'From that moment I vowed that I would make my father acknowledge me for who I really was. That one day I would hear him call me his son, no matter what it took.'

The hard mouth firmed, setting into a ruthless, unyielding line, and Lydia shivered faintly inside at just the thought of that pitiless determination being set against anyone, even the proud, cold-hearted old man his father obviously was.

'And I was even more determined when I visited Kuimar, first as a tourist and later to negotiate deals, to buy and sell the horses I bred—to watch them race. It quickly became my true home—as if I had never been away.'

Amir's broad shoulders lifted and fell in a resigned shrug of acceptance, jet-black eyes not leaving the fire, as if he was seeing in the wood and the flames the image of the country of his birth.

'I fell in love with the place and spent as much time as I could there. It's a country of such contrasts. The cities that are a dazzle of glass and chrome, and the wind-blown sand-dunes that are never the same shape from one day to the next. To the east there are the Hajar Mountains, to the west, the waters of the Gulf itself. I learned to love both the bustle of the city life and the still, eerie silence of the desert at night.'

'It sounds wonderful.'

Her soft murmur drew those brilliant eyes to her face, so that she saw the shadows of memory that still lingered in their depths.

'It is,' he said simply.

Kuimar is my country. The words she had heard him speak—was it truly less than twenty-four hours ago?—echoed inside Lydia's thoughts, making her wince inwardly in hidden pain. Had it really been only that morning that she had first heard him make the declaration that she knew spelled the death sentence for any foolish hopes she might have had of a future beyond the three days he had allotted her?

She might have been able to fight his past, or even the fact that he didn't love her—yet. But how did she fight a *country*?

'So that's why you only have three days? Because you're expected back in Kuimar—at your father's side?'

He took so long in answering her that she knew there was more to it than that, and her heart quailed inside her at the thought.

What more could there be? More than the fact that he was a Crown Prince and his father's heir. More than the fact that his heart belonged to his country.

'That's part of it,' he said at last.

'Only part? So what's the rest of it?'

Oh, *why* did she have to ask? Why couldn't she just keep quiet and leave it alone? Her time with him was almost up as it was. Did she truly want to complicate it now, with things that soon wouldn't matter?

Soon she would be gone and so would he. They would be thousands of miles apart, flying in opposite directions, going to different corners of the world. Soon his reasons for returning to Kuimar would be irrelevant because he would have gone and she would never see him again.

Today, she had the terrible suspicion that those reasons might just ruin what little was left of her three-day affair.

And still Amir was silent, looking down into her waiting face, his expression impenetrable as the face of a marble statue.

'Amir?' she prompted hesitantly, knowing that she had to have an answer and yet dreading the moment when he would actually say the words.

His deep sigh was even more worrying than his silence. Her heart clenched in fear as he raked both his hands through the darkness of his hair, ruffling it even more.

'Don't, Lydia,' he said, the softness of his voice doing nothing to calm her fears.

'Don't what?'

In contrast, her own tone was wild and sharp, revealing the turmoil of emotions she was struggling with.

'Don't ask? Why not? Is it something so dreadful?'

Her voice died on a small choking sound as he laid a finger over her mouth, silencing her.

'Can't we leave it as it is?'

She almost gave in to him. Almost nodded in agreement. Almost said yes, fine, they could leave it unsaid, she didn't want to know.

But she couldn't. Because she *did* want to know. Whatever it was.

And so with a movement that tore at her heart she pulled away from that gently restraining finger and shook her head firmly.

'No. We can't leave it.'

'Lydia…'

His sigh destroyed what was left of her self-control, shattering her ability to stay calm and wait.

'Amir! *Tell me!* Tell me now.'

'All right.'

His tone was heavy, lifeless.

'You asked. I have to return to Kuimar to get married. My bride is waiting for me there.'

CHAPTER ELEVEN

IT HAD been one of the longest nights of her life.

If Lydia had thought earlier that she would find it difficult to sleep, now she found it impossible. She lay there in bed, staring at the ceiling, seeing nothing, and all the time in her head Amir's words repeated over and over.

'I have to return to Kuimar to get married. My bride is waiting for me there.'

If anyone had told her that the man she had fallen head over heels in love with was going to say those words to her, and asked her to predict her reaction, she would have thought that she would scream or shout, certainly that she would cry out. She might have thought that she would slap him, or at least pummel her fists against his shoulders, demanding to know what he was doing, why he was treating her in this appalling way.

She had done none of those.

Instead, pride had come to her aid, giving her at least an outward dignity that her inner soul didn't possess. Inwardly she was screaming and weeping with the best of them, but her outward appearance revealed nothing of her distress.

She was proud of the way that she hadn't even uttered a sound. That she had got slowly to her feet, her head high, chin lifted defiantly. She had even managed to look Amir straight in the face with a strength she hadn't known she possessed. That strength had kept the tears away too, leaving her totally dry-eyed in spite of the knowledge that a torrent of weeping was building up against the dam inside her heart.

'And when were you going to tell me this?' she asked,

134

her voice as stiff and cold as her tightly held body. 'At the end of the three days? As you waved me off at the airport?'

'Never.'

The single word almost destroyed her. Blindly she reached out for the back of a nearby chair and held onto it with a desperate grip that turned her fingers white against the gold upholstery.

'Never?'

The ebony eyes were totally expressionless, blank and opaque.

'It wasn't relevant to our relationship.'

'Relevant!'

A mixture of fury and pain made her spell out every single syllable of the word coldly and precisely.

'You don't think that the fact that you're engaged, that you're getting *married* to someone else has anything to do with us!'

Big mistake, Lydia! You know there *is* no 'us'! That even Amir's use of the word 'relationship' was just politeness. He told you from the start that three days were all you'd have. Deep down, you know that the reality is that emotionally this means as little to him as that one-night stand you thought you were at the start. It just happened to stretch out a bit longer, that's all.

And if she'd needed any confirmation of that fact, then Amir's cold, tight smile as he got to his feet gave her it in spades.

'My relationship to my future wife is strictly between her and me. It has no bearing on this situation at all.'

'Except in that she is why you only have three days to spare to dally with me? I take it that you would have flown out to her two days ago, if the snow hadn't got in your way?'

'That is where I was going.'

Cold and clipped and curt, his words were like a death

sentence to any foolish hopes she might have harboured that she'd got it wrong.

'And, yes, if the snow hadn't closed the runways, I would have been in Kuimar by now.'

'And happily married and off enjoying your honeymoon somewhere in one of Daddy's better palaces, no doubt!'

'Not exactly. A royal wedding is a weeklong affair.'

Amir wished he could find a way to handle this situation better, but his mind seemed to have gone totally blank. All he could think of was how white and still she had gone, how darkly bruised her eyes seemed, deep as pansies above ashen cheeks.

She hadn't actually stepped away from him, but her withdrawal was as total as if a huge, impassable chasm had just opened up between them, yawning at his feet. If he made the wrong move she would turn and run and he would lose her for ever.

He wanted to reach out and enfold her in his arms, to kiss away that frozen look and tell her that it was not as it seemed, not as she thought, but the time wasn't right for that. Not yet. So instead he stuck to telling her the strict truth, even if it seemed to make matters worse for the moment.

'The ceremony wouldn't have been performed yet.'

'Oh, I'm glad to know that!'

Lydia didn't recognise her own voice in the one that spat venom into Amir's impassive face, savage bitterness hiding the agony that clawed at her heart.

'I'm glad to know that you wouldn't actually be being *unfaithful* to your fiancée just yet! I'm sure that must salve your conscience—absolve you completely.'

'Lydia, don't be bloody stupid!'

Amir's hands flew up and out in a gesture of total exasperation.

'I'm not looking for absolution! It's not relevant...'

'You're very fond of that word!'

'It's the most appropriate one I can think of!' As always his accent deepened and darkened with his rising temper.

'And was it because it wasn't *relevant* that you never mentioned this small matter of the fiancée you had? The wife-to-be who was just waiting for the ceremony to be performed.'

'I never lied to you.'

'No, you never *lied*! You just omitted a few vital facts. Didn't you think it would have been more honest to tell me everything? To give me all the details so that I could make an informed choice?'

'You knew where you stood from the start.'

'Oh, yes, I knew where I stood!'

And where she stood was precisely nowhere. She had just been a passing fancy to him. Someone with whom to while away the unexpected interval of waiting for his flight out to Kuimar and his wedding. And she had fallen straight into his honeyed trap.

Amir's dark head lowered so that he was looking straight into her ashen face. His eyes were brilliant and cold, devastating in their complete withdrawal from her.

'You knew exactly what the situation was. I told you I could offer you no more than three days. And you accepted. You went in with your eyes wide open.'

But he hadn't told her the whole truth! And that being so, she had foolishly, naively, *idiotically* let herself hope that, given time, she might change the situation for the better. She had actually allowed herself to believe that she could change his mind, win him round to loving her.

She couldn't have been more wrong.

He had no love to give her. He was already committed to another woman.

She had to get out of here. She couldn't stay in the room a moment longer. Not long ago, she had watched his stunning, expressive features in the firelight and known that she loved him. Now she didn't know if she loved him or hated him. She only knew that she couldn't look into his dark, handsome face and maintain any degree of composure. If she didn't escape she would break down completely and risk telling him exactly how she felt about him.

'I'm going to bed,' she said through lips that seemed to have been formed out of ice, they were so stiff and cold and awkward. *'Alone,'* she added pointedly when he nodded and half turned towards the door.

She would break completely if he so much as suggested that he came with her. If he touched her or tried to kiss her, then she would disintegrate into a shaking heap of despair, crumbling at his feet. As it was, she barely felt that her legs would support her on even the short walk to the door.

But Amir said nothing, made no move. He simply nodded and the rush of relief at the thought that he was going to let her go without a fight gave her an unexpected renewal of strength.

'I'm going to—to *my* room,' she managed, though the words almost stuck in her throat. 'You said that I could be totally private there. I trust you will respect that.'

'Of course.'

If his face had been carved from marble, his eyes as sightless as a classical statue, he couldn't have looked more distant from her. It was impossible not to contrast his expression now with the way he had looked at the time when he had made her that promise, on the second night she had spent in this apartment.

'I wondered if you were free tonight?' he had said when he'd phoned her up. 'If you'd like to do something—a meal—a film maybe.' And in a rare moment of reality in this whole fantasy affair, they had done just that.

After they had made love on their return from the shops, they had lain together for a long time, just holding each other. Then eventually they had got up, showered, dressed, and gone out. They had seen the latest Hollywood blockbuster, sitting in the back row, cuddling and kissing like teenagers, and then gone on to a restaurant for a meal.

Arriving back at the apartment, decidedly more high on atmosphere, pleasure, and the sheer intoxicating force of Amir's personality than on the couple of glasses of wine she had drunk, Lydia had consulted the 'sensual stages' magazine article and turned to him with a mock petulant pout.

'I'm supposed to be able to invite you in for coffee, but it can't be done. I don't have anywhere to invite you to! This whole apartment is yours. There's nowhere that's mine alone.'

That was when he had taken her by the hand and led her up the stairs. On the large, wide landing, he had turned in the opposite direction to his bedroom, finally stopping outside a door at the far end of the corridor.

'Here,' he had said, flinging it open to reveal a huge elegant room, beautifully furnished in soft shades of gold and cream. 'This is yours.'

It was more than a room, Lydia discovered. It was a whole suite, with a luxurious bathroom, a dressing room where the clothes he had bought her had already been unpacked and hung up, and a small sitting room on one side.

'This is your private space for as long as you are here. I promise you I won't come in here. I won't even cross the threshold, unless you give me permission. It's yours and yours alone to do with as you please.'

And then, while she had still been staring in delight and disbelief, he had come closer, cupping her face in one hand as he'd turned her face to his.

'So now…' he had whispered huskily, ebony eyes burning down into her darkened ones, telling her forcefully without the need of words just what was in his thoughts '…invite me in.'

Of course, apart from that one night, she'd never used the room as her own. She'd never needed to—until now.

But tonight the thought of somewhere private, some personal sanctuary that she could run to and hide, was like a haven from the torment of being with Amir and knowing how he had deceived her. Blinded by stinging tears, Lydia blundered up the stairs and along the corridor, diving into 'her' suite like a small, terrified animal seeking refuge from a ruthless predator.

Slamming the door shut, she fell back against it, holding it closed as if afraid that in spite of his promise Amir might still come after her, still demand that she let him in.

But of course he didn't. And even though just a few moments later she heard the heavy sound of his footsteps on the stairs and tensed, it soon became clear that he had turned in the opposite direction, heading for his own room.

And it was only then, as she sank down on the edge of the bed, and let her misery wash over her, that Lydia finally gave way to the despair that was in her heart.

It had been one of the longest nights of his life, Amir told himself as he headed down the landing to Lydia's room later that morning. He had hardly slept at all. Instead, he had lain awake for hours, knowing he'd made a pig's ear of everything, and trying to think of a way to sort things out.

There was only one way, of course. And that was to tell the whole story and then let Lydia make up her mind what happened from then on.

And that was the really terrifying bit. The putting everything into Lydia's hands and waiting for her to decide. He'd never let any woman have that much power in his life before. If he was honest, he'd never let any woman have *any* power in his life at all. He'd run things his own way, and that had always suited him.

So what had made things so different? he asked himself as he rapped sharply on the panels of the firmly closed door. He couldn't begin to explain. He only knew that when he'd seen her walk away from him last night, it had been the hardest thing he'd ever done to let her go. Harder even than accepting any of the rejections his father had handed out to him. But he'd also known that, right then, going after her had *not* been the thing to do. She hadn't been ready for it, and it could only have made matters worse.

And all the hours he'd spent in the big double bed, lying awake in the darkness, the thing he'd been conscious of was the space beside him. The cold emptiness of the sheets where Lydia's warm, softly scented body should have been. It seemed impossible that after only a couple of days she should have made such an impression on him, and yet, dammit, he'd *missed* her.

'Lydia? Are you awake?'

Silence.

Perhaps she was still asleep.

No, that explanation didn't convince. The memory of her white, miserable face swam before his eyes and he knew, without having been told, that there was no way that the woman who had left him last night would have been able to sleep, any more than he had.

She had to be awake, but not responding to his call.

'Lydia! We have to talk.'

Still no response. But then he knew she was stubborn as a mule.

A faint smile touched his mouth as he recalled the way she'd blanked him at first. The struggle he'd had to even get her to let him sit down, let alone talk to her. He'd had to work hard to win her round, even to the point of making it look as if he'd been about to walk away...

Not that he could have done it.

The smile became rueful as he shook his head in despair at his own foolishness. Even then he had been so totally under her spell that he hadn't known what he'd been doing. From the moment she had walked into the lounge at the airport he had been trapped, entranced, caught up in her spell and unable to break free. Even if he *had* walked away, he knew he would have had to go back. She had got to him so badly that his mind, his actions hadn't been his own.

They still weren't.

'*Lydia!* I know you're listening. Open this damn door, will you?'

This was crazy. If he had any sense at all, he'd leave it right here. It would be for the best all round.

All he had to do was to walk away, and things could go back to how they had been. How they had been three days ago, before he'd first set eyes on her. Then he'd had his life all planned out, totally clear-cut and defined. He'd known exactly where he'd been going. What had been going to happen to him. And then Lydia's appearance had turned everything upside down, thrown his plans into chaos.

He hadn't thought beyond that first night. But when he'd learned that the airport was closed for the next couple of days, he'd grabbed at the chance to spend more time with her because by then she'd really got under his skin, and there had been nothing he'd been able to do about it. But three days was all he'd said. And those three days were almost up.

'Okay, forget it! I know you're awake; I know you're listening. But if you don't want to talk, then that's up to you. I'm going downstairs to make some coffee… If you want to join me, fine. If not…'

If not, then this time he wasn't turning back. This time he'd walk away without a second glance. If she wanted to end it now, then that suited him. He'd have his life back under control and it would be as if this uncharacteristically crazy, irrational interval had never been.

And that suited him fine.

So why did he find himself filling two mugs with coffee? And heating the milk to add to one, just as Lydia liked it?

He was just going to try and get her to see sense, he told himself as he headed for the stairs again. Just going to get her to talk…

His foot was on the first step when the phone in the hall rang, loud and shrill.

Lydia heard the phone from behind the security of her locked door. The sound of Amir's voice didn't reach her, but she knew from the way that the faint buzzing sound stopped that he had answered it almost at once. Which meant that he was not going to come back—not yet at least.

But he would come back at some point, she was sure of that. He had sounded so cold, so ruthlessly determined when she had heard his voice on the other side of the door, that she knew he didn't intend to give in without a real fight.

'We have to talk', he had said, and she knew that, inevitably, at some point they would have to. But she couldn't face him, didn't know what to say to him. And so she had hidden away behind the locked door taking the refuge of silence, when all time every sense had been on red alert to even the faintest sound he made.

He would be coming back any minute. With the phone call answered, he would be heading back upstairs. She couldn't stay holed up in this room all day long.

But as she waited the time ticked by, seconds turning into minutes, and still there was no sign of Amir, no sound of movement from outside.

Was he coming back? Or was she just deceiving herself that it even mattered to him? Perhaps he'd given up on her completely? After all, the three days were almost up. Would he really think that the final few hours were worth all the effort of fighting for?

Eventually she couldn't bear the waiting any longer. It

was obvious that, whatever Amir was doing, he wasn't coming back. And as she couldn't stay in her room for ever, she would have to face him some time, sooner rather than later. Hastily she dressed in her own clothes, the ones she had arrived in. She didn't feel she could wear anything that Amir had bought her.

'Amir?'

The silence in the house was oppressive as she came down the stairs, looked in all the rooms.

'Amir? Are you there?'

No answer. Had he gone out, then? Certainly the weather looked clearer, heavy rain turning the snow to slush very quickly.

So what did she do now? What could she do but wait? But first she'd make herself a cup of coffee. Perhaps with something warm inside her she'd feel stronger.

Somehow without Amir's presence the kitchen seemed to have lost some of the cosy friendliness of before. On the table lay the magazine Lydia had brought with her and as she waited for the kettle to boil she flicked through the pages desultorily, skimming the sections she hadn't looked at before. Suddenly a familiar face in a photograph caught her eye and she froze, staring down at it.

'Eligible royal bachelors' read the heading to the article and there was a picture of Amir, tall and proud, raven head windswept and tousled, mounted on a magnificent Arab stallion. The article enthused in decidedly breathless prose:

Sheikh Amir bin Khalid Al Zaman might have been brought up and educated in England, but at heart this gorgeous Crown Prince is truly a magnificent son of the desert.

Lydia could barely read any more through the burning tears that filled her eyes, blurring her vision so that she had to blink hard to drive them back. Only brief sentences here and there caught her attention, and all of them were guaranteed to add to her already bitter discomfort.

'Love 'em and leave 'em seems to be his philosophy when it comes to women. No single female, however lovely, has ever caught his heart and held it for more than a few blissful months... But when the break-up comes, this Prince of Kuimar knows how to sweeten the pill with a vengeance. Every one of his former lovers has been sent on her way with a jewel or two worth something close to a king's ransom. Not enough to mend a broken heart perhaps, but very nice just the same.

'Sweeten the pill, indeed!'

Unable to take any more, Lydia tossed the magazine away from her, careless of the fact that it slid along the polished surface of the table and tumbled onto the floor.

The idea of the coffee no longer appealed and instead she made her way out into the hall, where she lingered at the doorway into the living room.

All trace of the Christmas decorations had been cleared away, the magical atmosphere disappearing with them.

'Face facts, Lydia,' she told herself aloud. 'There never was any magic there in the first place. It was all a delusion.'

As she spoke the sound of the phone rang out again, cutting into her words. Automatically Lydia moved forward to answer it, then stilled again as the answer machine clicked on.

On the table beside the telephone were the two pages torn from the magazine—was it really only two days before?—and she stared down at them, missing the beginning of the message.

'You asked us to let you know when flights were leaving again,' the disembodied voice spoke onto the tape. 'The runways are just about clear now, and we hope to get back to a normal service very soon…'

So that was it, Lydia reflected unhappily. The three days were over, even sooner than Amir had anticipated. The time she had spent here, with him, had come to a close.

The message clicked off but she was hardly aware of the silence. Slowly she ran her finger down the page, seeing how so many of the stages had been checked off, completed, done.

'First date, coffee…' she whispered, picking stages out at random, remembering bitterly. 'First kiss… Going to bed together…'

'Some of them we've rather jumped the gun on.' From nowhere, Amir's words slid into her mind, stabbing at her painfully. It was no wonder that he had grabbed at his opportunity. He must have thought that she was easy, cheap. He'd had only to click his fingers and she had jumped to do as he'd wanted.

But not any more. Now it was all over. Wincing as she recalled her own naïve enthusiasm, Amir's bemused reaction, Lydia saw that almost all of the stages detailed in the article had been ticked off.

'I promised you the affair of a lifetime.' Once more an echo of his voice tormented her. *The affair of a lifetime.* Oh, yes, he'd given her that all right. For a second she allowed herself to remember how it had been yesterday, the magic of every moment. But now nearly all the necessary stages were behind them. There were only the final few left on the list. Just number twenty-four and…

Twenty-four.

'The cost is a pittance and you'll need it for number twenty-four.'

He'd said that to her in the dress shop. She could still remember the saleslady's widened eyes, the look of shock on her face.

What *was* number twenty-four? Picking up the page, she turned it over, looking for the item she was seeking.

'Stage Twenty-four—he takes you somewhere really special. The best restaurant in town, or a really funky club. Perhaps he has an extra-special proposal in mind?'

'Never!' Lydia found herself saying out loud.

'Or perhaps this is his way of letting you down gently.'

But by moving the magazine page, she had disturbed something else. A note, she realised, her heart clenching on a thud of shock. It could only be from Amir; the firm, confident scrawl could be no one else's.

'Lydia,

Called away unavoidably. Sorry—but it really is important. I know I promised you three full days, and now I can't deliver. But I'll be back tonight and then I'll make it up to you. We'll go out—anywhere you want. Wear the blue dress, the one I bought for just this occasion, and we'll make the last dinner of this three-day affair one you'll remember for ever.

He hadn't even bothered to sign it, she thought miserably. He hadn't needed to. No one else but Amir would simply issue a decree like that and expect her to obey it.

'Wear the blue dress...and we'll make the last dinner of this three-day affair one you'll remember...'

'Oh, Amir!'

She didn't know if what she was feeling was agony or fury. She only knew that it felt as if her heart was shattering into tiny, irreparable pieces, splintering away inside her. His name was a moan of pain on her lips and she folded her arms tight around her body, trying desperately to hold herself together.

It was as she spun away from the table that she saw it. A large box, coloured in a soft turquoise with elegant black lettering on the top. The name of one of the most expensive and exclusive jewellers in London.

'But when the break-up comes, this Prince of Kuimar knows how to sweeten the pill.' The words of the article she had read just moments before came back to haunt her with a terrible bitterness. 'Every one of his former lovers has been sent on her way with a jewel or two worth something close to a king's ransom.'

'We'll make the last dinner of this three-day affair one you'll remember for ever.'

Was she really going to wait around for Amir to come back just so that he could take her out, say goodbye properly, maybe even take her to bed one last time—and then give her her jewelled handshake?

Once she might have dreamed that given time he could have come to love her, but now she saw her dream for the delusion it truly was. Tonight their affair was to come to an end, he would reward her for services rendered, and then he would walk away without so much as a backward glance.

No!

She had more pride than that.

The airport had said that the runways were clearing. If she was lucky she could get on a plane and be gone before Amir even came back.

She'd take the initiative from him. It was the only thing she could do for herself now, the only way she could preserve some dignity. Better to cut off the relationship hard and sharp than drag out goodbyes until they became unendurable.

Picking up a pen and pulling a second piece of paper towards her, she reached for the phone.

CHAPTER TWELVE

'MISS ASHTON, the manager would like to speak with you in his office. Immediately.'

Lydia's nerves tightened on a twist of apprehension as she turned and headed in the right direction, crossing the ornately tiled floor of the hotel foyer.

She supposed that one day, eventually, she would be able to respond to a summons like this without some such reaction. That she would be able to settle into her new job without constantly looking over her shoulder and worrying and wondering if Amir was going to appear. But not for a long while yet.

She didn't know what malign fate had meant that the very first posting she had received from Halgrave had been here, in Hafit, the capital of Kuimar; she only knew that she wished it could have been anywhere else. But because it *was* her first post, there was no way she could turn it down, though she'd tried to fight against it, and so, desperately unwillingly, she had now been living and working in Kuimar for three days.

'Come!'

The voice that greeted her knock on the door was muffled by the wood and no sixth sense alerted her. But as soon as she stepped into the room and saw the tall, upright figure standing by the window she suddenly knew that she was in very deep trouble.

He was standing with his back to her, and the fact that he was wearing the traditional Arab robes, together with the white *gutra* headdress bound with a black and gold cord or *igal* meant that she couldn't see his face, or even his colouring. But she didn't need to see. Every instinct had immediately gone straight onto red alert, telling her just who was in the room with her.

'*Amir!*'

He turned slowly. So slowly that it seemed as if her heart had time to stop beating entirely, only to start up again in a thudding, uneven pulse as they finally came face to face.

It seemed impossible that she could have forgotten the impact of that imposing height, those stunning features. That just over six weeks' absence could have blurred the edges of her memory and dimmed the brilliance of those polished obsidian eyes, the hard, high line of the forceful cheekbones, the beautiful bronze tones of his skin.

She would have said that time had been merciful in helping her that way, except that now it meant she was subjected all over again to the stunning realisation of just how beautiful he was. And, after all this time without it, just the sight of him was like a draught of the coolest, clearest water to someone dying of thirst in the desert, an indulgence for which all her senses clamoured loudly and hungrily.

'Good afternoon, Ms Ashton.'

The greeting was accompanied by a faint inclination of his head, too slight to be anything but condescending, too condescending to be anything other than sarcastic. The sleek suited businessman, the casually dressed Amir she had seen so briefly in London had totally disappeared. Here, in his native land, he was a Bedouin ruler from his head to his feet.

'What a pleasure it is to see you again.'

It was a struggle to keep his voice even, Amir admitted. His mind seemed to be splitting in two, one half delighting in the sight of her again, the other flooded with dark anger at the memory of the way she had left without a word. He didn't know if the throbbing pulse at his temple was in response to the sensual appeal of that lovely face and the long, slim lines of her body in the smart navy-blue dress that modestly covered her arms and her knees in respect of local convention, or a bitter fury that threatened to break out of control.

'I have missed you.'

He laced the words with enough acid to make her wince visibly, though she covered it up hastily.

'I'm sorry I can't say the same about seeing you!' Lydia flashed back. 'Quite frankly, I would have been much happier if I'd never set eyes on you again. I never wanted to come to Kuimar. It was the last place on earth I would have chosen to work, if I'd had the choice—but of course I didn't.'

'No, you didn't.'

Something in Amir's voice, the faint smile that flickered on his beautiful mouth and then off again, tugged sharply at Lydia's nerves.

'And what, precisely, does that mean?'

Suspicion sharpened her tone, sparked in the blue depths of her eyes, earning her a swift, reproving frown.

'My dear Lydia, I was simply agreeing with you that the choice was not yours to make.'

'And whose precisely was it?' she questioned edgily, struggling to ignore the cruel edge to that 'my dear Lydia'.

'Why, mine, of course.'

This time, his smile was pure malice, turning her blood from heated anger to cold discomfort in the space of an uncertain heartbeat.

'Yours! And what did you have to do with it?'

Once more that calculated smile was switched on and then off again, never once touching his eyes, which remained as cold and hard as jet.

'Kuimar is not a country that welcomes single European women to its workforce. Before filling the position in this particular hotel, the manager and the directors of the Halgrave Group had to submit a list of possible candidates from which I, as Crown Prince, made my selection. Knowing it was the company you worked for, I suggested that your name was on that list. Then, naturally, I chose you as the most suitable applicant.'

'Naturally,' Lydia echoed hollowly. Then suddenly she shook her head sharply. 'No, it's not *natural* at all! I can see no reason on earth why you should want to have me here in your country after what there was between us! I would have thought that you were far more likely to be glad to see the back of me and never want the two of us to come face to face again.'

'You couldn't be more wrong.'

Lydia was coming to detest that smile. If a deadly cobra could be capable of smiling in the moments before it struck, then that was exactly the sort of expression it would assume. It was both hateful and dangerous, a threat and a warning all rolled into one, and with nothing pleasant about it at all. And it made a sensation like the slow, creeping slither of something icily nasty slide uncomfortably down her spine just to see it.

'Since your unexpected departure from London six weeks ago, I would have moved heaven and earth to find you again.'

'You would? But why?'

'We have unfinished business between us. A three-day affair that lasted only three quarters of its time. Promises that weren't kept. Certain *stages* that were not worked through.'

'I think we accomplished all the vital ones. No?' Lydia queried as Amir shook his dark head slowly.

'No,' he stated, harshly unyielding.

'What did you want—*blood*?'

'Not blood, my darling. Something much more vital than that. Our affair did not end the way I wanted it to.'

'Well, tough!'

Lydia marched up to the big polished wood desk that

dominated the office and glared at him fiercely across it. He'd got every damn thing he'd wanted out of that affair. He'd had his fun with her, then tossed her aside in favour of the poor, betrayed bride who had been waiting for him here in Kuimar.

'It ended the way *I* wanted it. I'm perfectly happy with the way things turned out.'

Liar! her conscience reproached her bitterly.

If you were perfectly happy you wouldn't have wept into your pillow so many nights since then. And your heart wouldn't have ached just at the mention of Kuimar and its Crown Prince. And if you had wanted the affair to end then you wouldn't have spent every day since you knew you were coming to this hotel in the dread of just such a meeting as this, knowing it must be inevitable.

'But I'm not happy,' Amir declared coldly. 'And I intend to rectify that. I had plans for that last night.'

'Oh, I'll just bet you did! And I suppose you thought that I'd go along with them, no matter what! Well, I'll tell you this, Your High and Mightiness! I do have some moral standards, and one of them is that I don't have affairs with married men.'

'I am not a married man.'

'Near as dammit! It may not matter to you, but in my book an engagement is well on its way to being as binding as a wedding. I don't believe in being unfaithful to anyone...'

'Neither do I,' Amir inserted smoothly, stopping her dead.

'But—but you were going back to Kuimar, to your bride. You were getting married. You're married now!'

She choked her words off again as Amir held up long, elegant hands, spreading them so that it was only too evident that there was no ring on any of his fingers.

'And is that supposed to convince me?'

Desperately she tried for scorn to hide the way that cruel

acid was eating away at her heart. Now, when she was least able to cope with it, when it was the last thing on earth she wanted to remember, her mind would keep throwing at her the memory of how it had felt to have those strong yet gentle hands on her skin, the pleasure they could arouse with just a touch. Every secret, hidden pleasure spot on her tingled into wakefulness and wanting as something primitive and potent called from Amir's body to her own.

'Credit me with a little intelligence, Amir! It would be the easiest thing in the world to take off your wedding ring, leave it at home!'

'Then if I swear it on my honour, will you believe me?'

Lydia flung a fulminating glare into his dark, cold face.

'Do you think for one minute that I believe you have any honour to swear on?'

'I'm not married, Lydia. I have no plans to be married in the near future. I'm not even engaged to anyone.'

He *sounded* sincere. It terrified her how easily she was tempted to believe he *was* sincere. But it was a risk she dared not take.

'I don't believe you!'

'Believe it!' he insisted harshly. 'Because it's the truth. I *am not married*. Nor am I likely to be married unless things change very dramatically.'

'But—what happened?'

Black eyes locked with blue, making her fear that he could read her thoughts and see in her face the sudden, irrepressible flare of delight at knowing that he was still free that would not be held back, no matter how she tried.

'You happened,' he stated flatly.

That floored her.

'Me? I… How could I…?'

'The marriage was part of my father's plan for me. It was to be an arranged marriage. He had picked out a bride for me. A bride of perfect character and breeding for her role as my wife and the future Queen of Kuimar. I had never met her.'

She shouldn't be feeling relieved. She *shouldn't*!

None of this meant that he had cared any more for *her*. It wouldn't have changed a thing about their relationship. But just knowing that this unknown bride had not been his choice, that she had not been the bride of his heart, eased something of the cruel nagging ache that had been her constant waking companion, ever since the night Amir had told her about his impending marriage.

'I didn't even know her name.'

'And yet you would have *married* her?'

'Why not?'

His shrug dismissed her question as totally irrelevant.

'You didn't love her!'

'I'm Arab enough to feel that the western emphasis on love was heavily over rated. I'd never been in love with someone strongly enough to want to commit my life to them. Never met anyone I couldn't just walk away from in the end, so this was no great sacrifice to me.'

Well, that put her squarely in her place! 'Never met anyone I couldn't just walk away from in the end.' She had known that anyway, but somehow it hurt so much more to hear him actually speak the words, to see the coldness of his eyes as he looked at her.

'Love doesn't come into an arranged marriage.'

He had to get her off this uncomfortable line of questioning. He was beginning to feel as if he had been edged into a corner, with his back very firmly up against the wall. They were heading into territory where none of the beliefs he had had about himself held true any longer. But he didn't know yet just what he could put in their place.

'If the couple is lucky, that may come with time, but it isn't a prerequisite of a successful union.'

'But—what was it you said—character and breeding is?'

'Character and breeding and my father's approval.'

'Oh, of course!'

She'd forgotten about that. Forgotten the one thing that gave his bride an advantage above and beyond all others. That she could help him win the thing he wanted most out of life—the kingdom he believed was his birthright from his father.

'Except that none of those matter now because the marriage isn't going to take place.'

'You haven't explained why.'

Don't let yourself hope, she warned her vulnerable heart silently. Don't even *dream* that it could have been because of me.

'Why?'

Amir reached into a pocket, pulled out a piece of paper and tossed it at her, watching stony-eyed as it fluttered down onto the polished top of the desk.

'That's why.'

Lydia stared in shocked consternation at the newspaper picture of herself and Amir, taken on their first day in London, when they had paused for a meal during the shopping expedition. Their heads were close together and she was smiling straight into his eyes.

And anyone but a fool could have seen the way she felt about him, she told herself on a shiver of apprehension.

'Who took that?'

'Some reporter with nothing better to do. They don't matter. What matters is that Aisha saw it. My father saw it. The wedding was called off.'

And he was *furious* about it. It glittered in the depths of his ebony eyes, drew every muscle in his handsome face tight over his amazing bone structure.

'Which is why you are here.'

'Me?'

Lydia's pulse started to throb a warning, and instinctively she took an unsteady step backwards away from the danger signals she could see in his eyes.

'I'm here to work!'

'Do you really think I went to the trouble of ensuring that you came here just so that you could manage an hotel?'

'It's what I'm trained for! What I want to do!'

'I have other plans for you!'

She didn't like the sound of 'other plans'. And when had he moved? She hadn't noticed him coming towards her, prowling across the thick rug with the silent pace of a hunting cat. And yet suddenly he was in front of her, reaching out to still her when she would have turned away.

'You have no right to have any plans for me whatsoever! You've no part in my life...'

Her voice cracked, croaked, died completely as she saw the way he shook his dark head.

'I have every right. You see, my father believed he was getting not just a son, but a dynasty. Heirs to his throne. That's why he arranged this marriage. The marriage that has now been called off—because of you.'

'Because of *you*!' Lydia tossed back, her chin coming up, blue eyes blazing defiantly. 'You seduced me!'

'We seduced each other, sweetheart,' Amir drawled, injecting silky menace into his tone. 'And this picture proves it.'

There was no denying that, Lydia admitted miserably, looking again at the photograph and at the hands linked on the top of the table, the total concentration of the man on the woman and vice versa, the heads so close they were almost touching.

'My father still wants those heirs. He wants grandchildren.'

Lydia's head flew up again, her eyes widening as the full impact of his words hit home with a vengeance.

'You can't mean...'

'I want to give my father the heirs he craves. To do that, I have to have a bride. Because of you, the bride who was chosen for me is no longer prepared to marry me. The only solution that I can see is that you should take her place.'

'Oh, no! No, no, *no*! No way! You can't do this to me! You can't make me!'

'I am Crown Prince, heir to the throne.' The declaration was pure arrogance, undiluted by even the tiniest touch of hesitancy or conscience. 'I can do as I please.'

'You still can't force me! I didn't come here for you, I only came because of my work. I just want to get on with my job.'

'In order to work in this hotel you will need the permission of a member of the royal family.'

'In other words, you? Then I'll find another job—any job!'

'In order to do *that* you will need the permission of the royal family.'

'Then I'll resign—go home...'

Once more she caught the dangerous glint in his eyes.

'No, don't say it! To do that I will need the permission of a member of the royal family! That can't be true! There would be an international incident if you kept me here!'

'Do you really think that you are that important?' Amir scorned. 'Besides, how would anyone know?'

'I'd phone the embassy—or...'

That hateful, cobra's smile was back, totally destroying what little was left of her shattered composure.

'You can't do this, you know!' she tried again in desperation. 'All I have to do is to go to the airport, get on a plane—any plane going to anywhere...'

'No plane can take off or land at the airport or fly anywhere without the permission of a member of the royal house. It is not a law that we usually trouble much about enforcing...'

'But in this case you'll make an exception,' Lydia finished drearily, knowing that she was staring defeat right in the face. 'But this is barbaric. You can't force me into a marriage I don't want.'

'Your tongue says you don't want it…' Amir murmured softly.

Reaching out one long hand, he trailed the backs of his fingers softly down her cheek, watching intently as, in spite of herself, her eyelids drooped in languid delight at the gentle caress.

'But does your body agree?'

'Yes…' Lydia tried to begin, but he had moved faster than her thoughts and the word was crushed by his lips, the sound of it smothered into a sigh. And in the tiny space between one breath and another she knew she was lost.

Her head was swimming, her pulse beat wildly. She couldn't get enough of his kisses and she knew that with every movement of her body, with the small, moaning cries that escaped her, she was encouraging him to kiss her harder, caress her more. His hands roamed urgently over her, sparking off tiny infernos wherever they touched, and her own fingers tugged at the unfamiliar lines of his robes, seeking some way of reaching the intimate warmth of his skin.

When she couldn't find that, she laced her hands tightly in the raven strands of his hair, pulling his head down to hers to deepen and prolong the kiss. And all the time she was hotly, hungrily aware of the thick, potent force of his arousal pressed into the cradle of her hips.

'Enough!'

With an abruptness that tore at her body and soul, Amir wrenched up his head and put her from him, long hands gentling her, holding her upright as she swayed unsteadily on her feet.

'This is not the place for this. When I take you to my bed again, I want the privacy of my own room, not to provide a public spectacle in one of Kuimar's best hotels.'

When, Lydia noted ruefully. Not *if*. He was totally sure

of his conquest of her. And who could blame him? She hadn't even tried to protest, to assume a pretence of modesty or reluctance. And there was no point in trying to do so now. She wouldn't be convincing anyone, least of all herself.

'You're very sure of yourself,' she managed, her voice shaking weakly.

Amir looked down into her clouded eyes and smiled.

'No, *habibti*,' he murmured softly. 'I am sure of *you*.'

'I haven't said yes yet!'

'Perhaps not.'

He shrugged off her protest with supreme indifference. 'But you will.'

She didn't even dare to think how right he was for fear that he might read it in her face. Could she really turn down a chance to be married to this man she loved so desperately even if he didn't love her?

'And it would be worth the sacrifice, would it? In order to get this kingdom of yours and your father's approval? You'd tie yourself in marriage to a woman you don't love?'

'I was prepared to do it once. I will happily do it again.'

If only she knew, Amir thought. If only she realised *how* happily he would do it. And for reasons that had nothing whatsoever to do with the kingdom or his father.

For the past six weeks he had felt as if he were only half alive. He had lost all his zest for life, his interest in anything. But not now. Now after just an hour in her company his whole body was buzzing with a feeling like an electrical charge and he felt more animated, more awake, than ever before.

'And when the woman involved is as beautiful, as desirable as you are, then it will be no sacrifice at all. To keep you with me, by my side in the daytime, and in my bed at night, I would sell my soul to the devil himself.'

If she hadn't been looking down at the newspaper picture as he spoke, then Amir's words might not have had quite the same impact. But Lydia had just glanced down as he spoke, her gaze drifting to the revealing photograph.

Just moments before, she had been horrified at what it had revealed about her feelings for Amir, but now, suddenly, she was seeing it in a very different light. The couple in the picture were like mirror images in the way their heads were inclined towards each other, hands linked. And although Amir had his back to the camera and so his face could not be seen, it was evident that both pairs of eyes were intently locked together.

To keep you with me… I would sell my soul to the devil himself.

Was it possible? Or was she just deceiving herself? Was she letting fantasy take control of her mind so that she was seeing things that she wanted to see?

'So,' Amir said harshly. 'What is your answer?'

If he really wanted her in any other way than his hard-hearted declaration had made clear, then he was doing a wonderful job at hiding it. But perhaps he was the one who was hiding?

And how would she ever know if she didn't take a chance to find out?

'My answer?' she said carefully, exerting every ounce of control she possessed over her voice so that it didn't give away just how important this was to her. 'My answer is this. When we met in London, you promised me three days and the nights that went with them. You promised me the affair of a lifetime. You still owe me that.'

Something in that arrogant, ruthless face had changed. The onyx eyes were suddenly hooded and a muscle worked in the stubborn jaw. But did that mean that she was right in her hopes—or that she couldn't possibly be more wrong? Either way, her whole future could depend on what happened.

'I'll take those three days all over again, Amir. But this

time we'll have them here, in your country. Show me
Kuimar. Show me why you believe it's worth selling your
soul for. And when the three days are over, then I'll give
you your answer.'

CHAPTER THIRTEEN

ONCE again Lydia had three days.

But this time she didn't need the full seventy-two hours. This time she knew from the start what her answer would be. She knew exactly how she felt. She just didn't know what was in Amir's mind.

And that was the most important thing of all.

Because she had always known that she didn't need three days to make up her mind. She had known what her answer to Amir was going to be in the first second that he had made his intentions plain, and there was no going back.

She was so deeply in love with him that there wasn't even a question to answer. He was as essential to her life as the air she breathed, the blood pulsing in her veins. The weeks they had been apart had taught her that she could no longer live without him, no matter what it cost her to live with him.

And by the end of the first day after her declaration, she knew she was also falling in love with Kuimar as well as its prince.

In the hotel, where most of the duplex suites even had their own *en suite* swimming pools, she had already had a taste of some of the luxury available, but now she encountered some of the real sights, sounds and smells of Amir's birthplace.

'I'll never need to wear perfume again!' she exclaimed when they were alone on the evening of the first day, a day she had spent meeting the female members of his family. 'My clothes are saturated with the scent of that aromatic wood they burned. What was it you called it?'

'Oudh.'

Amir smiled, lazily watching her as she put her nose to her sleeve and inhaled appreciatively. He hadn't been able to look away from her all day. She was like some brilliant, gloriously coloured butterfly, drawing and holding his gaze with every movement, every gesture, every laugh. And when he had thought he would never hear it again, the sound of her voice was like the flow of gentle water in his ears, washing away the confusion of the past and filling up the empty spaces inside him.

'It's burned as a sign of welcome. Obviously, it would originally have been used in a tent, to perfume it ready for the arrival of a guest, and at women's parties every guest would waft the smoke over her head or settle over the burner to allow the scent to permeate her clothing.'

'Presumably taking care not to set herself on fire!'

'If you think the air was perfumed tonight, you wait till you visit the spice *souk*. There the whole market is drenched with the scent of cinnamon, frankincense and dried roses. I'll take you there tomorrow.'

'And I want to see the gold *souk*—and the silks...'

'You don't have to visit the markets for those.'

Amir stretched out on the huge, luxurious bed and clasped his hands behind his head, leaning back against them.

'I can have anything you want brought to the palace.'

He wanted to give her everything she desired. Everything she'd ever dreamed of. If she let him, he would fulfil every fantasy she had and some she'd never even begun to think about.

If she would let him. That was the real problem. He had resorted to threats and bluster, behaved like a primitive Neanderthal to keep her here, but could he maintain the pretence? Could he really hold her captive, imprison this beautiful creature, just for his own happiness? To do so would mean breaking her bright spirit and he knew he could never forgive himself if he did that.

But she had promised him three days. And when he had thought that she had gone out of his life for good, then three days seemed like an eternity. He was determined to put them to good use, try every trick in the book.

'You only have to say. As my wife…'

'I'm not your wife yet, Amir!'

His indolent self-assurance set Lydia's teeth on edge.

'I haven't said yes! I haven't even given you any sort of an answer.'

And he hadn't given any indication of the way he was feeling. Oh, he had been unfailingly attentive, indulgent and good-humoured all day. But if he felt anything deeper he had shown no sign of it.

'I could still say no.'

Try it, those glittering black eyes warned, sending a shiver down her spine. Just try it and see where it gets you.

'You could,' Amir said slowly. 'But after today would you want to?'

'After today?' Lydia questioned, deliberately misunderstanding. 'Oh, you mean now that I have seen the palace—the luxury you live in? Now that I've walked on marble floors, had my way lit by spectacular chandeliers, bathed in a bathroom where all the fitments are made out of gold. You think that I would marry you for *that*?'

'Many women would. I've met enough of them.'

'Then I'm not one of many women. Don't you think that if the money was what mattered to me, then I'd have made sure I took all the clothes—everything you bought me—when I left the first time?'

She'd hit a wrong note there, bringing a dark frown to his handsome face. Clearly he'd taken it as an insult that she had rejected his gifts, leaving them behind when she had gone to America.

'I had them all flown out to you here.'

He could never admit to her how he had felt, the sense of loss that had hit him like a blow when he had opened the door to 'her' room in the London apartment and seen all her clothes still hanging in the wardrobes. Her perfume had lingered on the air as well, tugging at his memory, haunting him for days. He had spent more hours than he cared to remember sitting in that room, in the darkness, just breathing in her scent.

'So you did, but clothes won't influence my decision. You forget, Amir, I'm not happy with the idea of an arranged marriage. I told myself I would only ever marry for love. To me, a marriage without feeling would be as dry and arid as the desert out there beyond the mountains. It would be empty and barren and all the wealth in the world couldn't turn it into a temperate oasis where flowers and trees would grow.'

He was trying completely the wrong approach, Amir told himself. It was time he changed tack swiftly.

'Don't you like the idea of being a queen one day?'

If she could be queen of his heart, it would be a different matter. That was the only place she wanted to reign.

'I really hadn't thought about it,' she said honestly.

'Well, think about it!' Amir growled. 'Think about being Queen of this country and mother of the heirs to the throne—'

'Which reminds me,' Lydia broke in impulsively. 'When do I get to meet your father?'

Now what had she said to put that scowl on his face?

'My father has gone to his palace in the mountains for a few days. Perhaps when he returns…'

'Perhaps!'

Lydia's blue eyes flashed with an indignation to match the anger in her tone as she swung round to face him.

'Perhaps! What is this, Amir, do you not think I'm fit to meet your father?'

'Don't be foolish!' Amir tossed back at her. 'As my prospective bride, you are fit to meet with anyone. It's just that…'

Just that if King Khalid met Lydia now, before he had her promise to marry him, then the old man would surely let slip the truth about the marriage to Aisha and the reasons why it had fallen through.

'Just that…?'

She had to blink in astonishment as she saw the way that his frown suddenly disappeared, swept away by a smile of such deliberate brilliance, such sensual provocation that it made her toes curl into the softness of the rug.

'Just that for now I want you all to myself.'

One hand lifted, curved into an imperiously beckoning gesture.

'Come here,' he said and the lordly, arrogant tone grated on her raw nerves, stripping away a protective layer of skin so that she stiffened in instinctive rejection.

'Please…' he added very gently, his eyes softening, seeming to plead with her. And immediately all her resistance melted with a speed that made her sag weakly like a puppet whose strings were cut so that it fell in a limp heap on the ground.

Somehow Amir had sensed her reaction because, even as she thought she might fall, suddenly he was there beside her, the strength of his arms coming round her, supporting her, bringing her gently down to the bed to lie beside him.

'You are wrong about the desert, *habibti*,' he murmured, pressing warm lips against her cheek, trailing kisses down her throat to the point were her pulse beat at the base of her neck. 'It may be dry and barren, but it is not empty or dead. And it can be very, very beautiful.'

His tone soothed her, held her still, as his hands smoothed the dress from her shoulders, slid it down her body.

'The dunes can be as smooth and rounded as the curves

of your flesh, and every bit as warm,' he murmured, stroking his hand along the long line from shoulder to waist, then up over the arc of her hips. 'Or they can be wild and inhospitable, blown into tortured shapes by the wind.'

Leaving her dressed in only the briefest scraps of silk and lace, he turned his attention to her hair, pinned up into a neat chignon because of the heat. Long hands gently eased out the pins, then combed softly through the bright strands, massaging her scalp with his fingertips while all the time his lips kissed her into a state of mindless oblivion.

'You are too tense, sweetheart,' he said suddenly, and she heard the frown in his voice rather than saw it on his face.

'Too much coffee,' Lydia offered, trying to make light of the matter.

She didn't want him to suspect that the real reason for her tension was his presence. That inside a private little war was raging between her gloriously aroused senses and the strict demands of self-preservation.

One side had already half yielded to his caress, the heavy, honeyed ache of desire starting up between her legs. The other side warned despairingly that to give in to Amir's lovemaking now would only leave her far too vulnerable in the future. How could she ever hope to say no to marriage if she said yes now?

'You should have warned me that the way to show I'd had enough to drink was to turn my cup upside down.'

The finger she had lifted to his face to administer a small tap of reproach refused to obey her, gentling instead and turning into a slow caress down the lean plane of one cheek.

'And as for the *halva* and those pastries! I swear I can still taste the sugar on my lips now.'

Teasingly she let her finger run over his mouth, tracing the firm outline of his lips.

'There's even some still here on yours,' she told him, looking deep into his eyes.

The flare of hunger she saw there told her everything she needed to know. Unexpectedly for Amir he lay back, his head cushioned on the downy pillow.

'Kiss it away for me,' he murmured lazily, sensual hunger thickening his voice.

Lydia slid over the silk covers until she was half lying on top of him, supported by the hard wall of his chest. With deliberate slowness she brushed her mouth against his, lingering softly, letting her tongue slide out and follow the same path as her fingers. Under her caress she heard Amir's low sigh of surrender and she angled her head more so as to deepen the kiss.

Her senses had won, she realised hazily as heat flooded her body. They had swamped any sort of rational thought, drowning it out completely with the throbbing pulse of sexual hunger.

Only then did she become aware that Amir had not been lying submissive as she'd thought. While she had concentrated on his kisses, he had removed the final slivers of her clothing, replacing them with the heat and strength of his hands. And now he shrugged off his own clothing, coming back to her proudly naked and fiercely, powerfully aroused.

Lydia gave a small, shaken gasp as he pulled her towards him, then lifted her bodily until she was straddling him while he lay on his back, the hard, hot strength of him probing the centre of her femininity. Looking down into his hard-boned face, she saw the blaze of colour along the carved cheekbones, the shimmer of desire in his eyes.

'Never fear the desert, darling,' he told her roughly. 'Not when I am with you. The sands may shift and swirl until you can't see where you're going, but I'll take care of you. I'll make sure I'll always keep you safe.'

She had opened her mouth to answer him, only to find

that no words would come out. There was nothing in her thoughts but the need for his possession, the longing to feel him deep inside her, filling her completely.

She no longer cared about self-preservation or the wisdom or lack of it in what she was about to do. She had never really planned to say no to Amir's demand for marriage. To do so would be like cutting out her own heart and throwing it on a fire. She couldn't live without Amir, and even such a loveless marriage as he proposed—on his side at least—would be better than nothing.

'Promise?' she managed, her voice raw with the need she couldn't hide from him as he stroked her intimately, with devastating effect.

'On my life,' he assured her harshly, shifting slightly so that he could thrust up and into the innermost core of her; a shaken gasp escaping him as he felt her tight muscles close about him.

And as she took him into her, abandoning herself to the burning pleasure his passion triggered all over her body, Lydia told herself that it would be enough. He might not love her, but he wanted her. And for now that was enough.

CHAPTER FOURTEEN

HE'D waited long enough, Amir decided. At least, he'd waited as long as he could bear.

Okay, so technically the three days weren't yet up. They still had one more night. Eight, ten more hours before Lydia had promised to give him her answer.

But he couldn't stand not knowing.

He couldn't endure one more sleepless night lying beside her, hearing the gentle sound of her breath, inhaling the scent of her skin, feeling her soft, slender body curved against his, and wondering if she planned to stay or go.

Because if she decided to go then he knew that he wouldn't be able to stop her. For all his attempts to intimidate her, his threats to force her into staying, he knew now that he could never carry them out. Even as he had made them he had known that they were just so much empty air, forced out of him by sheer panic and desperation. The knowledge that, having found her again, he couldn't let her go.

And if he had felt that way then, now it was all so much worse.

Because now, at last he had admitted to himself just what she meant to him. And by doing so he had acknowledged that if she went she would take his whole world with him.

He had to know now what her answer was. He'd waited long enough.

'Move over…'

She looked up at him in astonishment, her eyes widening slightly at his tone, the hard set to his jaw. And that was hardly surprising. Only a few minutes before, they had been sharing a shower and putting the heated enclosed space to more sensual use than simply getting clean.

So what had brought about this change of mood? Lydia wondered as she shifted position on the couch, giving him room to sit beside her. What had happened to the relaxed, smiling Amir of just seconds ago?

'I know now why you love this country so much,' she said in an attempt to distract him from whatever unwelcome thoughts had darkened his mind. 'I've never seen anything as spectacular as the desert in the moonlight, or heard anything as eerie as the sound of the wind amongst the dunes.'

She tried to smile as she spoke, the warmth fading rapidly from her face as she met with a stony, flint-eyed response. Without a word, he took from her hand the comb that she had been using to smooth the tangles from her freshly washed hair and began to ease it through the shining bronze swathe.

'Mmm, that's *good*…'

She let her head fall back, giving herself into his hands, enjoying the gentle tugging sensation. If she left it, surely he would tell her what was wrong in his own good time. Making him feel pressured was certain to make him clam up even more.

'I think— Oh!'

She broke off on a cry of surprise as, abruptly as he had picked it up, Amir tossed aside the comb and pulled her back until she was lying almost in his lap, her head supported by his strength, long, still-damp tendrils of hair spread out over his arm. The only place to look was up into his dark, handsome face, and what she saw there set her nerves painfully on edge.

'What's wrong?' she began hesitantly. 'What…?'

'What's wrong?' he echoed so harshly that she winced as if the words had actually been cruel blows falling onto the delicacy of her exposed skin. 'I'll tell you what's wrong—*we're* wrong. You and me.'

'You and me,' Lydia echoed shakily. 'What—*why* are we wrong?'

Had he completely rethought his plans? Had the second three days been just long enough to make him change his mind? Had he decided that he no longer wanted to marry her?

'Because we're neither one thing nor the other! We're not having an affair, nor are we doing anything else.'

'And what would you want us to do?'

'You know what I want! I want you to marry me.'

'To be your princess and one day your queen?'

His only response was a brusque nod, his black eyes opaque and unreadable. If that was the only reason she had for staying, he wasn't going to argue. Just so long as she stayed he didn't care *why*.

'To give your father the heirs he wants? To win you his approval and make you truly the Crown Prince of this country?'

'Yes, dammit. Yes! For that, for anything, for whatever else you want! Lydia, I can't wait any longer. I need you to tell me. I need to know what your answer is.'

'My answer…'

She didn't know why she hesitated. She only knew she suddenly couldn't get the words out.

She had known that this moment would come. That at some point she would have to give him his answer, and she had fully resolved just what that answer would be. She knew he didn't love her. She also knew she could cope with that. She could cope with anything if he only stayed with her. If she could only be his wife.

So why could she not say it now?

'Lydia…'

His low, raw-toned use of her name was a warning not to try his patience too far. He had already risked his father's disapproval because the marriage to Aisha had been called off, and he was not prepared to do so again. To win back the old king's affection, he needed a wife, and he intended that that wife would be her.

'Never fear the desert, darling.' The words Amir had spoken barely two days before came back to haunt her now. 'Not when I am with you. The sands may shift and swirl until you can't see where you're going, but I'll take care of you. I'll make sure I'll always keep you safe.'

In her mind she had a vision of the desert as they had ridden through it only that evening, the brilliance of the stars glittering against the night-dark sky. The dunes had been a vast and silent void and looking at them she had suddenly known what true emptiness must be like. Without Amir, her life would be as desolate as that, but with him, knowing that he could never love her, wouldn't she know another desperate form of loneliness?

'I'll always keep you safe,' he had said. But this hurt was one thing he couldn't protect her from. Because he didn't even know it existed. And just the thought of that terrible emptiness made her shiver deep inside.

'My answer...' she tried again, fighting the stab of anguish that made her voice quaver. 'My answer is yes.'

'*No!*'

She couldn't believe what she'd heard. He couldn't have said it, could he? Had he...?

'Amir?'

But he was already hoisting her up into a sitting position, getting to his feet. Striding away from her, his long straight back taut with rejection.

'Amir? What is it? Please look at me.'

She saw the muscles in his shoulders tighten, but even then she wasn't prepared for the white, drawn expression on his face when he whirled round to face her, the blaze of rejection in his eyes.

'Amir, I—I said yes.'

'And I said no. I've changed my mind, Lydia. I don't want this. I never wanted this.'

'I don't understand—what are you trying to say?'

'I'm not trying to say anything! I can't make it any clearer. It's over! Finished! I don't want to marry you.'

At least, not like this. He had been a fool to think that he could cope with this. That he could take so little when he needed so much. He had hoped that she felt something for him, even if it was only the white-hot desire that burned them both up when they touched. But now it seemed that even that had gone.

He could have taken anything. But not that look of fear in her eyes.

When she had looked at him like that something had died deep inside him. He felt as if his heart had shrivelled into ashes, crumbling away.

There was no way he could keep her with him if she felt like that. No way he could look at her every day and not see that moment of panic, no matter how bright the smile, how cheerful an expression she tried to hide behind.

The thing he had most feared was breaking her spirit and now it seemed that he had come desperately, dangerously near to doing just that.

'Amir?'

He couldn't meet her eyes for fear that she would see how close he was to breaking too. But he couldn't let his feelings show now. The one thing, the only thing he could do for her was to set her free as soon as possible. But if he looked into her face then it would destroy him completely. And so he stared at a point in the distance, deliberately not focusing on anything.

'The whole idea was a mistake. A stupid one on my part. I thought I could still have everything, but now I see that I don't want it after all.'

'I don't want it after all.' Could he have said anything

more cruel, anything more savagely hurtful, more guaranteed to destroy her totally? 'I don't want to marry you.'

I don't want you.

If he had ripped out her tongue by the roots, he couldn't have done more to make sure that she didn't argue or protest. Every single word had died in her throat, her tongue froze in her mouth. She could only stand silently and watch as he suddenly leapt into action.

A tug on a bell-pull summoned servants. A few brusque, barked commands sent them scurrying to do his bidding. A click of his fingers, and a mobile phone was brought and a stream of unintelligible Arabic poured into it. Only when they were finally alone again did he draw breath and turn his head in her direction.

'It's all arranged. You can leave tonight.'

'Tonight!'

Lydia shook her head in dazed disbelief. This couldn't be happening. Only moments before, she had been ready to answer his proposal of marriage, anticipating the prospect of spending the rest of her life with him. But now he had turned that hope of a future upside down.

He couldn't wait to get her out of his life, it seemed.

'But I can't—I haven't...'

'Your bags are being packed as we speak. A car will be here for you in ten minutes. The jet will be waiting for you at the airport. It will leave as soon as you are safely on board.'

'So this is goodbye?'

What else could she say? A tiny, desperate voice at the back of her mind was shrieking at her to protest, to argue, to fight her case, but even as she opened her mouth to do so she knew that even to try was futile.

'Yes. Goodbye. Have a safe journey.'

His eyes were as bleak and dead as his voice. He might be looking at her, but she was sure that he didn't *see* her in any way at all.

'Amir, please don't do this.'

It was a last-ditch attempt. Short of going down on her knees and pleading with him not to do it, she couldn't think of any way to get through to him. Perhaps if she had been able to cry, if he could see desolate tears pouring down her cheeks, then he might understand just how terrible she was feeling inside. But of course now, of all times, was the moment that her eyes chose to be burningly, painfully dry, her heart breaking secretly, inwardly, without any sign on the outside.

'I don't want to go.'

'And I don't want you to stay.'

He couldn't take much more. If she had to go then he wanted her to leave *now*, straight away. He couldn't cope with standing around, making stilted, awkward conversation as if she were just some passing acquaintance, someone he'd shared a few pleasant hours with, and not the woman with whom he had wanted to share the rest of his life.

In fact he couldn't bear to see her walk away.

'There's no point in dragging this out. I never was one for long drawn-out goodbyes. Far better to make it short and sweet and have it done with.'

Short and *sweet*!

He actually held his hand out and expected her to take it. She couldn't touch him. If she did she knew that the flimsy barriers that were all that were holding her emotions in check would splinter totally, letting the flood tide of anguish and misery pour through. And she would never be able to pick up the pieces.

Far better to keep her dignity now and at least walk out with her head held high.

'Goodbye, Amir,' she said stiffly, ignoring the proffered hand. 'I wish I could say it's been nice knowing you.'

At least she had the satisfaction of seeing him wince at that. But if she had got through to him then, a moment later he had covered it up, his emotional armour back in place.

'I hope your father won't be too disappointed about the grandchildren.'

Amir's smile was brief, hard, and totally emotionless, no trace of light in his eyes at all.

'Oh, I'm sure my father will understand. In fact, he'll probably have another bride lined up for me within the month.'

'Then I hope you'll be very happy together.'

If she opened her mouth again, she feared she might actually be sick. Her pain was choking her, gathering in a tight, bitter knot at her throat, cutting off the air so that she had to gasp for breath.

Luckily at that moment one of the servants that Amir had sent off to carry out his orders appeared in the doorway to be greeted by a swift, curt question.

Evidently his answer was the one Amir had been waiting for because he nodded, snapped a dismissal, and turned to Lydia.

'Your car is here; Kahmal will take you to it. The driver knows where to go. If there's anything you need on the plane, you only have to ask.'

He had turned on his heel and was gone before she even had time to register that she too had been dismissed, striding away from her and out of the room without so much as a backward glance.

Left alone, Lydia could do nothing but turn and follow the servant who led her out into the enormous hall where, amazingly, her bags were already waiting, and from there to the main door of the palace where the car stood ready, engine purring. The sound of a clock striking behind her stunned her with the realisation that Amir's orders had been obeyed strictly to the letter.

The car would be here in ten minutes, he had said. And precisely ten minutes later she was stepping into the powerful vehicle, sinking down wearily onto the soft leather of the back seat.

Ten minutes exactly. That was all it had taken to shatter her dreams. Ten minutes ago she had thought she was about to marry Amir, to be with him for the rest of her days. Now, just that brief, terrible time later, she was on her way out of his life for ever, never to see him again.

The journey through the darkness was a nightmare. Lydia refused to let the tears fall and instead sat tautly, perched on the edge of the seat, her arms wrapped tightly round herself, struggling to hold back the welling pain, the burning bitterness.

At the airport she was hurried through the building and out onto the runway without even the formalities of departure. Clearly Amir's orders had made sure that nothing would stand in the way of her leaving. The plane, Lydia saw with a terrible sense of inevitability, was a private jet, with the flag of Kuimar on its side.

'In order to do *that* you will need the permission of the royal family.'

She could hear Amir's words in her head as clearly as if he had been sitting beside her. Well, it was obvious that he had given his permission this time—with a vengeance! He had clearly wanted her gone as quickly as possible.

Huddled miserably in her seat, she heard the plane's powerful engines start to throb, in a few moments she would feel the movement as they taxied towards the runway. Suddenly plagued by a desperate need to have something of Amir with her in these last few minutes in his country, she reached for her handbag.

The letter Amir had written her on the last day in London was the only thing she had kept. Even though its contents were so painful that she had never been able to bring herself to open it again until now, it was the only example of something so personal to him as his handwriting. It had been in her bag ever since.

The sound of the engines changed, the jet lumbering into movement as Lydia opened the letter for the first time since that morning in London.

'Lydia…'

The letters of her name blurred as tears threatened at last.

But as her fingers tightened on the paper the feeling had her stiffening in surprise. Looking at the letter more closely, she felt her heart jolt in shock at the sudden realisation that there was an extra sheet, attached to and folded behind the first. A part of the note that she hadn't read.

'We'll make the last dinner of this three-day affair one you'll remember for ever,' was the last sentence on the first page. The point where she had thought it ended. But what she read now made her breath catch painfully in her throat.

But before that dinner, there's something I'd like to ask you to think about. These three days have been truly special to me, Lydia. So special that I can't imagine living the rest of my life without you in it. I have a lot to explain, I know, but I'd also like to hope that you would consider the possibility of turning this three-day affair into something permanent.

With love, Amir.

With love, Amir.

Looking back, Lydia was seeing those last terrible moments with Amir all over again. Seeing the bleakness in his eyes, the emotionless set of his face. Seeing it from a very different point of view. One that translated his anger into pain, turned his coldness into a terrible, agonising restraint.

'Wait!'

The pilot couldn't hear her but she didn't care. She was already scrabbling with the seat belt, getting to her feet.

'Wait! Oh, please, please *wait*!'

Amir kicked open the door, strode into his room and flung himself down in the nearest chair, not even troubling to switch on the light. Darkness suited his mood better. It matched the shades in his mind.

He supposed that one day, some day, eventually, he would get used to the feeling of loss, of emptiness, but it would take one hell of a long time. Right now he couldn't imagine how he was even going to face the coming dawn without her.

He had given up trying to rest hours ago, and gone out riding on one of his favourite Arab stallions, hoping to exhaust himself into sleep. It hadn't worked. His body might ache with tiredness, but his mind refused to let go of Lydia's memory.

With a groan he buried his face in his hands, but in the same instant a faint sound on the far side of the room had him jerking his head back up, eyes searching the darkness.

'Who's there?'

Leaping to his feet, he flicked the light on, wincing at the sudden brightness.

'Who the hell are you?'

The woman stood between the bed and the wall. She was tall and slender, that was as much as he could tell because her whole body was enveloped in the all-covering folds of the *abaya*, the traditional long black robe with gold border embroidery that Arab women wore in public. A black scarf was draped over her head and wrapped around most of her face so the only things visible were her eyes and they were deep in shadow.

'What are you doing here?'

'I came to you, Highness.'

Her voice was soft and husky, muffled by the concealing veil.

'I thought you might be lonely.'

'Lonely?'

The palace grapevine worked faster than he'd ever thought.

'Lonely. Yes, you could say that.' Desolate would be more like it. 'But if you also thought that this was your chance, then I'm sorry, you couldn't be more wrong. I'm not in the market for any sort of comfort you might be offering.'

'No?'

She had moved, was coming towards him now, her bare feet silent on the marble floor. Lydia had walked like that, with that same subtly sensual sway, her body tall and elegant.

'No!'

The word was as much to deny the memory as to answer her.

'Look, I don't mean to be rude, but would you just *go*! I'm not in the mood for female company—*any* company right now. If I tell you that the woman I love has just gone out of my life, perhaps you'll understand. And there's no way on earth that anyone could fill the hole that she's left behind.'

Beneath the flowing *abaya*, Lydia's heart kicked sharply in joy. In the moment that the light had gone on she had been shocked by the change that a couple of hours had effected on Amir's face. He looked pale and drawn, black eyes like bruises above deep shadows on his cheeks.

If she had needed any proof of the truth of his declaration, it was there for anyone to see. And what a declaration of love! No woman in her right mind could ask for more.

'But perhaps I could try.'

Amir shook his head violently.

'No…'

It trailed off into a puzzled frown.

Was he seeing things? The eyes above the folds of the veil were blue, deep, vibrant blue. And that voice…

'Who…?'

The hesitancy in his voice, the shadows in the eyes tore at Lydia's heart. It was time to put him out of his misery.

'Oh, Amir, don't you know—haven't you guessed?'

The veil was hastily unwrapped, tossed away. Amir stared, black eyes stunned.

'Lydia…' Her name was a raw, choking sound. 'You came back!'

'I couldn't leave,' she said simply. 'This is where my heart is.'

And this time there was no room for doubt. This time her smile, the light in her eyes told him that there was no fear, no uncertainty, in her reply.

His arms were open wide and she ran into them without a second thought, feeling them close around her, hold her tight, and this time she knew instinctively that he would never let her go.

'But how?' he asked eventually when the first storm of feeling had ebbed, the first snatched kisses had eased some of the emptiness in their souls. 'My men had orders…'

'Oh, Amir…'

Lydia's smile was light-hearted, teasing.

'Don't you know that no plane can take off or land without the permission of a member of the royal house? So if the Crown Prince's bride-to-be gives the order that the plane must not leave the tarmac, then—well…'

She shrugged her shoulders lightly.

'He couldn't disobey me.'

'Bride-to-be…'

Amir echoed the words with a thread of awe in his voice.

'Is that what you truly are, my love?'

'If you'll have me.'

'Have you! Darling, there is nothing I could want more in the whole world.'

'But you made me go…'

A faint echo of the pain she had felt then clouded her eyes, and Amir bent his head to kiss her again, driving away the distress with his caress.

'I did it for you. I thought that you only said you would marry me out of fear. That you could see no way out. So I gave you one.'

In spite of the pain, the distress it had caused him, he had still been prepared to set her free.

'What I was afraid of was never having your love. But loving you the way I did, I knew it was a risk I was prepared to take.'

'I thought I'd trapped you. When you told me about Jonathon, I thought that I was your rebellion, your moment of wild irresponsibility, nothing more. I knew what it felt like to need someone's love and have it withheld and you had told me you would only ever marry for love. That a marriage without feeling would be empty and barren as the desert. I couldn't tie you to that.'

'And *you* said that you'd never loved anyone strongly enough to want to commit your life to them. Never met anyone you couldn't just walk away from in the end.'

Amir had the grace to look a little shamefaced at that as he took her hand in his and led her to sit down on the bed beside him.

'That might have been true before I met you, but from the moment you walked into that airport lounge I knew I was lost. That's why I told my father that the wedding he had planned could never take place. What?' he questioned, looking down into her upturned face, seeing her bewilderment. 'What did I say?'

'You told your father that the arranged marriage was off?'

Amir nodded his dark head, his expression sombre.

'I told Aisha too. She's a lovely girl, very sweet, very attractive, but I knew that to me she could only ever be second-best. She would never be you. She deserved better than that. She deserved someone who could love her as the one and only person for them.'

'And you did this when I'd already gone? When you thought I'd left you? You risked your father's approval? The kingdom—for me?'

'I had no choice. You were the only woman I could ever feel this way about. But…'

Suddenly his expression lightened, the sensual lips curving up into a smile.

'I knew I was going to get you back. I *had* to get you back. That's why I made sure you were sent here.'

'I would never have gone, you know, if I'd read your note properly.' Lydia's voice was soft, her eyes glistening with tears at the memory.

'I only thought there was one page. I didn't read the second one until now.'

Amir's smile grew, and the eyes that looked down into hers were touched with a teasing light.

'I had already rung my father to say that I couldn't go through with the arranged marriage. I thought you would have guessed—number twenty-four,' he prompted when she still looked bemused.

'Number twenty-four?'

Gropingly, she tried to recall what the magazine article had said.

'Number twenty-four—"he takes you somewhere really special… Perhaps he has an extra-special proposal in mind?"'

'You…?'

'I was going to propose to you that night. That and your birthday were the only stages we hadn't covered. That was why I wanted you to wear the special dress. I was going to take you out and…'

Suddenly he astonished her by getting up, her hand still in his.

'And I was going to go down on one knee…'

His gaze fixed intently on her, he suited action to the words. Lydia could only watch, her heart thudding wildly in her breast.

'And I was going to say—Lydia, love of my heart, light of my life, would you make me the happiest man in the world by agreeing to marry me?'

'Oh, Amir, yes! Of course the answer's yes.'

The kiss that followed was long and deeply passionate, so intense that it left them both breathing raggedly. Looking into the darkness of Amir's eyes, Lydia knew that her future was sealed and that she would never be lonely again.

And as Amir gathered her up onto the bed beside him and began to slide the black silk of the *abaya* from her willing body, she had just one thought left in her head.

'If that was the something extra special, then just what did you have in mind for my birthday?'

'Can't you guess?'

Amir paused for one moment to smile into her eyes that shone with love for him.

'Your birthday, my love, was—is—to be the day that you become my bride.'

Lydia's answering smile said it all. She couldn't have been happier. Couldn't have wanted anything more in her life.

'Perfect,' she sighed. 'Just perfect.'

And as she gave herself up to his passion she knew that was how it would be for the rest of her days.

MILLS & BOON®

Modern
romance™ *Extra*

More passion for your money!

In August, Mills & Boon Modern Romance is
proud to bring back by popular request,
Raising the Stakes,
and have added a new-in-print linked story,
The Runaway Mistress,
as a bonus. Both come from bestselling,
award-winning author
Sandra Marton.

Sandra has written more than 50 Modern
Romances and her Barons stories have
pleased many readers:

'**An unforgettable read overflowing with
exciting characters, a powerful premise and
smouldering scenes.'**
–Romantic Times

MILLS & BOON

It was impossible to control their

DISHONOURABLE

Desires

JULIA JUSTISS JOANNE ROCK

On sale 5th August 2005

Available at most branches of WHSmith, Tesco, ASDA, Martins, Borders, Eason, Sainsbury's and all good paperback bookshops.

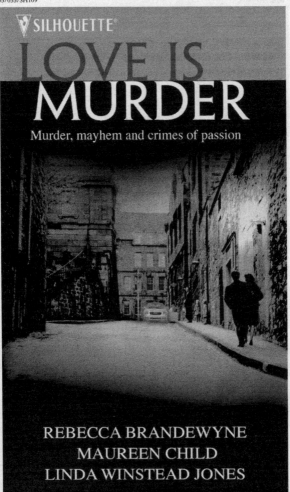

LOVE IS MURDER

Murder, mayhem and crimes of passion

REBECCA BRANDEWYNE
MAUREEN CHILD
LINDA WINSTEAD JONES

On sale 16th September 2005

Available at most branches of WHSmith, Tesco, ASDA, Martins, Borders, Eason, Sainsbury's and all good paperback bookshops.

SILHOUETTE®

A Hot Pursuit

MARIE FERRARELLA

BRENDA NOVAK

With danger all around, could their love survive when the sun went down…?

On sale 17th June 2005

Available at most branches of WHSmith, Tesco, ASDA, Martins, Borders, Eason, Sainsbury's and all good paperback bookshops.